GOLD RUSH

# GOLD RUSH

## Yu Miri

Translated by Stephen Snyder

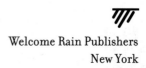

Welcome Rain Publishers
New York

GOLD RUSH by Yu Miri
First Welcome Rain edition 2002

Original Japanese edition published by Shincho Sha Co., Ltd.
English translation rights arranged with Kodansha Ltd. on behalf of Yu Miri through
Japan Foreign-Rights Centre/Writers House, LLC.

Library of Congress CIP data available from the publisher.

Direct any inquiries to:
Welcome Rain Publishers LLC

ISBN 1-56649-283-1
First Welcome Rain Edition March 2002
Design by *like white on rice*

1 3 5 7 9 10 8 6 4 2

There was no one to notice the boy as he walked along Isezaki Street in the unnaturally bright sunlight. When the shops lining the road gradually fell into shadow, his pace slowed and he turned suddenly to the left, disappearing down an alley.

It was not so much that this neighborhood, Kogane-chō, seemed to be shunning the light, but that a peculiar heat was concealed within, so hot the sun itself avoided these streets. Though it was midday, the whole area seemed shrouded in cave-dark shadow, as if the inhabitants needed to turn on the lights. To outsiders, the violence and corruption of Kogane-chō were almost audible, discouraging them from coming near. To the uninitiated, it was a dangerous place to be carefully avoided. Here, desire had settled in and set up shop. Other places like this had come and gone with the times, but Kogane-chō had never lost sight of its basic commodities, continuing to offer sex and drugs at a fair price.

The boy in the alley exhaled slowly and checked his watch: just past four-thirty. The watch, a Rolex, was a present from his father when he had turned fourteen the month before. Still twenty-seven minutes, he told himself as he passed out of the alley and into the street that fronted the Ōoka River. A signboard proclaiming the work of the Kogane-chō Environmental Clean-Up Council had fallen over in a stand of dead brown azaleas withering in the merciless midsummer sun, and next to it an assortment of pots and pans, a futon, and a drying rack protruded awkwardly from a broken old handcart. A powerful body odor engulfed the cart, marking the owner's property.

The boy stood looking down at the river. The black, stagnant water, like used tempura oil, showed no sign of movement. He caught sight of a white mass bobbing on the surface. Realizing that it was the body of a cat, it occurred to him that even if it had been a dead baby, he probably would not have gone to the police—but the thought flitted through his head and vanished like the foam on the river. The evening was beginning to release its stench, and waves of odor pulsed through the hot, humid air: onions frying in the cheap restaurants under the train tracks; the smell of the whores in the alley, like perfume dumped in sour milk. The boy opened his mouth and filled his lungs with the familiar smells.

Eleven years earlier, his mother, Miki, had learned that the disease afflicting her eldest son Kōki—something called Williams Syndrome— was incurable. And from that time on, she had left her daughter, Miho, and the boy in the care of the housekeeper and devoted herself to Kōki. Their father, Hidetomo Yuminaga, ran a pachinko parlor known as Treasure Ball Hall in front of Kogane-chō Station. He began to take Miho and the boy along to work, assigning an employee to look after them. Yasuda lasted longest as their nursemaid; he was barely thirty, but he had five- and six-year-old daughters of his own to look after and he was already going bald. After his wife left him, Yasuda had begun playing high-stakes poker. One night at a casino, he'd met Hayashi, a manager at Treasure Ball Hall. Hayashi had talked to Hidetomo, and Yasuda had been allowed to move into the pachinko parlor's employee dormitory along with his daughters. Before his wife had run off, Yasuda had been a technician at an electric company. The only time the light came on in his eyes now was when he was repairing broken toys for the boy. Often, when Yasuda was lost in thought, the boy would try to get his attention; if there was no answer, he would kick his shin as hard as he could. Even then, Yasuda would simply raise an eyebrow and smile, baring his pale gums. He would take the boy by the hand and suggest they go find something to do. The boy had been in second grade when Yasuda had hung himself from the fire escape with his daughter's jump rope.

He didn't recall much about the incident, but less than a week later, Yasuda's girls had disappeared from the dormitory, and no one mentioned him after that.

The boy didn't like the young employee who succeeded Yasuda as his guardian. He did take him quite often to the game arcade across from Treasure Ball, but as soon as the boy pretended to be engrossed in a game, he would disappear. Left alone, the boy would wander out of the arcade and follow a passing stranger through the neighborhood. He didn't care whom he followed, as long as he could match his footsteps to theirs. Ignoring people headed in the direction of Isezaki-chō, he would choose someone walking along the river or the elevated tracks and follow them from Kogane-chō to Hinode-chō, invariably losing his guide somewhere along the way. After that, he would wander until evening through gray, decaying streets, seemingly unchanged since the war, colored only by the graffiti sprayed on the walls under the tracks.

As it grew dark, lights came on in the tiny bars and restaurants crowded along the streets, shining dimly, like insect traps, through cellophane shades. Inside, glowing violet and red, were cheap stools lining counters barely long enough for four or five customers. Doors stood open, and in the front of each shop was a woman waiting for the men who passed by. Some were middle-aged, their faces beginning to decompose like squashed pomegranates; some were clearly foreigners, big women blooming like hothouse flowers. They would appear just after noon, and while it was light, when the streets were still empty, they would stop the boy as he passed and give him candy or take him on their knees and rub his head. But once the sun had set, he became invisible, as they turned their attention to the men, unbuttoning sheer blouses to show more breast or hiking miniskirts up their thighs— anything to catch the eyes and slow the steps of a customer. Their entreaties, like the cries of the sick, full of hope and desperation, filled the boy's ears.

"Ten thousand yen!"

"Hey, good-looking. I'd do you without a rubber."

"Best pussy around!"

"Talk dirty to me, mister."

The names of the bars were all simple words even the boy could read: Lamplight, Mimi, Panda.

During his last year in elementary school, his father had made Kogane-chō off-limits, but he would say that he was meeting friends at the Nogeyama Zoo and go instead to get lost in the maze of bars and brothels. Now, turning several corners, he entered a narrow, gray building and without slowing his pace began climbing the stairs. The boy didn't know why this building was nicknamed the "Pillbox." In the late fifties, on the banks of the Ōoka River, there had been a cluster of small huts known as "pillboxes" where drugs were sold. They had long ago been converted into apartments, cheap hotels, or shops, but the name "pillbox" was preserved here.

He felt a little light-headed as he reached the landing on the third floor, but instead of stopping, he ran up the last two flights of stairs, two steps at a time, and pounded just once on a metal door on the fifth floor. As he stood waiting, he felt as though something hard and black were lodged deep in his head, something he should pluck out and put into words, but at the moment he didn't want to think about it.

He could sense someone approaching the door on the other side. The peephole went dark for a moment, then the sound of the chain being drawn and the deadbolt unlocked, and the door was opened by the usual young man. The boy had been coming here for more than a year now, but it was always the same guy, the same white T-shirt over the same gray sweatshirt under the same crew cut. His left hand, which usually held a cigarette, opened the door just wide enough for the boy to pass in the bill he had fished from his pocket; and in return the man would hand him an envelope with three gram bags. In a matter of seconds, the door had closed and the boy had tucked away the envelope and was charging down the stairs.

As he walked, his scalp grew damp and began to itch. He licked at the drops of sweat that had collected above his mouth and started to raise his arm to check his watch but let it fall back. Walking more slowly, he looked up at a window above a bar. A blue plastic curtain blocked the view, but the window was open and adorned with a bra and panties hung out to dry. Hearing a low moan, he pictured the woman, legs spread out on an old futon, sheets yellowed with sweat and semen. He wiped his forehead with the back of his hand. On his walks through Kogane-chō he sometimes heard sobs or shouts or screams, but they were as much a part of the neighborhood as the constant rumbling of the Tōyoko Express trains passing overhead.

"Kazu!"

The boy stopped and glanced around nervously. He was sure that no one had been standing there when he passed, but now a woman was leaning against a door and waving at him. It was Ryōko.

Ryōko had been doing business in this alley for as long as the boy could remember, but the image conjured up by her girlish name had little to do with the middle-aged whore standing before him. The pink bra, visible through the sheer purple polka-dot blouse, could barely contain her enormous breasts, which hung nearly to her waist. She wasn't particularly fat. On some women it might have looked healthy. But her skin was loose and pale, like a corpse that had been soaking in formaldehyde. Her makeup was streaked with blue and red, as if she'd been beaten, and the tiny eyes that peered out of her bloated face were like pencil points poked into little lumps of clay.

"Kazu!" Her voice sounded rusty, like a machine that hadn't been used in some time. "You're getting so tall. Seems like yesterday I could hold you on my lap." She stumbled toward him, swaying on her ancient high heels, and wrapped her sweaty palm around his elbow. "You been keeping up with your studies?"

"Yes," he answered, pleased in spite of himself, like a five-year-old child.

"That's my boy!" A shudder ran through her powder-caked cheek and she let out something resembling a laugh. But almost immediately, she dropped the boy's arm and pressed her hand to her stomach, falling into a coughing fit, as if her laugh had failed to come out and had run amok in her belly. As she slouched forward, the boy reached out to keep her from falling. But she retreated a step, vomited something yellow into the gutter, and looked up at him while wiping her mouth with her hand.

Watching him, Ryōko felt a kind of nostalgia for Kazuki's childhood, though she had never had a real childhood of her own. Memories of her youth, like cats tied in a bag, would thrash in her head from time to time, but they only made her feel how trapped she was, how miserable and wasted her life had been.

Ten years ago there had been a rumor in Kogane-chō that Ryōko had given birth to a baby girl and had left it with her sister. It was said that the baby had died in a fire, but since it was only a rumor, no one had ever come to her to offer condolences. No one even bothered to check whether the rumor was true or not. Kogane-chō was not the sort of place where you settled down and built relationships; then as now, most people who drifted in were simply hoping to get out again as soon as possible. And Ryōko herself went on as before, always the same clothes, the same doorway, always another customer. The rumor was soon forgotten. Yet deep inside, where no one could see, she had slowly and quietly gone mad. Her body had blown up like a balloon and her hair turned white as she forgot to dye it. No one would have cared now had they simply carted her away. The street had been taken over by young girls from Thailand, and Ryōko could no longer get a man to stop, even when she offered her services at half price.

"For you, Kazu, I'd do a freebie. You being all grown up now." His Rolex had caught her eye. The boy could feel the smile on his face suddenly freeze and then fade, as if it were floating away. Thrusting his hands in his pockets, he walked off staring down at the pavement. For a moment, he heard the clicking sound of high heels following him, but it stopped so quickly he glanced back to see what had happened.

"Here kitty, kitty." She was holding out her hand to a tortoiseshell cat. It approached warily and sniffed at her fingertips. Satisfied, it rolled on its back, stretched its paws in the air, and began to purr. Ryōko squatted over the cat, and when she did, a glimpse of her bright red panties appeared between her legs, stabbing the boy's eyes as though a knife had been drawn across his skin. As he watched her crouching there, the scene suddenly went flat, screenlike, silent, except for the rumbling in the cat's throat as Ryōko rubbed its belly.

When the boy passed through the tunnel under the train tracks in Kogane-chō he was always afraid he'd be trapped. He could never simply walk straight through, but would turn around several times, as if wondering which way he should flee. When the fear was worst, he would press his back against the wall and inch sideways in one direction or the other. As the express rattled overhead, he would sink into the dark pit of his memories.

At four o'clock on February ninth, the boy had gone to a karaoke rental studio in Kannai with two classmates, Kiyoshi and Takuya, and a boy named Reiji who was a year ahead of them. On the way to their studio room, they passed two high school girls, and Reiji invited them in. The girls agreed. At five-thirty, one of them went home, but the other stayed for more singing. About seven, while doing a duet with the girl, Reiji put his arm around her and invited her back to his house. They took two cabs, and arrived at Reiji's place in Kuboyama at seven-thirty. Reiji lived with his mother, but she worked at a bar in Hinode-chō and never got home before one o'clock, if she came home at all.

Reiji put some cans of beer out on his desk, but no one touched them.

"I'm thirsty, but I *hate* beer," said the girl. "Don't you have juice or something?"

"How about Pepsi?" Reiji asked, getting up. "I think that's about all we've got."

"While you're at it, make some ramen, too," said Takuya, tossing the comic book he was reading from the bed and flipping onto his stomach.

"For me, too," said the girl.

The conversation died as Reiji shut the door and they listened to him go downstairs. The silence turned to heat and enveloped the room. The girl felt sweat begin to gush under her arms. The boys listened as her breathing became heavier, but they kept very still. Kazuki held his breath, willing himself invisible. Her panting, echoed by the pounding of their hearts, began to stir the air in the room. But just then the girl glanced down at her watch.

"Oh no! It's so late. I've got to get home," she said, standing to go.

"But the ramen will be ready in a minute," said Takuya nervously. "Why don't you have some before you go?"

"But it's so hot in here," she countered, a wrinkle forming between her pencil-thin eyebrows.

"We can fix that," said Takuya. Kiyoshi grabbed the remote control sitting on the table and lowered the thermostat. At that moment, Reiji came in carrying a tray on which he was balancing cups of ramen and cans of Pepsi. The girl tucked her dyed hair behind her ears and set to work on the ramen. When she finished the noodles, she lifted the cup in both hands and slurped the soup noisily. Then she lit a cigarette. Though the boys all seemed to be looking elsewhere, they were watching her. Takuya and Kiyoshi held their breath, wondering when Reiji would go for the kill, while Kazuki inched toward the door, his back pressed against the wall.

The girl flicked the ashes from her cigarette into the half-empty can of Pepsi. "I always forget after I do that and end up drinking it, don't you?" she laughed. "Then I spit it all over the place when the ash gets in my mouth." Her smile vanished after a few seconds, fading to a frown as she crushed the cigarette into an ashtray. Then she poked around in the empty cigarette box.

"I've got Casters," said Reiji, fishing a new pack from his pocket. The girl fidgeted quietly, squeezing her hands between her knees.

Sure, she was thinking, she'd felt that nice tingle that went all the way to her crotch when men watched her cross her legs in a miniskirt on the train. But this was different; this was some kid's room, with a lock on the door—the warning lights were beginning to flash. She blamed herself for not going home after the karaoke studio.

"Well, I've got to get going," she said, tugging at the hem of her skirt. "See you around." She gathered up her book bag and stood to go, but as she made her way toward the door, Reiji tripped her and she fell. "What are you doing?" she shrieked, but Takuya and Kiyoshi had pinned her arms and legs almost before the words were out of her mouth. Reiji peeled up the secondhand sailor suit she wore on top and grabbed her bra. She thrashed her arms and legs, trying to scratch them with her long fingernails; and even after she could no longer move and they'd gagged her, she continued to writhe and squirm, her eyes bulging and her neck twisting.

"Do it!" said Reiji, glaring at Kiyoshi. Though Kiyoshi was clearly nervous, he immediately let go of the girl and unbuckled his belt, while Takuya slid off her underpants and spread her legs. Kiyoshi clutched his penis and tried to enter her, but because he wasn't hard enough yet or she wasn't wet enough, he didn't get very far.

"Use some spit," ordered Reiji. Kiyoshi dribbled some saliva into his palm, rubbed it on the end of his penis, and shoved it in, collapsing on the girl with a loud groan.

She lay limp now, tears forming in her eyes and spreading dark circles of mascara onto her cheeks. The boy could not make himself look away, and sat staring intently at the tears. She was quiet; no sobbing or sniffling, just the tears and the periodic rise and fall of her chest as she gasped for air. Takuya pulled off the shirt of her school uniform and unhooked her bra. Then he slid her skirt over her hips, leaving her naked. He squeezed her breasts as if trying to crush them, but she didn't even whimper. Reiji spread her legs from behind, dipped his index finger into her, and then held it up. Her thighs were dripping with semen. Catching her by the hair, he yanked her halfway up onto the bed.

"Try her from behind," he told Takuya, whose pants were already down around his knees. The bedsprings creaked as he pulled her up by her hips. Her breasts swayed back and forth, but her mouth was fixed, teeth clenched. Still, as Takuya's thrusts grew more violent, she let out a gasp.

The boy watched all of this with a vacant look, his senses so dulled that he could barely tell what he was seeing, what sounds he was hearing. At first he was only conscious of wanting to get away; but then he began to feel hatred, as though he would vomit with disgust for this woman.

When Takuya was done, Reiji draped himself over her and began to slowly thrust his hips. "Now watch how it's done, boys. I'll get a rise out of her. Check it out—she's wet now." He started to pant as his hips moved more rapidly, and at the last moment, he pulled back and shot onto her stomach. "If you know what you're doing, you don't come inside," he said, lighting a cigarette as he quickly got dressed. Seeing him, Takuya and Kiyoshi jumped up and scrambled into their pants. "They're done," Reiji said, turning to look at the boy. "You want a turn?"

"I . . . already came just from watching," Kazuki answered, hoping to sound as pitiful as possible. The air in the room was stale, heavy with semen and sweat. The boys were suddenly overcome—not by what they had done but by the filth they sensed emanating from the girl's body. They shrank from the bed, backs against the wall, as if to avoid a shower of defilement.

"We're finished, bitch," said Reiji, catching the girl's bra with his toes and dropping it on her face. "Hurry up and get dressed." She pulled herself up on her knees and clenched her fists over her eyes. Then slowly, moving like a blind woman, she began scraping her clothes together. She hunched her back, as if it were a protective shell, and began to dress, hoping to conceal the body they had smeared with spit and sweat and cum. Her zipper made a rasping sound as she pulled it up; her hand trembled violently as she smoothed her bangs. As she tried to get to her feet, a low moan escaped her mouth and she clutched her belly. She crouched there for some time before finally managing to pull up the panties that hung around her right ankle. Stepping into them with her left leg, she stumbled to her feet and out the door. With one hand against the wall for support, she made her way carefully down the stairs.

Their chests felt tight as they listened to the stairs creak, and they sat perfectly still until they heard the front door closing. The heater stirred the smells of their bodies, their warm breath. Reiji used the remote to turn it off. He mopped the sweat from his brow with his sleeve. "Sure is hot!" he cried, stripping off his shirt to wipe his back and under his arms. Then he pulled the cigarettes from his pocket. Kiyoshi hurried to give him a light with his Zippo.

"I like ganging up on them like that, but she was really too young," he said falling back onto the bed. "I don't even feel like doing it unless they're over twenty."

"Here," said Kiyoshi, fishing a knee sock from among the sheets and dangling it over Reiji's face.

"Fuck off," muttered Reiji, brushing away the sock and kicking Kiyoshi in the ass. He quickly lit another cigarette to cover the look of panic that had spread over his face and grabbed a can of beer from the table. Pulling the tab, he lapped at the foam that oozed through the hole before pronouncing it lukewarm and spitting it into the ashtray.

"She'll probably tell," said the boy, eyeing the sock.

"No way," said Reiji, wiping some foam from his jaw with the back of his hand. They sat in silence as the light faded to the point where they could barely see one another, overcome with the feeling that the room would dissolve and they would be trapped inside.

"I came inside her," Takuya blurted out, sounding panicky.

"Me, too," added Kiyoshi, a large drop of cold sweat dangling at the tip of his nose.

"If she's knocked up, her parents will find out. Fuck!"

"She's probably on the pill. She sleeps around, and I hear she even does her old man about every night," Reiji added, trying to reassure them.

"If we're caught, it won't be in the papers and on TV, will it?" Kiyoshi sounded tense.

"No way," said Reiji. "They can't show pictures of minors, or print names. But I don't think she's even going to the cops. She liked it, boys.

She's not telling nobody. No way." Fighting the urge to hit something, he wrapped his arm around Kiyoshi's shoulder.

The scene, everything that had happened in the room, replayed itself in Kazuki's head, and as the fear began to dissipate, the details emerged in distinct outline. "I didn't do anything," he muttered. "I just watched." He glanced around coolly at the other three.

"We should have taken pictures," Reiji murmured darkly and shuddered.

"Why?" asked Kiyoshi, glancing at Reiji and then starring at his feet.

"We could've blackmailed her, told her we'd spread the pictures around if she talked." Ignoring Kiyoshi, Reiji watched Kazuki, but the cruel, unfeeling look on his face made Reiji look away.

"Well, if things get sticky my father knows a lot of big shots. I think he even knows the chief of police," said Kazuki, getting up as if he were weary of the whole subject. Reiji snorted and shot Takuya and Kiyoshi an irritated look.

"So that's our story, if we need one," said Reiji. "Yuminaga didn't go through with it, but the three of us did. Got it?" Takuya and Kiyoshi looked as though they were either going to laugh or burst into tears. "But it's not gonna happen. Nobody gets done by a bunch of guys and goes telling the police." Reiji laughed nervously. "But if she does, you tell the police that we did it, and Yuminaga wasn't even here," he added, signaling Takuya and Kiyoshi behind Kazuki's back. They nodded gravely. "So, Yuminaga, where were you, exactly?" he asked in a theatrical tone, putting his arm around Kazuki and driving his finger into the pit of his stomach.

The passage under the tracks was lined with billboards: "End the Influx of Foreign Prostitutes," "Prevent AIDS!" "Rid Our Streets of Prostitution and Gangs."

Kazuki heard someone calling and turned to find Kanamoto coming toward him. Kanamoto, as he told it, had worked the docks when he was young but after an accident, more than thirty years ago now, had drifted into Kogane-chō. But Kazuki had his doubts; he thought it more likely he'd been the leader of one of the gangs. When he was still a little boy, Kazuki played the video games at his father's pachinko parlor. Often, in the middle of a battle, Kanamoto would show up, ask to take over, and then proceed to shoot everything in sight, clearing the board as if by magic. It was Kanamoto who had, in effect, given the boy a passport that allowed him to go anywhere in Kogane-chō. He had taught him how to clench his fists when he hit someone and told him stories about buying smuggled pistols off ships at Honmoku Pier. From time to time he would roll up his sleeves to show the boy scars where his father used to grind out cigarettes when he was little, and he had told him how his dad used to kick him until he had nearly gone blind. For a time Kazuki had called him "Boss" and pestered him for more stories. But when he turned ten, he found he no longer wanted to talk or listen to anyone at all, and he began avoiding Kanamoto and his endless chatter.

When he turned twelve, they'd bought him a middle school uniform. But about the time that it got too tight to wear, Kazuki became convinced that the only way to prove that he was an adult was to cut himself off from everything that had to do with his past. In twelve months, beginning during the summer of his last year in elementary school, he grew seventeen centimeters. He knew that smoking and drinking and talking like a man were a good start, but after that he wasn't quite sure what it took—until one day when he realized that the only thing that separated an adult and a child was that one had power and the other didn't. When you looked at the world with the benefit of this special X ray known as "power," what once seemed chaotic and random suddenly appeared for what it was: a neat system that divided everyone into the haves and have-nots. Fathers, teachers, policemen—they all commanded respect because they were powerful; if they lost their power, they were nothing but garbage. But what was power, really, except another word for money? You could buy authority and influence with money; in fact, was there anything you couldn't buy with money?

And that meant poor people were nothing but losers, children really; and just about everyone in Kogane-chō was a lot like his brother who had Williams Syndrome: caught in some twilight zone between childhood and the adult world. To Kazuki, the one thing that a powerful person could never afford to lose was compassion, but he decided early on that he would have to become an adult as soon as possible.

"You're looking well, Kazuki." He stared at Kanamoto's kindly face. The gold in his teeth was so bright you might think he was using some special polish. His stubbly, familiar jaw and his nose were both warped and crooked, as if someone had given his face a terrible beating. The few hairs that clung to his forehead had been smoothed back over the top of his head. Kanamoto pulled a cigarette from his shirt pocket, put it in his mouth, and lit it.

"You're looking pretty good yourself," said Kazuki. Kanamoto had puckered his lips into a circle to blow a smoke ring, but a sudden fit of laughter spoiled the attempt. Kazuki could smell whiskey on his breath.

"I'm thinking you got some of this," said Kanamoto, running his tongue across his gums and raising his little finger.

"No sir!" Kazuki dropped his eyes bashfully and kicked at the asphalt with the toes of his sneakers like a little boy.

"I thought you'd stopped hanging around Kogane-chō," Kanamoto croaked, frowning. "It's not the kind of place for you. You should stay away or you'll end up in trouble." The boy looked away shyly, muttered something inaudible, and shuffled off. Out of the corner of his eye, he could see Kanamoto waving good-bye; until quite recently he would have waved back, but he was too old for that now. He kept his head down, fingered the bag of cocaine in his pocket, and kept walking. He didn't look up until he turned right onto the bridge over the river and heard the sound of something being dropped in the water. Just ahead, he could see the silhouette of a woman leaning out over the railing. For a moment, the groans of the high school girl came back to him and he froze; but this was a middle-aged woman, listing over the railing like an abandoned ship. He looked down at the river, studying the black hulls of real ships tied up under the bridge. The river, he thought, was actually a graveyard for boats. The owners would come in the dead of night to leave these broken tubs to rot, and now there were so many that the police could barely tell if there was a new one from day to day, much less trace them. The river water sat in stagnant pools around them, still and dark in the day, animated only at night by the flickering of pink and blue neon.

The air, too, was hot and utterly still. But just where the woman stood, if nowhere else, a breeze seemed to be blowing, stirring her full, white skirt and rustling the long black hair that hung down her back. Her mouth seemed to be forming words.

"I'm so frightened. I want to die. Why doesn't anyone understand that a woman like me is better off dead?" The woman threw out the words, but no one answered. "Don't you know, master? Is that my only choice? To die? Then give back the bag, please. It's all I have left . . . Give it back, now!" She screamed and then began to laugh quietly. The sound of the laughter seemed to settle on the river, sinking to the bottom and just as quickly ripping back to the surface before it passed away. "That's why I'm telling you to give it back, master!" The laughter changed to sobs as the woman went on talking, but the rest of it was unintelligible. Kazuki was overcome with the feeling that the woman was vomiting darkness itself, which was spreading like ink over the river, threatening to flood the city and dye it black. The woman was herself some dangerous shadow, a phantom. It occurred to him that she might be a ghost, and despite the heat he was suddenly covered with gooseflesh. He started to run, talking to himself as he went. If the signal changed to red by the time he reached the crosswalk, the curse would kill him. If he made it through the crosswalk and to the next corner without meeting anyone, he'd be safe. Eventually, he convinced himself that the curse was real, and he sprinted along faster than he had run in years. Sweat was dripping from his forehead by the time he reached the door of the restaurant known as the Golden Pavilion.

There was just one customer inside: a white woman whose ample bottom was spread over one of the chairs at the counter. She turned and looked at Kazuki as if sizing him up. Her face was caked with powder, except for her cheeks, which were heavily rouged. A strong stench of cheap perfume wafted from her body. The only thing about her that seemed real was the lemon-colored silk of the chiffon scarf wrapped around her neck.

"Who's this?" she asked. The old man behind the counter glanced up at Kazuki and then back down at his pot. He fished some noodles from the water and drained them before he spoke.

"My grandson."

Kazuki had been hanging around the Golden Pavilion since he was five. Long ago, he had taken to calling the old man Grandfather Sada and the bedridden woman on the second floor, Granny Shige. He loved them both very much. The old man had opened a greasy spoon in this same location before the war, converting it to the Chinese Restaurant Golden Pavilion in the midfifties. Kazuki took a chair down the counter from the white woman, who studied him out of the corner of her eye as she stabbed a dumpling with her chopsticks. She shook her head and sighed nervously.

Someone on the TV laughed, and Chihiro, who was washing dishes, stopped and turned to look. Kazuki couldn't tell whether she was staring at the smoke from the white woman's cigarette or trying to catch the joke that had amused the celebrity on the screen. He had often thought that Chihiro might make a good companion for his brother and had even thought he might invite her over to the house. But in the end he had decided against it; you couldn't really pick friends for someone else, he'd concluded. If his brother were to play piano for Chihiro, he wondered, what would she think?

"Water," Kazuki said, but Chihiro continued to stare at the screen. So he stood and took one of the plastic cups from the tray on the counter. Noticing the fingerprints and dirt on it, he leaned over to rinse it under the faucet while asking Chihiro very slowly for a Fanta Grape.

One day, when he had come into the Golden Pavilion, he had found this woman, Chihiro, standing next to the old man washing dishes, just as if she'd been doing it for years. In those days she had been thin and scrawny, like some botanical specimen; but each time Kazuki came back she had gained weight, until now she was whiter and plumper than the woman at the counter who was just preparing to attack her bowl of ramen. Chihiro was a mystery, but Kazuki knew that even if he were to ask about her, the old man was unlikely to tell him anything. For the old men and the hookers and drug dealers of Kogane-chō, the past was a person's only real possession, and they guarded it as though they were locking memories in a vault and hiding the key.

The woman at the counter stared up at the TV with a bored look as she sucked the soup scum from her teeth and spit it back into the bowl. Her hair was cut in a sharp line just below her ears, but it had probably been more than a month since her last dye job and dark roots were beginning to show in the blond mass. Under the raised tracks on one side of the Ōoka River was an area where prostitutes from Thailand, Malaysia, the Philippines, and other Southeast Asian countries charged ten thousand yen for twenty minutes. But the other side of the river was crowded with cheap hotels; here, the going rate was twenty thousand for an hour plus money for the room, and the women were white, from Russia or Colombia. None of the women, though, was here for long. They stayed until they'd earned enough money, and then went home. If a regular customer didn't come around for a while, when he finally did come back, he'd find the woman gone. But every once in a while, one of them lingered on in the neighborhood and became a fixture, unable to find her way back out.

"Stir-fry veggies!" As the woman placed her order, the room began to shake from a train passing overhead—about the same as a fairly strong earthquake, Kazuki noted as he waited calmly for it to subside. The woman, however, glanced uneasily at the ceiling.

"You want something to eat?" the old man asked Kazuki when the shaking had nearly stopped.

"Nope." No matter how often Kazuki ate there, the old man refused to take his money. Once, eighteen months ago when he'd entered middle school, he left a ten-thousand-yen bill on the counter. "Keep the change," he'd said, but the old man had made a point of tearing up the bill right in front of him.

"Okay if I go upstairs?" he asked. The old man merely nodded. "Three guys are coming by. When they get here, could you send them up?" Without bothering to wipe the suds from her hands, Chihiro poured the Fanta into a glass and set it on the counter. "How's she doing?" Kazuki asked, taking a sip.

The old man glanced up from the onions he was chopping. "It won't be long now," he said, his voice flat and emotionless, as if he were clearing his throat. The pile of onions on the cutting board looked like enough for a month.

"What do you mean?" said Kazuki. "You're not going senile on me, are you? Granny'll die when you die. If you hurry her off like this, you'll probably go first."

The old man set a wok on the stove. He had long ago made a decision about the boy. No matter how busy he was with the restaurant, no matter what kind of trouble he was in, he would always make time to listen. And whatever Kazuki did, he would accept him and defend him—that much he knew. He had a clear memory of the day Kanamoto had first brought Kazuki into the Golden Pavilion. It was, for Sada, perhaps the only pure and innocent thing that had ever happened to him. Though he could never quite put it into words, afterward he often thought that it was as though a baby crane, snowy white and gangly, had wandered into the shop. Kanamoto had called out "Ramen for the young master," and lifted him onto a chair, but Sada had stood frozen, staring at the boy. Even when Kanamoto had become a little irate, he hadn't been able to rouse himself. Finally, he had managed to tell them that he didn't have the skill to make ramen for such a fine boy, that they should please go elsewhere.

"What are you talking about? You think I kidnapped the kid?" Kanamoto had shouted. "Just get us some ramen!"

"But I'm telling you, I can't make anything good enough for him. I mean it: now shut up and get out!" Sada's eyes were fixed on the young Kazuki. The boy stared back as Kanamoto lifted him down from the chair.

"I want to eat Grampa's ramen," he muttered.

"Really?" Sada had whispered even more quietly than Kazuki, and he dropped a serving of noodles into the boiler. After Kanamoto led the boy out of the shop, the woman who would one day be Granny Shige had found her husband sobbing as he cleared away the empty bowl.

Kazuki was incapable of admitting that Shige was dying. Could someone who had lived so long just disappear without a trace? Still, he knew that she was worse every time he came to visit. But why did they leave her up there? Was it the money? He pushed his chair back and balanced on two legs. He didn't really mean to ask, but as the chair fell forward it just slipped out.

"Why don't you put her in the hospital?"

Sada turned so that Kazuki could hear him over the noise of the wok. "She says she'd be better off going straight to the cemetery rather than going to the hospital." He grimaced as though some oil had splashed on his hand, but there was a hint of laughter in his voice.

Chihiro craned her neck to see who was whispering out in the street just as Reiji peeked in under the awning.

"This map you faxed us is a piece of crap."

"We were *seriously* lost," said Kiyoshi, his voice cracking. The white woman looked skeptically at the newcomers for a moment; then, realizing they were Kazuki's friends, she began murmuring something that sounded more like curses and incantations than Russian.

"Looking good, Kazu," said Reiji, raising his palm. Kazuki raised his own hand to slap Reiji's, noting the dark sweat stain on the front of his T-shirt. "So, where should we do our homework?" Reiji asked, glancing around the shop.

"Up there," said Kazuki, nodding toward the stairs.

"Hasegawa's late," Reiji said. A train rattled overhead as Kazuki slapped the counter and pushed back his chair.

"Let's go on up."

The three boys slipped out of their shoes at the bottom of the stairs by the toilet in back. Kazuki had been wearing his Reeboks since noon, and they were damp from the heat. He flipped the switch on the wall and a dim bulb lit up as if exhaling light onto the stairs. The building had not been renovated since it was built in the fifties, and it groaned when the three boys started up. The staircase was no more than a dozen stairs, but the darkness, thickened with smoke and smells from the kitchen, made it seem longer. At the top, Kazuki took hold of the doorknob.

Reiji and Kiyoshi followed him into the room but then froze, their eyes fixed on the futon. Kazuki knelt by Shige's pillow.

"Granny, how are you feeling? We're going to use the room." The old woman's eyes watered as he bent over her, and her wrinkled lips opened as if tearing apart. "Have a seat," he said. The two boys advanced a step into the room but seemed puzzled as to where they should sit.

An assortment of objects covered the walls: a moss-colored sweater on a hanger, a clock stopped at 3:25, a calendar featuring a blond nude stretched out on a beach, some sort of framed certificate, and a clipping from an old newspaper stuck up with a thumbtack. On the tatami were just a few scraps of furniture—a low table, a rocking chair by the window, a hotplate, and a small chest of drawers made of paulownia wood. On the chest was a beer bottle in which someone had stuck a single sunflower that had long since dried up and lost its petals. The dark center drooped over like a head lolling on a neck. The only things in the room that appeared relatively new were the sheets and pillowcase on the futon; everything else gave off an odor like wine that had turned to vinegar.

"Have you got it?" Kiyoshi whispered, looking up at the ceiling. A tie-dyed sash was draped over the lamp shade.

"Let's go somewhere else," said Reiji, lowering his voice.

"It's safe here," said Kazuki, smiling.

"But . . . ," Kiyoshi stammered, looking at the old woman on the futon. Averting his own eyes, Reiji sat down at the low table.

Kazuki fished a gram bag of cocaine from his pocket and set it on the table.

"He's late. I'll go look," he said, leaving the room. As he walked through the restaurant, the white woman was fishing pieces of cabbage from her bowl and stuffing them in her mouth while trying to make conversation with the old man behind the counter. Kazuki was slipping into his sandals when Takuya appeared under the awning. The woman glanced in their direction but turned quickly back toward the counter, crossing herself and muttering some foreign words. Kazuki had no idea what she was saying, but he knew it was some kind of prayer; it was probably because he couldn't understand the words that they sounded so much like a prayer. As he listened, an uneasy feeling settled over him like a white shroud.

"Are they here yet?" Takuya asked, panting a little, as if he'd run all the way.

"Upstairs," said Kazuki, glancing toward the back of the shop.

The cocaine on the low table had already been divided four ways. Reiji smiled up at them and pulled out a silver-plated cigar case. Laughing, he shook it like a maracas and patted his side, then flipped open the lid and extracted two short straws. He passed one to Kiyoshi, and the two of them bent over, carefully snorting the powder deep into their nostrils. Then Takuya took Kiyoshi's straw and bent over the table.

In a few minutes, the three of them were talking feverishly, telling stories about their experiences in juvenile centers and reform schools. Kazuki had decided not to snort until he was sure the other three got what they wanted. He assumed they were exaggerating about reform school to make it seem worse than it was, probably to get a better deal out of him.

"Why don't we give Granny a line," said Reiji. "Fix her right up." Takuya and Kiyoshi collapsed in fits of laughter. "They come wake you every morning at six," Reiji said, continuing his story. "If you're still asleep, they kick the shit out of you. You swear you'll get back at them when you get out, but if you say anything they only hit you harder," he said, half smiling at Kazuki.

"Really?" Kazuki responded flatly; by his count it had been about thirty minutes and the effects would be wearing off soon. He wondered whether he should give them another bag or wait for them to ask.

"The whole time I was in, I kept thinking what I'd do when I got out, the first thing I'd do . . ." Kiyoshi glanced at Reiji and Takuya.

"But you know," said Reiji, ignoring him, "reform school and juvy are about as different as kindergarten and college. Juvy's hell," he added, putting the straw in his nose and sniffing.

"They don't even have reform schools anymore, do they?" asked Takuya, a gargling noise rising in his throat. "The name changed; now they call them 'Self-sufficiency' something or other," he added, though nobody was listening.

"That exercise crap they make you do all morning, that's torture. Nothing but child abuse, really. They make you do fifty push-ups, and if you get even a little behind, they start beating you. Then they give you about thirty seconds' rest and start in again—a hundred times, two hundred times. Everybody has to count while you do it, 'one, two, three . . . ,' and if you aren't loud enough, they're right there with the stick. Who the fuck can do that anyway? Hundred push-ups, two hundred push-ups? So in the end, everybody gets the crap beat out of them. You think that's funny?" Reiji looked at Kazuki who, instead of answering, pulled another plastic bag from his pocket. "Shit, boy," Reiji muttered, "if you've got more, why didn't you say so sooner?" This time he measured out half the pile for himself. Then Takuya passed the straw to Kazuki and he bent over the table; but he took only a short sniff before handing the straw back. Still, in a few minutes he felt refreshed, and his hatred for the three of them had begun to dissipate, replaced by a feeling of calm and well-being. Reiji was rattling on now about the physical exams they had been given in the reform school, but Kazuki hardly heard him. The sounds in the room seemed to fade into the distance, while those in the distance became clear, as if he could distinguish them one by one. Ignoring the chatter around him, Kazuki strained his ears to hear other voices. Like a faint whisper, the Russian prayers of the white woman below came to him.

Suddenly, Takuya fell silent, and as the violent motion of his mouth stopped, his face froze, exactly like a Noh mask. Just at that moment there was a hesitant knock at the door. Kazuki opened it a crack to find Chihiro with a tray laden with dumplings, chopsticks, and pots of soy sauce, hot pepper oil, and vinegar. When Kazuki had taken the tray from her, Chihiro wiped a drop of sweat from her nose and stood blinking.

"Smells good!" called Kiyoshi, his voice cracking. "We're in luck. A care package!"

"Thanks," Kazuki murmured, shutting the door and setting the tray on the table. Reiji grabbed a pair of chopsticks and broke them apart with his teeth, but by the time he had mixed sauce from the bottles, he had forgotten the chopsticks and began stuffing dumplings in his mouth with his fingers. As he chewed, bits of pork and cabbage oozed from between his lips and fell on his lap. Watching them eat, Kazuki was overcome with the impression that Reiji was a dog, Takuya a cat, and Kiyoshi a pig. The idea struck him as so hilarious that he broke down in a fit of laughter, pointing at them as he bellowed, but they hardly seemed to notice, barely glancing up as they continued to stuff their faces.

Kazuki had been sitting uncomfortably for a long time, his back resting against a knob on the dresser, but he no longer felt the stiffness or the tingling in his legs. He continued to stare at the others, but now they were looking back, like mirrors set facing one another, but somehow drifting apart. His heart soared like a bird streaking into the sky, while his body was swept away by the crash of a tidal wave. Body and soul were free, floating lightly in the pitch black. Suddenly, for no reason at all, he felt happy. He had no desire to leave the darkness, but then someone's voice opened a hole and pale light came streaming in.

"They made you keep a journal every day." It was Reiji, still talking about reform school. "And if you didn't write down all this embarrassing stuff, they said you weren't reformed. I busted my butt writing that crap . . ."

"Is it raining?" Kazuki asked, but his own voice sounded distant and he stuck his fingers in his ears to clear them. A roar of laughter bounced off his eardrums like a trampoline. He shook his head to drive it away. "It's the train," he said, but before his voice had died away in the laughter, he felt a wave of sound sweeping over him. He clasped his hands over his ears to protect them from the sound, a buzzing like a great swarm of locusts, but as he did, his hearing returned to normal. The euphoria faded, leaving a hollow place that was the only proof the happiness had ever existed. Then the darkness, gathering in around him, filled the hole. He caught a glimpse of flickering light from someone's cigarette. But it wasn't tobacco that Reiji and the others were smoking; it was cocaine. There was someone else in the room, he suddenly remembered. Kazuki strained his eyes toward a corner that was particularly dark, where his mother lay on the futon—at least it seemed to be his mother.

"Does it hurt?" he asked, stroking her hair, but she said nothing, as if she had departed, leaving her eyes behind. Still, those eyes, he felt, could see through everything. He used his fingers to wipe away the gummy residue that clung about her lashes and then pressed his palms lightly over her eyelids to close them. Wringing out a washcloth in the basin of water next to her pillow, he carefully wiped the old woman's face; then opening the collar of her robe, he mopped the sweat from her neck and under her arms. He rinsed the cloth and rolled up the hem of her robe. As he washed her, the deep tracework of wrinkles on her calves and legs reminded him of the veins on a leaf. After cleaning her thighs, he removed her disposable diaper and went to get a clean one and a fresh robe from the chest. He had almost finished washing the soiled places where the diaper had been when she opened her eyes. He pulled his hand back. "You want me to stop?" he asked.

Her eyelashes fluttered. "Want me to do your back?" More blinking. "We'll do it next time," he said. "Let's get you changed." He slid his hands under her body and slowly turned her on her side, skillfully maneuvering her out of the old robe and into the new one.

When he looked up, he saw the other three rolling on the floor and laughing. He looked at them doubtfully, as if eyeing a group of rare and remarkably ugly animals. Why would they be laughing at me for taking care of my sick mother?

"What's so funny?" he asked, but they just laughed harder, convulsed in uncontrollable fits. Kazuki stood and walked over to Kiyoshi. Grabbing him by the front of his shirt, he punched him in the face. "Asshole! There's nothing funny about nursing your mother!" For a moment he stroked Kiyoshi's head as he kneeled before him, covering his face with his hands. Then, as he watched Reiji frantically brushing something invisible from his legs, the haze that had been clouding Kazuki's mind began to clear.

Reiji, however, was eyeing an enormous swarm of ants that was emerging from his toes and making its way up his legs, over his thighs and belly, and on up to the tip of his head. When his whole body turned black with ants, he thought, he would probably scream for help. Now and then he grabbed at his shirt, mistaking the sweat stains for tarantulas and cobras. His eyes were wide with fear, and his mouth made a sputtering noise, spindles of saliva dangling from the corners. His whole body shook.

This performance sent Takuya and Kiyoshi into new fits of laughter, but Kazuki began to feel nervous. He wiggled a straw into Reiji's nose and set a line of cocaine at the other end.

"Take it!" he shouted, and Reiji sniffed the powder into his head. A few seconds later, his body went limp.

The amount of coke Reiji used had increased rapidly since he and Kazuki had become friends. Last autumn, Takuya and Kiyoshi, whom he barely knew, had brought Kazuki to the video game center in Isezaki-chō. At first, Kazuki seemed like a boring rich kid and Reiji wanted nothing to do with him, but then the four of them went out for a hamburger. As he listened to Kazuki, he began to sense that all the polite talk and nice manners were fake, meant to cover up something that was badly cracked, like dabs of glue barely holding together a shattered pot. But the pot was crumbling anyway, the cracks spreading out like radio waves, surfacing in a pattern of petty crimes. Reiji had casually asked for a loan of a thousand yen, and Kazuki had handed it over so readily he seemed to be making change at a convenience store. When Kiyoshi mentioned that Kazuki's father owned the pachinko parlor known as Vegas, Reiji had barely been able to stop himself from shouting "Bingo!" This was a big fish, and he was just the guy to land it.

A few days later, he had invited the three of them to go out for karaoke and then back to his apartment where he had left the bait: half a gram of coke. That first time he had given them two hundredths of a gram apiece and done just three hundredths himself; they'd all stayed high for three hours. From that time on, Kazuki had taken to paying for the drugs, no questions asked. A gram of cocaine cost about thirty thousand yen, but it seemed to Reiji that for Kazuki this was like buying a pack of gum.

"So, have you got it?" Reiji's question came out of the blue. "We kept our promise; you keep yours." His tone was syrupy and slightly obscene.

"How much?" Kazuki asked icily.

"A hundred thousand for them. But I was in juvy, so make mine two hundred."

"That okay with you?" Kazuki said, looking around. Takuya looked at him blankly; Kiyoshi's nose was dripping blood. He looked back at Reiji, who opened his arms and moved toward him as if to give him a hug, but Kazuki shoved him away and opened the window. He thought he saw the woman they'd raped, looking up at him. As he watched, her hand rose and her fingernails began to grow, twisting toward him through the night. He screamed and slammed the window.

Kazuki looked up at the exterior of Vegas. Above the white metal and glass door was a huge mirrored arch in the middle of which were red, green, blue, and yellow neon lights stacked up like a rainbow. Otherwise, though, there were none of the gaudy billboards, lights, or floral banners that decorated most pachinko parlors. Vegas would have looked right at home next to the fashionable boutiques in Bashamichi or Motomachi.

Six years ago, Kazuki's father, Hidetomo, had torn down Treasure Ball Hall, the aging pachinko parlor his father had left him, built this modern place, and christened it Vegas. The new name had never quite taken, and the locals still called it Treasure Ball, but Hidetomo had changed more than just the name of the hall: the management company, which had been Beneficial Enterprises, Inc., became Group Icarus. No doubt the changes were due in part to the fact that pachinko halls that looked like hotels or restaurants were doing good business; but it was rumored that the real reason was that Hidetomo had been made a trustee of Hōsei Academy.

Kazuki attended Hōsei, a nationally known prep school. Its success rate for getting students into Tokyo University was among the best, and its soccer team regularly made it to the national tournament; but Hōsei was also a crassly commercial place where even the teachers would admit that they concentrated on training only the top two hundred students while the rest were there simply for the steep tuition they paid. Hidetomo was in the habit of telling everyone he met that the south building of the new elementary school Hōsei had founded four years ago was built with his donations. Though no one ever believed he could have given more than part of the building, his boast was, in fact, true: in six years' time he had given over five hundred million yen, two hundred million of which he had realized in a tax evasion scheme. Getting Kazuki and his sister into the school without the entrance exam was only a minor consideration in all of this; Hidetomo's real interest was in the circle of contacts he would make as a trustee and Hōsei's close ties to the worlds of high finance and sports. He envisioned expanding Group Icarus, which consisted of eight pachinko parlors strung out across the country, into a conglomerate of hotels, restaurants, karaoke bars, and sports clubs. With that in mind, he also made private donations—more than thirty million yen over six years—to the chairman of the board of trustees, a noted economist who had graduated from Tokyo University but who now could be heard at the city's best clubs and restaurants calling Hidetomo his "right-hand man."

Kazuki did a quick inspection as he moved through the hall. The high green-and-white ceiling had been glassed over to make it appear higher still, and the aisles were so wide that two men waving their arms could pass along them without bumping one another. In back, on the right, was a lounge with a soundproof phone booth and an array of vending machines, but it was empty. The customers were mesmerized by the silver pachinko balls dancing in their tiny, brilliant universe, a cross between Disneyland and Las Vegas. A steady stream of customers was returning from the rest rooms and prize window in back. As they passed, they studied Kazuki briefly before concluding, apparently, that he was there looking for his father. The employees, on the other hand, fluttered around him like sparrows, bowing hurriedly in his direction and then ducking out of sight. His head was swimming, and he stopped for a moment, closing his eyes. Yellow flashes, like sunspots, spread out across the backs of his eyelids—yesterday's coke, most likely. His hands were slightly clammy, but he felt cold. The cool, dry air seemed charged with static electricity, and Kazuki realized that the air-conditioning must be turned up too high. That's sure to drive customers away, he thought, looking around for Hayashi.

Though he hadn't put up any money, right from the beginning Hayashi had worked with Kazuki's grandfather, Hideaki, to make Treasure Ball a success. They had collaborated on every aspect of the business, Hideaki as manager and Hayashi in charge of floor operations. He was usually stationed at the front of the hall, hair neatly parted, face clean shaven. His reading glasses were gleaming gold, his shirt carefully starched; his suits were English, his ties Armani or Versace, his socks black silk, his shoes highly polished. He might almost have been mistaken for a bank manager, yet there was also something in his attentive manner that suggested a hotel bellboy. Though the name had long since been changed to Vegas, Hayashi continued to run things just as he had in the Treasure Ball days.

Hidetomo liked to read books on business strategy, especially biographies of successful managers. When he found out that the president of one large company had started training to be a manager at thirteen, he began having Kazuki, who had just entered middle school, attend the branch managers' meetings; and he gave strict orders that his son was to be treated as his proxy whenever he showed up at one of the halls.

"I don't see Hayashi," Kazuki told the clerk behind the prize counter. "Have Sugimoto ring his cell phone and get him here at once." Startled by the cold, mocking look in his eyes, the woman, a plump forty-something who had only been with the company for six months or so, fumbled with the telephone and poked at the key for an inside line. Kazuki glared around at the hall, listening vaguely to the background music—an electronic symphony of pachinko machines. His slightly parted lips were slowly broadening into an ecstatic smile. To his eyes, this crowd of adults huddled around the machines appeared to be a herd of livestock. Whenever a picture of a barn or a pigsty came on the TV, Kazuki inevitably thought of the customers at Vegas. He had heard from his father that an estimated twenty-seven million players poured fifteen trillion yen into pachinko machines annually, adding four hundred billion yen to the national coffers; and he had decided that these adults, who did nothing but feed the little balls all day long, were somewhat lower than cows or pigs in the scheme of things, perhaps about equal to chickens. Then again, even chickens, in their short lives here on earth, were raised to do society some good. The pachinko players were a step down from barnyard fowl. In the end, the feeling spilled over to other areas: when it occurred to him that college students, housewives, businessmen, and teachers were potential pachinko players, he felt nothing but contempt for all of them. He wanted to shout "Welcome to Vegas!" to the whole adult world.

Sensing someone hurrying up behind him, Kazuki spun around. His eyes met Hayashi's for a split second before they both looked down.

"I was out at the Sakuragi-chō shop. Sorry to be late getting back," Hayashi muttered, bowing at a perfect forty-five-degree angle and then looking up. He folded his arms in front of him, cocked his head to the side, and looked expectantly at Kazuki. The corners of his mouth were turned up in something resembling a smile, but behind his gold-rimmed glasses his eyes were serious.

"It's cold in here," said Kazuki, conscious that there was no way Hayashi could have made it back from Sakuragi-chō in five minutes. "Let's turn down the air-conditioning." He glared down at the older man as if to remind him that he was now the taller of the two.

"Right away," said Hayashi, turning to the woman at the prize window who had been hanging on every word. "Go ask Fujimaki to turn up the thermostat," he told her, pointing out where she should go. Instantly, she came fluttering out from behind the counter.

"Anything out of the ordinary?" Kazuki asked.

Hayashi answered as if reporting to his boss. "Three days ago we found some counterfeit prize vouchers. Since we caught them early no damage was done, but they were the best ones I've come across. They were in denominations of five thousand yen, so they didn't amount to much; anybody doing the books would catch them at the end of the day. The prizes are different at each hall, so they can't get away with it all over town." Faced with Hayashi's polite tone and withering look, Kazuki began to feel like a miserable child.

"But don't some people say we should use the same prizes, at least at all the shops in the same prefecture?" He had taken his hands out of his pockets and folded his arms across his chest.

"We're already moving in that direction in Tokyo, as the police and the trade board suggested, but it will take some time. As you say, though, standardization does seem to be the key. By the way . . ."

"Where's the boss?" Feeling his own energy fading as Hayashi gathered momentum, Kazuki decided to cut him off.

"We haven't seen him in the hall much lately. If he's here, he'd be in the office."

"Thanks," said Kazuki, turning on his heels. Bowing slightly, Hayashi watched him go, thinking that he was looking more like his father every day.

The office was on the second floor of an old brick building next door to Vegas. The first floor was rented out to a restaurant that specialized in grilled meat. As Kazuki peered through the gold-lettered "Icarus" painted on the glass, two Dobermans charged the door barking hysterically. Behind them, a grinning Sugimoto appeared. She stroked the dogs as they stood, front paws on the glass, and with her free hand she opened the door. Reaching down, she put one arm around the neck of each dog—Door and Bell, as they were called—and let them lick her face, sticking out her tongue now and then to lick back.

"Come . . . in . . . Kazuki," she managed between licks. Sugimoto had worked in the office for more than twenty years as Hidetomo's financial secretary. Behind her back, she was referred to as the empress of Vegas. She released one of the dogs and wrapped her free arm around Kazuki. "Would you like some barley tea? Or maybe a cola?" she asked, but Kazuki didn't answer.

Hidetomo rose and started toward Kazuki, but thinking better of it, he pushed a button on the intercom. "Call Hayashi!" he bellowed. He glared at Kazuki as he stood frozen on the other side of the office window, eyeing him slowly up and down. "I've decided I don't want you coming here," he said at last. "Come to think of it, for the time being let's forget all about the Little Mr. Pachinko routine. And since when have you stopped going to school? Did you think I wouldn't find out? Shimada tells me everything. I couldn't give a shit about that fucking school, but you should be taking it a little more seriously so soon after your little 'incident' . . . And I don't want you hanging out with that bunch of losers," he continued.

"I hear they got out. I guess gang rape isn't such a big deal? What do you think of that, Sugimoto?" He picked up the glass she had set on the desk and drained it in one gulp.

"Oh my!" she gasped, a smile playing around her mouth. "I guess I'd better watch myself."

There was a knock and the door opened. Hayashi, his back straight as a rail, advanced into the room. When he was a few feet from Hidetomo's desk, he stopped and bowed precisely.

"Hayashi! What's your daughter's name again?" Hidetomo asked.

"It's Yōko, boss," he said, forcing a broad smile onto his face.

"They tell me she's an actress. I think I've seen her in the weeklies or somewhere. Hard to believe, with an ugly puss like that."

"Now, boss," Sugimoto scolded. "You know that's not true. She's darling, absolutely darling." But Hayashi's smile just widened.

"I've known Hayashi and his girl since before you could fit a matchstick in her cunny. She's done porn video, hasn't she?"

"I prefer to call them 'art films,' boss," said Hayashi, his smile becoming brittle.

"So can you explain the difference to me?" Hidetomo demanded.

Hayashi cocked his head to one side like a dog that had failed to understand a command, but then he brightened and looked up smiling. "Excuse me?" he said.

"I repeat," Hidetomo shouted, pounding the desk with his fist. "What the fuck difference is there between porn videos and your 'art films'?" He spat out the words.

"Well, porn videos are dirty films made for grown men, while 'art films' are . . . well . . . art. I have to admit I've never actually seen them, but I think that's the difference."

"Is that so? Well, whatever. Anyway, I want you to bring your daughter around tomorrow."

"Very well," said Hayashi. "And what is it you'd like her to do?"

"When was the last time you did it with a woman?" Hidetomo asked him. The roar of an express train covered Hayashi's silence. "I want to buy your daughter, of course! About how much do you think you owe me, anyway?"

Blood suddenly roared into Kazuki's head, and his brain began to race. His father, Sugimoto, and Hayashi all seemed to be moving in slow motion. He circled around behind Hidetomo and out of his field of vision. As he slowly slid an iron from the golf bag propped against the wall, a frightened look came over Hayashi's face and his lips started to move. Kazuki took aim and swung the club at one of the Dobermans. But he missed, and instead of the sharp crack of club head on skull he was expecting, the narrow shaft sank into the dog's abdomen. The Doberman yelped in pain, but having absorbed the first attack, it leaped back, baring its teeth and snarling as it eyed the raised club. Kazuki spun around and struck again, this time at the other dog, which was about to spring at him. The club grazed the dog's ear and bounced off the linoleum floor. Sugimoto's shrill, grating voice filled the room as Kazuki made a third swing. This time his aim was better and the club hit the dog in the head, spraying a shower of blood. The dog squealed and toppled over, bloody foam dripping from its mouth. Its legs twitched for a moment and then went limp, but its chest continued to heave. Kazuki felt a shock run through his body, numbing him from the top of his head down through his neck. The room began to spin and his nerves seemed to splinter into fragments. He stepped back, took aim, and swung the club again. Sugimoto buried her face in her hands as the dog's skull shattered. Its close-cropped coat was damp with blood now, but Kazuki couldn't stop. He swung at the motionless body again and again, aiming first at the back, then the flanks. The horrible sound of bones snapping could be heard with each stroke. His Reeboks and the bottom of his pants were stained with blood and with the brains that had burst from the misshapen skull. The dog's eyes stared up at him blankly, like those of a drunk passed out cold. The body was still and lifeless. Now Kazuki turned on the other Doberman whining in the corner. Again he raised the club and aimed at the head, but suddenly he found himself staring into the dog's mournful, upturned eyes and he realized what he had done. The three adults stood watching him, frozen in horror.

"You're disgusting!" he screamed. The muscles in his face twitched; his stomach was churning and his throat stung. He edged past the dog's bloody, mangled head and turned the knob on the door. It wouldn't budge, but he tried again, pulling harder, and finally it flew open, nearly knocking him over. Someone spoke and he turned to look, but the people in the room were now just flickering shadows. As he bolted outside, his lungs were flooded with hot air and the agitation and tension turned to nausea. Sensing he was about to vomit, he rested his hand against the wall to steady himself and staggered down the stairs. As his feet hit the pavement, his head began to spin as though he were drunk.

He shuffled along the sidewalk like a toddler in his first pair of shoes. Anyone passing by would have noticed that he was trembling, but the street was empty. His face and body were wet. From the acrid smell drifting up from his pants, Kazuki could tell that he had pissed himself.

"Been playing golf?" someone asked. Kazuki looked up to find Kanamoto smiling at him like a detective who has just cornered a criminal. He tried to loosen his grip on the club, but his fingers resisted and it just swayed back and forth in his hand. As Kanamoto pried it loose, Kazuki noticed that they were under the train tracks.

"Shall we go and have a coffee somewhere?" Kanamoto asked.

"What's gold selling for?" Kazuki asked. Kanamoto shuddered at the almost childish tone in the boy's voice and wondered whether he had, in fact, just killed someone.

"Why don't you rest here against the wall," Kanamoto suggested. As he helped Kazuki steady himself, he thought back over the thugs he'd known for the last thirty years in Kogane-chō. Committing murder had made some of them seem suddenly older, while others had reverted to childhood. When Kazuki was quite young, Kanamoto had more or less driven off the Treasure Ball employees assigned to watch him and had taken on the job of nursemaid and playmate himself. It had always struck him as odd that the boy would rather wander in Kogane-chō than be taken to department stores or toy shops, but there was no better guide than Kanamoto, and together they had explored every inch of the neighborhood. Recently, however, the boy had grown distant, and when they met he would exchange a few quick words before hurrying off.

"You know, those little gold ingots," Kazuki muttered, ignoring Kanamoto. "How much does one cost?" Though they were standing in the shade, Kanamoto's face seemed to glow a brilliant yellow. The words he was trying to say stuck to his gums and tongue like the scum on steamed milk, and he had no idea why he was asking about the price of gold.

"Hmm." Kanamoto pondered a moment. "Last I checked, a kilo of gold was going for just over a million yen, but it's been a while since I've been in the market. If you really want to know, I'll check for you. Why so curious, anyway?"

"Uh, no particular reason. Just thought I'd ask," Kazuki said as warmly as he could, hoping somehow to repair the crack he could feel opening up between himself and Kanamoto, between himself and the words coming out of his own mouth. But his head was still spinning and he saw how stupid his question had seemed, how ridiculous he must look.

"You look a little out of it, Kazuki," Kanamoto said, suddenly concerned at the boy's vacant stare.

"No, I'm fine," Kazuki assured him. He caught a glimpse of the gold caps on Kanamoto's teeth as he started to say something, but then Kanamoto bent over to sniff at the head of the club.

"Be seeing you," Kazuki said, waving vaguely, as he walked out into the sunlight.

"I think I should get you a cab," said Kanamoto, grabbing his arm.

"Let go, please," said Kazuki, shaking his head and smiling. "I just killed a dog. It seems weird to take a cab home. I'll walk a while and then catch the train." Kanamoto let go of his arm and watched as Kazuki walked away, surprisingly steady on his feet.

Kazuki could hear the persistent thud of machinery from a building site somewhere nearby, but the elevated platform was hemmed in by the tracks like an island in a delta and he couldn't see the construction. He could, however, see the roof of the building that held the business office for Vegas. A crow fluttered up from the roof and came to rest on the water tank. He wondered how many crows would come around if they left the dog's body up there, recalling a documentary he'd seen on TV about someplace where they buried people by leaving them out for the birds to pick over. On TV, eagles had circled gracefully over the body and the whole thing had seemed like a sacred ritual, if a little cruel. But if you thought about it, there was something grotesque about the sight of a corpse covered with flapping wings and all that cawing and picking at eyeballs. He thought he remembered the announcer saying that they would carry the body out to a spot where the birds were sure to find it and then the family would slice it up to make it easier to eat. They exposed the muscles and tendons and pulled out the organs before they left it for the birds. Kazuki could feel the dark cavity deep inside his brain slowly begin to fill with viscous blood.

A white sheet hung out to dry near the water tank began to flap in the breeze. Why would they have laundry out there? No one lived in the building, and anything you hung up would be filthy before it dried. Maybe it was a tablecloth from the restaurant on the first floor; but whatever it was, the wind was about to take it. Realizing he was thirsty, he ran his tongue over his cracked lips and got up to go to over to the vending machines, but at that moment the red train came gliding into the station, its din swallowing up the construction noise.

It was a weekday afternoon and the car he boarded was empty. Since his pants were still wet, he sat gingerly on the worn blue seat and waited for the scenery outside the window to begin moving. He thought he'd like to ride all the way to the end of the line at Misakiguchi, but in order to get home he would have to change trains at Yokohama Station.

The car seemed to shake more than usual, perhaps because it was old, or because they were running on elevated tracks. He wasn't sure why, but from the time he was little, every time he rode the Tōyoko Express he was petrified that it would fall off the track.

Just one man got on at Hinode-chō. Though he had the whole car to choose from, he sat down directly across from Kazuki, folded his arms in front of him, and crossed his legs. Kazuki looked down, but he was conscious that the man was staring at him. He tried to tell himself that he was just looking out the window behind him; but if he wanted to look out the window, why had he made a point of sitting directly across from Kazuki? He could feel his hands begin to shake. Maybe the man was a detective? It occurred to him that he should move to the next car, but his body seemed frozen. Or maybe he was a drug dealer? Or a narcotics agent posing as a dealer? He unconsciously closed his hand around the pendant under his shirt.

It was the day before he started elementary school that his father had first led him down the stairs to the underground room. Hidetomo usually made a great deal of noise going down those stairs, as if he were trying to attract attention, but that day he had crept down silently like a cat stalking its prey. He stopped in front of the door at the bottom of the stairs and selected a key from among the cluster on his key chain. He inserted it in the lock, opened the door, and signaled for Kazuki to come in.

Bottles of whiskey and brandy lined a shelf to the left, in front of which was a double bed. On the right was an elaborate stereo system. Beyond the bottles was a large display cabinet that held a collection of swords, and in the center of the room was a Persian rug on which a black leather couch and a table had been arranged. There were no other furnishings in the large room.

"Take your shirt off," his father said, and Kazuki had pulled his sweatshirt over his head. His father produced a gold pendant from his pocket and hung it around Kazuki's neck. His name, address, and telephone number had been engraved on one side of the medal. Hidetomo fiddled with a knob on the stereo and the strains of Debussy's "Two Arabesques" filled the room. "I like Tchaikovsky and Debussy," his father said, "and I don't want you listening to anything but classical music either. That thing I gave you is a dog tag; American soldiers wear them. If you're in an accident or something, they'll know how to get in touch with me. It's like a lucky charm, so don't lose it and don't show it to anybody."

Kazuki was rubbing the pendant between his thumb and middle finger, enjoying its silky smooth texture, when his father asked him to help move the sofa and table off the rug. After the furniture had been removed, his father rolled back the rug and pried out some floorboards to reveal a concrete cellar about five feet square. Hidetomo pointed silently at the hole, so Kazuki knelt to peer inside and found it full of neatly stacked gold ingots. It was absolutely quiet, as if sound itself had been converted to light waves. When Kazuki turned around to look at his father, he found that he was staring at the gold, transfixed.

He wasn't sure how much time had passed, probably no more than a minute though it seemed much longer, when his father suddenly turned down the volume on the stereo and spoke again.

"Someday this will be yours," he rasped, as if the words were sticking in his throat. He seemed to be moaning rather than speaking. "By rights it should go to Kōki, but it wouldn't do him any good. It'll all be yours eventually."

"When?" Kazuki had asked.

"When I die," Hidetomo responded. His tone sounded as though he had already lost something.

He hadn't intended to take a taxi, but as he came down the steps at Ishikawa-chō Station and caught sight of the line of cabs, his hand shot up. A lot of drivers objected to being ordered around by a kid, so to avoid any trouble he gave his address in a faint, sickly voice. Having checked that his pants were almost dry, he settled into the seat and rested his head on his hands, as if he were ill. The plan seemed to work.

"You say you live near St. Joseph's? It'll only take about ten minutes, but you let me know if you're feeling sick." Sounding worried, the driver made his way slowly up Jizōzaka.

Kazuki peered out at the scenery through half-closed eyelids. Branches from the trees growing inside the walls of the mission school hung over the road. Whenever he came along this street, Kazuki thought that it looked like a scene on a postcard. If you took a picture and told someone it was America, they'd believe you. He had the driver let him out in front of St. Joseph's, and, walking a few yards down the street that led to Motomachi, he stopped in front of a big iron gate. The wall surrounding the white, fortresslike house was more than twice Kazuki's height, and there were no windows visible from the street. No doubt it was designed to keep out intruders, but it could as easily be seen as a prison for those inside. Kazuki's grandfather had planned and built the house three years before he died. The gate was equipped with a device for reading palm prints. Kazuki pressed his hand to the plate and the gate swung open. Hidetomo had installed this security system after it occurred to him that Kazuki or his brother or sister might be kidnapped, but Kazuki suspected that he'd done it more out of fear of having to pay a large ransom than from any real concern for the safety of his children. It was probably just his way of letting everyone know that he was rich enough to be worried about kidnapping. Inside the gate, a black Mercedes and a red Porsche were parked under a wide portico; his father must have taken the silver BMW.

As he walked along the stepping-stones that led across the lawn from the gate to the entrance, Kazuki could feel a slight breeze on his cheek. The smell of grass tickled his nose. Portulaca was in full bloom in the stone planters that flanked the door. Though no one bothered to give them water or fertilizer, the flowers always bloomed in summer in a riot of red, yellow, and white. There was a terrace to one side of the entrance, and a table and deck chairs had been arranged on it, but anyone coming too close would notice that the furniture had been so badly damaged by the weather that it was little more than junk.

Kazuki knew his brother had almost certainly heard him coming up the path. Kōki was extremely sensitive to noise, so much so that the sound of the refrigerator or the air conditioner could distract him from his reading, while a helicopter flying overhead caused him actual pain. As Kazuki's sweaty hand fumbled with a knot of keys, the smell of metal stabbed his nose. He slid the key into the lock and opened the door. His brother's smiling face greeted him.

"You're home!"

"Apparently," Kazuki muttered, as Kōki jumped barefoot down into the entrance and embraced him. Kōki held him tightly for a moment in silence, as if trying to communicate something through his arms, and then looked up at him with his kind, bright eyes that always seemed to be pleading for something. His face, with its prominent brow, wide-set, bulging eyes, and slightly slack cheeks, resembled that of a bisque doll. In fact, when he was small, he had been so cute that people had often stopped in the street to comment on his doll-like appearance. As he grew older, however, Kōki's flat, upturned nose, thick, half-opened lips, and other childlike features came to seem strange.

"I'm tired," said Kazuki. "I've been to Vegas."

"Well then, you should go upstairs and fill the bath with hot water, scrub yourself, and have a soak. If you still haven't chased all the monsters out of your head, then rub yourself with a towel, dry your hair with the dryer, put a pillow under your head, and dream some dreams. Kazuki, please don't think I'm a baby. I want to be smart, just like you." Kōki's metallic voice rang in Kazuki's ears. His voice was not changing, nor did he have a cold. From the time he began talking, when he was four years old, he had spoken with the gravelly voice typical of Williams Syndrome. A broad grin spread over his face and he reached up to hug Kazuki again. When he was in third or fourth grade, he and Kōki had been about the same height, but eventually Kazuki had passed his older brother, and now he was several inches taller.

He patted Kōki's long, giraffelike neck and sloping shoulders and pried himself loose.

Kyōko was watching them, as if making some sort of comparison between the brothers. Normally, Mrs. Shimamura served as both housekeeper and Kōki's companion, but without telling his father, Kazuki had begun asking Kyōko to come on days when Shimamura was off. He had met her at the end of last year when he ran into Hayashi's daughter, Yōko, while the two girls were wandering around Motomachi. The three of them went to a café. "Don't you recognize her?" Yōko had asked as soon as they sat down. "Why should I?" Kazuki murmured, looking at his lap. "Look again," Yōko urged. "She hasn't changed at all—it's Kyōko Yasuda. We used to play with her when we were little." Laughing, she poked Kazuki gently in the jaw. Yasuda's daughter . . . the Yasuda who committed suicide. According to Yōko, after Yasuda died, Hayashi had put Kyōko and her younger sister Haruko in an orphanage. A few times a year he would bring them home to his house or take them to Disneyland. Kyōko, who was seventeen, the same age as Yōko, had stayed in the orphanage until she finished middle school. After that, Hayashi had found her a job as a waitress in a restaurant in Sakuragi-chō. "Don't give him your phone number," Yōko warned her friend, laughing. The faintest of smiles had passed across Kyōko's face as she looked at Kazuki.

It had been Kazuki who called her. The first time they went out, she gave mostly one-word answers to his questions. But Kazuki, who was usually quiet himself, talked for almost three hours without a pause—until he realized what he was doing and felt embarrassed. He had wanted to buy her some sort of present but couldn't figure out a way to ask what she'd like; so as they were saying good-bye, he tried to hand her thirty thousand yen. "You want me to sleep with you?" she asked, apparently offended, and he had abandoned the idea of a gift. He knew he had no idea how to express affection, but her words had hurt him all the same. "Okay if I call you again sometime?" he'd asked rather curtly, and they'd parted.

"Kōki, Kyōko and I have some studying to do in my room," Kazuki said.

"I understand," said the older boy, and folding his arms around his protruding stomach, he waddled off to the living room like a woman about to deliver a baby.

The first time she'd entered Kazuki's room, Kyōko had been shocked at how normal it was: posters, cassettes, video games and movies, then the textbooks, notebooks, and assorted pens and pencils scattered about—the average middle school boy's room. His indignation at her surprise made her laugh.

The sound of the piano came floating up the stairs and crept through the crack under the door. When he closed his eyes, Kazuki could picture his brother's fingers, bent in that odd way he held them, flying rapidly over the keyboard. Kōki couldn't read music, but while their mother was still at home a piano teacher had come once a week for lessons. He must have learned how to play by watching her hands. Now, if he liked a particular piece of music he would listen to the CD a few times, then sit at the piano practicing until he could play it. Kazuki had no idea why people who suffered from Williams Syndrome should have perfect pitch.

Kyōko sat on the edge of the bed. Kazuki lowered himself into a chair and for a while they listened to the music.

"Close your eyes," he said at last.

"Okay," Kyōko said, closing them and resting her palms on her legs. Kazuki pulled his T-shirt over his head and then slipped out of his pants and underwear. He stood before her naked, with only the pendant clinging to his chest.

"I stink, don't I?" he said.

"Yep," she agreed. Kazuki found he couldn't say anything more. He moved his lips but nothing came out. He stood there in silence for several minutes.

"I pissed my pants," he managed at last.

"Why?" she asked. She cocked her head but her eyes remained closed.

"I killed a dog."

"Why'd you do that?" she said.

"I don't really know," he said. Kyōko opened her eyes and stared at Kazuki's face. Nodding vaguely, she stood up and left the room. A few minutes later, she came back with a damp towel. He clenched his teeth as she knelt in front of him and began wiping his body. He could feel himself becoming erect. When she had finished cleaning him, she took a neatly folded T-shirt and a pair of underpants from the chest and helped him get into them. He put his hand on her arm. She rested hers on his in return, and they stood looking uncertainly at one another, unsure what to say or do. He put his arms around her neck and closed his eyes, and as she felt his lips approach, she closed hers too. They fell over on the bed, lips pressed together, and lay there for a moment. Kazuki suspected that she wouldn't refuse him if he tried to have sex with her, but he wasn't really interested in that now. The piano melody mingled with the murmuring waves deep within Kyōko's chest. Kazuki pulled himself up and sat on the edge of the bed. She looked at him, and then sat up next to him, listening to the music.

Several minutes passed before she rested her hand on his shoulder. Kazuki turned to face her, and she gently rubbed his shoulders and neck in time with the music until she was cradling his face in her hands. As she pulled him to her, the music rose, filling the room, and Kazuki prayed that gravity might be suspended and he could remain forever floating in her arms. He strained his ears, listening for the beating of her heart and the sound of the piano.

"Kōki should become a pianist," she said. It seemed to Kazuki that her voice was echoing not in his ears but directly in his hollow body.

"I doubt he could," he answered.

"He'd be so happy if you could arrange a recital in a little hall somewhere," she said, putting into words a thought that had occurred to her as she'd sat listening to Kōki play for a long time that afternoon. "Or you could just invite people here to listen . . ." She had barely spoken when Kazuki interrupted.

"Go home," he said, standing and turning his back on her. Kyōko straightened the bed and left the room; she knew there were times when Kazuki became angry for no apparent reason. When he was stirred up this way, it was useless to say anything. He really didn't even want to be placated, content apparently to simply abandon himself to the fury. And though the source of this anger seemed to be located somewhere within him, he lacked the strength to confront it.

It was July. The leaves of the ancient ginkgo tree outside Kazuki's window had grown thick, cutting off the light of the setting sun. As a breeze shook the tree, the few rays that found their way through the leaves danced on his face as he lay on the bed. But gradually the light faded and he dissolved into the gloom of dusk. He closed his eyes and waited for something to appear in the inky darkness. For as long as he could remember, whenever he shut his eyes and concentrated, he'd had the feeling that something was squirming out there in the dark; but it always vanished just before he could tell what it was. In order to see something that was invisible, Kazuki knew, he had to create some sort of crystal that would refract even the darkness in his head; and if that proved impossible, there was nothing to be done but split open his skull and let the light in directly. Still, he had no idea how to go about discovering this alchemical secret, how to convert the darkness to light.

The house was silent. Perhaps the humming of the refrigerator or the creaking of the foundation was bothering Kōki's sensitive ears, but Kazuki could hear nothing but the faint rustling of the ginkgo tree. He grimaced, catching another whiff of the Doberman's blood that seemed to have dried in his nose. He poked at his nostrils with his knuckles and then sniffed his hands. Nothing but sweat, as far as he could tell. It seemed to be gushing from every pore on his body, making him feel clammy all over. He recalled the face of a corpse he'd seen on TV a long time ago—the man had died from a disease that made blood spurt from the pores. Doctors, in protective white clothing that looked like space suits, had been hovering over him, covering the body in order to stop the virus from infecting other people. To Kazuki, this was the worst possible way to die—to be eaten up by a virus. It suddenly occurred to him that you would go crazy if a virus invaded your brain, and that perhaps one had already taken over his brain cells. He jumped up on the bed, pressed his back against the wall, and clutched his head like someone who has just been passed a basketball. Fear and darkness had teamed up and were coming for him. He wasn't usually afraid of the dark, but fear, like hope, had a way of absorbing everything else. Still, he preferred fear to hope; hope was a sickness only adults could contract.

From the time he learned to talk, Kazuki had been convinced that some sort of disaster was always looming; a car crash, suicide, insanity, kidnapping, viruses—he was used to being terrified of any and all of them. And it seemed to him that the only way he would ever conquer these fears would be to grow up, that he would be an adult when he had overcome the fear. But this was still sometime in the future, and until then he could only wait, passing the time between home and school. He was waiting to throw away his fear as one would throw away flesh that has been flayed from the body. His naked fear. Nevertheless, he had continued to postpone the time when he would have to confront these fears, and this knowledge bothered him. He knew that the only thing that could overcome fear was anger, and he waited for the day when fear and anger would bump heads. But he was well acquainted with the restlessness and anxiety you felt when something that should happen doesn't.

Kazuki waited for the smell of fear to fill his head. The dog's blood was gone now and he felt like smoking a cigarette, but when he reached toward the pack on the desk, he grabbed a Hall's instead and tossed it in his mouth. Reiji and the others had told him all about reform school and juvenile hall, but were they really so different from his life here? If there was a difference, it was just in terms of the limits placed on his freedom. He was free to play video games or go out to a convenience store, to drink and smoke. But if those freedoms were really worth something, then why was he lying here in the dark? Why did he feel trapped, as though his body were encased in a plaster cast? Why did the fluorescent lights at the store remind him of a prison he'd seen once in a movie? And why was it that Reiji and the others couldn't see that fear was lurking there, fangs bared, somewhere inside this freedom?

He had erupted at Kyōko because she had spoken out of turn about his brother. Who knew what might happen if he let Kōki play for other people? If it made him happy, then Kazuki would have to get together an audience every day. Couldn't she see how cruel it would be to give Kōki the hope that someone really wanted to listen to him play? Kōki's own anger came from the knowledge that he was unable to live on his own, unable to enjoy the freedom of other boys his age. But you couldn't even call it anger—it was just a vague suffering that came with being shut in the house, suffering that could be relieved simply by taking him out. Kōki's pain began when he first realized that there was a world outside; so to remind him of that world—even through the pleasure of playing for people—would be cruel. Why couldn't Kyōko see that?

Fortunately, Kōki was incapable of feeling real fear, but he knew his own problem had more to do with anger, anger that was just about to reach the boiling point. It would be a good joke if the moment he had been waiting for, the moment he finally became an adult, had already come and he just hadn't noticed. But if he decided to stop waiting and let his anger out, the fear would probably show its true colors as well. He grabbed a mirror that was lying on the desk, fell back on the bed, and examined his own face. The nose, mouth, everything seemed horribly blurred, as if he were looking at a double exposure of pictures of an adult and a child. He clenched his teeth and glared into the mirror.

At the sound of the gate opening and a car coming up the driveway, Kazuki jumped up and turned on the light. He peeled off his sweaty T-shirt, took a fresh one from the drawer, and pulled it over his head as he ran down the stairs. Hidetomo gave him an icy look as he came through the door, but he quickly looked down and busied himself with taking off his shoes. It was too late, though, Kazuki had caught a glimpse of fear in his father's eyes, fear of the boy who had killed the Doberman, and it sent a quiver of pleasure through him, a kind of agreeable itching sensation.

"What's so funny?" Hidetomo demanded. Kazuki could tell at once when his father was drunk from the way he seemed to tilt to one side.

"Nothing," he said, trying to look serious as he knelt by the entrance. He straightened his father's shoes, toes slightly apart, just as Hidetomo had taught him when he was a small boy.

"Get me a drink," he called over his shoulder as he vanished down the stairs that led to the basement. By the time Kazuki had gathered the bottles from the kitchen and carried them downstairs, his father had settled into the sofa and propped his feet up on the table. He was smoking a cigarette. With practiced movements, Kazuki mixed a Scotch and water and set it on a coaster.

"Is Miho home yet?" Hidetomo asked, without looking at Kazuki. He took a sip of his drink.

"I don't think so," said Kazuki. His father grunted and downed his whiskey. He fumbled with a pack of cigarettes, dropping several before he was able to catch one between his thumb and forefinger and guide it to his mouth.

"What time is it?" he asked. Kazuki glanced at his Rolex.

"Ten forty-seven," he said, wondering how it had gotten so late. It was still light when Kyōko left, probably around five or six o'clock.

"Did you know your sister quit going to school more than a year ago? It doesn't really matter, since she'd made it as far as high school; but legally you still have to go, which is why that homeroom teacher of yours, Shimada, keeps calling me. I don't care if all you do is sleep in the nurse's office, I want you to start showing up." Kazuki had no intention of discussing his school problems with his father. As long as there was no pressure from Hōsei to transfer to a public school, he would continue to go when he felt like it. At any rate, they were sure to call his father in for a conference before handing down any final decision, and if he was right, he could let things ride for another month or two before that happened. And when the time came, the school, his father, and he could lay their respective cards on the table. But in the meantime, it seemed that the best he could hope for was a compromise among the three parties. Schools and parents seemed to feel they had an obligation to see a child got an education; but Kazuki himself had long since lost any sense that he had a responsibility to attend school. He had enormous respect for his grandfather, who had barely finished elementary school but had still been able to build the foundation of what was now Vegas. He wanted to work like his grandfather. If he was just going to inherit Vegas anyway, what could possibly be wrong with starting to work there now? But if he had to put up with this law requiring him to go to school until he was fifteen, he at least wanted someone to explain to him why he should have to. When he tried to get an answer out of Shimada, his homeroom teacher, however, he would blow him off.

"Now that's a *real* tough one, Yuminaga. I doubt the minister of education could figure that one out. I suppose I should say 'to become a worthwhile human being,' or something like that, but you and I both know that's not likely. Still, there's a part of the Constitution called the Basic Education Law that says you have to, and basically that's why: you have to." Kazuki could still hear the sarcasm in his voice, but he had not seen how Shimada had gone back to his office and taken a copy of the school legal code off the shelf. He had flipped through the pages until he came to chapter three, article thirty-six, which outlined the "Goals of Middle School Education." "He may have to be here," he muttered, "but that looks like the only rule we aren't breaking."

"You'd be surprised to know what your sister's been up to now that she's quit school," Hidetomo continued. "But I just don't get what's wrong with you two. I'm not even asking you to get good grades or anything. I know better than anybody what you're capable of. I'm just telling you to get your ass to school—not even every day, just often enough to get by! I think I see why you're skipping school, but can you tell me why she is?" Kazuki looked away in embarrassment, realizing that he had never seen this wounded, forlorn expression on his father's face. Could it be that he was really worried? That he suffered like other people?

"Just show up at school three or four times a week," Hidetomo added suddenly, apparently having forgotten his concern for Miho. "And then you can do whatever you want for fun. As long as you don't get in trouble with the police, I don't care what you do. If you want women, I'll buy them for you. I can fix you up with real lookers, fashion models, whatever—just let me know. That's no trick for your old dad. Now what do you say? Does anybody else have a dad like yours?"

Kazuki shook his head in silence. He was calculating the best moment to ask for the four hundred thousand yen. His father had never once asked him why he needed money, but this time the figure was a little too large.

"I would like to borrow four hundred thousand," he blurted out.

"How much do you owe me now?" Hidetomo asked.

"About nine hundred thousand yen, I believe."

Hidetomo could tell hear the note of contempt concealed under Kazuki's polite tone, but he had no grounds for accusing the boy of sarcasm. And, too, he couldn't risk widening the gap between himself and his son, who was effectively his eldest. Through elementary school, he had been a smart kid, easily getting into Eiko Gakuen, one of the top schools in the prefecture and a step above Hōsei; but under pressure from the director of the board, Hidetomo had put him in Hōsei. And then, during the summer of his first year in middle school, something happened and his grades took a nosedive. As his body grew, he seemed to become a different person. Outwardly, he remained the same serious, methodical boy he had been in elementary school, but Hidetomo knew something had changed. He almost felt it would have been easier if he had grown his hair wild or started talking tough. He remembered the uneasy feeling it had given him to watch Kazuki smoothly repeating his alibi to the detective during the rape investigation. Sometimes, he wanted to grab the boy and shake him until he realized whose blood it was flowing through his veins, but he always stopped himself out of fear that he would release some unimaginable, ominous stranger hiding inside his son.

Hidetomo had never hit Kazuki. More than once, he had been on the verge of doing so, but when the boy looked at him with those eyes that reminded him of an animal caught by infrared camera, he always lost heart.

"Take a guess how much that dog was worth," he said, draining his whiskey. He set the glass down on the coaster and pushed it away with his index finger. Kazuki measured some whiskey into the glass, added ice, and filled it with mineral water. As he set the drink down, he wondered when it was that he'd begun playing bartender for his father, and for a moment he savored the superiority a bartender feels when he watches his customers across the counter. He suddenly wanted to play the part to the hilt: Can I freshen that up for you, sir? Another round, buddy? At times he had amused himself by adding extra whiskey to get his father drunk. "Both the father and mother were all-Asia champions, and they were planning to enter it in the national show this year. Two million. The dog was worth two million, and then there's the iron. It was custom made, worth about a million and a half." There was no hint of anger in Hidetomo's voice, just a touch of plaintive bitterness in the way his sentence trailed off. His whole body seemed crushed with worry over the loss of something much more valuable than the dog or the golf club. It occurred to Kazuki that he should be feeling pity for this man rather than contempt, but in the end, there was nothing to be done with a grown man who had lost all sense of pride but get rid of him.

"Do you know how much your last little escapade cost me?" Hidetomo asked. "I paid a million to each boy's family to keep them quiet. And did you know that I ended up handling the settlement with the girl's family? I paid the lawyers two million and then put up five million more to keep the case out of court." Hidetomo took the drink Kazuki offered him and poured it down his throat. "You said you didn't rape her, but I know you did. I see through that bull you fed the police.

So here's your punishment: you're no longer allowed at Vegas, at least until you finish high school. You're grounded until further notice, got that?" Hidetomo reached down to pull off his socks, but he suddenly noticed the cigarette he was holding. Annoyed, he transferred it to his mouth, stripped off the socks, rolled them in a ball, and threw them as hard as he could against the wall. His pale bare feet rested on the floor like cheap hotel slippers. The doorbell rang and Kazuki and his father glanced at one another.

"What time is it?" Hidetomo asked, his voice sounding angry but tired.

"Eleven-thirty," said Kazuki, glancing at his Rolex.

"Doesn't she have a key?"

"She probably lost it. Shall I bring her down here?" Kazuki asked, standing to go.

"I'll come up. You're my heir; no one else is allowed down here." Hidetomo grinned oddly. As Kazuki was running up the stairs, the bell rang again. He stepped down into the entrance in his bare feet to open the door, and Miho slipped in.

"Sorry! Were you asleep?" she said, but then she caught sight of Hidetomo's shoes and froze for a moment, her eyes darting around nervously. She staggered as she tried to take off her high, platform heels, but when Kazuki reached out to steady her, she brushed aside his hand and sat down heavily on the stair. "Is he asleep?" she asked, rubbing the left foot that she had finally managed to extract from the shoe.

"He's awake. I think he's been waiting up for you," said Kazuki, going over to the glass door that led to the living room. He looked in at his father who was scowling, and then glanced back at his sister.

"Fuck him!" Miho spat out the words. "I came home, didn't I?" Just a week earlier, Hidetomo had kicked her when she'd returned late, and she was still dragging her left leg as she headed off toward the bathroom. As she passed him, he caught a whiff of shampoo and realized that her hair was damp. Frowning, he followed her into the bathroom where she had started to rinse her mouth at the sink.

"Don't you think it might be better to just stay at a friend's house?" he asked. What happened between his father and sister didn't concern him, but he needed to get some sleep. Now that she seemed to have given up on herself, he didn't feel inclined to protect her.

"It's too much trouble to get back into my shoes," she said, wiping her mouth with the back of her hand. Her eyes bore into the boy's reflection in the mirror. "You never actually run away, Kazuki," she said, "but you always seem to be hiding." She walked out of the bathroom and stopped in front of the door to the living room. Fastening a button on her blouse and smoothing back her hair, she went in.

As he watched his sister sit down on the couch across from Hidetomo, Kazuki realized that they were almost identical: the same brown hair, same narrow nose, same heavy eyelids. His father's eyes were clouded with meanness and treachery, while somewhere behind his sister's he sensed that something was slowly coming unhinged. Unlike Hidetomo's cringing look, however, her gaze was fixed and resigned as she stared at the blank television screen.

He could see the gears turning in his father's head as he calculated the best way to hurt his daughter, to humiliate her so completely that she'd want to die. Draining his glass, Hidetomo signaled to Kazuki, who immediately refilled it with whiskey, added a splash of water, and set it down again in front of him.

"You've been at that sleazy hotel in Yamashita-chō, haven't you?" Hidetomo said, staring at her as he took a sip of his drink. "Do you rent the room by the hour?" Kazuki studied his sister, who seemed to be growing uglier by the moment. When he'd first seen her at the door, he hadn't noticed that her hair was soaking wet, but now it was obvious. Her forehead and the tip of her nose were peeling, and he guessed she must have spent the last two nights sleeping on the beach. As he glanced down at the thighs protruding from her short skirt, he could suddenly see her lying under some man, legs spread wide, and he had the strange sensation that all the doors of all the bars in Kogane-chō had been flung open and the women had come out laughing. "I know the place," Hidetomo continued, swirling the whiskey in his mouth and then swallowing it noisily. "The one below Harborview Park." His face, already tanned from the golf course, flushed a deeper red, and the veins in his throat stood out.

"Hotel?" said Miho, her gaze shifting to Kazuki. He noticed that her cheek was twitching, as if she were about to burst out laughing.

"That's right," said Hidetomo. "You know the place: the rooms stink like pussy and cum."

"Never been there," she said.

"Don't lie to me," Hidetomo snorted, shaking the ice in his glass. Kazuki stole a glance at his face as he poured more whiskey. His father should have been passed out drunk by now, but the adrenaline from his rage must have suppressed the effects of the alcohol. It would be better if he'd just hit her or kick her and get it over with, he thought, fighting a yawn. If he thought all this chatter made the rough stuff more interesting, then his father was stupider than he thought. He might have been able to salvage some respect for him if Hidetomo had just hit her without saying a word and then gone back to the basement. What was the point of words anyway?

Resigning herself to the situation, Miho crossed her legs and cast a defiant look toward Hidetomo. Her right hand absently rubbed her left as she wondered whether her father had really had her followed all the way to the hotel. There was that incident three years ago when she'd been picked up by a bunch of guys in front of the mall at Yokohama Station and gone to a private karaoke box with them. They were just starting to have some fun when Sugimoto showed up out of the blue. She'd been taken by taxi to the office in Kogane-chō and made to sit before her father, much as she was now. They claimed then that Hidetomo had his ways of finding out who came into every single karaoke club in the city. But how had they picked her out? She wasn't wearing the Hōsei uniform—she hadn't worn it since she'd stopped going to school after the first semester of eighth grade. And he couldn't have spread her picture around town like a wanted poster. Besides, the karaoke places were all understaffed, often with just one person manning the register, serving drinks, and cleaning up afterward. No way they would have time to check every customer. Could he have surveillance cameras with feeds into the Vegas office? Not possible. She didn't really believe what he said, but it was a fact that she had started to frequent the karaoke clubs and video game parlors in Kawasaki and Ōfuna about three years ago. And if he really knew that she'd been at that hotel today, then he must have had her followed. The flunkies at Vegas would do anything they were told; and then there were his yakuza friends. For that matter, he could easily afford to hire a private detective. Miho could feel her hatred for the man overcoming her pain, feel it creeping up from her calves and thighs to the nape of her neck.

"So, you think there's nothing wrong with skipping school, going to the beach to make out with some guy, putting out at that hotel?" Hidetomo drained his drink. "He's in his late forties, wears a white polo shirt, about five feet six; square, black glasses, Vuitton bag. Before you went to the hotel, the two of you stopped in at a drugstore, and what do you think you bought? Two thousand yen worth of rubbers. But as luck would have it, the owner of the drugstore was a friend of Sugimoto's and he gave us a call." As he finished his harangue, Hidetomo shoved his hand in his pocket and fished out a roll of ten-thousand-yen bills. Licking his finger, he began to count. "Okay, Kazuki, here's your loan: four hundred thousand." When he'd finished, he tossed the bills at the boy's feet and fanned the rest in Miho's face. "So can you tell me? Why should Yuminaga's daughter be fucking for cash? You can have all the money you need. But this time, why don't we try sticking it in your cunt. That'll teach you a lesson."

"Who the hell am I hurting?" Miho shouted. "Tell me that!"

"Don't give me that crap. You're hurting me, that's who: people laugh at me, say my daughter's a fucking whore. They're the only people who sell it without hurting anybody; are you telling me you're a whore?" Miho grimaced as if she'd been sprayed with filth, but she wasn't really hurt. Hidetomo, in his secret apartment with his five women—he was the filthy one. And why should she care if that pig called her names? The women he did it with would do any geezer as long as he had money; but she'd never sleep with an old fart like him, no matter what he paid her, and her friends wouldn't either. She wasn't a pro; she could pick who she did it with. She was *not* a whore. She was simply doing something she wanted to do of her own free will. And she didn't live on the money she made; she spent it on whatever she felt like—could a whore do that? For the first time she noticed her father's body odor, the smell of his breath. She didn't find it particularly offensive, but it did make her realize that he was just a man, and that thought relaxed her, made her want to laugh in his face. Still, she fought the urge as best she could. Refusing to look away, she raised her eyes to meet his gaze. Probably due to the whiskey, his face was dripping with sweat, but the look on his face betrayed something other than anger.

Hidetomo was beginning to understand his own frustration, for which he had only his own confused life to blame. His home, which he had fenced off in one corner of the kingdom of his desires, was turning out to be a barren field from which he could expect no yield. Nevertheless it was his; the sign out front said so, and as such, it could not simply be abandoned. Then again, Hidetomo had no strategy for disposing of this sort of nonperforming asset. In the old days you would simply disown the kid and that would be that; but now, even if you did cut her off and throw her out, if she ended up in the scandal sheets it would do no good to remind people that she wasn't yours. As long as she was a minor, he would be expected to clean up after her. But how long would she go on flaunting that crotch of hers? And those chubby thighs! I wouldn't pay a thousand yen for them, but there must be plenty of guys who would. It's the school uniform that gets them, and a Hōsei uniform at that; when you look at it that way—thirty thousand to take off a Hōsei uniform—shit, it's a bargain. But she's not even doing it for the money. She's doing it because she wants to. But if she wants it so bad, why doesn't she just get a boyfriend and shack up with him? As it is, the rumor's going around that she's turning tricks. Maybe I should be finding her a man, Hidetomo thought.

"So, do you have a guy?" he asked. "A boyfriend, I mean."

At that, Miho erupted. "You should be ashamed of yourself, you old fucker!" she shouted, and rose to go, but as she turned her back on him she could feel her hair being yanked from her scalp, hear the sound of tearing skin. Hidetomo had grabbed her and pulled her back, rubbing the wad of money in her face. Then, letting the bills flutter to the floor, he swung his arm around and slapped her face.

Kazuki had no idea what they were screaming about. He felt he was listening from a great distance to what were perhaps cries for help; but his ears were also ringing with sounds that seemed to well up from deep inside his own body, sounds that could be screams or curses. When words lost their meaning, violence was the only thing you could count on. His legs started to move of their own accord, as if trying to establish an alibi, to force him to be elsewhere; he took long, deep breaths, feeling his mind, too, begin to absent itself. It floated through the glass door and hovered quietly in the dark. At the sound of flesh being struck, however, Kazuki came to himself and found his sister shoving Hidetomo with all her might. His father gave a startled cry and fell, legs thrashing, between the couch and the table.

Almost immediately, though, he pushed the table aside and pulled himself to his feet, shoulders heaving. His face was crimson with whiskey and rage, and the eyes set in it were no longer their father's. Without warning, he lashed out, striking Miho in the face. He caught her just above the eye, sending blood gushing down her face. His knee came up savagely, striking her leg with a sharp cracking sound and sending her crumpling to the floor.

Kazuki listened intently to the bloody murmur filling the room as he went to stand by his sister. Her left leg stuck out from under her like a broken bat. Her face was covered in blood, and her eyes had already begun to swell. More blood was dripping from between her lips, as if her mouth were cut inside or she'd broken a tooth. Kazuki glanced up at his father. Perhaps because of the alcohol, or because he didn't want to see what he'd done, his eyes were hooded and sleepy and his body was rocking back and forth. Hidetomo's head was spinning, but he had the feeling there was one more thing he had to take care of before going to bed—if he could just remember what it was . . .

"Shall I call an ambulance?" Kazuki asked, surprised how calm his own voice sounded. If it had affected him so little, perhaps none of this was real? He picked up the phone and began dialing, but Hidetomo grabbed it out of his hand and flung it against the wall. He stared at the phone lying on the floor and wondered if that was what he'd forgotten to do.

"Whogivesashit," Hidetomo mumbled and stumbled down the stairs to the basement.

When he was gone, Kazuki squatted next to his sister and spoke in her ear. "Do you want me to get an ambulance?" he asked. He would have preferred that she go to sleep now and then get herself to the hospital in the morning; but if she died overnight, there would be trouble. To check whether she was conscious, he whispered the name he had called her when they were little. "Miho-ane?" Her eyelids fluttered in response, so he went to the bathroom and wet two towels. Returning to the living room, he put one in Miho's hand. When he saw that she couldn't lift her arm to her face, however, he took the other towel and wiped the blood around her eyes. As he worked, her fingers began to move and her eyes opened slightly, so he asked again if he should call for help. A murmuring sound emerged from the back of her throat, indicating he shouldn't. "Can you stand?" he asked. As he was helping her to her feet, words seeped from her mouth.

"Kazu, get my bag." He looked around the room and spotted it under the couch. Picking it up, he brought it close to her face. "There's a pillbox. Can you see it? It says 'Bon Voyage,' in French." When Kazuki produced the case from the bag, Miho raised her hand but was unable to hold it. He opened it for her.

"Is that speed?" he asked, as he poured her a glass of water. Raising her head, he rested it on his knee and slipped one of the pills into her mouth. He pressed the rim of the glass to her lips and she took several swallows. He had been right: two of her front teeth were broken.

"Is there someone you can trust at Vegas?" she asked. Kazuki lowered her head back to the floor as he thought for a moment. "How about Hayashi?" she continued. "No, not him. Isn't there anyone, an adult you can trust?"

"There is someone," he said.

"Who?"

"How about Kanamoto?"

"Him? Fine, then could you get him to come tomorrow?" Kazuki nodded. "Umm," she murmured, almost happily, "I thought speed would do the trick."

Just as Kazuki was reaching for the case to try some himself, he realized that his brother had come into the room. Kōki's expression reminded Kazuki of the head of a deer that had been stuffed and hung up on the wall; his mouth was stretched wide open, as if he were trying to swallow something, and the look in his eyes seemed to tell of the disaster he had just witnessed, of the indignation and astonishment that had caused him to flee. Kazuki went over to him and cradled his face in his hands.

"Kōki," he called to him. His body was rigid. Kazuki rubbed his thumbs over Kōki's eyes to close them, and then, like a child working with clay, he pressed his lips together. But as he folded his arms around Kōki and tried to lead him up to his room, his eyes suddenly opened and he looked up at Kazuki. He blames me, Kazuki thought, biting his lip.

"I was just teasing," Kōki suddenly said. Kazuki stood for a moment, startled by his brother's joke, but then behind him he heard a soft chuckling. Miho's laughter was bubbling from her mouth and spreading out across the floor.

He had the feeling that he was living in a picture; or perhaps he was standing outside the frame looking in. He sensed that he was free to go in or out of the image at will; but at the same time, it seemed that his head existed as a faint shadow in the upper left corner, observing everything that transpired. He was dreaming a dream of himself dreaming.

In his dream, the animals were all sleeping: tigers, giraffes, bears, ostriches, monkeys. Only the field mice were stirring. Kazuki threaded his way through the sleeping animals, heading for a wild horse, but no sooner had it occurred to him that the horse might be dreaming, too, than he was sucked into the horse's dream. He could see a group of shadow figures, gathered in a circle. As he drew nearer, he saw that the shadows were peering into a hole. One of the shadows held a sheaf of newspaper in his hand; when he opened it, the severed heads of a giant frog, a chimpanzee, a dolphin, and a sheep appeared and the shadow dropped them into the hole. When he turned to look back, the animals were all fast asleep, but just as he was about to shout "Wake up!" the horse's head was lopped off and dropped in the hole. It was falling at a tremendous speed—and it was Kazuki's head! Aaaahhhh! As he fell, utterly terrified, he tried to tell himself that it was only a dream; but then suddenly he was in a pillbox, seated at a roulette table. He had a feeling that a wizened old dope peddler with a crew cut was sitting next to him, but when he tried to check whether he was wearing a white T-shirt and a gray sweatshirt, he couldn't see any clothing at all. Rather than numbers, the spaces on the roulette wheel were marked with the words "Yes" and "No," written in spidery letters. Kazuki stood and walked around the interior of the concrete pillbox; he was in a doorless room—a hospital room. A naked woman was lying on her back, hooked up to an IV drip. She stared at him as she repeatedly crossed and uncrossed her legs. The words on the neon signs outside the window were reflected on her stomach. Kazuki went over to the bed to have a look at her face, but the fluorescent lights were flickering and he couldn't make out her features. When he bent still closer, suddenly curious to know who it was, her arms and legs wrapped themselves around him and caught him in a viselike grip. He screamed.

Ouch! Even after he was awake, the aching numbness continued. Wondering why he would still be feeling the pain from the dream, or whether he was really awake, he raised his head to look around. He was in his own room. The television was on, but the volume was turned down—he remembered doing that before falling asleep. He thought for a moment about who the woman could be, but nothing came to him. The horse and the hole and the roulette wheel drifted as fragments through his head, but there was nothing to link them to one another. He stared around the room while the pain gradually receded. There were perhaps six billion people on earth, he thought, and every night each one of them dreamed. But dreams were utterly useless, so why did people go on dreaming them? Or maybe they did have some purpose? Kazuki had no idea. No two people on earth ever dreamed the same dream, so perhaps they were a symbol of individuality itself, an expression of one's real abilities. He decided he would try to make up a story that connected the horse, the hole, the roulette wheel, and the naked woman, filling in the gaps in his memory. He was galloping the horse on a plain; black clouds streamed across the gray sky. The horse came up to the hole—now he remembered: the animal heads were falling into the hole. From there he wanted to find some link to the roulette wheel, but he was unable to go on with the story. Dreams were probably human spirits, though they no doubt concealed something real. But if they were spirits, they were surely trying to tell us something. Most dreams were crazy, so maybe they were meant to give us a clue about the relationship between madness and sanity. Maybe that explained the roulette wheel?

Remembering that he had to call Kanamoto, he grabbed the cell phone on his desk, fell back on the bed, and punched the number. He checked his Rolex: 4 A.M. No one answered; no one was there when he called before going to bed. He glanced over at the TV. An emergency message was scrolling across the top of the screen: Earthquake centered in Shizuoka Prefecture, Itōoki. Local magnitudes: magnitude 5, Itō and Numazu; magnitude 4, Hamamatsu; magnitude 3, Tokyo.

It had registered a 4 in Yokohama; he must have slept through it. Underneath the earthquake alert, an old white woman was working her abs on an exercise machine.

Kazuki switched off the phone and tried to remember how far he'd gotten remembering his dream. The horse, hole, wheel, and naked woman were still there, but they were nothing more than bits of memory sinking quietly into his subconscious. He started to get up, but it occurred to him that he had nowhere to go. As he tried Kanamoto's number once more, he chuckled at the thought that he had dreamed right through a strong earthquake.

"Who is this?" a hoarse voice croaked.

"It's Yuminaga," Kazuki said. Kanamoto had told Kazuki his number more than three years ago, but this was the first time he had called it.

"Kazuki? What's happened?" Kazuki felt himself relax at the sound of Kanamoto's calm voice.

"Miho's badly hurt," he said. The thought immediately occurred to Kanamoto that she'd been raped. He tried to recall what she looked like, but no image came. "Could you come to the house this morning?" Kazuki asked. Before calling, he had been convinced that Kanamoto would agree to help; but somehow, over the cell phone, his voice sounded small and distant, and Kazuki began to worry. "I'd like you to take her to the hospital. I don't really know what to do," he added, almost in tears.

"I understand, I'll be there at seven," said Kanamoto, barely able to conceal how happy he was that Kazuki had trusted him enough to call. "Or should I just come now? That would be fine with me." The weariness had gone out of his voice.

"She's sleeping now; seven should be fine." Kazuki hung up, unaware how cold his these last words had sounded to Kanamoto.

On the TV, a young couple in leotards were testing out the exercise machine while the earthquake alert floated along over their heads. Kazuki could not understand why people were afraid of earthquakes. Either the house would fall on you and you'd be killed or seriously injured, or the furniture would fall on you and you'd be less seriously injured. It was as simple as that. If the Big One came, you had to be ready to die; for a smaller one, there was nothing to do but wait until the shaking stopped. Why did people waste their time worrying in that valley between life and death? Fear was itself part of both, not something that existed in that vague space that separated the two. For Kazuki, it was the trembling deep in his own soul that really scared him.

He pushed open the door to his room and went out into the hall, not so much to do anything as to check whether anything was happening. The bottoms of his bare feet felt an aftershock. He headed downstairs, wondering whether Miho had noticed it. Entering the living room, he found her sprawled out like driftwood.

"You want some more speed?" he asked, bending over her.

"It's all gone," she said. The Bon Voyage pillbox was clutched in her hand, but the two pills it had held the night before were missing.

"I've got some coke, if that would help," he said.

"No thanks," she said, with a faint smile. Kazuki gathered up the ten-thousand-yen bills that lay scattered on the floor. "Have you quit going to school?" she asked suddenly, her voice sounding exactly like their mother's. Kazuki looked down at her.

"I go when I feel like it," he said.

"You're lucky," she said.

"Why do you say that?"

"You'll get Vegas when he's gone."

"I'd just as soon it went to you," he said.

"Idiot!"

"Why? Why shouldn't you get it?" Kazuki sat on the couch and began laying out the whiskey-soaked bills on the coffee table.

"I won't get anything," Miho said.

"Why wouldn't you?"

"Not one thing," she said. Not knowing what to say, and feeling a bit like crying, Kazuki rose from the couch. "I know I'm not very smart," she continued, "but I've thought about things. There's not one thing in life I want to do, not one thing I've ever thought of myself. That's why I end up doing what everyone else is doing; but that's no fun either. But I can't keep doing speed forever . . . Oh! Ow! That hurts!" Grimacing, she hid her face behind her hands.

"Should I call an ambulance?"

"No," she said, shaking her head. "They might report it to the police." Kazuki put the pillow he'd brought from her room under her head and spread a blanket over her. He made a mental note to add his sister to the list of people to be pitied, and he vowed to protect her when the day came that he would be in charge. But if it was true that her suffering was due to the fact that there was nothing she wanted to do, then what could he ever do to help her? He heard a faint sniffling from under the blanket.

"Isn't there anything you'd like to do?" he asked quietly.

The sniffling gradually stopped and the house was silent. She must have fallen asleep, he thought. Up to this point, he had taken care of his brother with the help of the housekeeper. From now on he would have to look after his sister, too. At most, his father came home two or three times a week, so there was nobody but Kazuki to take charge. The house had been placed under his jurisdiction, but it didn't exactly bother him. In fact, he was proud to have taken on the duty of watching over the family.

"I wouldn't mind being a model," she said suddenly, "but it'll never happen."

"Why not? You could be a model, I know it. I promise, you could!" he said, sounding positive.

"Could you make me a model?" she asked, poking her head out from under the blanket. "But how?" she added, laughing faintly.

"I promise, I will," he said, pounding his fist on the floor.

Miho closed her eyes and took a deep breath, a smile playing over her lips. In a few minutes, she was sleeping peacefully. Stuffing the wad of bills into his pocket, Kazuki went out into the hall. He could hear a sound, like shells being scraped together, something clearly different from the normal creaking of the house. It wasn't exactly like metal rubbing on glass, but it was equally as grating. He gave a shudder as he realized it was coming from the basement. Wondering what his father could be up to, he headed down the stairs. The door stood ajar and a pale light was leaking from the crack. The eerie noise grew louder as he approached the door. As he reached the bottom step, his body tensed with the effort to be quiet. He silently swallowed the spit that had collected in his throat and wedged his shoulder into the space between the door and the frame.

His father was collapsed on the bed, as if someone had beaten him. The noise was coming from him—*kari, kari, kari, kari*—from his grinding teeth. Kazuki walked slowly over to the bed, avoiding the pool of vomit that smelled vaguely of Chinese food, and stood looking down at his father. He had been drawn by the noise, *kari, kari, kari, kari, kari, kari,* and now he bent over, peering down into the sleeping face. Though he had been clean shaven when he came home, stubble had appeared on Hidetomo's face during the night. Kazuki wondered why he should be looking so closely at his father's face. It wasn't so much that there was something he wanted to do as from the desire to understand the meaning of these grinding teeth.

Kazuki, too, was sensitive to noise, though in a different way than Kōki. Any sort of unusual sound echoed in his head like tidings of some disaster. If you stripped words of their meaning, only the sound remained. But if sound then tried to recapture some meaning, it became so much noise—like his father's grinding teeth.

He took a cigarette from the pack lying on the end table. He put it in his mouth, but unable to find the lighter, he clicked his tongue in annoyance, crushed the pack, and threw it down on his father. The grinding continued. He had never really thought about what went on inside his father before, but apparently he kept an enormous amount of bitterness and hatred shut deep inside. On the surface of things, Hidetomo seemed to have inherited a good deal from his father and had gone on to develop even greater wealth, so that now he could satisfy nearly all his desires. But Kazuki suspected that these grinding teeth were proof that he was really a man who had lost his reason for living, who was tormented by self-doubt. What sort of future was there for a man who beat his daughter and then passed out drunk? Kazuki averted his eyes from his father, who seemed to have been caught by death like a fish on a line, and he reminded himself that he must never allow anyone to see his father asleep. He suddenly pitied the man who had this hideous sleeping self trailing after him like a shadow even when he was awake.

Kazuki sat on the sofa and crossed his legs. He didn't really see the point in working to protect this man's property until he died, but then he didn't really have any other options. For Kazuki, however, anything beyond the satisfaction of his own desires was pointless. He didn't remember how he came to this conclusion, but somehow he had known, from the time he was a small boy, that things that were given to you were worthless. You had to find something that you could believe in absolutely, or you would be doing little more than spinning your wheels until you died.

The gnashing stopped. Hidetomo's mouth opened and he seemed to be waking up. Kazuki knew that he should get out of the room, but he couldn't take his eyes off his father. He stared into his mouth. The teeth were yellow with nicotine stains, the spaces between pitch black. His nostrils flared slightly and he began to snore with his mouth still hanging open. In a moment, the snoring had grown louder and fallen into a rhythm. Kazuki knew he could relax.

Then, feeling as though someone was watching him, he looked up and caught sight of the display case that held the collection of swords. He got up and walked over to the case, placing his hand on the knob. A few months ago, he had taken advantage of a moment when his father was out of the room to try to door, but it had been locked. Now, however, it swung open easily. He pulled a scabbard from the case with a flourish and slowly extracted the blade. For a moment, he was mesmerized by the beauty of the steel; a chill ran up his spine and he shook himself. For the first time in his life, he was in the presence of a perfect entity, a thing that lacked nothing, with nothing extraneous. He held his breath as a cold, spectral light engulfed him. Reaching out, his finger traced a slow arc along the blade, leaving a thin trail of blood. Perhaps the sword had become beauty incarnate precisely because it was no longer permitted to perform its true function: to kill. But even if it were allowed once more to do what it was meant to do, Kazuki doubted there was anyone in the world worthy of killing with this perfect blade. Certainly not this man, not his father. How could someone who possessed a blade capable of imparting such nobility end up himself like a rotten fish head that had been hacked away by a rusted kitchen knife? Kazuki decided that ownership of the sword must pass to him, and that he must learn many things, train himself relentlessly in order to become like the sword. He slid the blade back into its scabbard and returned it to the display case.

He went over to the briefcase his father had dropped on the rug and reached inside. He pulled out a key ring, removed the key to the basement, and pocketed it. Next time he would look for the key to the case. *Kari, kari, kari, kari*—the grinding had started again. Recalling the flash of light that the naked blade had released in the infinite darkness, he left the room and shut the door behind him.

The window in his room was gray with early-morning light, as if the color had been sprayed on. Going over to close the curtains, he noticed that the glass was thick with the bodies of tiny white and brown moths and other winged insects. He lost interest in the window and collapsed on the bed. He squirmed out of his T-shirt and shorts, stuffed a pillow under his head, and curled up in a ball. As he dozed, the sound of rain, like the furious flapping of wings, echoed in his head, and then suddenly he was sitting bolt upright, blinking his eyes. A glance at the Rolex told him that there was still an hour until seven, when Kanamoto was due, but if he went back to sleep he wouldn't be able to get up so he might as well stay up. He took a bag of cocaine from the drawer of his desk and snorted a line through a straw.

Kanamoto arrived exactly at seven, and Kazuki explained the situation. Kanamoto listened without interrupting and then called a taxi. He helped Miho out to the gate and lowered her onto the backseat. When Kazuki tried to get in with them, he stopped him.

"Don't worry. Please leave it to me," he said, tapping his chest. "We'll go straight to the hospital, and you should go to school. Everything will be fine."

Going back in the basement, he found Hidetomo still asleep, snoring loudly. He went up to his room and flopped on the bed, but he couldn't sleep. Instead, he changed into his school uniform, gathered up his book bag, and wandered aimlessly down to the entrance hall. On days he went to school, Kōki would always be standing by the door with a smile on his face, waiting to see him off.

"See you later!" he would say, hugging Kazuki, and then he would scuff into his shoes and follow him out the door. He would stop on the porch and lean against the door, waving brightly until Kazuki was out of sight. But today, Kōki was nowhere to be seen. Kazuki opened the door quietly, slipped out, and closed it behind him. Then he started to walk.

He stopped in front of the American school to try to catch a taxi. The gate to St. Joseph's was wide open and groups of white and black and Asian children, elementary school age to high school, were chattering in English as they filed in. Kazuki, who had hardly been to school since seventh grade and who hadn't even been awake at this hour in three months, was dumbfounded to see that everyone else was still showing up for class. His hand closed around the basement key in his pocket.

It was nearly fifteen minutes later that a taxi finally stopped and he slid down in the backseat, escaping the eyes of the St. Joseph's students. As the car headed for Ishikawa-chō Station, Kazuki yawned, thinking he would find some complaint to keep him in the nurse's office until school let out. But then he remembered what his sister had said: "You never actually run away, Kazuki, but you always seem to be hiding." Not me, he answered in his head. I could be skipping school altogether and wandering around town. He'd been stopped by the police lots of times when he was playing hooky, but he always told them that his mom was sick and he was going to find her at the hospital and they let him go, no questions asked. He had read somewhere that schools in the early days had really been nothing more than prisons for kids. And even today, if children were needed for labor, they were never sent to school; in some countries they worked like slaves, in others they carried guns and fought in battle.

The sidewalks on either side of the road up the hill were swarming with girls in various school uniforms: Ferris, Futaba, Kyōritsu, Yokohama Academy. At the top of the slope was a small shrine housing several images of Jizō, patron god of children, thus the area had been named Jizō Hill, though the residents called it Maiden Slope.

A train was just pulling in at the overhead platform as Kazuki climbed out of the cab in front of the station. A flood of uniformed girls poured down the steps in a cloud of laughter and chattering voices. Kazuki had no desire to climb the stairs against this flow, so he stood by the ticket gate, hands stuffed in his pockets, waiting for it to run its course. He should have taken the cab all the way to Hōsei, he told himself.

An hour and a half and three transfers later, he arrived at the school gate. But as he stood watching his classmates, in uniforms identical to his own, marching into the building like a column of ants, his chest contracted and he felt as though a wad of newspaper had been stuffed down his throat. He slipped away along the wall that lined the school grounds, walking with his head down. I'm not like them anymore, he thought; I'm in a whole different place and there's no use trying to go back there. He found a spot where no one could see him and bent over double, opening his mouth to spit out whatever was choking him. He shoved his fingers down his throat but nothing came out except a dribble of spit. He wasn't sure what was happening to him: Was he throwing off the yoke and trying to run away? Or was he being hunted down like a wounded animal? He mopped up the spit with his sleeve and waited for the bell announcing the start of class. When he heard it, he turned his back on the school and walked away.

He took the train to Shibuya and went straight to Tokyu Hands, where he had the basement key copied. Back in the station, he retrieved his book bag from the locker where he'd stored it and headed for the ticket gates of the Keihin Tōyoko Line. At Yokohama Station, he transferred and got off at Kannai. He followed Isezaki Street for a few hundred yards and then turned into the maze of alleys, coming at last to the Ōoka River. There, he took off his book bag and punted it out over the water. He didn't really expect to rid himself of school so easily, but he felt suddenly lighter, relieved of the bag. He wandered off, whistling badly as he melted into the alleys of Kogane-chō. Puddles of blue were beginning to appear in the overcast sky, but in the quarter it was still a long way from a pleasant midsummer day. It seemed as though the humidity and mustiness of the rainy season were lingering on here in Kogane-chō, if nowhere else.

An old woman he did not recognize was standing in the middle of the alley. There was no one else in sight, but the air seemed to be filled with a whispering sound like the fluttering of insect wings. The sound increased with each step, and it was impossible to tell whether it was welcoming Kazuki or trying to drive him away. But it hardly mattered; he had just escaped from enemy territory and now he was home. He walked along the street with a smile on his face, until he came to the old woman. She was staring straight at him and gave no sign that she intended to get out of the way. As Kazuki approached and tried to pass her on the right, she spoke at last.

"You're Chang Yong-ch'ang's son, aren't you? How you've grown!" Her voice seemed to come from somewhere deep inside rather than from her lips.

"Sorry, you've got the wrong person," he said, shaking his head.

"Then you're his grandson," she answered. Kazuki shook his head once more. "Really?" she said, spitting on the asphalt and chewing her lips. "You look just like him."

Crazy old bat, thought Kazuki. Look just like him, she said, but she had obviously mistaken him for someone else. He had never even heard of Chang-Yong Chang. Looking back over his shoulder, he saw that she was still standing in the middle of the road, staring at him. Scary, he thought, but just then the rhythm of a taiko drum came vibrating from under his feet. He took off down the street again, pressing the pendant on his chest through his shirt and wondering whether he could have the basement key copied in solid gold.

He checked his Rolex as he reached the top of the gently sloping street: 2:32. As he pressed his sweaty palm against the security panel, the gate swung open and a tinny voice blurted out of the speaker. Shimamura, the housekeeper, was trying to stop Kōki, who was apparently determined to go out.

"I told you that I'd be going shopping in an hour. Just wait till then!" This woman, who was usually so obsequious, so soft-spoken, was screaming now in a neurotic frenzy. "When I say no, I mean no! You just play your piano; that's all you know how to do. Why do you want to go out? What could possibly be so interesting? All you do is walk straight ahead like a crazy person. And you couldn't do the shopping even if I gave you the money, so what could you possibly want to do out there?" She was prying Kōki's fingers from the knob as he wrenched the door open and struggled to get out; finally, she grabbed him by the collar and hauled him back in the house.

Kazuki charged up to the door, threw it open, and caught Kōki just as he was about to fall. Looking up, he was confronted with Shimamura's grim face, like a color copy of the mug shots on the police ledger in the newspaper. He reached out and shoved her, sending her flying against the wall. She slid down on the rug and lay in a heap.

"Why, why did you do that?" she stuttered, getting up on her knees.

"Please don't." She crawled into the hall and tried to escape to the back of the house.

"I told you to look after my brother! If he wants to go out, you forget the other stuff and take him. I'm paying you fifty thousand extra a month just to keep him company! Why won't you let him go out? Tell me!" Even when he kicked her from behind, Shimamura held her tongue.

Go ahead and kick me, she thought. Just so he doesn't pull a knife. He's crazy . . . got to keep calm. She tried to remember the words to the sutra. She'd been saying it morning and evening for twenty years . . . how did it go? "Namu . . ." But what came after that? Fool! "Namu . . ." How could I forget? "Namu . . ."

"Shut up with that shit!" Kazuki screamed, kicking her again.

Ouch! As long as he doesn't get a knife . . . Concentrate on the sutra. She suddenly realized that the boy wasn't standing behind her anymore. Should she hide in the bathroom? Better move, she thought, but as she tried to get up, she felt a blow on her back and pain shot through her. Groaning, she looked around to find the boy standing over her, brandishing the umbrella stand.

"Get up!" he shouted. "Can't you understand? Get up!"

She struggled to her feet, shielding her face with her hands, and backed against the wall. "I'm so sorry. Please, forgive me!" she pleaded, inching toward the entrance. "I beg you, Kazuki, don't do this. Forgive me! Please! Just let me go home. I'm sorry, really. You were right, I beg you!" She darted toward the door, arms flailing, but Kazuki threw the umbrella stand at her. As she lurched forward, groaning, he caught her arm and dragged her back into the hall, shoving her up against the glass door.

"Thought you could get away, did you? Don't fuck with me, lady. Now tell me again, why wouldn't you take him out? Tell me!" he bellowed, thrusting his face in hers.

It didn't hurt so much as feel numb, like when she'd had a tooth pulled at the dentist. I guess this is it . . . I knew there was something weird about this house. So this is what it's like to be murdered, she mused, vaguely watching the boy's heaving chest and shoulders. But then his hot breath on her face revived her a little and she realized she had to try to do something . . . and at the same time she began to realize that she really had mistreated Kōki.

"I'm sorry," she managed. "I was doing the laundry and I couldn't leave it. Please believe me, Kazuki. I meant no harm . . ." Before she could finish, he shoved her to the floor, but she muttered on. "Forgive me! It'll never happen again. I'll take him out for a walk right now, really I will," she sobbed, clasping her hands together and bowing before the boy.

"Apologize to my brother!" Kazuki shouted, beginning to cough. "On your hands and knees!"

Shimamura pressed her forehead against the floor. "Namu kara tannō tora yaya! Namu kara tannō tora yaya!" She was nearly shouting the sutra, happy to have remembered it at last. "Namu kara tannō tora yaya! Namu kara tannō tora yaya! Namu kara tannō tora yaya! Namu kara tannō tora yaya!"

"It's okay," said Kōki, covering his ears, "it's okay!"

"You're fired," Kazuki screamed, beginning to wonder whether Shimamura was putting a curse on him. The housekeeper made one last bow. She waited for a moment, rose slowly to her feet, and then scurried off to the kitchen to collect her things.

Left standing there, Kazuki felt suddenly empty—but also a bit sleepy. He gave a big yawn. "We'll go for a walk later," he told Kōki, and then went up to his room. As he was taking off his uniform, he heard the front door close. Yawning for the fifth time, he went downstairs carrying a change of underwear and the key. He opened the basement door and dropped the key next to the smear of vomit.

He went up to the bathroom and took a shower. He soaped up his pubic hair and stroked his penis, but it refused to get hard. After the shower, he was still sweating, so he left the bathroom naked and began leafing through the phone book for nurses and housekeepers. The woman he had just fired was the third housekeeper they'd had, so some of the names had already been crossed out. How about starting with the W's today, he thought, picking up the phone and carefully punching in a number. Seven A.M to 6 P.M, six days a week, Sundays off, care for a mentally handicapped eighteen-year-old—Kazuki smoothly repeated the specifications. The word "handicapped" bothered him a little, but it was almost impossible to explain Williams Syndrome over the phone.

"What's the salary for a job like that?" he asked.

"Somewhere between four hundred fifty and five hundred thousand a month, I should think," said the voice.

"And when could you send someone for an interview?"

"At your convenience, sir."

"Fine, then let's say the day after tomorrow at eleven." After giving his address and phone number, he pressed the button to end the call. Then it occurred to him: if he was going to pay five hundred thousand, he might as well ask Kyōko to take the job. He dialed her number, but no one answered.

"I see your balls!" Kazuki turned to see Kōki laughing at him. "The phone in your room is ringing," he added.

Stuffing his legs into his underpants, Kazuki ran up the stairs. Fortunately, the phone was still ringing when he grabbed it from the desk. He pressed the button and held the phone to his ear. It was Kanamoto.

"I waited until four so you'd be home from school. Miho is in the hospital. She has a broken leg, but it doesn't look too bad. They put a cast on it, and they say she should rest in the hospital for a week or so."

"Where are you?" Kazuki asked.

"A clinic near Hiranuma Bridge in Takashima-chō. They know me here. They agreed to say in the report that she fell downstairs. I'm calling because Miho wrote down a list of things she needs and I want to come by and pick them up."

"I was just about to take Kōki out for a walk," Kazuki said.

"I'm at the station. I can be there in ten minutes." When the phone went dead, Kazuki put on some shorts and a T-shirt. He took the stack of ten-thousand-yen bills from the desk drawer, counted out twenty, which he tucked in an envelope, and returned the rest to the drawer. Shoving the envelope in his pocket, he went back downstairs.

Kōki was lying on his back on the living room floor. "They sure looked funny," he blurted out, glancing up at Kazuki. "Your balls, I mean." He started to slap his palms against his stomach and slowly curl his body, but when the buzzer on the intercom sounded, he jumped to his feet and ran to the door. Kazuki checked to see that it was Kanamoto's face on the monitor.

"Come on in," he said into the speaker as he pressed the button to open the gate. A few moments later, the bell rang and he opened the door.

"These are the things she needs," Kanamoto said, handing him a slip of paper. Kazuki ran upstairs to his sister's room. He found her black Prada suitcase and began filling it with the things on the list: pajamas and underwear from the dresser; a brush, hairpins, rubber bands, a hair band, and tissue from her makeup stand. In the bathroom, he found her toothbrush, toothpaste, a cup, soap, facial cleanser, lotion, cotton balls, shower cap, washbasin, two washcloths, and a towel. He packed everything into the suitcase and then checked the list again.

When he got back to the entrance hall, he found Kōki resting his head in Kanamoto's lap and reaching up to rub the stubble on his cheek. He was giggling quietly to himself. Most people found Kōki's strange intimacy disturbing, but Kanamoto acted as though it were the most natural thing in the world.

"Hey," Kōki said, hopping up suddenly, "we should go, too." He shoved his hands under Kanamoto's arms and tried to pull him up.

Kōki's innocent, puppylike playfulness reminded Kanamoto of Kazuki when he was four or five years old. He didn't know the name for the older boy's condition and he assumed that it was a form of retardation, but he was also sure that if you could strip away the egotism from a human being and give him an extra measure of sociability, you'd come up with someone like Kōki.

"This is a map showing how to get to the hospital," said Kanamoto, fishing two sheets of paper out of the breast pocket of his linen suit. "The phone number's written on it. You'd better ask your father to notify her school. Here's a copy of her medical record for him to show them."

"How much will the bill come to?" Kazuki asked.

"Hmm, I'll have to ask. They'll probably want you to settle up when she gets out."

"Here's two hundred thousand. Be sure to take the cab fare and the rest out of this, too." As Kazuki held out the envelope, a crooked smile appeared on Kanamoto's face.

"Very well," he said, slipping the envelope in his coat pocket. It was the first time that Kazuki had seen Kanamoto dressed in a suit and tie, and it occurred to him how useful it would be to have someone he could trust with this kind of thing. He would want Kanamoto to be there in any tight spot.

They had been walking for only a few minutes, but the wind had already scattered the clouds and patches of blue sky were appearing. The sloping path they followed was lined on both sides by large homes. Trees from the gardens shaded the walk, but here and there it was dappled with sunlight. Kōki made his way haltingly, his small head wobbling on the long, thin neck that protruded from his sloping shoulders. Kazuki and Kanamoto followed behind. From time to time, Kōki would stop, turning around and grinning like a small child as he waited for them to catch up. When they were quite close, he would jump up and grab Kanamoto's arm, hanging on like a monkey. After that, he would walk holding his hand for a few yards before going on ahead by himself once more.

"I've never met anyone like your brother before," said Kanamoto. "He has eyes like an angel." He had the feeling that he had witnessed some sort of miracle in Kōki's eyes, and his tone was full of awe. They had come down Jizō Hill and were approaching the shops in Ishikawa-chō when Kanamoto spoke again. "Please don't tell your father that I was the one who took Miss Miho to the hospital," he said, shifting the Prada bag from his right hand to his left. "He should probably hear it directly from me at some point."

"It looks like you stole the bag," said Kazuki cheerfully. "You'll probably get arrested." Kanamoto chuckled and moved the strap to his shoulder, as if intending to make it more noticeable. With that, he disappeared down a side street without saying good-bye to Kōki, who was walking several yards ahead.

A moment later, Kōki turned and waited for Kazuki. The smile had left his face.

"Where's Kanamoto?" he said.

"He went to take Miho her things at the hospital."

"Is he coming back?" Kōki asked, once again staring straight ahead.

"He'll come," said Kazuki.

Kōki stopped when he reached the window of a store that sold imported housewares. In front of the fake brick facade stood an enormous wooden rocking chair, large enough for a giant to sit in. The faded green paint on the chair was beginning to peel away in places like sunburned skin. The chair was almost identical to one that Kazuki's grandfather had used right up until his death, and whenever their grandfather had gone out, the boys had fought over the right to climb up and be rocked by their mother.

"Remember?" asked Kazuki.

"Granddaddy's chair," Kōki answered. Kazuki had lost interest in the chair before he was five, but Kōki had gone on with the game. Because of his condition, he was not allowed to use the sliding board or swings at the park, so the chair had served as his playground. At some point after their grandfather had died, however, the chair had disappeared.

"You want one?" Kazuki asked.

"Uh-huh," Kōki said, a grin spreading across his face.

"I don't have any money with me now, but next time I'm by here I'll order one and have it delivered." Kōki held out his tiny, crumpled little finger and Kazuki locked his gently around it to seal the promise.

Continuing down the street, Kōki stopped next at a toy shop. As he spread his fingers on the glass like miniature frogs coming to rest, he noticed Kazuki's reflection behind him and smiled. Suddenly disturbed by the image in the glass, Kazuki shifted himself out of the frame like a tourist dodging a persistent photographer. Kōki darted into the store and began looking around at the toys, picking up whatever caught his eye: puppets of Snow White and the Seven Dwarves; a stuffed rabbit that gave a pained cry when its belly was pressed; a yellow sports car that ran around in a tight circle; a patrol car driven by a policewoman; and a little dancing skeleton that seemed to be made out of wire. He would weigh an object in his hands, then place it back on the shelf. Finally, he picked out a silver-plated music box and turned to look at Kazuki.

"Was this made in a faraway country?" he asked. Kazuki took the box from him, turned it over, and read the tiny letters engraved on the bottom.

"France," he said.

"Is France farther than America?" Kōki asked.

"Yes, I think so," Kazuki answered. He wound the key on the music box until it wouldn't turn anymore and then opened the lid. Kōki closed his eyes, concentrating on the melody. When the mechanism ran down and the tune became slurred, he opened his eyes.

"It sounds a little funny, but I still think it's pretty," he said, smiling. Kazuki remembered reading in a magazine that some company was making special-order music boxes for lovers to give to one another with their favorite tune.

"We could have one made to play the songs you play on the piano," he said.

"No, I don't think so," said Kōki. "I think we could make a CD, but not a music box."

"No, we could. All we have to do is record you on the piano, and they can make a music box from the tape," Kazuki said, as if quoting from the article. Kōki wound the key again. He stuck out his sharp jaw. A wrinkle creased his broad forehead, and his wide-set eyes bulged open as he set the music box on the palm of his hand.

"Yep, it sounds funny," he said. "I don't think I really want one."
The melody wound down and stopped.

Until he was almost three, Kōki had slept very little. Their mother, Miki, had suffered a great deal during those years, trying desperately to get the baby to sleep, but whenever she thought she'd succeeded, he would suddenly begin crying again. In fact, he cried almost continually through his infancy. After making the rounds of various clinics, she had finally had him examined at a large university hospital, where they determined that he had a hereditary defect that prevented him from metabolizing calcium properly, resulting in high blood pressure and elevated levels of calcium in the blood. Unfortunately, other than regularly testing his calcium levels, they had no treatment to suggest. During the final diagnostic session, they had simply informed her that he would have developmental delays and that they intended to watch him carefully.

Less than three months after Kōki was born, Miki had become fed up with Hidetomo's temper and had moved to a separate bedroom. But Hidetomo, determined to have a male heir, had called her to his room like clockwork three nights a week. In two years' time, Miho had been born; two years after that, the child Hidetomo considered his eldest son.

Until he was four, Kōki continued to grow so that it was barely possible to distinguish him from a normal child, but he had not started to say even the simplest words. Then one day, while playing with a broken flashlight, he turned to Miki and his first intelligible words emerged: "Mama, I have ruined it."

"What did you say?" Miki blurted out, doubting her ears. Kōki repeated himself.

"I'm sorry, Mama, I have ruined it. Will that be a problem during earthquakes or blackouts?" He stared up at his mother with a worried look. He still spoke rarely after that day, but when he did, what he said was much more sophisticated than other children his age and his vocabulary was enormous. At five, he was still unable to go outdoors by himself, but he displayed a miraculous memory, repeating endless lists of insect names or countries until someone told him to stop. Miki, who had started to believe that he wasn't sick at all but some sort of genius, devoted all her energy to Kōki as Miho and Kazuki seemed to disappear from view.

About the time Kazuki turned five, Kōki took to following him around and pestering him to play. But to the younger boy, this strange older brother was a liability, and he took to pinching him and knocking him down as punishment for having stolen his mother's attention. It was when Kazuki was eight that Miki took Kōki and moved out of the house. A month later, Kōki came home by himself. Kazuki's persecution of his brother escalated after that; once, he pushed him down the stairs, and another time he chased him around the house with a lighter, blistering Kōki's hand. But then one night his attitude toward his brother completely changed.

That night Kazuki killed someone in his dreams. He didn't know who it was he had killed or why, but he did know that he lived right next door to the police station and that there were no walls between his house and the station. Policemen were constantly wandering from the station to the house and back again, but the fact that they didn't seem to suspect him had the odd effect of making him even more terrified. Then the scene changed and he was walking down a street in the neighborhood. A man in work clothes pried the cover off a manhole and cloudy water came pouring out. As Kazuki watched, a man's naked torso bubbled out of the hole, and the thought occurred to him that this was the corpse, that they'd found it, that it was all over for him. Fear oozed from him like oil paint from a tube as he studied the workman's face. But the workman continued to pump out the hole without a word, showing no sign that he'd seen anything out of the ordinary. But a body washed right by him! As the water level receded, the profile of the corpse emerged—it was Kōki. Kazuki's own scream woke him. Getting out of bed, he stripped off his pajama top and wiped the sweat from his chest with the sheet. Then, wanting a drink, he stepped out into the hall. But suddenly a horrible grief-stricken cry shook the floor and froze him to the spot. Was he still dreaming? He had stood there for a long time, but at last he opened the door, went in the room, and took Kōki's hand as he sat crying on the edge of the bed.

"I'm so lonely I'm going to kill myself," Kōki had sobbed, shaking off Kazuki's grip and burying his face in his hands.

"I'm here," Kazuki had said without even thinking. "You can't die. Mama'll be back, I know it. I'll bring her back. I promise." He held Kōki in his arms, then lay down next to him while he fell asleep. As Kazuki lay there, he decided that he had a duty and a responsibility to take care of his brother. Kazuki was eleven at the time, Kōki, fifteen.

The two boys cut through Motomachi and then made a loop around Harborview Park. After that, they headed for home. The street that led from the park to their house passed through the most expensive real estate in Yokohama, and it was lined with spacious, Western-style houses. As they made their way along this route, Kōki, who was walking a bit ahead, came to a sudden stop. One of the houses had been torn down, leaving just the cinder-block wall and a black iron gate. A white rectangle on the wall marked the spot where the nameplate had been removed, suggesting that the demolition had been rather recent, but the healthy growth of ivy on the wall hinted at a longer period of neglect, perhaps a half year or more. Though he had passed this way many times, Kazuki could not recall the house that had stood here. Kōki carefully took hold of the handle on the gate and pulled it, and as he did, a yellow tabby cat leaped out of the weeds. The family who lived here probably left it behind when they moved, Kazuki thought. The cat ambled toward Kōki, collapsing a few steps away to roll over and scratch its back on the weeds. Kōki bent down to gently rub the cat from its throat to the stripes that ran across its white belly; but then he straightened up suddenly, stepped over the cat, and walked into the weeds. Stopping in the middle of the lot, he closed his eyes and listened for a moment. Then, like a conductor listening to a symphony, he began murmuring the names of the bugs: "blue pine cricket, bell cricket, grass cricket . . ." *Chirii, chirii, chirii, chin, chin, firi, firi, firi, firi.*

The empty lot was not really empty; countless insects made their homes there, and as if to announce their presence, they kept up a constant chorus. Kazuki had thought that the city had banished the sounds of nature, replacing them with man-made noise, but he was wrong. The city was filled with the sounds of an astounding number of creatures living their lives. For city bugs, this vacant lot was a forest. For Kōki, who could distinguish every sound, from the lowest to the highest pitch, the insect voices were almost three-dimensional, like the sound from the best stereo equipment.

Kazuki was not sure what had happened, but he mimicked Kōki's posture, closing his eyes and listening. He found that he could hear the bugs faintly, but all of the cries sounded the same to him. Kōki was unusually afraid of loud noises such as drills or thunder, but Kazuki knew how fond he was of quieter sounds, like the chirping of crickets or grasshoppers. As he stood there, Kazuki could hear the songs of sparrows concealed in the grass, then, the piercing sound of a helicopter and other noises, and as they grew, a peculiar anxious feeling came over him. As if suddenly hypnotized, he sank into a mire of sound . . .

When at last the world grew quiet again and he opened his eyes, his brother had disappeared. Kōki was barely five feet tall, but he would still have stood out above the weeds. Kazuki called his name, but his voice sounded weak and insubstantial, as if absorbed in the grass. Thinking that he must have left the vacant lot, he walked to the gate, but there was no sign of Kōki in the street. The only sound now was the beating of his own heart. The grassy patch had fallen silent again, and the air above it shimmered with heat. A shiver went through him and he suddenly felt that the weeds were about to burst into flames. He filled his lungs with the scent of damp grass and earth and called Kōki again, beginning to push through the tallest weeds with both hands. The sharp leaves cut his arms like razors, but he pushed on, ignoring the pain. Images of his brother falling headlong into a bottomless pit, of his body washing up on a spout of cloudy water, flitted through Kazuki's mind; but just as he was beginning to wonder if he were dreaming, the older boy's head popped up in the grass.

"Kōki!" Kazuki shouted. Kōki thrust his clenched fist toward Kazuki.

"Jiiiyo, jiiiyo, jiiiyo," he chirped, slowly opening his hand. A cricket sprang from his palm and disappeared in the weeds, but almost immediately a cry exactly like the one Kōki had been making rose from the spot where the insect had landed. The resemblance was so perfect it almost seemed that the bug was imitating the boy.

As they made their way down the slope past the high wall that surrounded their own home, Kōki suddenly stopped again and looked intently toward the house, then shifted his gaze to his brother.

"The phone's ringing, Kazuki, and it sounds loud. Must be something important." Kazuki couldn't hear the phone but he grabbed Kōki's hand and began running. As he turned the key in the lock and pushed open the door, it was still ringing. Convinced that it was someone calling with bad news, Kazuki felt numb as he slipped out of his tennis shoes and ran to the living room.

"Kazuki?" It was Kanamoto. There was a moment of silence as he seemed to collect himself, and Kazuki clutched the receiver tighter, expecting to hear that his sister had taken a turn for the worse. "Granny Shige at the Golden Pavilion died." It took several seconds for this information to sink into Kazuki's brain.

"Died? When?" His voice caught in his throat. "I'll go over right away." He hung up the phone and stood frozen for a moment. Thoughts and feelings jostled in his brain, taking time to digest, like food eaten too quickly. As he chewed absentmindedly on his thumbnail, an image of his grandfather's funeral floated suddenly into his head, and he realized he should not go to see Granny Shige in shorts and a T-shirt. Running upstairs, he changed into his school uniform and stood in front of the mirror to knot his tie. He rubbed some mousse into his hair and combed it neatly; and when he'd finished dressing, he took the stack of ten-thousand-yen bills from his desk drawer and shoved it in his pocket.

Kōki was waiting for him when he came downstairs.

"Not now!" Kazuki screamed, but his tone betrayed more sorrow than anger. He ran back upstairs and found a white shirt and navy blue pants in Kōki's room. Back in the hallway, he changed Kōki's clothes. "Granny died. Not your grandmother, Granny Shige, she died," he muttered feverishly as he forced Kōki's feet into his socks.

The two boys climbed from the taxi in front of the Golden Pavilion just as Kanamoto was crushing the butt of his cigarette under his heel.

"I came directly from the hospital," he said. "I hadn't had anything since breakfast, and I just wanted a bowl of Sada's noodles. I guess it was some sort of premonition. They said she died right at dawn." There were tears in his voice but he managed to force a smile. "Let's go in."

As they entered the restaurant, all eyes turned to look at them. The neighborhood shopkeepers and streetwalkers, along with some random customers, were sitting at the counter and around the two tables, drinking beer and sake in an informal wake.

"Wait right here," Kazuki told Kōki. "Do *not* go out in the street."

"I'll look after him," said Kanamoto. "You go on up."

"I didn't know her," Kōki said, sitting down on one of the stools at the counter. "The dead lady was calling you, so you'd better go up. I'll just pour some drinks. Kanamoto-san, will you buy something?" He wrapped his arm around the man on the next stool.

Signaling for Kazuki to go, Kanamoto went around behind the counter, took a bottle of beer from the refrigerator, and flicked off the cap.

"Who is this?" the man sitting in Kōki's embrace asked Kanamoto.

"I'm Kōki. What's your name?" he said.

"You're a strange one," said the man. "I'm nobody you should know, but call me Kimura." Kōki went around the room, asking each person's name in turn. Some seemed amused, others reluctant, but everyone in the shop eventually introduced himself and the mood grew festive. Having memorized what they told him, Kōki began pouring beer, calling each person by his name.

Kazuki went up the stairs and opened the door. A woman sat fanning vacantly, perhaps toward the body, perhaps toward the old man nearby. She looked up as Kazuki came in, jagged teeth visible in her gaping mouth. It was Ryōko, the whore from the alley.

"Ah! Kazu-chan! You came? Granny'd be happy. That's so nice of you." She stood and pulled Kazuki by the arm as she would one of her customers. "Granny! It's Kazu-chan. Kazu-chan's come to see you. You see! Kazuki's come." She was nearly shouting at the corpse. "Sit over here, near her," she said, beginning to sob. She turned over a cushion for Kazuki and sat him next to her.

A faded bath towel was draped over Shige's face. As Ryōko lifted it, he could see the sunken eyes and cheeks, the dried, mummylike skin.

"She's all shriveled up, like those chicken bones she put into the ramen soup, but her face is still just like a baby's," Ryōko said, pulling back the quilt. The body had been dressed in a gaudy pink kimono with a border of white chrysanthemums along the hem. "I found this in the back of the wardrobe. Grampa said it made her look like a minstrel or a streetwalker, but he's just old-fashioned. I put it on her anyway. I'm sure there's some story to it—part of her trousseau or some such."

It was so humid the room itself seemed to be sweating. Chihiro sat properly up on her legs, but her head threatened to nod over as she craned her neck, struggling to stay awake. Her face shone with moisture. Ryōko and Grandfather Sada, too, were dripping wet. It struck Kazuki as odd that only Granny Shige's body was dry as a bone without a drop of sweat. Dressed in the pink kimono, she reminded him of a performing monkey; but still, he thought, pressing his hands together unconsciously in prayer, were she to be installed in her own little shrine just like this, she'd probably become a buddha. He reached down and stroked her wrist, gnarled like a withered branch.

"Gramps! Kazuki's come. See! You haven't left us, too, have you?" Ryōko shouted, tapping her fan on Sada's hand as he sat by his wife's body. "Oh, he's hopeless, he is. He's left everything up to us. We divided up the chores: somebody called the doctor to get the death certificate, somebody took it over to city hall, someone else went to get the cremation license." In the midst of her soliloquy, Ryōko apparently remembered something she'd forgotten and hopped up. "Oh! Excuse me a minute," she said, shuffling out the door and stomping down the stairs.

"Would have been better if she hadn't come," the old man muttered without looking up. They could hear Ryōko downstairs.

"Why aren't the fans here yet? If we don't get some going, Granny'll start to stink. Go find them. And why the hell do you all look so jolly? I know it's a wake, but you're going to give the old girl regrets . . ." Several voices could be heard answering her, and then a burst of laughter.

Kazuki wasn't quite sure that what he was feeling was sadness. The emotion swirling in his head felt more like white-hot anger. It didn't seem right. How could her whole life end like this? Someone ought to weep for her, but who? Kazuki didn't know.

"Call up the liquor store and tell them to send over plenty of beer and sake," Sada said. Chihiro stood up without a word and left the room. Kazuki sat daydreaming about what a funeral might be like, picturing a little pink boat floating slowly down the Ōoka River with crowds of people lining the banks. And in the boat was Granny Shige, covered in white chrysanthemums.

"Go home now," Sada said, addressing Kazuki for the first time. "Granny can rest in peace."

"I told you she should have gone to the hospital, didn't I?" Kazuki blurted out. When he reached the bottom of the steps, he found the restaurant in chaos, with the shopkeepers of Kogane-chō embarked on a party to rival the liveliest neighborhood festival. Kazuki had never seen Kōki in such good spirits, as his high, tinny laughter echoed through the room. A Thai prostitute was planting kisses on his cheeks and forehead, leaving smears of lipstick as she flirted with him.

"Shall we get rid of them?" Kanamoto called to him, but Kazuki shook his head. He felt no anger toward them. They didn't seem to feel sad about Granny Shige's death, but this was probably just the way they did things; they were probably imagining themselves drinking sake that Granny herself had poured. Kazuki's eyes fell on Chihiro, who was running around the shop like a cat in heat making sure everyone's glass was full. Granny's soul must have migrated into her, he thought.

At some point, he realized that Sada's apron-clad figure had appeared behind the counter.

"Hey, Gramps. You open for business?"

"I've never heard of a guy dishing ramen on the day his old lady died!"

"Relax, come have a drink with us."

Sada lit the burners under the pots for boiling the noodles and simmering the broth. Then he set to chopping onions and slicing pork.

"You got a karaoke machine in here?" someone called.

"They have one at Mimiko's place!" another voice answered, and several men ran out the door.

"Gramps, how about some chāshū ramen?" a woman from the Philippines called out in broken Japanese. Soon afterward Chihiro was carrying steaming bowls of noodles and the room was filled with a chorus of slurping.

"Not quite funeral fare," someone said, but the words were lost in the din. The sound of voices singing could be heard in the distance, and someone stood and stepped outside.

"They've got a mike pulled out in front of Mimiko's." Kazuki recognized the old Korean folk tune that echoed through the neighborhood.

When the song was over, the men came one by one to give their condolences to Sada and then went quietly home. Ryōko had passed out drunk, but someone hoisted her on his back and carried her away. Kōki had curled up in a ball and was fast asleep at the bottom of the stairs. Kazuki sat at the counter, his head supported on his arm, nodding off from time to time.

"We should have sent them home?" said Sada.

"Kazuki," Kanamoto said, standing and resting his hand on the boy's shoulder. "Let's get going."

"You'll be taking her to the temple in the morning," Kazuki muttered, his eyes half closed. "I want to go, too."

"Go on home," said Sada, spitting in the sink. "What do you want with her bones, anyway?" Kazuki said nothing, and a moment later his head flopped over on the counter.

"Carry them home," Sada said to Kanamoto.

"I can't take both of them," Kanamoto pointed out, draining a cup of sake someone had left. "And anyway, you'll need someone to help you with the funeral." Grabbing the bottle of sake, he poured himself another drink.

The coffin was already loaded in the black hearse when Kazuki woke the next morning. Chihiro, in a gray dress, was in the backseat, with Kōki's head resting on her lap. After waiting for Kazuki to come out, Sada locked the door of the Golden Pavilion and climbed into the passenger seat. Kazuki and Kanamoto got in the limousine that was waiting for them. The hearse pulled away with the other car following.

"Where are we going?" Kazuki asked.

"The Kuboyama Funeral Hall," Kanamoto said.

"Is there a convenience store around here?" Kazuki said, looking over at Kanamoto.

"I don't think there's one before Fujidana," he said. "Do you want to go there?"

"Uh, sure," said Kazuki. After passing through the shops in Fujidana, the car headed toward Hodogaya. As they came up on a convenience store, the driver slowed and pulled to the curb. Kazuki signaled for Kanamoto to come with him as he stepped out of the car.

He could not have said why, but the tight rows of potato chip bags and tissue boxes lining the shelves set his nerves on edge. He felt disoriented, unable to tell what all these shapes and colors meant, what all these products were used for. He wandered the aisles, finally returning to the stationery section as he recalled what it was he wanted. Sandwiched between the plain business envelopes and the elaborate ones for wedding gifts was a small stack of the special envelopes used for funeral offerings. Kazuki pulled one from the shelf.

"Is this the right kind?" he muttered, as if talking in his sleep.

"Yes," said Kanamoto.

"You write something, don't you?"

"Just your name."

"Here?"

"Yes, there." Kazuki took the envelope and a brush-pen to the register and paid for them.

"Could I borrow your counter a minute?" he asked the clerk, twisting the cap off the pen. He waited for the ink to fill the bristles and then carefully wrote his name. "Damn. That's no good," he muttered, crumpling the envelope in his hand. "Go get another one."

Kanamoto placed the new envelope on the counter, and the clerk ran the scanner over the bar code. Kazuki paid and then ripped the wrapping from the envelope. He spread out the ruined envelope and practiced several times before finally moving his arm awkwardly over the new one.

"That's still no good," he said when he'd finished.

"It looks fine," said Kanamoto, picking up the envelope.

"How much do you put in?" Kazuki asked.

"Well, I suppose ten thousand yen would be appropriate," Kanamoto answered, watching the boy's serious expression. He started to smile, reassured somehow at the innocence of Kazuki's question, but as he watched him pull a huge roll of bills from his pocket, warning lights began to flash in his head. Kazuki peeled bill after bill from the stack, smoothing it neatly before inserting it in the envelope. When he was done, he tucked the offering into the breast pocket of his uniform and breathed a satisfied sigh.

Up the hill in front of Western Yokohama National Hospital stood the Kuboyama Funeral Hall, a newly renovated version of the old crematorium. The limousine stopped in the parking space reserved for microbuses.

As Kazuki climbed out of the car, a light rain was beginning to fall on the stands of oak and magnolia trees that dotted the grounds. He had imagined a sinister, factorylike building with a tall, dark smokestack sending the remains of the deceased up in smoke, so he was surprised to be heading toward a pinkish building that might have been mistaken for a hotel. "Creepy," he muttered, glancing nervously about. The crematorium was the officially sanctioned facility where city dwellers, shielded as they were from the reality of death, could send their loved ones off to the land of the dead with all due formality, but there was no sign of a dead body to be seen anywhere.

"Where's the hearse?" Kazuki asked, returning to the land of the living.

"I wonder," said Kanamoto, looking over at the main building. "Come back in a couple of hours, and have some coffee on me in the meantime," he told the driver, handing him a thousand yen. As he spoke, the hearse pulled through the gate and stopped next to him. The window on the driver's side slid down.

"Sorry, I made a wrong turn at Kuboyama Slope," the young man said, smiling at Kanamoto. "I have to get the coffin into the building. Could you give me a hand?" He craned his neck around and asked his passengers to get out.

"Kazuki, please have everyone wait at the entrance," Kanamoto said, getting in by the driver. The hearse drove around to the back of the building.

"We should have had her embalmed," Kazuki said, coming up to stand by Sada. The old man said nothing as he stood watching Kōki and Chihiro. Kōki had wrapped his arms around Chihiro, who was twisting and squirming in an attempt to escape the embrace. Their laughter rang through the funeral hall, less a note of cheerfulness than an echo in the void of life.

We should have had her embalmed. Kazuki's peevish comment was like a slap in Sada's face, but he merely looked out at the rain, falling more steadily now, and then walked into the building.

They went to the lounge where they found Kanamoto and the driver already seated at a table. After pouring a cup of tea for the old man, he asked the others if they wanted something to drink. There was no answer.

"Well, I'll just get something then," he said, getting up and going over to a row of vending machines.

Kazuki sat with his hands clasped on his knees. "Do you have a family grave somewhere?" he asked Sada. The old man took a sip of tea and shook his head. "Well, what do you plan to do? If you don't have a grave, there's nowhere to put the ashes." He could barely conceal his irritation that Sada seemed so unmoved by Shige's death. Why weren't the shopkeepers who had been at the wake here at the funeral?

"Maybe I'll make ramen soup from the bones." Kazuki thought he heard Sada laugh as he said this, but it was just a sigh escaping through the gaps in his teeth.

Kōki was clasping Chihiro's hands as they lay on the table. They had apparently invented a private game: Chihiro would slide her hands out across the table and then pull them back as Kōki tried to grab them. They played again and again, clearly enjoying themselves. Kanamoto came back with cans of Coke and orange juice and set them on the table. He pulled a small bottle of sake from the pocket of his coat and offered it to Sada and the driver in turn. When they refused, he set it on the table in front of him. As he did, he suddenly thought of the head of the neighborhood association, a man named Takakura who managed three massage parlors in Kannai.

"Is Takakura coming?" he asked the driver, twisting the top off the sake.

"Hmm," the young man murmured, cocking his head and scratching his neck. He had introduced himself by saying that he'd worked for Takakura. "I had a part-time job at a funeral parlor a few years back. I guess that's why he let me handle things."

"You worked at a funeral parlor with blond hair?"

"I just did this three days ago," the driver laughed. "Back then I had a pompadour, but nobody cared."

Kazuki had taken great care not to crush the envelope in his pocket. He took it out now and set it on the table, but Sada merely glanced at it and continued sipping his tea.

"I want to give this for Granny Shige," he said, pushing the envelope forward with his fingertips.

"Then give it to her," Sada said.

"Don't make fun of me!" Kazuki shouted. "She's dead!" Kōki and Chihiro jerked their hands to their laps, but Kanamoto calmly tapped the end of his cigarette on the table where they had been playing and studied Kazuki's face.

"That's right," Sada murmured. "Dead. Gone, like so much smoke."

"But she needs a grave!" Kazuki's mouth felt dry. His eyes stung and his head was beginning to ache.

"Gramps," said Kanamoto, picking up the envelope, "you should take it. The boy wants you to have it. Don't be stubborn; he's not your grandson." He moved over to where Sada was sitting and tucked the envelope in his bag.

"What's all this going to run?" Sada said, fishing his reading glasses from the bag and setting them on his nose. He glanced at the driver and then opened his cracked leather wallet and peered inside.

"Uh, I think Mr. Takakura will take care of it," the young man said, looking embarrassed.

"Don't be an idiot," Sada barked. "The neighborhood association doesn't have that kind of money. I look after Shige." The driver looked sheepishly at Kanamoto and then pulled a receipt from his back pocket and handed it to Sada.

After studying it for a moment, he looked up. "Fifteen hundred yen? They're going to cremate her for fifteen hundred yen? That would barely pay the gas bill." He handed the receipt to Kanamoto.

"That's what it says all right," said Kanamoto with a laugh.

"I thought it sounded strange when they gave it me," the driver said. "It seems they charge Yokohama residents fifteen hundred yen; outside the city limits it's seven thousand five hundred."

"It's about what they'd want to haul off a pile of garbage. Shige would have had a good laugh to know that her funeral cost about the same as a beer, some ramen, and a plate of dumplings." Shaking his head, Sada laid two thousand-yen bills on the table. He thought for a moment and then added a ten-thousand-yen bill to the pile.

"I can't accept this," the young man said, but Sada grabbed his hand and pressed the bills into it.

Kazuki stared out at the large drops of rain pelting the window. It occurred to him that it was probably a typhoon, and for some reason the thought comforted him, providing the first relief he'd felt since he'd learned of Shige's death.

"They said it would take about an hour, didn't they?" Sada's voice sounded like a fading flame.

Lightning flashed and the rumble of thunder shook the room. Kōki covered his ears and buried his face in Chihiro's breast. There were nearly forty people in the lounge, three mourning families, but at that moment everyone fell silent and listened to the storm outside. The room darkened, as if the shadow of death had passed over, and then the intercom crackled with an announcement.

"May I have your attention, please. Preparations for the bone gathering for the Nakata party have been completed. Will all those attending this funeral please proceed to the hall adjacent to Furnace No. 3." The six mourners gathered at the elevator and rode up to the hall.

"Are we all here?" the attendant asked when they reached Furnace No. 3.

"All here," the driver echoed.

"Then we'll begin." The attendant pressed a button and the door to the furnace slid open. A platform containing the ashes and bones emerged. The bones of the arms and legs had crumbled, but the skull and ribs were intact.

"The family will now please gather the bones. Working in pairs, please grasp them with the chopsticks and place them carefully in the urn." The attendant made a polite bow. Sada and Chihiro went first, then Kazuki and Kōki, and finally Kanamoto and the driver. The attendant, clearly embarrassed at how quickly they had finished, asked them to remove more of the bones. This time they worked slowly, fishing the small bones from the ashes and dropping them carefully in the urn.

When they were done, the attendant bowed again and began removing the larger bones. As he grasped the skull, the chopsticks pierced the bone and it crumbled.

"Stop!" Kazuki screamed. The man peered around, a stunned look on his face. "You think you can just break her bones? Her head?" Kazuki yelled, pouncing on the man.

"Kazuki!" Kanamoto shouted, grabbing his arms and holding him back.

"My job," said the attendant, controlling his anger, "is to carefully transfer the bones to the urn and deliver it to the family. In twenty years, I've never had any complaints. Who do you think you are, shouting like that? Everyone else managed to stay calm. What do you think this is?" He finished crushing the skull and ribs and dropped them in with the other bones. Then he raked up the remaining pieces.

"I'll smash your head!" Kazuki's scream was even more frantic. He struggled to get loose as Kanamoto dragged him toward the lobby.

When Sada came out, cradling the urn, the lightning and thunder were coming in waves, and rain was streaming down the windows, completely obscuring the view outside. They climbed back into the limousine, Sada next to the driver and Kanamoto, Chihiro, Kōki, and Kazuki in back. The car headed for the boys' house. It seemed as though they were driving through a waterfall as the windshield wipers pulsed back and forth, fighting the torrent. Kōki, who had been resting his head quietly on Chihiro's shoulder, suddenly spoke up.

"Can Chihiro stay at our house tonight?" Kazuki stared out at the rain without answering, so Kōki repeated his question.

Thoughts raced through Kazuki's head as he sat silently watching the storm. How was he in a position to say yes or no to Kōki if he hadn't even been strong enough to stop the man at the funeral hall? Real power extended only to things you actually owned, and Chihiro didn't belong to him. The man at the funeral hall didn't either, nor did Kanamoto, nor Sada. But that thought suffocated him, as if he'd been buried alive in a narrow coffin.

"Kazuki, only cowards don't even answer!" Kōki's voice was high and brittle. Kazuki drew in a deep breath but it caught in his throat. He took in more air, still unable to let it out, as his fingers and toes started to grow numb. The numbness seeped into his head and he began to panic, continuing to suck air.

"Kazuki, are you all right?" Kanamoto asked, peering at him. His thin chest was heaving and his teeth were clenched.

"She can stay," he managed to mutter. His face was bright red as he looked over at Kōki.

"No she can't," Sada said quietly.

"Please let her," Kazuki suddenly pleaded. "It won't be any trouble. Just for tonight, please."

"Well, if it's that important. But have her back at the shop tomorrow," Sada said.

"Thank you! Hear that, Kōki? That's great!" He rubbed his hands through his brother's hair.

"Kazuki's great!" Kōki chirped

"Not a coward?"

"Not a bit!" Kōki grasped Kazuki's hand and rubbed it against his cheek.

As soon as he had slipped out of his shoes, Kōki took his brother and Chihiro by the hand and led them around the house, looking for a room where the lightning and thunder could not reach. He took them into the bathroom and had Chihiro squat down in the tub with him.

"We're out of the rain, and we can't get a shock here," he sighed, squirming behind Chihiro. He lifted her slightly in both arms and settled her on his lap, giggling quietly.

Kazuki looked on, a scornful laugh welling up in his throat. He wondered what they would do if he poured boiling water on them from the shower. They'd yelp like dogs, he thought, and they wouldn't cuddle up together like that again anytime soon. But the laughter stuck in his throat as he remembered how he and his brother and sister used to close themselves in the sauna for fun. Kazuki had been in charge of coming up with the storyline—usually they were trapped in a landslide or a cave-in, waiting in the dark to be rescued. Then they would sit and grumble to one another about how horrible it was until someone got claustrophobic and went running out the door. The rules were simple: whoever left first was the loser. Miho always lost, but he and Kōki had sometimes stayed in for almost an hour at a time.

Noticing a horrible stench that seemed to be coming from Chihiro's body, Kazuki opened the bathroom door. The storm seemed to be over.

"No more thunder," he said.

"Kazuki," said Kōki, glaring at him, "close the door!" Startled by an arrogant tone he had never heard from Kōki, he turned to go.

"Take a bath!" he yelled back at Chihiro.

Back when Granny Shige had been healthy, she and Chihiro had gone together every evening to the public bath. But about six months ago Shige had become bedridden, and Sada had been taking her only once a week, asking the prostitutes he knew to help her wash herself. In the last three weeks, as Shige had gone into her final decline, the old man had not even had the energy to get himself to the bath.

"I wonder if you even know how to wash yourself," Kazuki said, stopping in the door.

"You use soap to wash," Chihiro murmured, her eyes drooping.

"I think I should wash her!" Kōki suggested.

"No you don't," said Kazuki, setting the temperature on the bathtub.

"The police will come, if you wash her," Kōki said.

"I'm not going to," said Kazuki. "Wait a minute. I'll go get her something to change into." He ran up the stairs, taking them two at a time, and went into Miho's room. Opening the drawer to her dresser, he pulled out a pair of pajamas and some underwear. He was panting when he got back to the bathroom and handed Chihiro the clothes.

"Put these on when you're done in the bath," he told her.

"Small panties!" she laughed, holding up the pink lace underwear in both hands. As she hiked up her dress to pull off her stockings, Kazuki ushered Kōki out of the dressing area.

After ten minutes, Kazuki began to worry. He opened the door to the dressing room and called through the frosted glass door of the bath.

"Are you done in there?" he said, but there was no answer. Kōki had followed and stood next to him listening intently. Elbowing him aside, Kazuki knocked on the glass. "We're coming in," he said.

As the door slid open, they could see Chihiro, sunk deep in the tub. She turned slowly to face them, her pimply brow, plump white cheeks, and round nose peering out over the rim of the tub. Her sleepy, hooded eyes blinked.

"Aren't you going to wash me?" she stammered, as her grinning face sank below the surface of the water. The brothers had started to get a little worried at how long she'd been under when she suddenly thrust her head out of the tub and shook it wildly, spraying drops around the room.

"We've got to get her clean," Kazuki sighed to Kōki. "Just wash her, that's all." They pulled off their socks, rolled up their sleeves and the cuffs of their pants, and stepped down into the bath area.

Kōki wet a washcloth and rubbed it with soap as Chihiro rose out of the water and straddled the side of the tub. Her body swayed, shining brilliantly in the cloud of steam, her curves smooth and gentle in the haze. Kazuki was overwhelmed by her flesh, richer and whiter than any nude picture he had ever seen. Kōki busied himself lathering her back. As he rubbed along her spine, her ample breasts began to rock back and forth. Red nipples rising from the large areola. A mole lost in the valley between. The gentle curve from her navel down over her abdomen. The pale, round buttocks fading into the steam. Kazuki imagined himself pressing his thumb into her throat, watching it disappear into her flesh.

"Kōki, no!" he said, coming suddenly to himself. His brother's face was just inches away from Chihiro's breast when he grabbed his collar and pulled him back. They were both covered in bubbles and soaked from the splashing. "You do your front," he told Chihiro, handing her the cloth. Watching from behind as she rubbed in big circles from her chest to her belly, he felt he was looking at a sow, but also at the warm, ripe body of a woman. She lay the washcloth on her lap and, rubbing the soap into her palm, began washing noisily between her legs. Kōki studied her intently, his broad forehead shining like a plastic implant and his wide-set eyes wandering wider still, like a monster from a science fiction movie.

"I'll do her feet," he blurted out, grabbing an ankle and beginning to scrub with a sponge. Chihiro squirmed, laughing like a newborn baby.

"Now your hair," Kazuki told her. "Close your eyes." She pursed her lips and screwed up her eyes as he poured water over her head and squeezed out a handful of shampoo. Kōki sank his fingers into her hair and began to rub.

"Now we're rinsing!" Kōki suddenly shouted, grabbing the hose from Kazuki and spraying Chihiro's head. As the soap washed away, her hair flowed down her back, black and lustrous. Staring at this firm, plump body that would seemingly have turned aside any injury or disease, Kazuki was filled with respect, something close to awe, for this perfect example of the power of life itself. He had always thought of a woman's naked body as something indecent, a dangerous thicket, but Chihiro reminded him of a picture he'd once seen in art class at elementary school of a young girl praying in a shaft of brilliant light.

Having changed into shorts and a white T-shirt, Kazuki called to order a pizza while Kōki began to play Beethoven's "Moonlight Sonata." Chihiro, in Miho's red-checked pajamas, came into the living room and sat on the sofa. When the food arrived, Kazuki watched his brother and the woman as they wolfed down pizza and gulped soda, smears of tomato and cheese growing around their mouths. He felt as though he were studying the habits of animals through the bars of their cage. Their gluttony embarrassed him, but at the same time he hated himself for being unable to reach out for one of the last two slices of pizza. He couldn't remember the last time he'd eaten a proper meal, or much of anything at all for that matter—it had probably been at least three days— but he could control his hunger by force of will. These two, however, were completely intent on the food, chewing madly without a word. Kazuki had no idea why people had to eat. He had never particularly enjoyed eating. Upper teeth grinding against lower, saliva mixing in, and then swallowing—and then the next bite. And they all repeated this pointless procedure two or three times a day. Why? Animals stored up energy for their necessary life functions, but human beings, cut off from the terrors of the hunter and the hunted, still seemed to have no limits to their appetite. They eat every available thing, simply to keep their mouths busy, and the more they eat, the weaker and flabbier they become. Eventually, they have no way to use up this stored energy, and they grow fat as it backs up in their bellies.

When they had finished the pizza, Kōki and Chihiro wiped their sticky fingers with damp tissues, burping and yawning in turn.

"Bedtime," said Kazuki, standing up, and they bobbed up with him. Kōki waved to Chihiro on the landing, wished her good night, and went into his room, as Kazuki led her into Miho's room. She fell over on the bed and lay on her back, eyes wide open and hands clasped on her chest, like Granny Shige in her pink kimono. Kazuki took hold of the blanket and yanked it out, laying it carefully over her. "You should get some sleep," he told her. She lay still, her jaw jutting slightly, as if wait- ing for a kiss. Reading the signals in her eyes, Kazuki backed toward the door. "Lights out," he said, hitting the switch and slipping into the hall. He heard snoring as he passed his brother's door, so he crept quietly to his own room, closed the door behind him, and threw himself on the bed.

Beyond a certain point, exhaustion itself became an obstacle to sleep, but Kazuki wrapped his arms around his pillow and tried to will himself into unconsciousness. He was walking along on top of the railing of a tall bridge. As he went, the railing narrowed, until he lost his balance—but just as he fell, he woke . . . and then he was walking again, looking far down to the shuffling lines of cars and people below. He went on for some time, hovering between waking and sleeping, until he decided it would be better to just get up. Then he fell asleep . . . and woke again. The clock on the VCR was flashing 8:03. He'd been in bed for a little over an hour.

He listened to his own heart, which seemed to be beating out of sync with everyone else in the world. If it were to stop beating, who ,,ould really care? His brother and Kyōko—that made two, he told himself, ticking off two fingers. The third finger twitched for a moment, but he couldn't think of name to go with it. And anyway, it didn't mean much to be mourned after you were gone; what he needed was someone to feel sorry for him right now because . . . he couldn't get to sleep. He rubbed his lips with the still-trembling finger. A person's worth was decided while he was alive, by the number of people who felt sorry for him and the number of people he felt sorry for. He felt sorry for his brother and Kyōko, and perhaps for Miho and Sada. But there was not a living soul to feel sorry for him as he lay here now, unable to sleep. He felt he could pity even the birds that fly in the sky; but in reality, he had never once cried since the age of four. If you were unable to surrender to feelings of impotence, tears would not flow. Tears were just a way of comforting yourself, of wallowing in your own weakness. But whenever Kazuki sensed weakness in himself, he immediately set up a wall of hatred and anger, and he felt sorry for people who couldn't build their own barriers.

Kazuki suddenly had the feeling that a middle-aged man, someone he did not know, was at that very instant hanging himself. He could hear the rope biting into the flesh of the neck, see the face turn red like a pomegranate, sense the flash of light behind the eyelids, feel consciousness slipping away. Shit and semen oozed from the body; eyeballs popped noiselessly from the head. As it swung back and forth on the rope, the body vanished, replaced by the drowned corpses of two sisters, about ten or eleven, bobbing on the waves. The two forms were gradually swelling, as the creatures of the sea nibbled at them, drawing them farther off shore. Eventually, the pale forms faded into the whitecaps.

He opened his eyes. Chihiro's nude mass was floating near the ceiling, floating amid waves of Kōki's snores. As he sat up in bed, his heart began beating loud and fast. A voice whispered that it would be better not to get out of bed, but he found himself out in the hall, headed for his brother's room. Pressing his ear to the door, he could hear the strains of Josef Ranner's "Farewell Waltz." Puzzled, he moved on to the door of the room where Chihiro slept. He reached out and pulled the doorknob.

Was he dreaming? The room was filled with steam and the walls seemed to be oozing sweat. He sensed that he was looking at an image from outside the frame. The picture was vague, like a silhouette or, more precisely, a series of X rays projected in sequence. A woman's legs, or the image of the bones in her leg, spread wide; a man's tailbone thrusting violently; the bones of the woman's legs, arching into a bridge; the man catching hold of the woman's pelvis, his spine arching. Kazuki, rocking as if he were riding the waves, suddenly sensed a flash of lightning. He looked out the window, but he could see only the faint glimmer of the light by the gate. When he looked back, the image had transformed from negative to positive, and he realized that it was the naked bodies of Kōki and Chihiro he was seeing, rising out of the gloom. His brother's hands were massaging her breasts. His mouth had closed over one nipple, and Kazuki could hear his moan of tearful ecstasy: "Mama!"

"Mama!"

"What?"

Staring at Chihiro's mouth, Kazuki felt as though his soul had been scooped out of his body. But her mouth had not moved except for a quiet panting.

"Mama?"

"You're safe now. There's nothing to fear."

Kazuki's ears were buzzing as he listened to the clear, high voice. Chihiro's? His mother's? He had no way of telling. Lightning flashed. Just at the instant their naked forms were burned into his eyes, the bed seemed to float away like a raft taken by the current.

It was exactly 10:22 the next morning when he arrived home from returning Chihiro to the Golden Pavilion. As he was taking off his shoes, Kazuki wondered why he checked the time when there was really no need. It was 4:26 P.M. yesterday when they'd had made it home from the funeral hall in the downpour. He was probably still uneasy about cutting himself off from school, where they measured everything by the clock; so now, when time no longer meant anything, he continued to parse every minute and second in his head.

He checked on Kōki, who was sleeping, and then came down to the living room, but as he opened the door, his mind suddenly went blank, as if every synapse in his brain had simultaneously stopped firing. As he looked around the room, he had no idea why he had come here. When he was little, he was sometimes left alone at home. Then, he remembered, he had not suffered so much from loneliness as from boredom. On days when he couldn't think of anything to do, he would climb into a cupboard or a closet and play one-man hide-and-seek. He would sit there in the dark, afraid that a burglar might sneak into the house; eventually, that fear would change to anticipation, even hope, but his hopes would invariably be dashed.

The basement, where the probability of being found was the very lowest, was always locked. But just once he had found the door ajar. As he stepped into the darkness, he was frozen with fear. Unable to move, he stood wondering whether his body would congeal, begin to crack from the strain. When a voice suddenly asked "Who's there?" he thought his heart would explode. He remembered screaming, and the next thing he knew, he was cowering on the stairs, sniveling and wailing all at once. Had his father been down there that day? If so, what was he doing in the dark?

He went down the stairs now. Even after he'd started middle school, when his father would call him down to the basement, he would creep down quietly. He held his breath and pulled on the doorknob. It didn't budge. Locked. His father must have come home. But when? Yesterday? The day before? He turned to go, but suddenly his heart beat faster and he pulled the key he'd copied from his pocket and fit it in the lock. Looking around, he was sure his father had been home: the key Hidetomo had left lying on the floor was gone. He checked to make sure no one was there now, then quickly moved the table and sofa and rolled up the rug. Prying off the hatch to the vault, he hooked his arms over the rim and lowered himself into the hole as if he were doing a chin-up. Once the back of his legs had rubbed up against the smooth, cool surface—unmistakably that of gold bars—he let go and dropped down into the hole. Squatting on the floor of the vault, he snapped open the latch of a small suitcase and peered in at the stacks of ten-thousand-yen bills, neatly wrapped with rubber bands. He opened the lid of a cardboard box that sat nearby—it, too, held bundles of soiled bills. Kazuki stuffed one of the bundles in his pocket.

It was 10:54 by the time he had restored the basement to its original state and returned to his room. He felt as though he had just been a disinterested bystander at a well-planned burglary, but the sweat on his forehead and the pounding of his heart betrayed him. As he was hiding the money under his mattress, the intercom rang. He went down to the living room and found the face of a middle-aged woman staring out of the monitor.

"Who is it?" he asked into speaker.

"I'm from the Wakamatsu Nursing and Housekeeping Agency," the woman said. "My name is Shirakawa."

"Come in," said Kazuki, pressing the button to open the gate.

Kōki was waiting by the door when he reached the hall.

"It's not a visitor," Kazuki told him. "I'm interviewing a new housekeeper. We'll go to McDonald's when I'm done, but you have to wait in your room. Okay?" After checking to see that Kōki had gone, he opened the door.

"Is your mother or father at home?" the woman asked.

"We've been expecting you," said Kazuki, ignoring her question. "Please come in." He arranged a pair of slippers in front of her and then showed her into the living room.

"May I meet the master of the house?" the woman said, lowering herself onto the couch.

"Did you bring a résumé?" Kazuki asked, pronouncing the word with special care.

"Well, yes," the woman managed, clearly bewildered, but she reached into her purse, extracted a sheet of paper, and handed it to Kazuki. He glanced over the document. Forty-two years old. Two sons, ages twelve and fifteen. Six years' experience as a kindergarten teacher; licensed nutritionist. The column for "spouse" was left blank.

"You do have experience as a housekeeper, don't you?" Kazuki asked.

"Uh, is your mother here?" the woman countered.

"I'm in charge of the house," Kazuki said without looking up from the paper.

It was hard enough being interviewed by a child, but this boy seemed to be trying to make her nervous, to be testing her. No situation was as cushy as they'd made this one sound at the agency, but she wasn't going to let herself be caught in a loony bin. And she knew from experience—after all, she was the mother of two boys—that if you didn't let them know who was boss, you weren't likely to get a straight answer.

"I'm not asking about you," she said, almost shouting. "I'm asking whether your mother is in or not."

"She doesn't live here anymore," Kazuki said.

"And your father?"

"If you want to know who lives here, it's my father, my older brother, my sister, and me. In general, you can count on all four of us for breakfast. For dinner, it's usually just my brother and me; but you'd better make enough for four, just in case. Or five, if you're planning on eating, too. At the moment, we don't have any pets."

"Is your brother the only one at home during the day?" the woman ventured to ask.

"I'm usually here, too," Kazuki said, folding up the résumé. After giving her a brief run-down of the housekeeping duties, he went out in the hall and called Kōki. A moment later, his brother appeared, barreling down the stairs like a dog answering its master's whistle.

"I'm Kōki," he shouted, hugging the woman. Kazuki studied her reaction to Kōki's greeting. While she did seem taken aback, there was no sign of revulsion, so he handed her a ten-thousand-yen bill.

"Take him to the McDonald's in Ishikawa-chō, and on the way back, stop at the supermarket and pick up whatever you need to get started in the kitchen. If it goes well, you're hired." He wanted to stamp "passed" on her forehead.

The woman grabbed her bag and stood up. She had thought this sounded like the best possible setup: no lady of the house, just kids at home during working hours. But just as she would not want to work in a house that let snakes and lizards crawl around loose, she was not sure she wanted to be here. She imagined herself doing the laundry when suddenly she would hear a voice and turn to find this boy. She was sure she'd be scared out of her wits. If there was one thing she'd learned from her experience as a teacher, a housekeeper, and a mother, it was that strange children did strange things. Kids who were put in destructive situations always gave off warning signals, and this one's eyes were flashing red. Still, she took Kōki by the hand and led him toward the door, avoiding Kazuki's eyes.

He was on the phone arranging with Reiji where and when he would hand over the money when Kōki came back in the room, threw the crumpled ten-thousand-yen bill on the table, and ran out again. "Wait a minute," he said. Putting Reiji on hold, he followed Kōki into the hall. "Did you forget something?" he asked, but Kōki said nothing, backing up the stairs as if someone were chasing him. Kazuki went back to the phone and punched the button. "Okay, two o'clock. I'll be there," he said, hanging up.

"Kōki, what happened?" he called from the bottom of the stairs, but he had vanished into his room. He walked back in the living room and glanced down at the money. That woman must have said something terrible to him, he thought, couldn't be anything else.

I'm sure we'd get along, but I don't think I could deal with your brother. I'm really sorry, but I'm leaving now. Kōki couldn't tell his brother what the lady had said. He knew that he had no choice but to depend on Kazuki, but he also knew that Kazuki was pushing him out on a ledge, and he wasn't sure when he would let him fall off. He heard the sound of something breaking downstairs. He wriggled down under the covers and pressed his hands over his ears. "Mama," he whimpered, but he couldn't even remember what she looked like. Chihiro's breasts, belly, thighs, the shape of her hips came back to him instead. He wanted to see Chihiro.

Kazuki arrived at Yokohama Station well before two o'clock, so he went to the Yūrindō Bookstore in the underground arcade at the West Exit and killed time by browsing through the stacks of books. Then he waited in front of the window of Takashimaya. At two-fifteen, no one had showed up. He rubbed the sole of his Reebok in a puddle of spit on the sidewalk, and when he looked up, there they were, all three, running across the bus lanes.

"Sorry! Wait long?" said Reiji, slapping him on the head.

"This is it," Kazuki said, taking a manila envelope from his bag and handing it to Reiji. "Don't try asking for any more. I already checked with our lawyer; even if they found out I was there, they couldn't prosecute me."

"You really talked to a lawyer? Yuminaga, you're too much. But you'd get it if your father found out." Reiji rubbed his sweaty palms on Kazuki's T-shirt and then put his arm around his shoulder.

"That's no problem," said Kazuki. "He knows, anyway."

"You didn't think we were trying to blackmail you, or anything like that? Would we do that to you? We're buddies, right? You don't have to worry about us. But then, it does seem strange, your handing us money like this. Whatever. Let's go to catch some rays." Reiji said, dropping his arm.

Kazuki wanted to get away from them as soon as he could, but he liked the idea of getting a tan. His appointment with his father wasn't until three o'clock and he had nothing to do in the meantime, he told himself, setting off with them.

"Pretty cold for summer, the last few days," Kiyoshi commented, patting his pocket to make sure the envelope was still there.

"Weird year," said Takuya. "It was hotter in June. Really weird . . ." He wanted to tell them about the causes of the unusual weather he'd heard explained on TV, but the moment passed as he was trying to remember the technical terms they'd used.

"Three more days till summer vacation." Kiyoshi's voice dripped like the sweat on Kazuki's neck.

"Who the fuck cares?" said Reiji, rolling his shoulders in a lazy arc.

They'd been walking for about ten minutes when they came to the Sun Spot tanning salon. Reiji and the others, who already had dark tans, opted for the powerful halogen lamps, while Kazuki chose the fluorescent "Ringo 600." Last winter, he'd come with them a couple of times, but he didn't get very dark. This time, he thought as he took the locker key from the attendant, he would keep coming back until he got brown.

Wrapping a towel around his waist, he went to the tanning room. He had just stepped into a vertical machine and removed the towel when he came bounding back out.

"I'm leaving!" he shouted next to Reiji's machine. Reiji, who was listening to hip-hop turned up loud on his headphones, didn't hear what he said, but Kazuki walked back to the dressing room, opened his locker, and dressed quickly. The moment he was naked, he had been overcome with an unbearable feeling of shame. To burn your skin just to look cool and tough was nothing but an insult to the way you really looked. Your real strength, he thought, was in your blood and your brain cells. They should be heating up their blood and brains! Noticing how pale and thin his arms looked as he was putting on his T-shirt, he looked away, climbed into his pants, and left the dressing room. In front of the vending machines in the lobby was a cluster of high school girls, their skin a burned shade that could only have been achieved with chemical treatments. Why do they work so hard to be somebody else when they always wind up with their own hideous selves? He hurried toward the door.

"My son," said Hidetomo, nodding toward Kazuki as the two men on the sofa rose and slipped card cases from their coat pockets. "Don't bother. He'll inherit someday, but it's about ten years too soon for that. Since when do you give out cards to a middle school student? Even one from Hōsei."

Bankers or pachinko machine makers, Kazuki guessed. He left his hands in his pockets, his head cocked to one side.

"These gentlemen are from Ginrei Amusement," Hidetomo said, looking over at Kazuki. "They'll be in charge there by the time you're grown up, so I thought it would make sense for you to meet them now."

"Well, then, sir. We'll hope for your favorable response," said the older man. "We'll be going now." The two men bowed deeply and backed toward the entrance. After bowing once more at the door, they disappeared.

"I'm going to Korea," his father said. "You're free to go to the hall again, but make sure it's after school hours. Understood?" He seemed to be in unusually good spirits.

"The casinos again? When do you leave?" Picking up on his mood, Sugimoto's tone was more familiar than usual.

"In a few days," said Hidetomo.

"And when do you get back?"

"Today's Monday? Probably around the middle of next week."

"You're going gambling and you'll be back in a week? A likely story!" she laughed.

"If I stayed two weeks, I'd win more than you stiffs earn in a month. And the place would go to hell while I'm gone."

"I seem to recall another trip, lasted about ten days, when someone lost about a million wan. Heading back to Paradise Beach?"

"Um," he grunted.

"Have you made reservations? Suppose it doesn't matter, though— a regular like you is always welcome."

"I'll call before I go," he said.

"You want me to get you some cash?" she asked.

"Don't be an idiot," he snapped. "I don't gamble with company money."

"Oh right, right! Well, I hope you have a safe trip. I'll make a list of what I want you to bring me back, in case you win!"

Kazuki could remember having heard almost exactly the same conversation on a previous occasion. Didn't they realize they'd done this routine before? Or maybe they enjoyed the rhythm of the banter, like a bad husband-and-wife act. As he listened to them, he felt sure that Sugimoto had been among his father's mistresses.

"Don't stand there with your mouth open. Sit down," Hidetomo barked.

"Mrs. Shimamura quit," Kazuki said, sounding like an employee.

"Tormenting them again?" Hidetomo asked. "Well, can't be helped. We'll have to get the agency to send over somebody new. I'll leave it to you; hire whoever you want."

"Miho's in the hospital. Seems she broke a bone somehow."

"That so? I guess she learned a lesson. By the way, I've got your summer present ready." He pressed a button on the house phone and called his private secretary. Kawabata, the only college graduate working at Vegas, had been lured away from one of their banks, accepting a big raise to serve as front man for the organization.

Hidetomo remembered only bits and pieces of the night he had beaten Miho, but whatever guilt that lingered, like the remnants of a hangover, he felt not toward Miho but toward Kazuki. Even now that he knew he'd put her in the hospital, he felt nothing for her at all, his only thought being how he could placate his son. The word "love" was not part of his vocabulary, but if someone had pointed out that he doted on Kazuki, he probably wouldn't have denied it.

Kawabata entered and bowed, but Kazuki ignored him.

"I was wondering if I could ask a girl I know if she'd take over as housekeeper," he asked his father. "I think she would stick with it for a while."

"How old is she?" Hidetomo asked. He looked skeptical as he lit a cigarette. Kawabata jumped to light it.

"I think she's about twenty," said Kazuki.

"Nope, I don't think so. She's not old enough to handle a job like that. What do you think, Kawabata? Seems to me he's got it all planned. He gets this girl a job as our housekeeper, and then they can go at it all day long, right under my roof. How'd you get off when you were fourteen? Polish it yourself, did you?"

"Actually, I was a late bloomer," Kawabata said.

Looking down at the secretary's shiny black shoes, Kazuki noticed a beetle struggling on its back on the gray linoleum. Its six legs waved desperately, but it didn't seem to be able to turn itself over. The door opened without a knock, and a woman in a peach-colored camisole dress came in.

"You're late," Hidetomo greeted her. "I thought we said three-thirty. No big deal. Have a seat over here," he said, standing up to wave her toward a chair. Kazuki tried to flip the beetle with the tip of his shoe, but it had gone stiff, playing dead, and he couldn't manage it. Sugimoto, who noticed everything, saw what he was up to and wandered over.

"That's a scarab, isn't it? Must have gotten in this morning when I left the window open for some air. Should bring you luck at the casino, boss." She'd made such a fuss, Kazuki quickly squashed the bug under his heel. Sugimoto let out a little gasp and retreated to the desk, mouth hanging half open. Her face still seemed young, but a closer look revealed wrinkles and dark patches, and the roots of her layered brown hair showed white. She looked five years older than her forty-eight years.

As the other woman turned to look out the window, Kazuki stole a glance at the fake skull tattoo on her chest.

"Mind if I smoke?" she drawled. Apparently aware that she was being watched, she self-consciously flicked back her bangs and settled into the sofa.

"Be my guest," said Hidetomo, his eyes wandering from her face to her chest and down to her legs, as if he were appraising an expensive purchase. The woman opened her Prada bag and extracted a box of cigarettes. Her fingernails were long and covered in sky-blue polish with silver sparkles. She used them to slit the seal on the cigarette box. Opening the lid, she took a cigarette and placed it between her lips, which were the same peach color as her dress. She lit the cigarette and took a deep drag.

"That's Kazuki. Second year at Hōsei Middle School," Hidetomo said.

"Pleased to meet you," said the woman, recrossing her legs.

"Okay, Kazuki, I want you two to go out, have a good time." Reaching for his wallet, Hidetomo took out eight ten-thousand-yen bills and thrust them toward him. Kazuki, however, felt nothing but disgust for a father who took such pride in providing a woman for his son, who thought of himself as loving and tolerant for playing pimp. The woman was flirting with him, parting her lips and running her long nails through the wisps of hair hanging around her face. He glanced at her again, at the silver anklet, her calves, knees, thighs, the deep cleft of her breasts, her neck. The artificial red hibiscus in her hair was a joke, but there was no doubt about it: he would kill to meet a woman like this anywhere but here, in his father's office. Still, it was the money that wound her up. She was obviously for sale.

"I've got things to take care of," he said, looking down at the beetle. Its body was crushed and some sort of slime was oozing from its shell, but the two front legs were still twitching.

"Well then, how 'bout a date with me?" Hidetomo laughed, fanning himself with the bills still clutched in his hand. Shit! How did this kid get so fucking stuck up? His head must be softer than his cock. And after all the trouble I went to getting the manager at the massage parlor to send over someone I thought he'd like. Maybe he thinks I wanted her all along.

Suddenly realizing that Sugimoto, Kawabata, and the woman were all staring at him, Hidetomo wavered between hitting Kazuki and laughing.

The woman rubbed her bare knees and looked back and forth between the boy and his father.

"What's so important that you have to do?" Hidetomo said.

"I have to meet some friends," Kazuki said.

"I told you to drop that bunch of losers and perverts," Hidetomo barked, settling on the strategy of humiliating Kazuki to save face himself.

"Here's the doctor's report on Miho," said Kazuki, setting a sheaf of papers on the table. "I don't think they'll send it on to the police." His announcement had the intended effect of silencing his father.

Hidetomo was not even particularly angry at this point, just disgusted with himself for the idiotic thing he'd done. And too, he wondered why all children were so utterly worthless, why they were all such brats. But this one was particularly strange, not normal; and it's not that he's just at a difficult age, that he's hit an obstacle along the normal road to becoming an adult. Somehow he's made a detour into some horrible world all his own, and he stands there looking back, sneering at all of us. He'd better figure out that I only go along with him because he's the only option I've got. But if he keeps on like this, he's got another thing coming. Hidetomo was suddenly tired. Picturing himself stretched out on the beach at Saishūtō, lapping up the summer sun, he wanting to sink into the couch and fall asleep.

"I gave you money that night, didn't I?" he said wearily. "Pay the hospital bill and next month's expenses out of that . . . But then you wanted to borrow that much, didn't you."

"Forgot about that," said Kazuki, getting up and going to the door. "I'm going home."

"Suit yourself. Oh, but there's still the matter of the golf club."

"It's at home," Kazuki said, turning around impatiently. "How's the dog?" he asked Sugimoto.

She took a deep breath and held it for a moment before answering almost inaudibly. "We had it put to sleep." The sound of the express train swept over the room like a roar of laughter and then faded away.

Kazuki was about to pull his keyholder from his pocket when it occurred to him to try the knob. It wasn't locked. As the front door swung open, the cool air from inside rushed out like an evil omen. Kōki, who always heard him coming and was waiting by the door, was nowhere to be seen. He'd had a feeling it might come to this after he'd taken Chihiro back to the Golden Pavilion while his brother was still asleep, but he'd been afraid of the scene they would have had with Kōki awake. He would probably have followed her out the door. But now he was worried, having left him alone so long. As he opened the door to one room after another, images of a burglar's stealthy entry and Kōki's strangled body flitted through his head, making his heart race, his nervous system crackle. The lid on the grand piano was open, but Kōki wasn't there either. He went upstairs and into his brother's room. The stereo was still warm, so he must be somewhere in the house. Kazuki scoured the second floor, opening every door. How many times had he told him not to leave the house by himself? He charged down the stairs and out the door, his anger ballooning to white rage.

He ran on down the hill, the heat of the day brushing his face. He ran by the shops along Motomachi, slowing as he caught sight of the giant chair in front of the furniture store. He remembered now that he'd promised Kōki he would buy him a rocking chair and hesitated a moment, wondering whether he should get the chair now. No, he decided, he had to find his brother first, and he walked on by the shop. As he left Motomachi and came into the shadow of the expressway overhead, he stopped, suddenly struck by the difficulty of trying to find someone in the city. There was little chance of meeting his brother as he wandered through this complicated maze of crisscrossed streets. He looked up at the sky. Just at that moment, a cloud in the shape of a battleship drifted overhead, and as it passed he suddenly lost the heart to continue the search. He turned back and headed for the police box in Motomachi.

"My big brother's missing," he announced flatly, his voice betraying none of the anxiety he was feeling.

"How old is he?" said the officer, rising cautiously from his chair and rubbing his palm over the holster on his hip. The idea of a boy coming in to report his older brother missing was strange to begin with, but it was really the very presence of middle- and high-school-aged boys that set off warning bells, more than when he was dealing with old vagrants or even gang members. He knew how tense he got when he encountered a group of them while on his rounds.

"Eighteen," Kazuki said. "But he's sick, and he shouldn't be walking around alone. He talks normally, but he doesn't understand numbers and he has no sense of direction. He just follows people around without thinking, and he could get into trouble. If we don't find him soon, he'll be hit by a car or fall in the river. Please look for him; he's got a disability called Williams Disease."

"So, this is really like a lost child? Someone may show up with him, or one of us might come across him on patrol. I'll call around to the other boxes and see if I can find out anything." He phoned the three stations in the neighborhood but no one had reported seeing Kōki.

"Don't the police go out and look for missing persons?" Kazuki asked.

"We don't have the time or manpower," the officer said.

"Even if my brother doesn't come home after a few days?"

"If it came to that, we'd file a missing person report with the station in Kaga-chō, but that's about all we can do. There's no way the police can go door to door looking for someone. We have to wait for something to turn up, an accident or an arrest or something. Anyway, he's probably waiting for you at home right now."

"I told you, he has no sense of direction!" Kazuki shouted.

"Don't get excited," the officer said. "Write your father's name, your brother's name, your address, and your phone number on that form, and we'll let you know if something turns up."

The police have a duty to protect the people of the city, but they're too busy with bullshit to help people who are really in trouble, Kazuki thought.

"Fine," he said, setting down the pen and standing up. "I'm sorry to have bothered you. I'll go home. You're right, he's probably there by now. If we haven't found him by tonight, I'll talk to my father and report it to the Kaga Station." He spoke quickly, leaving the officer no time to reply, bowed once and slipped out the door.

Kazuki came to a halt amid the fancy houses halfway up the hill, conscious that he had lost not his sense of direction but some other important faculty. The streets were empty. The curtains in the windows were drawn, air conditioners running on high. The people must have been cowering in the cold rooms, worried that the fierce summer sun would harm more than their eyes and skin, that it might even stop their hearts. But even at night, when they could come out, there was nothing for them to do. It was a neighborhood full of people who had forgotten what they were waiting for, people who hated the sun. A place like that had to be harboring even worse villains than Kogane-chō itself. Kazuki suddenly pictured his brother trudging through the maze of streets. He was plodding along, tracking the trilling of the insects, the sound of the wind, Chihiro's scent, walking endlessly. And then, after a year, when his long journey was over, he would come home. Kazuki's mouth twisted into a smile of satisfaction with his own daydream. He thought he would like to take Kōki to a place where there were no buildings, nothing at all in any direction. When they got there, he imagined, a "sense of direction" would be of no use at all. But even for someone who has a sense of direction, if he doesn't know where he is and where he's trying to go, it doesn't amount to much. And even if you have the means to get where you're going, if you don't have anywhere to go, it amounts to the same thing. In point of fact, he was the one who should be reported as a "lost child." Overcome by the strange feeling that someone was searching for him, he peered around at the quiet neighborhood.

When, as a young boy, he had got lost in the streets of Kogane-chō, Kanamoto or someone from either the Golden Pavilion or Treasure Ball would always coming looking for him and lead him home. But who would find him now, who would lead him back to a safe place? He shuddered at the sudden idea that there would be a missing person report with his name on it filed in the computer at the Kaga Police Station. Anyway, at some point everyone had some problem, some disease or defect you could put a name to. In general, people got classified by their religion or the color of their skin or some such, but eventually the day would come when they got divided up by the names of their ailments.

Kazuki suddenly started to run, kicking his knees and pumping his arms. He sprinted along, imagining himself clearing the wall around his house, flying through the door, and leaping like a circus tiger out through the living room window.

The door was open, and Miho was staring at him as he dashed through it. He was out of breath, his hair and shirt were soaked with sweat, and his face was flushed. Even his eyes were filled with exhaustion.

"What's the matter with you?" Miho asked.

"Is Kōki back?" he asked, bending over and fighting for air.

"What do you mean, is he back?" she said.

"He's gone," Kazuki said, slipping out of his shoes and stepping up into the hall. He glanced at the cast on her leg and her crutches before looking up at her face. Both eyes were rimmed with dark bruises that had not yet started to fade to yellow, violet, or blue.

"I thought you were supposed to be in the hospital a week," he said. "I was coming to visit you tomorrow."

"I had a fight with the nurses. They treat the patients like babies. 'Oh, you're awake! Let's change your ice pack.' It was too awful, them acting like mother hens all the time. The one who came around to put out the lights last night told me that they'd be washing my hair today, that I should call them when I was ready. So when I woke up this morning I got ready and then rang for the nurse. But a different nurse came and said there was no way I could have my hair washed. I flipped!" Miho, who never wore anything but miniskirts well above the knee, was flouncing around in a longer, flared skirt today, perhaps to cover the cast. The broken front tooth caused her to mumble, but still she rambled on as if she'd had a few too many drinks. Kazuki listened quietly.

"I hate to ask, but could you take the insurance stuff tomorrow and settle the bill? And ask them when I need to go back to have all this looked at?" Kazuki picked up the phone without answering her and dialed a number. Kanamoto answered almost immediately.

"Miho had a fight with one of the nurses and now she's home. Could you take the insurance forms to the hospital tomorrow?" Kanamoto was taken aback by the boy's presumptuous tone. His phone call the other day had been the first in three years. But Kanamoto had been happy that he was once more being relied upon and had come running to take Miho to the hospital. The new request, and the way it came, made him wince.

"Fine," he said. "Tomorrow, then." As he was about to hang up, he remembered another piece of unfinished business. "And when I come to get the insurance form, I'll bring the golf club, too."

"Don't bother," said Kazuki. "You keep it."

"I don't play," said Kanamoto, looking as though he had just bitten into a cough drop by mistake. Kids grew up, that's natural. And they change. But you wanted to see them going in the right direction. No doubt the boy was trying to walk the line, but when you see him veering off like this, you want to let him know. Still, he must think he's on the right track, and if you told him otherwise, he wouldn't believe you.

That's just the way things were, and nobody said kids wouldn't stray now and then. "I'll bring it back."

"I said you can keep it."

"All right, then. Why don't you leave the insurance papers at Vegas and I'll stop by and get them."

Kazuki hung up and sank onto the couch. He wiped the sweat from his face with the bottom of his T-shirt.

"Where is he?" he moaned.

"He's probably just taking a walk," said Miho, sounding perfectly relaxed.

"What are we going to do if he doesn't come back? I know what I'm going to do—I'm going to burn down this fucking house!"

"As if," Miho laughed, but as she watched the way his face went suddenly blank, like a shutter had been slammed, she remembered how the two of them had played arson when they were in elementary school. At first it was just a game. They would build little houses out of empty soap or candy boxes, set fire to them, and bring their toy fire trucks to put out the blaze. But when they got tired of that, they started taking small wooden things or folding chairs out to the garden to burn. After that, things got out of hand. They began scouting distant neighborhoods for houses where no one seemed to be home. When they found a likely-looking place, they would sneak into the garden and set fire to the doghouse before running away. One day, no longer able to resist the desire to see their own handiwork, they set fire to several doghouses and then ran off to wait at a nearby playground. After fifteen minutes, they went back to look, but none of the fires was still burning.

"They're all out," said Miho, disappointed.

"Who put them out?" Kazuki asked, staring up at her. He had just turned seven at the time.

"I guess they never really got going," said Miho.

"Well, next time they will." The following day, Kazuki had spirited a paper cup full of cooking oil out of the kitchen and invited Miho to join him. They wandered the streets until they spotted a brand-new, blue-and-white doghouse with a little dog tied up outside. "How about this one?" Kazuki whispered, climbing up on the hedge and beckoning to Miho. She pointed to the ground, signaling that she would keep watch outside, and he disappeared into the thick growth. She had paced back and forth by the hedge, pretending to be lost but prepared to run at any moment. Eventually, she convinced herself he must have been caught and she was about to run away, when he suddenly came flying out of the garden. They ran as fast as they could, around a corner and along the street. When they were a hundred yards away, they slowed a bit.

"Was it burning?" she asked. Kazuki nodded, his face lit up with a broad grin. "I don't believe you."

"No, really," he said. "Want to go back and look?" He hid the empty cup behind a telephone pole and set off at the most casual pace. As the hedge came into sight, Miho could hear a dog wailing and a little boy screaming. When they passed by, she glanced sideways and caught a glimpse of the doghouse engulfed in flames and a woman trying to get near it. Terrified, she had started to run again, but when she looked back, Kazuki was walking calmly along behind her.

After that, neither of them had ever proposed the arson game again. But once, a few years later when she'd almost forgotten the whole thing, there was a small fire in the neighborhood.

"Was that you, Kazuki?" she'd asked half jokingly.

"Not me," he'd said, a thin smile playing on his lips. He pulled Hidetomo's Dunhill lighter from his pocket and lit it again and again. "I thought it was you."

Even now, there was no telling how far he'd go. But it would probably stop short of burning down his own house, she thought, reaching down to scratch an itch under her cast.

Kazuki calmly took one of his father's golf magazines from the magazine rack, ripped it in half, pulled a lighter from his pocket, lit the magazine, and tossed it at her feet. Shrieking, Miho stamped out the burning pages.

"What do you think you're doing?!" she cried. "Are you nuts?" Kazuki licked the sweat from his upper lip, turned his back on her, and went out into the hall. He locked the door to the bathroom behind him and turned on the hot water. The noise of the running water sounded to his ears like an audience jeering, but even when he turned off the faucet, the jeering noise continued. He turned the water on again and got undressed. Slipping down in the tub, he hugged his knees to his chest and closed his eyes. Submerged in the hot water, rocking gently, he began to feel sleepy, like a newborn baby in its first bath. But there was no way now that he could go back to that earlier state, all new and soft. It was too late for that. He had no choice now but to continue being absorbed in himself. He heard the doorbell ring and someone going to answer it, but he sat motionless, his eyes still closed.

"He's back," Miho said, knocking on the door. "One of the neighbors brought him home, I think." He opened his eyes and stood up. Wrapping a towel around his waist, he went out into the hall.

Kōki was standing in the entrance, holding hands with a middle-aged man Kazuki did not recognize.

"He was at the ticket gate at the station, but it didn't seem like he was going to buy a ticket. I live a few houses down the street, so I recognized him. Since I was coming this way anyway, I asked if he wanted to walk along with me. He grabbed my hand and here we are."

"We can't thank you enough," Kazuki said, bowing.

"You must be happy to be home, huh?" said the man. Prying his hand from Kōki's grip and patting him on the shoulder, he slipped out the door. Kōki looked up, his eyes vague and out of focus. Without a word, he began climbing the stairs to his room.

Like a stabbing pain, the thought occurred to Kazuki that he had gone in search of Chihiro. He remembered a story that one of the fired housekeepers had told to Hidetomo about the son of an acquaintance. The boy was autistic, and when he reached puberty, he began to pick out young women on buses or trains and touch them or tag along after them. His mother had no idea what to do, so she took him to the doctor.

The doctor suggested picking one day a week for him to masturbate and showing him how to do it. "The problem seems to go away by itself by the time they're in their twenties," the housekeeper had said.

"You saying you want me to give him a lesson?" Hidetomo had laughed. The housekeeper blushed and went off to the kitchen to do the dishes, but Kazuki, who had been eavesdropping on the whole conversation, had thought he should ask Kanamoto to take his brother to a massage parlor or someplace.

"If I moved out and lived by myself, how much do you think he'd give me a month?" Miho asked suddenly.

"How much do you need?" Kazuki said.

"Oh, maybe a hundred thousand. The rest I can earn working part time." Hidetomo gave him five hundred thousand a month for household expenses, and he could usually get more simply by making up some excuse. He could probably manage to give her the hundred thousand, but he wasn't sure it was wise to hand his sister that kind of money.

"What kind of part-time work? You aren't planning to turn tricks, are you?"

"You sound just like Daddy," she grumbled.

"If you promise not to, it's okay with me. A hundred thousand a month, and if you need more, you just have to ask and I'll try to do something."

"You mean it? Then how about the security deposit on a condo?"

"How much is that?"

"About five hundred thousand, I guess. But there's no hurry on that. At the moment, though, I'm flat broke. Could you give me twenty thousand?" Her voice sounded suddenly almost childlike.

Simply handing her money was not going to solve her problems, he was sure of that. He needed to try to understand what it was that she wanted; but he suspected she had no idea herself. If that were the case, then he had no choice but to try to find her something worthwhile to do. Kazuki could understand his sister's uneasiness. It came from an inability to discover her own true worth. She defined herself by the label "high school girl," as if it were some high-end fashion brand, and she pounced on each new fad that rippled through her little crowd. But three short years of high school would be over in the blink of an eye, and waiting on the other side were her twenties and the prospect of growing up and growing old. Though in the end, it wasn't aging that was terrifying but the prospect of getting to be twenty without having discovered value in anything at all. She and her friends partied so frantically, so constantly, exactly because they were terrified of being tossed out into society. But there must be something that you could latch on to, something that would give you the confidence to become an adult. Kazuki went up to his room, pulled the stack of bills from under his mattress, and peeled off fifty thousand.

Taking the bills, Miho shifted her weight on the crutches, opened her shoulder bag, and tucked them inside. She sat down on the ledge in the entrance and slipped her right foot into a sandal. Her left foot and the bulky cast were covered with a hospital slipper. She probably didn't know herself why she was so determined to get out of the house, despite the awkwardness of the unfamiliar crutches, but even if the doctor had told her she had to rest the leg at home or risk amputation, no doubt she would have been out the door. It wasn't anything grand she was looking for: a cozy karaoke box, a weak, sickly sweet whiskey sour, a cigarette, and some idle chatter. No man was probably going to go for her at the moment, with her broken tooth, bruised face, and clunky cast, but she didn't care. She'd rather get hurt out there than here at home. Holding her head high, she tucked the crutches under her arms and swung out the door.

Time seemed to be warped. It was too dense, like compressed air. He had a feeling that if he could just free himself from the constraints of time, he would be truly free to control his own body. To eat when he was hungry, rest when he was tired—from now on he would live according to his own free will. He changed into his pajamas and went barefoot down to the basement. As he lowered himself onto the leather couch where his father always sat, he felt a certain satisfaction. He had successfully invaded his father's little castle, his fort, and the victory had gone to his head. As his gaze came to rest on the swords in the display case, he could feel the particles of power dispersed throughout his body begin to come together. He got up and went to get one of the swords. He stared at the tiny reflection of his face in the blade, and though he held his hand quite still, he had the impression that his face was flowing along the blade like a raindrop on a window, being sucked into the blade, made one with it. In an instant, the light from the sword melted into his skin, illuminating the darkest corners of his body. Neither word nor silence, like some supreme music, the cold, white flame urged him to the highest heights.

"What are you doing?" Turning around, he found his father standing in the door. He opened his mouth to say something, but his tongue was tied in a knot. "What do you think you're doing? Imitating me? That's a waste of time. Put that away." Hidetomo seemed indifferent to the naked blade in Kazuki's hand. With a cold, contemptuous look that he might have given a particularly inept employee, he watched while Kazuki returned the sword to its sheath and placed it back in the cabinet. He took a dressing gown from the closet and tossed it on the bed, then pulled a pair of pajamas from the chest of drawers.

"We'll match," he said with a grin.

Three months earlier, Kazuki had bought two pair of summer pajamas for himself and Kōki, but the housekeeper must have put one of them in his father's drawer. Repelled by the idea of seeing Hidetomo in the same pajamas, he went to the door. As he reached for the handle, his father spoke again, as if he had been waiting to stop Kazuki as he was on the verge of escape.

"How did you get in here?"

"It was open." His voice sounded calm.

"Are you saying I left it unlocked? That I left the door open?" He didn't think his father would try to hit him, but if it came to a fight, he doubted he could win—they were almost the same height now, but there was still a big difference in their weights. "You don't look like me," his father said, his voice thick and sticky, like a leech slithering into Kazuki's ear. "You take after your mother. The more I look at you, the more I see her—her eyes, her nose, her mouth."

If he isn't going to beat me, I wish he would at least yell a little. As he reached out to turn the doorknob, he heard his father snap his fingers behind him. "It's locked now," he said. What was he up to? Kazuki looked down at the pool of dried vomit at his father's feet. "And I know it was locked before," his father continued. "I had a hangover after that night and I must have left it open, but I came back that evening and found the key I'd dropped right here. I know I locked it after that." No doubt about it, thought Kazuki, he's feeble-minded. If he's so sure, why ask? If he's convinced I did something wrong, then punish me and get it over with. But then, he doesn't know how to punish me. He thinks he can hurt me by tormenting me and sneering at me. In the old days, Kazuki felt, parents knew how to punish their kids; they used their fists or a whip, locked them in a dark room, starved them. But these flimsy, meaningless words were just so much bullying. He thought it might work to just keep insisting that the door had been open, but then he suddenly changed his mind.

"Now that you mention it, it was locked."

"Then how did you get in?" Hidetomo looked around like a hunter who had just lost a prize he thought he'd bagged. Kazuki knew that his father would prefer to forget the whole thing, if he would show a little remorse, but he couldn't bring himself to apologize for something he didn't think was wrong. What's more, he knew Hidetomo wasn't expecting a real apology; he just wanted to see Kazuki humiliated— which was all the more reason that he would never apologize. Kazuki, like most children, had no problem telling a lie, but if he was told he had to lie, he couldn't. How did he get in? To get into a locked room he had either used a wire or something to pick the lock or he had a copy of the key—there weren't many other options. If his father had been direct with him, he probably would have apologized with no trouble. Hidetomo might have said "Kazuki, you had a key made, didn't you? If you wanted to use this room, all you had to do is say so. If you'd just told me, I would have had a key made for you . . ." If he had, it would have been easy. That's the way adults did it: you apologized and then you were forgiven. It was the only logical thing to do in a relationship between equals. If someone offended you or made a mistake, an equal could demand an apology first, before forgiving the offense. But when an adult wanted an apology from a child, he effectively had to forgive the child beforehand. If he demanded an apology without first forgiving the child, then the apology was no better than an act, a lie forced out of the child. The adult who has lost the ability to really punish a child has few options left—wheedling, sarcasm, shouting perhaps. And the child, intent on protecting his own fragile interior world, soon becomes adept at distinguishing the various tones of voice that parents adopt.

"Shall I make you a drink?" Kazuki said.

"What are you? Some kind of fairy? This isn't a gay bar. I'll tell you when I want a drink." This wasn't the normal pattern, Kazuki noted. Today, unlike most days, Hidetomo seemed intent on moving in for the kill. Perhaps he had discovered the missing money? The thought made the backs of his legs burn. He shifted nervously. Perhaps it wasn't just Miho he was having followed? Impossible, he told himself—but it was certain that a side of his father he had never seen was showing itself, a combination of craftiness, vanity, dissolution and vulgarity, and this new Hidetomo made him very nervous. "You can explain about the key later. For now, bring the golf club," he said, his voice dropping to a whisper.

For some reason, Hidetomo was not placing any special emphasis on the fact that he'd caught him in a lie, but now he couldn't understand why he was driving him into a corner. If you were going to tell a lie, you might as well go all the way: he'd left it in his room, but now he couldn't find it. Someone must have stolen it; he'll report it to the police tomorrow. Or perhaps it was better to simply say that it had disappeared and leave it at that. "That iron cost a million and a half, maybe two million. How much do you think that sword you were messing with is worth? It's called the 'Bizen Osafune Nagamitsu,' and it cost more than ten million. Okay, go get the club. Now!"

Kazuki gave him a look that was meant to explain everything: I made a copy of the key and let myself in, and the iron isn't here right now. What would Hidetomo say to that? He knew, and he decided it would be best to say nothing. In the long silence that followed, Hidetomo's face twitched occasionally from anger and irritation. Finally, he couldn't stand it any longer.

"Didn't I tell you to go get it? If you'd told the truth, I'd have already forgiven you. I'll listen to your excuses when you get back . . . and then I want to have a talk about school and the rest of it. I'm thinking of sending you to board at school, and not in some cushy dorm, either. I talked with the chairman of the board and I've found a place that'll be stricter than any reform school. But we'll talk about it when you've gotten the club."

The unexpected threat hit Kazuki like a blow to the head. He staggered out the door and up the stairs. What could he have in mind? Was he going to send him to live with the coach of the sports club? He remembered that after the rape incident there had been talk of having a student from the karate club at some right-wing school as a tutor. A momentary image of the face of Isozaki, the rugby coach, flitted through his head. No one knew how to use the threat of violence as well as Isozaki. He had come after Kazuki on a number of occasions, leading him to believe that if his father weren't on the board of the school, he would have given him a serious beating. If he were going to live with Isozaki, it was all over. Not only would he force him to go to school every day, but he would have to join the rugby club where he would be bullied to death. Even when they weren't practicing, the players would follow him around like bodyguards, and if he did the least little thing that Isozaki didn't like, he was sure they would figure out a way to make sure he never did it again. There was no other choice: he would have to ask Kanamoto to bring the club. Without stopping to think, he rushed to the phone and punched Kanamoto's number. There was no answer.

Fear was something that he thought he could manage. If you kept quiet and bided your time, you could most likely find a way out. But at the moment Kazuki had crossed over the line; he had gone beyond fear to full-blown panic. As he was hanging up the phone, the room was filled with a sudden flicker of light and then went dark. But as he blinked, objects in the room floated up before him as if his eyes were flashlights—the vase, an electrical cord, the desk lamp. Making his way to the kitchen, he spotted a frying pan, a paring knife, a larger kitchen knife. Then, back in the living room, he felt a strange willpower expanding and surrounding him. He stopped trembling as the power welled up in him, irresistible power, power driving him forward. Suddenly calm, he picked up the vase, and at the instant he did, whatever it was that had been holding him back collapsed. With the vase tucked under his right arm, he went downstairs, opened the door, and slipped inside, locking it behind him. The click of the lock was the last sound he heard, as even the beating of his heart faded to silence.

Hidetomo was just taking off his pants. Kazuki walked straight up to him and brought the vase down on the back of his head. It shattered as he clutched at his head and toppled over, his legs caught in his pants. As his father struggled to his knees and turned to look at him in astonishment, Kazuki ran to the display case, opened the door, and pulled the sword from its sheath.

Should he run? Or should he face him here? But he's my son, my heir. Hidetomo took a deep breath, trying to regain his composure and calm Kazuki, but the person standing before him was someone else, someone he had never seen before. Just as he was drawing another breath to call Kazuki's name, he saw an arc of light. The blade sank into his shoulder, and blood gushed out. His knees buckled under him and he fell, turning as he crumpled to the ground. His arms and legs were paralyzed from the shock and pain, and he could feel the life draining from his body. He was being murdered . . . He struggled toward the door, but as he reached for the knob, he felt a searing pain in his shoulder and his head struck the frame. Hidetomo looked around at his son and tried to call to him, but his throat was rapidly filling with hot blood and no sound emerged. He lay there, still in shock that his son had stabbed him. It was inconceivable—but the one thing that did seem certain now was that he was going to die. His eyes were open but his field of vision was contracting, growing dark, until he could see nothing. Death itself seemed to be bending over him, and he kicked frantically, trying to drive it away, but as his legs thrashed about on the floor, he could feel the sword piercing his thigh. A shock, like a high-voltage current, went straight to his heart, and his legs shot out as if they were being yanked from his body.

The legs were still twitching slightly, and blood continued to spurt from the neck, splattering against the wall. He plunged the sword again into the area above the stomach, aiming for the heart, and then pulled it out. In again. Breathing heavily, he stopped to stare into his father's face. Was he dead? Perhaps not. As he stood wondering whether he should take his wrist and feel for a pulse, or perhaps listen to his chest for a heartbeat, the pool of blood spread out across the floor, coming slowly closer to his feet. He climbed up on the couch and looked down at his father. The cavities on his face, eyes, nose, and mouth, had become pools of blood, and his hair was clotted with thick red gore.

For a long time, he stood and stared at the body, unable to move. Then at last he reached down to touch his father's arm. Still warm. He took hold of the wrist and gave it a tug, but there was no resistance. He let the arm fall back and swung his feet off the couch, being careful to avoid the pool of blood. Leaning over once more, he listened quietly for a moment to the whispering sound of blood. The heart was still pumping, though not to circulate the blood through the body but to send it spewing out. He found himself wondering whether he still needed to stab the heart, and that suddenly made him feel like laughing; but then he caught sight of a gash of white flesh laid bare on his father's arm in a place he could not even remember cutting, and the laugh died in his throat. As if suddenly thinking of something, he dipped his little finger in the blood around the wound and then brought it to his mouth, licking it carefully. The sweetly familiar taste of blood melted in his mouth, filling him with a feeling of calm and comfort. And from deep within him, he could feel new blood, new power surging up into his head.

His hand still tingling with the feel of the sword, Kazuki moved the couch and the rug and lifted off the top of the hidden compartment. Lowering himself into the space, he began lifting out the boxes and bags filled with gold ingots and stacks of bills. When he'd emptied the vault, he climbed out and went over to the body. He tried grabbing it under the arms and pulling, but he slipped in the blood and nearly fell over backward. More cautious this time, he took hold of the ankles, dragged the body over to the opening, and let it fall out of sight. He realized that blood had been spurting from each of the wounds, and he suddenly felt suffocated by the stench. Every hair on his body was standing on end, and he clutched his hands to his mouth to hold back the lump of terror or disgust rising in his throat.

He replaced the cover on the vault and stripped off his blood-soaked pajamas. Finding a dry spot, he wiped the stains from the bottoms of his feet and went upstairs. He found a bucket, trash bags, and some towels and went back to the basement. The blood and everything stained with it would have to be cleaned up—but where to start? As he looked around the room, his eyes came to rest on the sword lying in the pool of blood at his feet. Grasping the hilt, he examined the blade on both sides. Then, gathering up the scabbard, he went back upstairs.

In the bathroom, he sprinkled shampoo on the sword and sheath and washed them off. He carefully wiped the blade dry and slipped it into the sheath before heading back downstairs.

As the towels became soaked with blood, he rinsed them out and wrung them into the bucket. He scrubbed the blood that had splattered on the floor and walls and wrapped the bits of broken vase in a towel. Dropping the towel into a trash bag, he resolved to bring the vacuum cleaner down tomorrow to get the smaller pieces. Finally, there were no visible bloodstains, but he wrung out the towel and wiped the floor one more time. As he stood up and stretched his back, however, he noticed that blood had splattered on the bed. He stripped off the sheets. The blood had soaked through to the blanket, so he stuffed everything in a bag, followed by the pillows and his father's slippers. He stood for a moment, rubbing his hands together, but when he looked down at them, he noticed that there were dark red stains under his long fingernails. His eyes drifted down to the floor, to the narrow cracks between the boards. He would have to be very careful, he told himself, grinding his teeth together.

He began thinking of ways to eliminate all trace of what had happened, using all his resourcefulness. But when he realized that he wouldn't be able to do everything right away, he ran back upstairs to his room and changed into a T-shirt and jeans. Going down to the living room, he took all the newspapers and magazines from the rack, carried them to the basement, and ripped them in shreds. Then he stuffed the paper into the garbage bags so that the bloodstained contents were invisible from outside. Double bagging each one and tying them tightly, he carried them out to the garden.

The neighborhood was fast asleep. Kazuki's heart seemed to beat louder the more he tried to calm it, but now it was muffled by the distant bark of a dog. He carried the bags out to the garbage bin by the driveway. As he was taking the last one, he heard a chirping sound at his feet. A cricket. Thinking he would give it to Kōki when he woke up, he reached down for it but it hopped off into the grass. "Shit," he muttered, and crushed it under his shoe. The table and chairs on the terrace, the house itself—everything looked like a slow-motion sequence from a movie. The air around him shimmered, like sunlight reflecting off rain-drenched leaves. He rubbed his eyes. It was time to sleep. At least tonight he felt like sleeping—for the first time in a long while. He would sleep long and hard, and tomorrow he would think it all through. That was enough for today.

He stretched his legs out in the tub, breathing deeply and indulging in the comfort of the hot water that was rising around his body. He puckered his lips and whistled the theme song from Macross, one of his favorite cartoons when he was little. Usually, when he hit the part with all the high notes, his pitch went off and he lost the melody, but today he managed quite well. The secret was to relax your lips and not force the sound. An odd sort of joy was bubbling up quietly inside him, and his head felt suddenly lighter. No, it was more than that: he was almost unbearably happy, on the verge of bursting out in laughter.

He went upstairs and opened Kōki's door. His brother was lying faceup on the bed, his eyes wide open. He lay so still that Kazuki was afraid for a moment that he wasn't breathing, and his brother's silence made him conscious of the frantic beating of his own heart.

"What's up?" Kazuki asked, his voice like a soft moan. He felt faint, but he managed to keep his feet by bracing himself on the door.

"I am," Kōki murmured, his voice melting into the silence.

"Since when?" Kazuki asked. He was barely able to move his tongue. Kōki stared him straight in the eyes, his look full of meaning. "Well, go back to sleep," Kazuki stammered, closing the door. He was suddenly unsure whether he'd locked the door, so he went back to the basement. Unlocked, just as he'd suspected. As he entered the room, his legs seemed to give out on him and he sat down heavily on the bare bed. He glanced over at the clock: five before five. He was fast asleep before his head hit the mattress.

The clock said seven o'clock. He reached for the phone and dialed Kyōko's number. The mattress had bothered him as he lay down, and now he realized that it reeked of his father's sweat and the cologne he always wore. Kyōko explained that she was due at the café early so she wouldn't be able to come. He spent a long time trying to convince her and found himself growing irritated at her reluctance. Under other circumstances, he would have shouted at her and hung up, but now he was driven not only by the need for her help but by a simple and overwhelming desire to see her. He hated the tense, wheedling sound of his own voice, but none of that really mattered: he simply needed her. He finally got her to say that she would come in an hour or so, and he hung up with a sigh.

He stood on the bed and looked around the room, inspecting it carefully for any sign. Then he closed his eyes and wished that none of it had ever happened. When he slowly opened them again, his eyes fell on the center of the Persian rug where the pattern seemed to be wriggling like a knot of snakes. As he watched, the rug seemed to bulge from the floor, buoyed up by the stench of death rising beneath it. Shaking the vision from his head, Kazuki thought of filling the vault with concrete and covering it with a wood floor; but, realizing that would involve having workers in the basement, he gave up on the idea. He got down on his hands and knees like a dog and crawled around sniffing at the rug. A horrible stench—blood or vomit, he couldn't be sure which—made him turn away. His knees and hands suddenly felt damp, and when he lifted them to look, they were stained red. Looking more closely, he discovered that the beige area of the rug was spattered with blood, and the brick-red design on it was also soaked. He took several sheets from the closet, spread them out on the rug, and rubbed them with his palm. As he watched, red blotches spread out across the material. When he doubled the sheets over and pressed on them, the blood soaked through the second layer as well. He spread out another sheet and stomped around on the damp areas, leaving scarlet footprints across the white cloth. He would have to dispose of the rug altogether. But in the meantime, he wadded up the sheets and stuffed them under the bed. Then, making certain he wasn't leaving bloody footprints on the floor, he went up to the bathroom.

At first, Kyōko turned down Kazuki's offer of the job as housekeeper, refusing him several times. But eventually his persistence wore her down and she agreed to take the position. Kazuki asked Kōki to play something quiet and beautiful in honor of her first day, so he started into Ravel's "Jeux d'eau."

"Where's your father?" Kyōko asked when she had finished taking off her shoes.

"He's almost never home, so you won't be seeing him." Kazuki smiled, sounding positive about this. "He's usually at his girlfriend's apartment. Right now, though, he's in Korea." Kyōko doubted that Hidetomo would agree to hire her as his housekeeper without first meeting her. She had never really been sure of the circumstances surrounding her father's suicide, but the manager, Hayashi, had hinted that Hidetomo had been involved, and she suspected that it had something to do with a reprimand Hidetomo had given him. But even if she were wrong and he had nothing to do with it, it wasn't likely that someone would want to hire the daughter of an employee who committed suicide as his housekeeper. On the other hand, who would have thought that she would become involved with the son of the man who probably drove her father to kill himself? Perhaps Kazuki knew something about the cause of the suicide. She resolved to ask him at some point.

"There's just one problem," Kazuki muttered quickly. "Sometimes Kōki gets a little horny so you've got to watch yourself."

"Don't be silly," Kyōko laughed, but she remembered that before Kazuki had come out of the living room, as she sat down to take off her shoes, Kōki had put his arms around her from behind and grabbed her breasts. She had been on the point of screaming with pain. "I'm not about to let someone like that bother me," she said, regretting the "like that" the moment it was out of her mouth. Kazuki was under the illusion that she was somehow pure and innocent because she'd been raised in an institution, away from real life. But he was wrong. There had been plenty of reality in the orphanage, and it had rubbed at you like sandpaper, filing down your existence, then and still now. It was hardly any surprise that the cruelty and taunting at an orphanage would be worse than at a regular school, since all the children there had either lost their parents or been abandoned by them. Kyōko herself had more than once had her slippers or gym clothes stolen, been stripped of her underwear, or grabbed by the hair and thrown up against a wall. By the time she was in middle school, she had spent most of her time and energy figuring out how to get away from the boys who pursued her. If they caught you, they demanded everything short of intercourse. The thing that frightened Kyōko most was having a penis forced in her mouth, but if you clenched your teeth and resisted, they just got rougher, squeezing your breasts until you couldn't stand it. In the end, she had simply opened her mouth without a fight. Even now, when something brought back those carefully forgotten memories, her blood would boil and pain would shoot through her body. She wanted to be rid of herself. She knew that the day would come when she would have to talk about this horrible wound that time would never heal; but today was not the day.

She realized that someone was playing Chopin's "Nocturne No. 4." Kazuki sat listening to the piano, his face blank except for a look of fatigue. A strange sighing, like the cooing of a dove, seeped from somewhere in his chest. Kyōko suffered from a fear of heights. When she found herself in a high place, she shrank back and her legs went weak, but she was overcome with an almost irresistible urge to throw herself off and be done with it. Looking at Kazuki's face now, she felt that urge. Perhaps this was the feeling that drove people to double suicides.

"I want you to promise about Kōki," he said, his voice sounding suddenly serious. She nodded.

As he reached the bottom of the stairs at Kannai Station, his sneakers seemed to take off along the sidewalk by themselves, running him through the intersection as the crossing signal flashed. The bright, midsummer sunlight made Isezaki Street glow like the image on a high-definition TV, clear and hyper-real. He asked an old man sweeping in front of a watch shop whether there was a store for Buddhist implements in the area.

"There's a bunch of them over on Noge-dori, a block down there," he rasped.

Kazuki walked by the shop windows full of household altars and other accoutrements, turning into the third store, whose sign read "Renjudō" in big, gold letters. As the automatic door slid open, the clerk looked up for a moment, but then turned back to his work. He was wearing a dress shirt and a blue-and-white-striped tie, and he seemed absorbed in dusting and rearranging the goods on the shelf. Kazuki made his way toward the back of the shop, studying the neat line of family altars ranging from enormous ones taller than he was to small ones less than two feet high. He had six hundred thousand yen in the pouch attached to his belt, but a there was no way to fit a large altar on the second floor of the Golden Pavilion. He decided he'd pick one that would suit Granny Shige: small but dignified. An image of her face seemed to appear inside one altar as he passed, so he looked at the price tag. 275,000 yen. Kazuki went up to the clerk.

"I'd like that altar," he said.

"An altar? Why don't you come back with your mother or father?"

"What do you mean?" Kazuki asked.

"Well, we would want to discuss the purchase with your parents. This isn't like buying a computer." Maybe the kid was doing a project on family altars during summer vacation, the clerk thought, convinced that he couldn't be serious about buying one.

"You mean you won't sell it to me?" Kazuki demanded.

"Listen," said the clerk, straightening up. He looked Kazuki in the eye and flinched, thinking that if the boy had a knife with him he wouldn't hesitate to use it. "I'm not saying I won't sell you one. Not at all. Sure, which one did you have in mind?" Kazuki walked back to the altar where Granny Shige's face had appeared. "Ah, our 'Winter Moon' model," the clerk said. There was nothing funny about this, but he wanted to laugh—laugh and go back to work.

"I'll take it," Kazuki said, pulling the wad of bills from his pouch. At the sight of the money, the clerk became suddenly animated.

"Very well, then. I'll just check to see if we have it in stock." While he disappeared at the back of the store, Kazuki peered in the glass cases full of bells, candlesticks, incense burners, and other implements. He knew that there were things you needed to go with an altar, but he could only remember the gong, the incense holder, and the memorial tablet.

He imagined that for the time being Grampa Sada would burn incense and offer a prayer at Shige's altar every day, but after he was gone who would be there? Chihiro? But who would be looking after Chihiro? Guess I'll just have to take care of everybody, he thought, and an ecstatic smile crept over his face.

The shopkeeper and the clerk brought the box containing the altar from the back of the store. Kazuki was still staring at the glass case, like a child at a toy store examining the computer games kept under lock and key.

"Can we help you with something else?" the shopkeeper asked, somewhat skeptically. The clerk had explained the situation in back, but the shopkeeper had felt they should treat the boy like any other customer.

"That and that," said Kazuki, pointing at a bell, an incense burner, and a small stand. They watched as the clerk took them from the case. "Do you have mortuary tablets?" he asked next.

"Has someone passed away then?" the shopkeeper asked, more formally now.

"My grandmother," Kazuki said.

"I see. Well then, you will be needing a tablet, won't you," said the man, unconsciously rubbing his hands together. Kazuki had to fight the urge to make up a story for the clerk as he was totaling the bill at the counter: he lived alone with his grandfather now that his grandmother had died; the old man had lost the will to leave the house and had sent him out to buy an altar for his granny . . . "It's a very important decision," the shopkeeper said, placing his palms together, "so please take your time with the selection." Convinced that Granny Shige would choose her own tablet by telepathy, Kazuki walked along the case, looking carefully at one after another. "That one is finished with real gold leaf. Ah, and that one's ebony. I wonder what would go best with the Winter Moon altar? . . ." The shopkeeper's attitude had changed completely now as he watched the filial grandson selecting a memorial tablet for his beloved grandmother.

"Okay, this one," Kazuki said at last, stopping in front of the case.

"The Double Romon. It should fit nicely in the altar. Yes, that should do quite well."

"Is there anything else I should have?" Kazuki asked.

"Well, there are a number of necessary items," said the shopkeeper, "but the most important is, of course, the image of the Buddha itself." He led the boy to a wall covered with scrolls and was about to launch into an explanation of the finer points of each.

"No. We don't need that," said Kazuki, turning away. Realizing that there were no price tags on the scrolls, the shopkeeper was afraid that the boy had perhaps misunderstood and thought they were extremely expensive.

"The image varies, of course, depending on your family's sect, but these run about three thousand yen," he said.

"No thanks," said Kazuki. The shopkeeper was just about to explain that it would be bad form to have an altar with no image, but the boy seemed to have no further interest in what he had to say, so he followed him to the counter.

"Just these four items, then?" he asked.

"What else do you suggest?" Kazuki said. He pulled the roll of bills from the pouch and set it on the counter, looking around the shop.

"Well," said the shopkeeper, trying to make his voice sound calm, "There is the offertory bowl, where you put the rice every day." His expression was very serious.

"No," said Kazuki.

"They start at just Y250," he said, but Kazuki's no was almost instantaneous. The shopkeeper felt like screaming—did a little money make this brat so fucking important?

"It's a ramen shop," said Kazuki.

"I see . . ."

"But we could use some candlesticks."

"Candlesticks . . ." The shopkeeper wanted to ask why a ramen shop wouldn't need an offertory bowl, but he simply set the candlesticks on the counter. The boy picked out some incense and candles and asked them to send everything to the Golden Pavilion. But then, realizing that he didn't know the address, he asked to borrow the phone book.

"So that's in Maesato-chō. It's only about ten minutes from here, so we'll have it to you by tomorrow, if that suits." The shopkeeper noted down the address and number from the phone book. Kazuki nodded. "And what is your grandmother's posthumous name?" the man asked. This time Kazuki shook his head. "Well, that is a problem," the shopkeeper said. "A memorial tablet without the posthumous name is like a body without a soul, and—how should I put this?—a family altar without the memorial tablet is like a . . . house with nobody home."

"Fine," said Kazuki, "make one up for her."

"That's usually done by the priest at the temple. Then we have a lacquer worker engrave the name in vermilion and we finish it with gold leaf."

"And what does it cost?"

"That's a bit difficult to say. It depends on the characters chosen for the posthumous name, but it can run anywhere from a few hundred thousand to several million. But at any rate, it all has to begin with the priest assigning the name."

Kazuki thought for a moment. "Okay. Forget it." he said, gathering up the money that had been lying on the counter. The shopkeeper's mouth fell open in astonishment.

"Uh, 'forget' what?" he stammered, staring at the boy. Kazuki headed for the door, shoving the money back in the pouch and fastening it closed as he went. "Wait," said the shopkeeper, running frantically around to the front of the store and stopping the boy. "We should be able to find some way to work this out." He led him back to the counter. "There are some people these days who give themselves their own posthumous names while they're still living, so here's what we can do. I'll assign the name, and then if your grandfather approves, we'll consider it official. How would that be?"

"Fine with me," said Kazuki. "Go ahead."

"And what is your denomination?"

"I don't know."

"You've never heard anyone mention that you're 'Nichiren,' or something like that?"

"No," said Kazuki. The shopkeeper wanted to scream and chase the boy from the shop, but he wanted to sell the altar even more, so concentrating on that thought, he wrote out several names.

"Please use these in the name," Kazuki said, writing out the characters for "mansion" and "faithful woman."

If you used "mansion," thought the shopkeeper, then you almost had to use the characters for "big sister"; but that was likely to bother the boy and then he'd end up with nothing. So be it, he thought, suddenly weary of the whole thing. He went to the back of the store and returned with several poem cards that he used for writing haiku in his spare time. Picking up a brush-pen, he began transcribing the name in neatly calligraphed characters: Sōgetsu-in Kōsen Myōshin Shinnyo. Frosted Moon Mansion Happy Spring Mysterious Heart Faithful Woman. Perhaps not much of a name, he thought, but his handwriting was particularly fine.

"How's this?" he asked, holding out the poem card. The boy nodded blankly.

"Write it on the tablet, please," he said.

"Why don't we put the card in the altar for now and we'll have the tablet properly engraved for you?" His voice was shaking with anger. If he tells me to scribble it on with a gold marker right now, I'll snap, he thought. "We could deliver it in four or five days. I promise you, that would be better."

"Fine. Do that, please." Kazuki paid the bill: Y342,800.

"And I'll send this with the delivery as a small token of our sympathy at the passing of your grandmother," said the relieved shopkeeper, taking out an offertory bowl and putting it with the other things.

"I said we don't need one!" shouted Kazuki, shoving past the man and out the door. Granny Shige had always eaten her rice out of the little bowls she used to serve soup with fried rice. She would fold her hands reverently over the steaming bowl before carrying the snow-white rice to her toothless mouth. She would eat each grain from the bowl with great care, using her fingers to gather up strays that clung about her lips. How could she ever have any bowl but that one?

"Kazuki." Someone had whispered his name.

"What?" he said, his voice soft and sweet, the way it had been when he was small. He stopped and waited for an answer, but it was just the summer breeze brushing against his ears.

He had all but forgotten about this kind of home cooking; but now, as he walked into the kitchen, the odors promised a world of pleasure. Salted salmon fresh off the grill, the steam from the rice cooker, the oil draining from fried chicken, spaghetti drenched in ketchup, a paste of mayonnaise and boiled eggs that would probably be used to make sandwiches. He felt a kind of joy well up inside him. The smells had stimulated his senses, but he did not feel particularly hungry. There was no sign of the girls who had made the food—Kyōko and Yōko. He wondered where they could have gone.

As she was leaving yesterday, he'd thought to ask Kyōko about going on a picnic; and later, when Kōki was napping on the couch, he had tickled the bottoms of his feet to wake him and shouted, "Picnic tomorrow!" He had named several places—Negishi Forest Park, Sankei-en, Hakkeijima Sea Paradise—and let Kōki pick. He said he'd like to go to all of them. "But if you had to choose one, which would it be?" Kazuki asked, beginning to calm down a little.

"The Kanazawa Nature Park!" Kōki said, his eyes bulging. "You know, the roses and water lilies and hydrangeas are all blooming; and they've got a Queensland koala, a black rhino, and a white Japanese goat. And an Indian elephant . . . but not an Indian peacock." Kazuki remembered that in one of the photo albums there was a picture of the three kids—Kōki, Miho, and Kazuki—lined up in front of an elephant's pen with their parents standing behind, arms around them. Miho was staring at her feet; Kōki's eyes were wandering off somewhere; and only Kazuki was looking straight at the camera. Was that at the Kanazawa Nature Park?

Kyōko had asked if it would be all right to invite Yōko, and Kōki had insisted that they ask Chihiro. After Kazuki had phoned the Golden Pavilion and it had been determined that they could both go, Kōki's celebration got out of hand, and Kyōko and Kazuki ran around the house trying to keep out of his way, like spectators running from the sparks of errant fireworks. After Kyōko had gone, Kazuki phoned the cab company and asked them to have two taxis waiting outside the house at ten o'clock the next morning.

"What are you doing, daydreaming like that?" Yōko called to him. "And where have you been, anyway?"

"Taking out the garbage," he said. "The kitchen was starting to smell." The two girls were washing their hands at the sink. Then they began making rice balls. Their laughter seeped down into Kazuki like a warm, sweet drink. They were beginning a new life, he thought, unlike anything he'd experienced in his fourteen years. The sounds and smells of life, the heat from living human bodies would warm the house, leaven it like yeast in warm bread. The death of one human being had thawed this house. He thought he might try telling a joke to the two girls, who were still laughing, but he couldn't remember one, so he went to wash his face. As he was drying himself, he could hear Kōki, who must have gone into the kitchen just as he was coming out, laughing his cymbal-crash laugh. Yes, he'd thought, he'd done the right thing, and everything seemed to be going well. He stared at himself in the mirror; small, reddish pimples had appeared on his forehead and right cheek. He had always hated the fact that his skin was smooth and babyish, and he grinned at this sign that his hormones were working normally. When he'd finished washing his face and shut off the water, he could still hear laughter coming from the kitchen, cheering him like the bell they used to ring at festival time. When life and death were so intertwined like this, it seemed to him that some people would be depressed by the gloomy rhythm of death while others would respond to the joyous rhythm of life. Everyone in this house, with the exception of that man, was making joyful music; he'd had no choice but to eliminate the discordant note, the one that threatened to disturb the harmony. He looked once more in the mirror at his refreshed face before going back to the kitchen.

Kyōko had her back to him as she took something from the refrigerator, and she gave a startled cry when she realized he was there. Yōko, even more surprised, wheeled around on him.

"What are you doing there?" she said.

"I need a garbage bag. Could I get under here for a minute?" Kazuki waited for her to step aside and then squatted down by the sink. He stole a look at her long, slender calf as he opened the cabinet door and pulled out a plastic bag.

"You aren't really thinking of housecleaning before we go, are you?" Yōko said.

"They come for the garbage today, so we need to get it out," said Kazuki.

"You want some help?" Kyōko asked.

"No," said Kazuki. "There's not that much to do." He tucked a garbage bag under his arm and left the kitchen. Gathering up a pile of newspapers drifted across the table in the living room, he carried them down to the basement and locked the door behind him. How many days had it been? Must be about three or four, his numb brain calculated. The body under the floor would be changing by the day, by the hour. He pulled the three bloody sheets from under the bed, folded them, and wrapped them in the newspaper. Then he double bagged them, making sure the bags were tightly tied. He looked around, feeling that the room itself was about to cry out at any moment, and his eyes came to rest on the rug, which seemed to dominate everything else. He had to think of some way to get rid of it; but when he did, he would have to buy a new one to replace it. Standing in the center of the rug, the section covering the entrance to the vault, he sniffed a moment. No odor yet. But eventually the flesh and the organs inside would begin to rot and decompose. What would he do if the whole room began to smell of death? He'd thought of burying the body in the yard, but to get it out there without anyone noticing and without ruining the floors, he would probably have to cut it up. He knelt down and pressed his nose to the rug, wondering how many days it took for a body to start to decay. There was a slight smell of rusty iron, and when he rubbed the spot, a small smear of coagulated blood came off on his finger. Startled, he jumped to his feet. His right knee was marked with a powdery red circle, which he quickly brushed away. Suddenly, the rug and the body beneath it filled his whole head, and he knew that he would never be free until he had found a way to completely dispose of them. Still, he couldn't afford to get excited and make a mistake; he had to take things slowly and carefully and do the job right.

He went out to the pile of garbage bags he had left by the driveway. It took him three trips, but at last he had moved five of them—all but the one with the pieces of broken vase—to the dumpster by the fence of St. Joseph's. The garbage truck hadn't come around yet, and it would be a disaster if a cat or crow got into the bags before it did. He stood listening for the familiar tune the truck played as it made its rounds. There was still no sign of the truck, but it would look suspicious to stand here on the corner, so he decided to cross the street to the bus stop and pretend to wait there while he kept a lookout. The sun beat down on his head, as if it were aiming at him, and he could feel his arms and shoulders scorching in the bright light. The precarious mountain of garbage bags stood out from the colorless, midsummer cityscape, shimmering like a stinking mirage. The sunlight seemed to pierce him to the bone, robbing the strength from his legs. Inside his head, the bags suddenly burst into flame. Perhaps I should wait by them, he thought, walking back across the street. Why haven't they come yet? His eyes, bloodshot with rage, shot up and down the block. And even when they pick them up, if the mechanism in the truck breaks the bags and bright red pillows come spilling out, the garbage men will notice. What would he do then? He picked up the first bag and was about to run back to the house when another thought stopped him: if he couldn't even get rid of the bags, how was he ever going to manage with the blood-soaked rug or the body beneath it? They would have to stay where they were, filling the basement with the stench of death. He let the bag drop.

Five minutes later, the garbage truck appeared. Two men hopped down and began throwing the bags in the back. They started the grinder and continued hurling in bags without watching what might have come out of them, and in a few minutes the pile was gone. When the whole load had been crushed, they got back in the truck and drove off to the next stop. After watching them go, Kazuki turned on his heel, shook a drop of sweat from the tip of his nose onto the asphalt, stepped over the guardrail, and crossed the street. Just a few minutes ago he had felt as though he were being crushed by fear; but now, having cleared this first hurdle, he suddenly felt lighter, almost cheerful. He kicked at the pavement with the toe of his sneaker and went running down the hill. He knew that in any game they usually made the first obstacle fairly easy to beat, and that the hurdles gradually got higher as you went along; but at the moment he felt as though he would win, no matter what. He was overcome by a sense of omnipotence, as if he could manipulate everything around him with complete ease. His arms felt like wings and he began to flap them as he charged down the hill, coming to a sudden stop in front of the house. Two taxis were just pulling into the driveway.

Two neatly packed picnic baskets were lined up on the table in the living room, and next to them sat a plate of food.

"Does it always take you so long to put out the garbage?" Kyōko asked.

"Have some breakfast before we go," Yōko laughed, picking up a bite of omelette with her fingers and popping it in her mouth.

"Hurry up and change," Kyōko added, picking up a basket. "We'll take the food out to the taxis." Kōki picked up the other in both hands and stumbled after her.

Yōko scooped up another bite of egg and mayonnaise and held it out for Kazuki. As soon as the food hit his tongue, he spat it out in disgust.

"What's the matter with you?!" Yōko screamed, jumping back.

"It's rotten," he said, spitting the rest of the mayonnaise from his mouth.

"It most certainly is not. I just tried some," said Yōko, dabbing some on her finger and licking it off. "There, see. It's delicious."

"It's rotten," said Kazuki, spitting again.

"Here," she said, pouring some barley tea from a thermos into a paper cup. "Have some of this." He took a sip of tea, but his hands shot instantly to cover his mouth and the tea drizzled out between his fingers.

"It's sour. It's gone bad, too." He threw the cup on the floor.

"You're crazy," she said, pouring some tea into the lid of the thermos and drinking it. "Kyōko and I both had some earlier. It tastes perfectly normal. It's store-bought, anyway."

"I'm going to change," Kazuki said, heading off to the bathroom. It must be my sense of taste that's gone bad, he thought. Maybe the smell of blood had seeped into his mouth and made his taste buds go haywire. He could test this hypothesis with some water, he thought, rinsing his mouth under the faucet. If his nerves were somehow shot and he didn't realize it, he might do something strange and attract suspicion. He hesitantly sucked in a small mouthful of water, but it was just lukewarm and unpleasant, not foul tasting. Then why had the mayonnaise and the tea been so horrible? Wiping his mouth with a towel, he decided that he wouldn't eat at the picnic.

He went back to the kitchen, but avoided looking at Yōko who was watching him suspiciously and cut through the living room on his way upstairs.

"We're going hiking!" Kōki, who had a canteen hanging over his shoulder, took a bit of fish from a plate and popped it in his mouth. "Hiking! hiking! hiking!" he shouted, running to hug Kazuki as he returned from changing his clothes. Kazuki squirmed, trying to free himself from his brother's grip.

"Let's get going," he said, patting Kōki gently on the back.

Kazuki got into the first cab alone and the other three followed in the second car. "Stop in Kogane-chō on the way," he told the driver, sinking back into the seat. Yōko was probably telling Kyōko about what had happened with the tea and mayonnaise earlier; he would have to tell them he wasn't feeling well or that he'd smoked too much, some sort of excuse. He tried to drive the memory of Yōko's suspicious look from his head. He wondered if Sada was lighting incense for Granny Shige upstairs at the Golden Pavilion—or perhaps he'd simply refused the altar when they'd tried to deliver it. He'd been pretty upset when Kazuki had tried to give him the condolence money. He bit his lip, assuring himself that he'd done nothing wrong. Or if he had, it was an honest mistake, like a traveler in a foreign country walking on the wrong side of the sidewalk. It was just that the rules were different. If everyone knew the rules, then you could punish someone who broke them. But there were laws against minors smoking or drinking, and yet he'd never met anyone who'd been arrested for breaking them. The cities were overflowing with whores, but the police generally let them be. If the people who made the laws were not willing to reform them when they'd outlived their usefulness, then people had no choice but to live according to their own personal rules. Why didn't they bother to try to control the prostitutes? It simply wasn't cost effective. And that was just the way it was nowadays: everything came down to the cost—and all evil stemmed from things that were low cost. If something or someone wasn't commensurate with its cost, then it paid with its life: traffic accidents, suicide, murder, AIDS, the Ebola virus, war—and still there wasn't enough death to go around. The world was desperate for death!

He rested his elbow below the window, looking out at the scenery as they turned the corner at Isezaki-chō. He told the driver how to get to the Golden Pavilion. Not wanting Sada to know that he was riding around in cabs, he had the driver stop at the corner down the street from the restaurant and he got out. "Wait here a minute," he called back to the other cab.

As he pushed through the curtain that covered the door, a cardboard box with the name of the altar shop printed on the side caught his eye. Though he'd told the store to take the altar upstairs and put it somewhere no matter what the old man said, he could imagine that Sada had threatened the delivery men, had told them he hadn't ordered the thing and that they had to take it back. They had probably dropped it and fled under his barrage. He felt a slight regret at not calling ahead to warn Sada, but more than that he felt furious with him for being so stubborn. He was just about to charge upstairs when Sada came padding down and, turning his back on Kazuki, busied himself at the sink by the bathroom. The thought suddenly occurred to him that it had been years since he had bothered to pray for his own grandfather at their family altar, and he began to regret his decision to force an altar on Sada. Still, just having an altar in the house meant something, he concluded.

Chihiro came downstairs, tied an apron around her waist, and went behind the counter. Opening the lid of the rice cooker, she filled a ramen bowl with steaming rice. Then she broke two raw eggs on top and dribbled soy sauce over the bowl, mixing the concoction noisily with her chopsticks. Kazuki suddenly noticed how empty his own stomach felt, and he wanted to grab the bowl away from her and gobble it down. As his mouth began to water, he heard the sound of Sada gargling behind him. He turned to face the old man and muttered an apology in his direction, but Sada simply bent over and spit into the sink.

"I'm sorry if it's been a bother," Kazuki said a little louder.

"How much was it?" Sada asked. "I'll pay you when you bring Chihiro back this evening."

"Don't worry about it. It's for Granny Shige," Kazuki said.

"I am worried," said Sada. "You know you can't simply take other peoples' things without asking? Well, it works the same for giving—you can't just give things simply because it suits you. I'll call the store later and ask. Now get out of here," he said, wiping his mouth with the towel he had hung around his neck. Kazuki grabbed Chihiro's hand just as she was about to break an egg over a second bowl of rice and pulled her out of the shop.

He walked a bit apart from the others as they strolled by the cages in the Oceania section of the zoo: a Queensland koala, an Australian wombat, a giant kangaroo. Zoos, he thought, were nothing but prisons. People had simply locked up these innocent animals in cages so they could feel superior to them. According to the zoo's pamphlet, they had constructed environments that matched the animals' natural habitats and had kept the public as far away as possible to reduce the stress on the specimens. But in the end, they were just fancy cages. And, he decided, since the animals weren't free, walking around and staring at them like this didn't really amount to seeing them. You had to go to Australia or to the islands of the South Pacific to do that. Birds without the sky were no longer birds. Furthermore, he told himself, a country that locked away innocent animals had long since lost the right to sit in judgment on human beings.

"Come look! Over here!" Kyōko was waving and calling to him, but he had no intention of staring at animals that had become no better than objects on display. A dirty business all around.

As they entered the bird house, Kōki became even more excited, startled by the chorus of songs. As the birds flitted among the trees, he would stop and stand perfectly still until they'd come to rest. Then he put his arm around Chihiro's shoulder and pointed them out one by one, using the names he'd learned from the explanatory plaques: gray starling, Japanese great tit, Chinese bamboo partridge. He chirped, imitating the bamboo partridge.

"You try it," he told Chihiro.

"I can't," she giggled, squirming out of his grip.

"You can too," he said. "Listen!" He imitated the call once more, *chotto koi, chotto koi,* but Chihiro continued to laugh uncontrollably. Suddenly, however, her laughter died and the smile vanished from her face. She stuck out her jaw and closed her eyes.

"Koi, chotto, koi, chotto, koi," she ventured, puckering her lips into the shape of the bird's beak. Kōki, overcome with joy, danced a little jig and ran to hug her, but she continued her chirping, eyes closed and face tilted up at the tree. The sound of her voice melted into the other noises in the zoo, the murmuring of a small stream, the buzz of the cicadas, the soft hooting of owls, and vanished into the artificial forest. Then a loudspeaker, drowning out everything else, informed them that they should not feed the animals, and they wandered on.

Kōki and Chihiro were most delighted with the roller slide in the children's play area. Red, yellow, and blue rollers lined the bed, making it much faster than a normal slide, and the two of them went down it again and again. There was a line of children waiting their turns, but they would simply push to the front and climb the ladder. Kōki would go down first and sit waiting at the bottom until Chihiro's breasts smashed into his back. Kazuki and the two girls moved into the shade of a cherry tree to wait for them.

"Nothing seems to bother them, does it," said Yōko, leaning back against the trunk of the tree and closing her eyes. A trip to the zoo had seemed ridiculous to her, but she'd had nothing better to do so she'd agreed to come when Kyōko invited her. But when she thought about it, she didn't ever have anything to do and wasn't likely to in the future. She'd had a couple of bit parts in TV dramas, not much better than being an extra, really, and she'd starred in a couple of porno movies, but it hadn't come to anything. And now the management company had even stopped bothering to send her around to auditions, probably convinced that she had no chance. In the end, she'd been forced to find part-time jobs or work at a phone sex club. Why did people even go on living? she wondered, and then laughed out loud for asking such a ridiculous question.

"What's so funny?" Kyōko asked, looking around.

"Oh, nothing," she said. She closed her eyes again, listening to the laughter of the children as they played on the slide. In order to escape from the emptiness, people spent unbelievable amounts of time and energy building their various hiding places. But these were all empty too: home, school, office. For your whole life, up till the moment you died, it seemed you were doomed to live in fear of that scary echo from the void. It suddenly occurred to her that the energy that had quarried the stones for the pyramids and piled them up in the desert was just another attempt to combat this emptiness. When she opened her eyes, even the children, who had looked as though they were having such fun, now seemed to be writhing desperately in an attempt to escape their boredom. "Give it your best shot," she muttered to herself.

"Give what your best shot?" Kyōko asked.

"Nothing," she said, turning to look at Kazuki. "Did you say the boss went to Korea?"

"Uh-huh," he grunted, standing up and walking off toward the slide.

"It's lucky his father's letting you take care of the house," Yōko said.

"It is," said Kyōko. "But I don't think Kazuki's actually talked to him about it yet."

"No kidding? Then he'll probably fire you when he gets back."

"Probably," said Kyōko, "but I don't really care. It seems he's almost never home, though. Kazuki says he stays over at his girlfriend's place." Yōko remembered that her father had once told her that Hidetomo was particularly careful on this point: he would never stay over at a woman's house because he was worried that she might start pressuring him about marriage or he might have to pay her more when he left her. And when he wanted to be with a woman until morning, he always stayed at a hotel. If that were true, why had Kazuki lied to Kyōko? Her eyes drifted over to the bottom of the slide where he was talking to Kōki. Did he want her in the house so much that he was willing to tell a lie that would become obvious almost immediately?

"Have you two done it?" she asked suddenly.

"Not yet," Kyōko giggled, hitting Yōko on the shoulder.

Why was she getting involved with him, Yōko wondered. Could it possibly be that she simply wanted to marry a rich man? She glanced over at Kyōko, whose face was smiling as if she hadn't a care in the world, though she had experienced nothing but care and unimaginable hardship her whole life. Then her gaze moved on to Kazuki, who was walking toward them. His body was bathed in bright sunlight, but all the same it seemed to be deep in shadow. It occurred to her that the two of them were probably very much alike: though they carried something dark around inside, they hid it well, confronting the world with a placid expression.

"They want to stay a few more minutes," Kazuki said, lowering himself onto the bench where he'd been sitting earlier.

"When's he coming back from Korea?" she asked, standing up and stretching her arms.

"In a couple of days, I think. But I'm not really sure . . . Hey, I wonder what would happen to these animals if we had a real depression. If people were going hungry and no one had the money to come here, do you think they'd wind up eating them?"

"Yuck!" said Yōko. "Is that what you've been thinking about the whole time we've been walking around?" Noting that he had changed the topic rather abruptly, she studied him a moment and then looked at Kyōko. "Shall we ask him?" she said suddenly. "You've been saying you want to."

"Okay," said Kyōko. "Why not?"

Yōko had developed the theory that her friend had gotten involved with Kazuki in order to exact revenge for her father's suicide. First she would make him fall in love with her, then leave him and drive him to kill himself. But when she explained her idea, Kyōko had denied it immediately, saying it sounded like the plot of a comic book or, worse yet, like a bad mystery show on TV.

"Hayashi says that your father drove Kyōko's dad to commit suicide. There's no proof, but it makes sense. Everyone at Treasure Ball seems to think so too, he says. Did you know about it?" It was only when she was talking with Kazuki that Yōko referred to her own father as "Hayashi," mostly because Kazuki himself never used "san" after his name. She glanced at him, afraid that he would be angry, but he was staring back at her, eyes brimming with joy. His expression made her uncomfortable and she looked quickly away.

"I knew," he said. "The bastard accused him of stealing money from the company. He didn't have any proof at all, but he kept after him. After he killed himself, they discovered they'd just misplaced the money."

"Really?" said Yōko. Another bad TV show. Still, since when did he start calling his father "bastard"? She expected a more submissive tone when referring to "the boss."

"I heard the whole thing from the bastard himself," said Kazuki. "You want to get back at him?" he said, turning to Kyōko.

"How could I when I'm not really sure," she said, a weak smile playing across her lips.

"I'm sure," he said. "He told me the whole story."

"There are a lot of people who like to make themselves out as the bad guy. The orphanage was full of them. They seemed to think it made them stronger," Kyōko said.

"Well, if it were me, I'd want to get back at him!" Kazuki was nearly shouting.

And . . . and . . . how would you do it? Yōko was on the point of asking when Kyōko suddenly twisted around and waved at Kōki and Chihiro, who were running toward them, hand in hand and out of breath.

"Let's eat," Kyōko said, standing up.

Kazuki studied the map of the area on a nearby sign. It claimed that you could see Tokyo Bay and Hakkeijima from a spot at the top of the hill. "Let's go," he said, starting up the slope. On either side of the path, purplish pink altheas were in bloom. Chihiro pulled Kōki by the hand, drawing him over to the flowers. She leaned down, stroking the petals with her lips. The trees gave out at last, and they found themselves in a grassy field on the side of the hill.

"This would be a good spot." Yōko, who had been walking ahead, turned to look back at the others. "There's plenty of shade and you can see the ocean." Kazuki hurried to catch up to her. A few thin clouds had appeared in the west and were floating slowly across the sky. They blocked the sun for the first time that day, but soon they had moved on and the sun came out again.

The two women spread out a sheet of plastic and set the picnic baskets in the middle. They brought out containers of food and sandwiches in plastic wrap, arranging them on napkins before passing out paper cups, paper plates, and chopsticks. When the rice balls appeared, Kōki and Chihiro immediately grabbed them and began to eat.

"So, what's Haruko doing these days?" said Yōko, wiping her sweaty hands on her pants. A slight damp spot appeared but dried quickly.

Kazuki, who was stretched out on the ground, looked up at Kyōko and tried to imagine what her sister, Haruko, must look like now. No image came. At any rate, if she were any good with numbers, he could let her have Sugimoto's job. That would probably make Kyōko happy.

"She lives alone in Tokyo," she said.

"How old is she now?"

"Sixteen. She was born less than a year after me. She has a part-time job in a convenience store."

"How long has it been since I've seen her? I think the last time was at Disneyland, so it must be four years at least. How's she doing?" Yōko said.

"I don't see her very often myself," said Kyōko. "But we talk on the phone."

Haruko would probably come to work for him at Vegas, Kazuki thought. Yōko, too, if she would give up on the acting and devote herself to the job. That way he could start building his own loyal group within the company. And maybe he should have the house torn down and build a new one where they could all live together. Perhaps in the shape of a hexagon, two stories high, with an atrium in the middle. He'd have a kitchen and a dining room, and built around them, each of them would have his own room. The atrium would have a skylight . . . But at this point, his daydreaming was suddenly interrupted as the cover to the underground vault seemed to swing open, smashing his fantasy. Shit! If only the whole place, vault and all, would sink deep into the earth, down to where hot magma would consume it. As he pictured this scene, it seemed as though the lava were pouring into his own head and he jumped up shouting. The four of them were all staring at him. He looked around at them, wondering whether there was some way he could burn the body. Or better yet, he might dissolve it in acid or some other chemical, he thought, smiling.

"Kōki, what did you ask your father to bring you back from Korea?" Yōko said. Kōki froze, his hand holding a forkful of spaghetti in front of his ketchup-stained lips.

"You don't ask someone like him for souvenirs!" Kazuki spat the words at her. Kōki looked at Kazuki's eyes, then his mouth, then back to his eyes; and then he slowly lowered the fork to his plate. He unwound the spaghetti and rewound it before lifting it to his mouth.

"I'll be right back," Yōko said, jumping up and brushing herself off. Her thick, uneven eyebrows were arched over her eyes.

"I'll go with you," said Kyōko, getting up as well.

As he watched them walk down the hill, Kazuki was suddenly overcome by an inexplicable happiness. He stretched out his legs on the grass and let his arms float lazily in the air. They seemed to cross themselves naturally behind his head and he leaned back, staring up at the sky. The clouds were racing by at an amazing speed. There was no wind to speak of where he sat, but it must have been blowing steadily at higher altitudes. A thick mass of cloud drifted in front of the sun, casting the meadow in shadow.

"Rain?" Chihiro wondered, brandishing a piece of fried chicken at the sky.

"I got mosquito bites," said Kōki, his nose twitching like a rabbit's. "They're itchy." He had three bites, one on the back of his neck, another on his arm, and a third on his ankle.

"Itchy, itchy," Chihiro murmured, as she began scratching his leg. Kōki's eyes narrowed in delight.

"If it rains, you can stay over at our house again," he gurgled.

Suddenly, Kazuki felt alone, left out as the others had paired off. He rolled over on his stomach and began plucking at the grass. Eventually his index finger reached the earth underneath, and soon he was digging feverishly with his whole hand. The hole was the size of his fist, but he kept on digging. If he had a shovel, he thought, he could dig a hole big enough for him to disappear into.

"What are you doing?" The sharp tone of Yōko's voice startled him and he glanced up. The girls stood over him, looking angry, while Kōki and Chihiro giggled. Kazuki looked from face to face.

"I'm searching for bugs," he said, laughing.

"What bugs?" Yōko asked, her voice trembling. Was digging a hole such a strange thing to do? Kazuki couldn't understand why they seemed so upset.

"Stinkbugs, worms, whatever," he said. "And look, it makes a mask." He leaned over and thrust his face into the hole, bringing it back out with dirt clinging to his forehead, nose, eyelids, even his lips. It felt terrible, but he was sure it would make them laugh. He waited for a moment but no laughter came. Why? When he looked up at them again they turned away. He rolled over on his back, face still covered with mud, staring at his own darkness in the lacy, red afterglow of the setting sun.

After reminding Kyōko to take Chihiro back to the Golden Pavilion, Kazuki headed off by himself in the direction of Sakuragi-chō Station. He bought a ticket for Okuzawa and boarded an express train bound for Shibuya. It had occurred to him last night that there were some things he needed to talk over with his mother.

For a year after she had left them, Miki had lived in an apartment in Eifuku-chō. Then she'd moved to Okuzawa in Setagaya ward, where she'd been for the past five years. It was the year Kōki turned seven that she'd been told by an authority on Williams Syndrome that his disease was incurable. After that she used every connection she had to obtain introductions to famous traditional healers, accupuncturists and practitioners of moxibustion, and began taking Kōki. When these proved useless, she starting going to a fortune-teller who an acquaintance said was unusually accurate. The fortune-teller informed her that someone among her ancestors had committed a great sin concerning money and that the disease was a curse. If she could live an exemplary life of poverty, then the boy would be cured. From that day forward, she changed her ways, choosing only the most modest food and clothing and developing a neurotic aversion to money that made it impossible for her to live in a place like Kogane-chō where there was little else. She urged Hidetomo to close down the pachinko parlor and look for other work, and if that were impossible, she begged him to at least move the business to another neighborhood. When he was out of the house, she would have the fortune-teller come to pray for the boy. One day, having learned what was going on from the housekeeper, Hidetomo returned in the middle of one of these sessions and drove the fortune-teller from the house.

Kazuki stood on the underground platform in Den'en Chōfu Station. A woman's voice came over the loudspeaker urging passengers to stay behind the white line, and Kazuki could hear a muffled noise coming from the tunnel. The thumping reminded him of the sound of his father beating his mother all those years ago. As Miki had shrunk away from him, Hidetomo had grabbed her blouse and pulled her close. He slapped her over and over, then kneed her in the stomach. Catching hold of her hair, he'd knocked her head against the wall and then punched her. When he finally left the house, she stood beating herself as if in grief, blood running from her ears, nose, and mouth, but she never made a sound or shed a tear. Miho was curled up in a corner of the room, sobbing, while Kōki lay on his back, beating his arms and legs like an infant and screaming in a voice that sounded like metal being dragged over glass. Kazuki himself had closed his eyes and stood absolutely still.

A year after that incident, Miki had left the house, taking only Kōki with her. Hidetomo soon found out where they'd gone, but he never went after them or offered to pay support. If he had offered, no doubt Miki would have refused. A few days later, divorce papers arrived by special delivery. Hidetomo, barely able to hide his pain and anger, ripped them to pieces right in front of Kazuki. He told Kazuki that since she'd run out on him he no longer considered her his wife, that he didn't give a damn what she did. But she was still the woman who had given birth to his heir and he wouldn't divorce her. Any man who agreed to a woman's demand for a divorce wasn't worth shit anyway.

Since she had to look after Kōki day and night, she was unable to find work, and within a month her money had run out. She brought him home one day, watching him go in through the gate before she ran off. For a time after that, she continued to see Kōki about once a month, but recently their meetings had become increasingly rare. The knowledge that this filthy money was necessary to protect Kōki made her hate it all the more. The life of poverty that she'd begun in order to cure her son developed into a kind of religious faith; and gradually, as she came to completely reject any hint of comfort or luxury, she no longer came to see her Kōki. She believed, it seemed, that her constant prayers to the image of Buddha, in whose arms Kōki was held fast, were sufficient contact with her son.

A call had come from her last fall, the first time in six months. Kazuki had taken his brother to her apartment, so he knew where she was living. He didn't know what kind of work she was doing, but she'd said that she was out from nine to five. She never ate out, however, so she was bound to be back by five-thirty. If she wasn't, she'd only be doing some shopping in the neighborhood, so he shouldn't have to wait more than a half hour or so. If she offered him dinner, he'd refuse, saying that he had to go home and eat with Kōki.

As he stepped onto the platform, the air seemed hotter and more humid than usual, even for a midsummer evening—perhaps because the air-conditioning on the train had been turned up too high, he thought. It was almost like walking through smoke, and he gasped as he made his way down the platform. He needed to pee, but he didn't think he could stand the filth of the station rest room, nor did he want to use the toilet at his mother's apartment. He left the station in search of a vacant lot where he could take care of the problem. Just as the crossing guard was lifting, he realized he couldn't hold it any longer. He ducked into an alley by a row of houses, turned to face the tracks, and yanked down his zipper. His back was trembling despite the heat, and it was several seconds before the pee came. As he was pulling up his zipper, he looked up. In the twilight, the shadow of a telephone pole appeared grotesquely long, and the ordinary little houses and apartments seemed to glow with a strange, jaundiced light.

"Flower Heights" stood facing the tracks. To its right was a two-story house completely covered in vines; to its left was a dentist's office in a small building. Kazuki stopped at the bottom of the staircase and grasped the metal railing.

The door at the top of the steps stood open, but a bamboo blind shaded the interior. Kazuki could hear the sound of a wind chime somewhere inside. It was nearly dark, but the lights had not been turned on. Taking one more step, he called out.

"It's me . . ."

Miki's stooping figure appeared as she lifted the blind. "Oh . . . I thought it was Kōki," she said, straightening herself and appearing startled. Her hand drifted up, fingers spread, and pressed against the base of her throat, and the faint light that had flickered in her eyes died away. The look on her face could hardly even be called disappointed, as if it had simply resumed the same lifeless expression it had worn before she heard his voice.

"He's fine," Kazuki said. Miki turned on her heel and shuffled back into the apartment without inviting him in. He stood for a moment, then ducked under the blind and closed the door behind him.

"It gets hot if you shut it," she said, sliding the only pillow in the apartment toward him. He sat on it. As she opened and closed the refrigerator door, he looked around. In front of a golden statue of the Buddha stood a bowl of overripe fruit—cantaloupes, grapefruit, grapes, watermelon—filling the room with the odor of decay. Pasted on one wall, floor to ceiling, was a long strip of paper covered with a sutra painted in black ink. The ceiling was completely covered with a border of green leaves surrounding crimson and white lotus flowers that hung down in the center. Tied to these were small slips of paper—fortunes, Kazuki thought—and when he stood to examine them he found Kōki's name, address, and birthday had been written on each.

It was a six-mat room, the same size as the one at the Golden Pavilion where Granny Shige had died; but unlike that room, this one was spotless and the furniture and windows shone from constant polishing. When she had lived at home, Miki had left all the cleaning and other chores to the housekeeper. Kazuki, who had never once seen her run the vacuum cleaner, wash dishes, or mop the floor, tried to imagine her doing these things. The law said that when a husband died, the wife would inherit half of everything he owned; so even a conservative estimate put Miki's wealth at more than a billion yen. Her circumstances were a little different: she'd been separated from her husband for the past six years. He would have to do a little research to see whether this affected her inheritance rights. It was hard to imagine that anyone would refuse an inheritance in the hundreds of millions of yen, but there was, of course, always the chance that his mother would do just that. Still, it took seven years to have a missing person declared dead, so this was all a long way off, Kazuki told himself, cutting short his speculations. More important right now was how to make sure he could count on her as an ally if things got sticky.

The night before he had been looking through some books on commercial law on his father's shelves, but he hadn't been able to find out whether the minor heir of a company president who'd gone missing could assume the presidency. If it were a publicly held company, then the person who held the most stock would probably take over, but his father had told him that in the case of his company, 100 percent of the stock was held in the name of their family as a whole. This much was certain, then: Vegas belonged to the Yuminaga family. But if someone were to challenge him, would his mother back him up? The threads that bound them together seemed no more substantial than a spider's web.

Hearing a train approaching, he glanced out the window at the tracks, now almost invisible in the deepening dusk. The sky and clouds, the houses and apartments crowded together on the far side of the tracks—everything had been dyed the color of wine. And the lace curtains hanging on either side of the window billowed again and again, as if someone were standing outside pushing on them.

"It's hot, isn't it?" Miki said, setting a glass of iced coffee in front of him. Noticing how tanned she was as she wiped her brow with her arm, he wondered what sort of work she was doing, but he couldn't bring himself to ask. At any rate, it was something that required her to walk around outside. "Hot," she repeated, reaching toward the fan near the window and switching it on. The sudden gust of air brushed her wavy bangs against her forehead as she pulled loose a strand of hair that had caught in her mouth. She took a sip of cool barley tea with one hand as she gathered her hair in the other.

She was a woman of average height. Her suntanned body was lean, her face unadorned with makeup. Her hair, parted in the middle, fell about her shoulders. Her nose, jaw, and cheekbones were sharp and angular. The dark circles under her eyes told of many sleepless nights. Kazuki could no longer remember why he had come to this apartment. It almost seemed he'd come on impulse; or then again, it was as though the whole thing had been programmed by someone else. If he told her that his father was dead, she would probably barely blink; if he said that he'd killed him, she might take notice, but then again perhaps not. There was no way of knowing. She might pretend to be completely indifferent; or, she might report him immediately to the police. Like an actor hyperventilating just before the curtain goes up, he took an enormous breath and spat out his line.

"He's gone to Korea for a while, so I was wondering if you'd come home?" He was determined not to let his feelings show as he said this;

not his pity or his disgust, not the anxiety he'd struggled with from the time he left the station until he'd entered this room. He studied her face, but her expression hadn't changed.

"I can never approach that den of iniquity, fouled by greed and hatred and ignorance," she said at last, the first sign of life glimmering in her eyes.

"If that's what it is," Kazuki said, "then how could you go off and leave your children there? Doesn't it seem odd to you that you got out but we didn't?"

"You must use your own power to escape," she said. "If you don't, you can't be truly saved. If you get out, I'll do everything I can to help you." He wanted to force her to look at her self-delusion, but the important thing now was to mend their relationship. She was crazy, he told himself, and you should never shake something that was already cracked. He managed to control his anger.

"But it looks like he won't be back for a month, maybe longer." Miki waved her hands in front of her face as if brushing away an insect. "Kōki needs you. He's started wandering off and getting lost. He needs someone to look after him." Miki looked out the window. Her profile seemed slightly crushed under the weight of her fatigue, but there was no sign of sorrow or that the past held any meaning for her. The pain that she carried around inside of her was no longer an emotion but had long since become the very basis of her existence. Of course, she had suffered when she lived with her family, but those were nothing more than the hardships that might befall any lost, lonely housewife. When Kōki, her firstborn, had been still in the womb, they'd told her she was at risk of losing him and she'd been hospitalized for two months. Then the labor she'd felt as though she would split open. After that, the pain of being told he had an incurable disease and would never be able to manage for himself. And she had still not gotten over the pain of having to give him up. She had no way of knowing how many more years she might live, but she was sure that she would have to bear that burden until the day she died—the burden of having parted from the one child she was sure she would always keep close to her, the one she would always support. She was sure she couldn't live without him; and no one could know how she had suffered that day when she'd left him on their doorstep, how she'd battled second by second to keep from going insane. She'd prayed for madness, but that was the easy way out, and the easy way was never permitted.

Once in a while she had allowed herself to imagine how things might have been had Hidetomo managed to escape from his evil desires, from the charms of all that money. The five of them might have gone off to live in a little house somewhere. Kōki would probably have been cured; or if he hadn't, it wouldn't have mattered. Perhaps all of them would have learned to live like people with Williams Syndrome, taught by that child to be like the angels. Casting off one's desire wasn't really that difficult; it just seemed hard because the evil ones were always spying on those who sought to rid themselves of desire. In order to escape their clever ploys, one had simply to accept suffering. Kōki had been ripped away from her, but she was still nurturing the pain that had been born between them. What was more, if he ever wanted to see her, he could come here at any point—why, look, there he is now, she thought, staring at the billowing curtains.

Their faces were nearly touching over the tiny low table. Unable to stand the close scrutiny, Kazuki took a cigarette from his pocket and lit it. His mother said nothing, but after a moment she stood up and put some water in a paper cup, offering it to him in place of an ashtray. Then she turned off the fan. The breeze coming from the window blew the smoke toward her face. The room had grown quite dark, but Kazuki could not bring himself to ask why she hadn't turned on the lights. As a train passed in the opposite direction, he found himself imagining the last light of the day, as if it were squashed flat, having been plastered to the rails and run over by a train. A pendulum was swinging back and forth inside his head, between hatred and some other emotion. He realized that for her, the idea of becoming his ally simply because she was his mother was not just wrong, it was a horrible sin.

The pendulum froze on hate as he pulled a wad of bills from his pocket and set it on the table.

"It's three million. Please take it," he said. For a moment all the parts of her face froze: the lines in her cheeks, the skin around her eyes, her mouth. But in the next instant they relaxed into an ironic smile.

"You look like Yuminaga," she said. "Exactly."

Only a few days earlier, his father had told him he looked exactly like his mother; today she was telling him the opposite. He stared at her as if studying his own face in a mirror.

Since when has he looked like this, she wondered. There was almost no expression on his face; or rather, there were two faint ones, anger superimposed over a smile, that seemed to cancel one another. A facial expression was something that was supposed to change as feelings changed, but this boy seems to have decided you can simply layer them one on top of the other. He must be in the grips of some vengeful spirit. The boy's father is incapable of doing or saying anything without his emotions playing a role, she thought, but Kazuki has deposited his feelings in some faraway spot and lives his life watching them from a distance. Is he really thinking that he'll corrupt his own mother with money and get her to do whatever he wants? This didn't seem like a trick Hidetomo put him up to—clearly, something strange had happened. She studied his tense mouth and taught cheeks drawn into an artificial smile, and then smiled back, softly and naturally, as if giving him a lesson. Here was her son, on the verge of drowning, and it was her duty as a mother to throw him the life preserver and pull him in to shore. She felt a slight twinge in her womb and shifted her legs. She had never felt any love for this child, but to save another living being from filth and corruption was the greatest act of virtue. And the power of money could only lead him to corruption and decay.

Since his mother was staring at the money on the table, Kazuki decided that she must be hesitating over whether or not to take it. He looked out the window. Take it, he thought. People who thought money was dirty were the ones who were really hung up about it. Money was neither clean nor dirty; it was more like a magic charm that was passed on from one person to the next.

At last, Miki began to speak, calmly and persuasively, as if showering him with petals from her sacred flowers.

"Please listen carefully," she said. "Your mother earns the money that buys the food she eats. I have no desire for anything beyond that. I make no provision for my old age. When I am old and can no longer work to buy food, I will simply starve to death in this room. Better that than bow to the power of money. Human beings who live by money will die by it. This is the utter fickleness of gold."

To his ears, she was chanting an empty sutra, but the anger that was welling up inside him gradually changed to radio static on a frequency that was jamming hers. Without warning she had launched into this phony sermon, casting her shameful spell. The thing that would actually destroy the human race was not money but the invisible war that had already begun. It was the final battle to determine whether the humans were worth saving and, if they were, whether they would actually survive. The weapon this time was more terrifying than anything in the nuclear arsenal: it was the threat of losing our very reason for existence. Destruction was waiting in the wings, and it didn't need anything as insubstantial as money to make itself manifest. Kazuki was at last understanding that he and his brother and sister had never done anything to drive this woman out of the house, and the realization plunged him into a black rage. His face grew bright red and his breathing became quick and shallow. His eyes glowed with the fury he had felt when she had betrayed and abandoned them back when he was eight. He stood up, slipped on his sneakers, and put his hand on the blind.

"Kazuki."

It was the first time she'd spoken his name since he'd come here. He turned to see her lighting the bundle of bills in the sink. She must have sprinkled them with cooking oil or something, since they caught fire immediately and the flames leaped up, dyeing her face a brilliant red. Crazy fool! he thought. Running back inside without taking off his shoes, he grabbed her by the collar and slapped her hard on the cheek.

Miki grabbed his arm for a moment, but then her hand fell limp at her side. After that, no matter how much he hit her or pulled her hair or slammed her head against the wall, she never cried out or even clenched her teeth, simply rocking her body gently back and forth between his assaults.

I've crossed some invisible line, thought Kazuki. Beating your mother is different than beating your father—he froze, suddenly terrified. "Forgive me," he muttered, his voice like the ashes of the burned bills.

He looked around the hall, feeling a frightening tension and at the same time a kind of exhilaration brought on by the electric noise of the pachinko machines, the CR-Drudge S7, the Junior Circuit S5, and all the others. He suddenly wanted to tell the customers and employees who held the real power in this place. His grandfather had started here in Kogane-chō with Treasure Ball Hall, opening three branches in his lifetime. Then his father had added four more. All he had to do was hold on to the eight existing shops until he inherited at eighteen, and then he would expand into a major chain, opening a new store every year. Running a business wasn't so hard. Vegas alone brought in about three billion yen a year, and he'd heard his father say that for all Group Icarus it was more like twenty billion. But all that really mattered was that income exceeded expenditures. He'd read manuals on how to run a pachinko parlor, and he already had good business sense. Once a month, Sugimoto would do the books, and if one of the shops was underperforming, he'd pinpoint the cause and figure out a way to fix it. He'd have to study more than if he were going to school, he thought, suppressing a feeling of self-satisfaction. His eyes followed Hayashi as he cut through the room.

Hayashi had always been good at straightening the nails on the pachinko machines, and so he'd been with them for more than forty years. Now, he was the general manager of Group Icarus. It had been barely six years since Hidetomo had taken over the actual management of the company. After Hideaki died, Hidetomo had changed the name from Treasure Ball Hall to Vegas and then suggested they remodel and update the whole place. Hayashi had opposed him, saying that pachinko was a neighborhood business and until Kogane-chō itself was updated like Isezaki-chō or Motomachi, there was no point in updating the shop. Hidetomo had ignored him, turning the second floor of the hall into an area designed specifically to attract female customers. He set up display cases filled with brand-name prizes, Tiffany necklaces, Cartier rings, Prada and Gucci bags, Chanel and Dior perfume. But his plan had gone awry, as the new look failed to attract any new female customers and even seemed to drive away some of the old-timers. Less than three months after the experiment began, it became clear that they would have to find a way to bring back the regulars; in the end, they hit upon the idea of increasing the number of double-bonus days and narrowly avoided disaster. In six months' time, Vegas had a reputation as a true original: a modern shop inside and out that nevertheless attracted the crustiest old men to its shiny new machines. Hidetomo took to bragging that profits were up as well, though when you took the cost of the renovations into account, the whole adventure had clearly been a failure.

Hayashi said nothing about this debacle, but when Hidetomo sent the managers of other older branches like Tachikawa and the three shops in Chaya to ask Hayashi about their own plans for renovation, he turned them down. At the managers' meeting last fall, the man who ran their branch at the west exit of Yokohama Station had stood up and boasted about his shop: "'Enjoy!'—that's the keyword; we're offering the customer an environment where he can 'Play and Shop,' our new motto." "Profits," Hayashi had sneered. "The 'keyword' is 'profits.' And in that game you lose to Tachikawa, who always has the highest profit margin."

Hayashi had been right: the transition from Treasure Ball to Vegas had been a failure. But, Kazuki thought, there was still no choice but to update every shop as they moved into the twenty-first century, and with Hayashi around, that was going to be difficult. If he told him he was being transferred to Fukushima or Okayama or some other distant branch, would he go quietly? Hayashi had known him since he was a baby, and that made Kazuki think he just might listen. Still, the younger employees barely nodded at him as they passed, and there was no one he could really talk to.

The other day, he'd gone into the bathroom and found shit all over the bottom of a seat and the toilet lid. He'd grabbed the first employee who walked by and took him into the bathroom. "What's this?" he'd yelled.

"That's not my job," the young man had muttered, turning to go back to the hall.

"Clean it up! Now! I want it to shine," Kazuki screamed.

The young man had wheeled around, as if Kazuki had thrown shit at him from behind, his face white with rage. He grabbed Kazuki by the collar. "What the fuck do you think you're doing? No little shit talks to me like that," he said, trying to force Kazuki's head into the toilet.

He'd grabbed the rim and resisted with all his might, but his forehead had gone under the water. "I'm sorry!" Kazuki screamed. "Forgive me!" He managed to get his hand in his pocket and grab two ten-thousand-yen bills, but when he tried to give them to the man, he'd kneed Kazuki in the stomach.

"Fucking brat! You think you can buy me off with that?" Grabbing the money, he threw it in the toilet and walked out. For a while, Kazuki had just groaned, but when he caught sight of the crumpled bills floating in the water, he reached for the lever.

"You're dead, fucker," he muttered, flushing the toilet.

He'd been looking for the same man today, but he was nowhere to be seen. Hayashi was wandering among the machines, tapping his palm with the hammer he used to adjust nails. Kazuki waved to him, signaling that he wanted to talk, but after bowing back, Hayashi turned to give lengthy instructions to an employee, then laughed loudly at a joke one of the regulars whispered in his ear. As he watched him, Kazuki could feel his anger mounting, until he wanted to grab the hammer from Hayashi's hand and beat him in the face with it.

"You wanted to see me?" Hayashi said, approaching slowly as his eyes darted around the hall, taking in everything but Kazuki's face.

"That guy," Kazuki said. "Did you fire him?"

"I thought it over and decided that for now it would be best to accept his apology and transfer him to the Mita branch. When the time is right, I'll see to it that he's fired."

"Didn't I say I wanted him out right away?"

"There's something known as the Labor Standards Act, and I believe it's Article Twenty where it says that you can't simply fire someone without proper cause. This is something that everyone in the business world struggles with, but the fact is, you can't do things the way we used to." The truth was that Hayashi had no intention of firing the young man who had attacked Kazuki, that he had, in fact, wanted to praise him for a job well done. He would make up some excuse for putting off any final decision until Hidetomo got back from Korea. "If we fire him, he might want to get back at you and there's no telling what he might do. But if you really want me to fire him, I can get him here and do it on the spot."

Kazuki knew somehow that Hayashi was toying with him, but he held his tongue. He lacked resources for a counterattack. These adults were more cunning than he'd imagined, and he suddenly felt hemmed in by the powerful network they seemed to have woven around him. He felt certain, however, that Kanamoto would have been able to take care of something like this with no fuss at all. He would have to hire Kanamoto, he told himself.

"I want to go to the San'yō showroom to look at some new machines," he said, changing the subject.

"But we don't have any plans to buy any additional equipment at this point," Hayashi said.

"I just want to see what they've got," said Kazuki. "If you can't go, I can take someone else with me."

"No, I'd be happy to go."

"My father always says that the machines are the heart of any good parlor. We wouldn't want someone scooping us with the latest stuff, now would we?" said Kazuki, grabbing Hayashi's hammer. His hands suddenly at a loss for something to do, Hayashi pulled at his bolo tie as he eyed his lost hammer. There was no getting around it, the boy was odd. In Hidetomo's case, he had been reluctant to take over the business and never had any real interest in the management until after his father died. As far as Hayashi was concerned, he could hardly wait until Kazuki's enthusiasm for playing pachinko hall owner started to cool.

A woman who worked at the prize counter came up to them.

"Miss Sugimoto would like to see you," she said to Kazuki.

"What does she want?" the boy muttered, walking away.

"Do you suppose I could have that back," Hayashi called after him as if reminding a small child.

"Later on, you can show me the statistics on the returns from each machine," Kazuki shot back over his shoulder, tossing the hammer to the floor as he left.

As he opened the door to the office, a woman turned to look at him. She was perched on the arm of the sofa in a tight, zebra-striped dress.

"This is Yuminaga's kid? He doesn't look a thing like him." Kazuki could feel himself being drawn by the woman's eyes, but he forced himself to look at Sugimoto.

"This is Miss Mai," said Sugimoto. "The boss's . . ." Unable to find the right word, her voice trailed off and she looked at Mai.

"Where is Yuminaga?" Mai asked, lighting a new cigarette and blowing smoke across the room.

"I believe he's in Korea," Kazuki answered.

"He was supposed to leave yesterday . . . with me," she said. "He said he'd pick me up at eight, but he hasn't answered his cell phone since then. Something's wrong, I know it. He's never done anything like this before."

"Perhaps he suddenly felt like going by himself," Kazuki said without looking at her.

"In case you didn't know it, your daddy can't do anything 'by himself.' He can't make a hotel reservation; he's never flown alone; he can't even buy a train ticket." Mai tossed her cigarette on the linoleum and stood to grind it out with her spiked heel. "I can see he hasn't been in touch with you either, but then where is he? Is it a new woman?"

"Absolutely not," said Sugimoto, her eyes fixed on the cigarette butt.

"And how do you know that?" said Mai, coming over to Sugimoto and standing so close she could feel her breath. Dodging around her, Sugimoto crouched down and retrieved the cigarette, depositing it in the ashtray. "Okay, so you're probably right. You know him better than anybody. Then give me your best guess, where do you think he is?" Kazuki wanted to tell her that no matter how many times she asked that question, no one was going to guess, but he knew that the most important thing at the moment was to get rid of this prying woman. He turned to look at her.

"And what is your relationship to my father?" he asked.

"Your daddy and I are friends," she said. "Very close friends." She paused a moment and then burst out laughing.

"You're his lover?" said Kazuki. "Then it seems to me you should just wait for him to call you. Showing up at his office like this can only cause problems." That should drive her off, he thought, glaring at Kawabata, who was pretending to shuffle papers at the desk while eavesdropping on their conversation.

"My, aren't we the fine little man," she laughed. "But you can't wait around forever without doing anything. What if some gang has him tied up somewhere?" She was suddenly serious.

"That seems highly unlikely," Kazuki said.

"If the owner of a big pachinko business goes missing, it's just common sense that he might have been kidnapped by the yakuza," she said. Her eyes were laughing but her lips formed themselves into a pout. Kazuki stared at her as if she were a rare animal. It's probably the first time he's seen a real woman close up, she thought. The conspicuous features: a simple brain and raw sexual attraction. The more willfully she acted, the more attractive she seemed. It occurred to him suddenly that he'd like to see her naked body bound in Saran Wrap, and he realized he was getting an erection.

Mai adjusted herself on the arm of the couch and crossed her legs, satisfied that the boy seemed to be responding to her pheromones. "But I just don't know what to do," she said, making sure he was watching as she wet her cherry-pink lips with the tip of her tongue.

"Why don't we check to see whether he ever got on the plane?" Kawabata put in at this point.

"I've got a list of airlines. I wonder if they'd tell us over the phone." Sugimoto ran back to her desk and produced a memo pad from the drawer. Flipping through the pages, she found the names of airlines Hidetomo had used in the past, JAL, Korean Air, and others, and began calling to ask whether they could check for his name on their passenger lists for the past few days. It soon became clear that the six airlines had some twenty-five flights to Seoul that he might have been on.

"Looks like it could take a while," said Mai. "Let's go get some tea." She walked out of the office without waiting for Kazuki to answer. The moment he was out the door, he was staggered by the screaming heat and the smell of her perfume, but he managed to stumble after her, conscious how pitiful he must look. Mai's hair and skin seemed to glow with a soft light, as if it had drunk in the last of the sun's rays. Suddenly, she seemed to him like a mad dog that was leading him into danger, but just as he was about to turn back, she held out her hand for a taxi. When it stopped, she signaled for him to get in.

As the car pulled away from the curb, she lit a cigarette. "Just keep going this way for a while," she told the driver. "You wouldn't know a place where we could get a drink at this hour? Even a glass of wine would do."

"Hmm." The man thought a moment. "It's nearly five. Hotel bars usually open about now." He sounded only vaguely interested.

"Fine, take us to the Pacific," she said, cutting off the conversation.

They got out at the hotel and Mai went straight to the bar. Glancing at the menu, she ordered whiskey and soda in separate glasses.

"I have to have something," she told Kazuki. "After all, your daddy's disappeared." The waitress brought the whiskey and soda and a tumbler filled with ice. Mai poured the soda into the glass and then added the whiskey on top, watching wide-eyed as the amber liquid filtered slowly to the bottom. Tapping her drink against Kazuki's juice glass, she took a sip, sighed, and drained the rest. "I love summer," she said, "but I also can't stand it." Her face twisted into a frown as she called the waitress. "Another of the same, but make it a double," she said. "Some guys like women who drink and some guys can't stand them. Which are you?" Kazuki looked away, avoiding her earnest expression. He fumbled for an answer, thinking that the only women he had ever seen drunk were whores. Her question was probably some kind of test; it seemed that all adults liked to give tests.

"The ones who don't like us drunk are fuckers," she said, giving away the answer. The whiskey was once more sinking into the soda. "It's just my intuition talking, but I think your papa's been murdered."

Kazuki suddenly thought he heard the low, droning call of the brown cicada. Aburazemi, higurashi, tsukutsukubōshi, minminzemi— he tried to recall all the names he knew for these insects but no more came to mind.

"Does that shock you?" she said. "I have to tell you, I may not be the smartest girl in town, but my intuition's usually pretty good." Kazuki thought that he'd like to ask Mai the name of her perfume so he could buy it for Kyōko to wear when they were together. He slowly admitted to himself that he was attracted to this woman who had just told him that she suspected her missing lover had been murdered and yet seemed on the point of getting up to dance to the Hawaiian music that was drifting into the lounge. As he imagined her in a bikini, dancing the hula on the blood-soaked rug in the basement, he nearly came in his pants. "A lot of strange shit goes down in this world," she continued. "What I said before, about the yakuza—I wasn't serious. I think it was probably one of the people who works for you, Sugimoto or Hayashi. If you see them doing anything suspicious, you let me know. I'll call you, okay?" She took an eyebrow pencil from her purse, scrawled the numbers for her cell and home phones on a coaster, and handed it to Kazuki. "Whenever somebody dies, somebody else gets a new lease on life. You pay attention. If somebody seems different somehow, you've got your killer."

In fact, Mai was far from convinced that Hidetomo had been murdered; she was simply saying the first thing that came into her head, in an effort to forget her fear that his name would show up on one of the passenger lists. She was afraid she couldn't go on living if he'd found another woman. But if he had, she planned to get as much out of him as she could before she let him go. She wouldn't settle for anything less than thirty million. He'd probably claim business was bad and offer her twenty . . .

Kazuki had been trying to guess her age. "How old are you?" he said at last, unable to come up with any estimate. He thought he would believe anything from twenty to thirty-five.

"How old do I look?"

"Twenty-four or five," he said.

"Thanks. I'm twenty-eight," she said, shaving three years off her age. She pinched the soft skin of his cheek and gave it a tug. "Hypothetically speaking, if your papa doesn't come back, what happens to Vegas?"

"I believe I inherit it," Kazuki said.

"But you're just a kid!" she said, her eyes widening and her voice growing louder.

"There's no one in line but me. My mother and my sister aren't interested, and my brother's not well. At any rate, my father intended to hand the business over to me, and in the past year he's been teaching me the ropes."

Mai nodded gravely. She could feel herself settling into a pleasant drunk, her fears suddenly evaporated for the moment. "Well," she said, "if he doesn't come back, we should sit down and have us a long talk about what to do." Grabbing Kazuki's hand, she set it on her thigh and closed her palm over the top. The boy seemed so desperate to save himself from pleasure, she thought, but she would call him tomorrow or the next day and get him to come to her apartment. And if Hidetomo did come back, she could use the boy as an ally. With his help, she might even be able to have herself set up like a real wife. If you could wrap up a man in the sex thing, you could make use of him whenever you needed him. And this one was the sole heir. If they'd had a little more privacy, she might have inched his fingers up under her skirt; but looking once more around the room, she gave up and let go of his sweaty hand.

Hayashi, Sugimoto, and Kawabata were lost in conversation when they walked in the office. As the door opened, all three hopped up, as if snapping to attention.

"He didn't get on any of those flights," Sugimoto said, biting her lips.

"That's what I've been telling you. There's no way he went alone. Am I right, Hayashi-san?" Mai sat triumphantly in the middle of the sofa. "I suppose he might have boarded under an assumed name, but I doubt it. That kind of tricky stuff's beyond him."

Hayashi was reluctant to speak openly in front of Kazuki, but his own opinion was that the next place they should look would be the expensive suites in first-class hotels around Tokyo and Yokohama.

Kazuki wasn't sure why, but he was somehow unhappy to learn that Hayashi and Mai were already acquainted. All these adults seemed to know one another, and he alone was excluded from their private circles. In this case, the link between them was his father—a question of power for both of them. As soon as possible, he would have to get to know more adults and position himself so he could take advantage of his new network. But how and when was he going to announce that he was the new boss of Vegas?

"I think we'll have to report this to the police. Please phone them," said Mai, fishing her cell phone from her bag and holding it out to Hayashi. She's just stupid enough to figure it out, Kazuki thought, his warning censors kicking in as he shifted his gaze to the breasts mounded up under her dress.

"I wonder if they'll take a report on someone whose been missing for less than a week," Hayashi said, looking over at Kawabata.

"Hard to say. If you tell them he's been missing a few days, I doubt there's much chance they'll do anything."

"It's not like one of you going off and not showing up for work. This is your boss; tell them he might have been kidnapped." Mai looked around at them and then winked at Kazuki.

"Who knows," said Hayashi, smiling politely. "He may very well have already shown up at your apartment." Mai glared at him as she punched the number for her condo into the cell phone. When it began to ring, she pressed the phone against his ear.

"Let's give it a couple more days. If we still haven't heard from him, we'll call the police." Handing the phone back to her, Hayashi adjusted his gold-rimmed glasses.

"I don't like it, but I guess there's nothing else we can do," said Mai. Waving to Kazuki, she headed for the door.

"Do you think he's dead?" he asked before she could leave. When she turned around, Mai's face was tense, as if being stretched in every direction at once.

"Don't talk like that. It's bad luck. I'm sure your papa's alive." Without bothering to wipe her tears, she turned and charged down the stairs.

"He's not dead," said Kazuki, looking slowly at the others. Their faces were dumbfounded as they stared at the door where Mai had disappeared.

After getting Sugimoto to copy the past week's balance sheets, Kazuki left the office. Once out in the street, he phoned home and told Kyōko to go ahead with dinner. It had been some time since he'd had a proper meal, but he wasn't sure whether he was gaining weight or losing it. His legs felt so numb and heavy that he wondered whether he should find a taxi, but he pulled himself along through Kogane-chō in the direction of Kannai Station.

He wanted something sweet to drink, iced tea or iced cocoa, but he didn't feel like stopping at a café. He would buy a canned coffee somewhere. He was reluctant to cut through the back alleys of Kogane-chō, not just because he wanted to avoid passing the Golden Pavilion but because he knew it would bring back memories of his childhood. He had an odd feeling that Kogane-chō itself would crumble when Sada died. Or at least the neon signs that bewitched people as they wandered by and the obscene buzz that droned on day and night—those would fade away. Some areas—Fukutomi and Akebono—had already lost their popularity as entertainment districts. Kazuki was surprised at the sluggish movements and gloomy expressions of the people he passed; they looked so odd, he blinked, thinking his eyes must be playing tricks on him. They were probably on their way home but had plans to stop off somewhere to have a drink with friends. But they seemed to be in a daze, beaten down by some irreparable failure, as if the whole street were filled with criminals walking off their crimes in a great pedestrian penance. The people around him began to look almost panicked, and he wondered whether a terrible tragedy had occurred nearby, but there was no sound of sirens, no sign of the accident. Perhaps these were just the faces of people who were convinced that since awful things had happened today and yesterday and the day before that, they would go on happening tomorrow and forever after. Why are they all so depressed? he muttered to himself. But at that moment his eyes met those of a young businessman who seemed on the verge of a nervous breakdown. I probably look just like that, he thought, stepping over the guardrail and waving for a taxi.

He found Kyōko and Kōki watching TV in the living room. "He said we should wait until you got home," Kyōko explained. "It'll only take a minute to heat up." She went off to the kitchen.

"I said to go ahead and eat," Kazuki muttered, feeling a bit embarrassed at having suddenly become the patriarch returning home for dinner. He led Kōki into the dining room and they sat down at the table.

"We went to Queen's East and had fried chicken, so we weren't hungry," Kōki said.

"What have you two been up to?" Kazuki laughed, feeling suddenly cheerful.

"We watched the ships going in and out of the harbor. Then we went to Kentucky Fried Chicken and rode on the train," said Kōki. Kazuki called into the kitchen, being careful not to make Kyōko think he was angry.

"You don't have to take him out more than once a week or so," he said. Kyōko laughed as she stirred the pan.

"The boats go right at each other but they never seem to collide. And they look like they're standing still, but before you know it they've gotten far away. When you take your eye off them for a minute, they disappear altogether. Pretty strange, isn't it? I wonder if I've ever been on a ship?" Kōki seemed to be gazing far off at the distant horizon.

"Pretty soon you'll get to go on a ship and a plane. If you like it, you can go as many times as you want to. Even overseas." Kazuki picked up his spoon and took a bite of the stew that Kyōko had brought to the table.

"Really?" Kōki said, his eyes still lost in the distance.

"Really," said Kazuki, trying to sound sincere. Kōki laughed and picked up his spoon.

Kazuki wolfed down his stew, bread, and salad, feeling rather pleased with their new family of three. Then he pushed his empty plate toward Kyōko for more stew. When they'd finished their dessert of grapes and grapefruit, a satisfied silence descended on the table.

"Kōki," Kazuki said at last, "I've got something to talk over with Kyōko, so would you go to your room and listen to CDs or something."

"I'm sleepy. I'll just go to bed with the music on." Yawning, he disappeared up the stairs.

"What did you want to talk about?" Kyōko asked as she stacked the dishes.

"Nothing in particular," said Kazuki.

"But you just said you had something you wanted to talk over."

"Did I?"

Last night and again this morning, Kyōko had caught Kazuki looking at her like a little boy who has something important to confide to his mother. She sat down directly across from him. For a moment they looked at each other, then glanced away. The moment passed, like the foam in a glass that bubbles up and then vanishes, and they were left in dejected silence.

"Guess I'll head home," Kyōko said, her voice slightly hoarse.

"Why don't you stay over?"

"I don't want to feel like a sleep-in maid, and besides, I can never sleep at other people's houses. If you've got something you want to say . . ."

"I said I didn't."

"Fine, then I'll be going." She slid her chair back from the table and stood.

"But I want you to stay!" he shouted. Noticing the look of utter terror on his face, she sat down again. His whole body was shaking.

"You look like you're coming down with a cold," she said, reaching across the table to feel his forehead. He didn't seem to have a fever. "Have you got anything to take?"

"I'm just a little chilled," he muttered.

"I'll stay until you get settled down," she said, turning off the air conditioner and sitting down next to him. In less than five minutes, the room was filled with hot summer air.

"Are you going to quit school?" she asked at last.

"I already quit."

"But don't you have to go until you've finished middle school? Will they really let you just quit like that?"

"I just don't go," he said, noticing that the trembling had stopped.

"Then what do you do?"

"Actually, I help out running Vegas."

Kyōko had no idea why a kid this age would be interested in the pachinko business. It made her think of a little boy donning a fireman's outfit and dousing the doghouse with a garden hose. When little boys played those kinds of games, it was funny and somehow cute; but she sensed that for Kazuki it was more than this, that there was something dangerous in his game. He didn't seem to care about the money. He could have had anything he wanted, but his clothes and other possessions were pretty much like those of any other middle school kid.

"You want to become a pachinko bigshot?" she said.

"Something like that," he said, feeling his body beginning to relax.

"So you'll be rich?"

"It's not that," he said. "It's more like a game. Life itself is a game. Those video things are for kids; but the boss of a pachinko parlor has all the machines in the world, and the game he plays is business—the most interesting one of all."

Kyōko had never played the video games the boys seemed so obsessed with. One of the high school students who had a part-time job at the café where she'd worked had once shown her a game strategy book called *The Complete Soul-Hackers*. In "Soul-Hackers," he explained, you made deals with the Devil, and sometimes outwitted him, trying to thwart his evil schemes and prevent him from destroying the world. The page the boy showed her was a discussion of a riddle that the Devil posed in the course of the game: "*I was never born, so I can never die! And you? Have you been born?*" There were four possible answers: 1) Of course; 2) I think so; 3) I don't know; 4) No. Yōko chose the second one. "There are many in this world who proudly claim that they have been born," the boy had chanted in a strange drawl. "Your answer is fair enough, but finally meaningless. Still, not to worry . . ." He then went on to explain the attraction of the game. To Kyōko, though, it all sounded like gibberish. The one thing she did understand was that the boys got lost in all the fighting in the hope of getting a taste of victory. She could understand people who loved sports or games like cards or chess where you competed with other people; but what was the point of these role-playing games that were all preprogrammed? And for Kazuki, was playing at being a pachinko boss reality or virtual reality? She had no way of knowing.

"I'm not much interested in games," she said.

"Then what do you like to do?"

"Something worthwhile, I guess."

"Whoa!" he howled. "And what is 'worthwhile.'"

"I don't know. I guess I'm still looking for it," she said, dropping her eyes in embarrassment.

"I doubt you'll ever find it," he said. "But that's the beauty of games: you decide what's worthwhile and what's not; you decide your own values. Of course, values keep changing as the games change. For a while everybody was big on that Christianity game; then it was the Buddhism game. Then they all seemed to quit playing them. But that wasn't because they lost their values; it was sheer boredom. They've all had their run: the Marxist game, the Hitler game. They all go out of style in the end."

Kyōko suddenly lost interest in the conversation. Talk itself was just another game, but no matter how much they rattled on, like a pachinko ball bouncing around among the nails, they would never come up with the right answer. No prize ball would be dropping from the shoot. She knew she wasn't likely to find that one indisputable value, but there must be something out there that would have meaning for her own life. She wanted to have this meaning explained to her, and not by some god but by a human voice. If religions came into being because they were absolutely essential for the human mind, it seemed strange to Kyōko that there were no new words of comfort for people like herself who were born long after almost everyone had lost the religious spirit. What they had instead were games: computer games, money games, almost any kind of game at all. But these games weren't about entertainment or even competition; they were commodities, machines for the consumption of human thought and will.

And now boys were enslaved by these video games, while girls danced like shrine maidens at the altar of something called "youth." For all of them, god was anyone who could satisfy their desires.

"I'm going," she said, disappearing into the maid's room to change her clothes. When she was ready to leave, she went back to the living room, but Kazuki wasn't there. He probably got mad and went to his room, she thought. As she was leaving, she heard a noise coming from the basement. She went down the stairs and knocked on the door.

"Kazuki? I'm going now," she called. There was no answer, but she had the distinct feeling that she could hear him breathing heavily on the other side of the door.

Kazuki had rejected Hayashi's suggestion that they meet at Vegas and go together, preferring to wait for him in front of the police station in Isezaki-chō. He knew that he couldn't stand to be in an enclosed space like a taxi with anyone for even a short time. He could imagine himself gasping for breath, overcome with anxiety. Not that he had a phobia about being with people, but today he was sure that even the least little comment would make him suspicious, set off black thoughts in his head. "Hot, isn't it?" he might ask, and Kazuki would wonder what he meant by such an inane remark; and while he was thinking of something to say in response, he'd become convinced that Hayashi secretly hated him. It was that kind of day.

He paid the fare and stepped out of the cab. There was Hayashi, waving at him like an idiot. He avoided making eye contact and hurried up the stairs to the entrance. The information desk was just inside the door on the left. Hayashi asked for the Public Safety division and the officer told him to take the elevator to the fourth floor. In the Public Safety office they found another policeman.

"Is Satō-san here?" Hayashi asked him. "I'm the one who called about the Yuminaga case."

"Oh, the people from Vegas," said a middle-aged man at another desk. He pulled some papers from a drawer and stood to greet them. He was dressed in street clothes: navy blue pants and an open-neck shirt. He signaled for them to join him at a conference table. "Still haven't heard from him? Is this the son?" He looked at Kazuki, his face a model of policeman's deadpan.

"He's the boss's second son," Hayashi said.

"Okay. Have a seat," the officer said. "So you want to file an official missing persons report on behalf of the company?"

"We've discussed it and decided that we should. That's why we've come today," said Hayashi.

"Where's your mother?" said the officer, looking at Kazuki.

"My parents are separated," he answered.

"I see. Well, Yuminaga-san doesn't seem like someone who'd just disappear, but why don't you run through things for me anyway." He took out a pen and a form for reporting a missing person and looked up at Hayashi. In response to the officer's questions, Hayashi reeled off Hidetomo's name, age, home and business addresses, and telephone number.

"Assuming this is the real thing," drawled the officer, not a trace of interest in his voice, "can you think of any reason he might have disappeared?"

"None whatsoever," said Hayashi. Kazuki hesitated, wondering whether he should tell them that his father was beating his sister, whether he should give them the impression that Hidetomo was so estranged from his family that they wouldn't know whether there were reasons for his disappearance or not. In the end, he just stared at his lap and shook his head.

The fawning tone of Hayashi's voice sickened Kazuki. Why should he be squirming like that when he didn't do anything? He's even sweating like a pig.

"Well then, can you tell me where we could normally expect to find Mr. Yuminaga?" said the officer.

"Actually, he was due to leave for Korea four days ago, but the airlines have no record of his departure," said Hayashi.

"Does he go there often?" the policeman asked, beginning to show some interest. He set down his pen.

"Two or three times a year," Hayashi answered.

"Okay, then. If he was supposed to go to Korea we can check with Legal Affairs to see if he ever left the country." He got up and went over to his desk.

Kazuki noticed that Officer Endō resembled a particularly tight-lipped science teacher at Hōsei. This was the first time he'd been inside a police station, but it was more bright and orderly than he'd imagined. If it weren't for the uniformed officers, it would be virtually indistinguishable from the city hall, where he had been once before. Looking around, Kazuki felt sure that the officer at the police box in Motomachi had been right when he told him that filing a missing persons report didn't always trigger an investigation.

"I don't think he ever left the country," said Hayashi, watching the policeman who was now making a call.

"Then where is he?" said Kazuki.

"I'm not quite sure how to put this, but given the circumstances I believe it's most likely that he met up with a young lady and they're off on a holiday somewhere," said Hayashi. Kazuki sneered inwardly at his conventional line of thought; he would have liked to tell him that in Mai's book Hayashi himself was a suspect. Suddenly remembering that his father had made good on ten million yen worth of poker debts for Hayashi and that he was repaying Hidetomo a bit at a time, Kazuki abruptly changed the subject.

"How's your luck been at poker lately?" he asked.

Hayashi began mumbling excuses, but just then the police officer returned.

"Looks like he never left the country. At any rate, I'll file this," he said, picking up the forms. His voice had taken on an edge. Hayashi and Kazuki had risen as he approached; the officer turned and led them toward the elevator. "I have a feeling he'll turn up in the next day or so. People with a certain social standing like Mr. Yuminaga just don't go missing. If there's still no sign of him after a few weeks, that'll be a different story. But if it's just been a week or so, he's probably off on a trip somewhere."

"And what happens if he's still missing after a month?" Kazuki asked.

"Well, that's hard to say. But I really don't think you have to worry about that just yet. And be sure to let us know if he does show up." He nodded as the elevator door closed.

"I'm sure he's right and we'll hear from your father soon," said Hayashi as they got out on the first floor. His voice was saccharine and low. "I've got a car waiting; can I give you a ride somewhere?" he asked, but Kazuki walked out into the street without looking back and hailed a cab. Flopping down in the seat, he stared at the back of the driver's head.

"Yamate, in front of St. Joseph's," he said.

As they were starting up Jizō Slope, the cell phone in his pocket rang. He answered, thinking it must be Kyōko, but the voice on the other end was Mai's.

Kazuki took the elevator to the eleventh floor. After checking the number, he rang the bell. The door opened almost immediately, as if she had been waiting for him.

"Come in," she said. She was wearing moss-green shorts that might almost have been panties and a pale pink bra. As he settled onto the sofa, Kazuki wondered whether this was some new fashion or just her underwear.

"I'll make us something to drink," she said, disappearing into the back.

The room reeked of perfume. His fear seemed to close in around him, as if he were being buried in hot sand. Mai returned with two glasses and set one down in front of him. "Cheers," she said, tapping her glass against his. She waited until he'd taken a sip. "How do you like it?" she asked, taking a puff on her cigarette.

"It's delicious," he said, guessing that it must be gin mixed with lemon soda.

"I've been doing some research," she said. "Filing a missing persons report doesn't mean a thing. Unless the police determine that a crime has been committed, they won't lift a finger. On the other hand, if he really has been abducted, we would have received ransom demands from the kidnappers."

"There's been nothing like that. The housekeeper's at home all day, and I'm there at night."

"Let me get you another," she said, stubbing out her cigarette in the overflowing ashtray and picking up Kazuki's empty glass. He glanced over at a photograph of his father, arm around Mai's waist, that was sitting on the ledge in front of the window. Then he studied the rest of the room. Sleek, fashionable furniture covered with an assortment of incongruously cheap pink, blue, and orange stuffed animals. Mai came back, glass in hand.

"Your father gives me about a million a month," she said. "He deposits it on the fifteenth, and then my rent, credit cards, phone, gas, everything is paid automatically out of the account. But when I went to the bank to check my balance this morning, there was only fifteen thousand yen left."

Kazuki's eyes were wandering around the room. He felt as though he could see his father's fingerprints everywhere, on the doorknobs, the sideboard, the glasses, the brandy bottle. "I'll deposit a million tomorrow," he said. Mai stared at him, mouth open, but could think of nothing to say. "What's your account number?"

"The other day you said that when your father died you'd inherit Vegas, but what happens to the rest of his estate?" she asked.

"I think I'll be in charge of everything," he said.

So my intuition was right, she thought. This boy could be extremely useful. I'm not sure I quite believe him yet, but we'll see what happens with the million tomorrow. I guess the kids usually do inherit their parents' property, so he probably is entitled to everything. Laughing to herself, she got up from the sofa. Taking Kazuki by the hand, she led him into the bedroom.

"Wait here a moment," she whispered in his ear before wandering back into the living room.

As Kazuki caught sight of the king bed, his body went rigid with fear, but his penis, which had been hard since the moment he walked through her front door, withered to a nub. Before he knew it, Mai was back, setting a fresh cocktail on the bedside table. Pushing him gently onto the bed, she took a sip of her drink and then pressed her lips against his. Whiskey and soda filled his mouth, mixed with her sweet saliva, and he swallowed. She set down the glass. "How old did you say you are?" she murmured, beginning to unbutton his shirt.

"Fourteen," he said, closing his eyes. His voice was a mixture of anxiety and resignation, like a patient answering a nurse's questions in the hospital. Mai slipped her tongue into his mouth and ran it gently over his tongue.

"This is a first—doing it with a fourteen-year-old. Go take a shower, and be sure to get your little asshole nice and clean for me. You never know whose tongue might end up down there. It's the purple door," she said, her voice low and rasping.

Kazuki came almost as soon as he had closed the bathroom door. He glanced at his rapidly shriveling cock as he hurried to wipe up the semen that had sprayed everywhere. He was somewhat afraid that he wouldn't be able to get hard again, but at least this would be better than coming too soon with her. After shampooing his hair, he soaped a washcloth to wash his body. He hesitated a moment and then scrubbed his anus as well. He let the warm water run down his body, rinsed his mouth, and then stepped out of the shower.

As he dried himself and turned toward the sink, he noticed that it was lined with the same kind of toothbrush, hair tonic, and shaving cream that his father used at home. He ran the blow dryer for a few minutes, sprinkled on some of the hair tonic, and combed his fingers through his hair. Finally, he sprayed his chest and buttocks with aftershave.

The overhead lights had been turned off and the room was lit only by the lamp next to the bed. Kazuki had wrapped a towel around his waist. Mai was nude. She lay against the headboard, legs crossed, and sipped her drink. The pale light of the lamp played over her beautiful breasts, the small, pink nipples, her gently rounded abdomen. She looked at him and slowly, without a word, began to spread her legs.

His whole body felt numb and he had no idea what he was supposed to do. Why doesn't she say something? She's trying to make a fool of me . . . I should beat her brains out, he thought, but at that moment she spoke.

"Come over here." As if being drawn into her eyes, Kazuki walked toward the bed. Setting down her glass and pulling the towel from his hips, she wrapped her arms around him. "My, you smell just like your daddy," she giggled; but then she noticed that the penis pressed up against her side was still soft. "I didn't mean it," she corrected herself. "To tell the truth, he smells awful . . . This your first time?" Kazuki shook his head. "Of course not. But I doubt there're too many boys who don't get a hard-on from hugging naked like this." She pushed him back and climbed on top of him. As she arched her back above him, he reached up to take her breasts in his hands. Thinking how much he'd like to crush them, he gave them each a hard squeeze.

"Ouch!" she moaned. "Gently, gently." He bent his neck forward and sucked her nipple into his mouth. Mai shifted her hips and rested her legs on his shoulders, wrapping her thighs around his head. He struggled for a moment but then ran his tongue along her inner thigh and buried it between her legs. Hearing her gasp somewhere over his head, he lapped at her like a dog drinking water. "Oh, lovely! That's soooo nice!" she screamed. The sudden knowledge that he could give a woman pleasure filled Kazuki with a sense of satisfaction and superiority, as though his class rank had just shot up.

She bent over and drew his tongue into her mouth as she guided his hand between her legs. He pushed his fingers in deeper and deeper, matching their motion to her breath, harder, then softer, then harder again. I can do this! he wanted to shout.

At first Mai had been overly conscious of Kazuki's age and she had exaggerated the moans a bit. But gradually, as she thought about the fact that this was Hidetomo's son and that she was teaching a fourteen-year-old boy about sex, she began to get excited. I wouldn't mind giving him a little now and then, she thought. And at a million yen a pop, it wasn't bad work. Once a month would be fine with her— even once a week. She wouldn't care if Hidetomo came barging in about now. She'd be a little afraid, but . . . ah, ah . . . let him. About now . . . he was probably fucking some new little pussy. He could at least have had the decency to call her before he went off. She'd given him her best five years, and he just dumps her when he's through—unbelievable! She thought she had him tied up hand and foot, but the ropes had snapped like so much thread . . . ah, ah . . . good, that's good. Reaching over, she pulled open the drawer of the bedside table and fumbled for a condom. After helping him put it on, she straddled him and lowered herself onto him. Ah, ah . . . good, *very* good! Slowly, she began to grind her hips, feeling him rise up into her. That's it, like that. A little harder, harder. Kazuki's hips bucked for a moment and then were still.

He lay with his eyes closed, listening to the sound of water running in the bathroom. He wondered whether he'd done a better job of pleasing Mai than his father. What if she were standing there in the shower grading them on their performance? The thought made his hands creep up to cover his withered penis. The hot wind of ecstasy that had blown through his body had died away. His desire had been so strong that had she refused him he might have strangled her. But once it was over, it was gone without a trace—like playing pachinko and suddenly realizing you had no balls left. If it were only a matter of coming, you could always masturbate. But this had been infinitely better than jerking off. He'd been with her—the woman he'd wanted from the moment he'd seen her at Vegas. But then it was over—and if desire were something that simply switched off once it was satisfied, then it wasn't really worth anything. Maybe it was more like food that got turned into flesh and blood. Maybe sex became a kind of energy that was stored up in the body and brain. If not, why would people get so worked up about it? But if that were the case, then why did he feel so wiped out now?

After sex with Hidetomo, Mai would always bring a damp towel back to bed and wipe his penis. As she did this now for Kazuki, she thought how cute he looked, all spent and limp. Older men always jumped out of bed as soon as they were done and smoked a cigarette or started fooling with the TV remote, but this boy was just lying there, soaking up the last drops of pleasure. She slipped in beside him and pulled the sheet up to her waist.

"How was it?" she asked. Kazuki said nothing. "Want to do it again?"

No, he thought, not bothering to open his eyes, this time he wanted to do it with Kyōko. He hadn't had sex with her before because he'd been afraid he couldn't do it. Now he knew he could . . . But what would he do if he had this same empty feeling afterward?

"Could you let me have some condoms?" he asked out of nowhere, surprised at the words coming from his own mouth. "I'll pay you for them."

"To use with who? Are you dumping me already?" She fell back, her body shaking with shrill laughter.

"I'm out of here," he said, sitting up.

"No, no," she sputtered, stifling her giggles. "I'll give them to you. As many as you want. Two boxes enough?" Grabbing his shoulder, she swung her body on top of his and wrapped her thighs around his penis. Instantly, the switch was thrown and the adrenaline began to flow. Kazuki sucked a nipple into his mouth and Mai moaned. "Again? You want to do it? Again?" Kazuki was moaning with her.

"I want to do it every day."

"Not every day," she laughed, pulling away from him. Kazuki, her breast still in his mouth, bared his teeth.

"Ouch!" she cried, cradling his head and pulling it off. "How about once a week?"

"I'll call if I feel like it," he said.

"But when your daddy comes back, it's over."

"He's not coming back."

The blank look in his eyes made her shudder and she pulled away. "Time to get up," she laughed, slapping his pale buttocks and reaching for her cigarette on the nightstand. "What did you mean, he's not coming back?"

"I didn't say that. I'm sure he'll be home soon." He grabbed the cigarette from her and took a deep drag.

"If I took up with you, how much would you give me?" she asked, her irritation suddenly showing.

"The same as my father gives you now," he said.

Is this kid crazy? What sort of middle school student can come up with a million a month? And didn't he just say that his father wasn't coming home?

"So do you have your father's cash card? And his bank book?" she asked. He smiled as he picked up her glass and took a sip of her drink. Mai closed her hand around his penis and began to move it slowly. When it started to get hard, she bent over and held her face close to him. "Tell me. If you do, I'll suck you. You want me to, don't you?" She stroked the end of his penis with her tongue. "Tell me!" she chirped before taking him deep into her throat.

"I've got the key to his vault," Kazuki moaned, his body writhing.

That was it! Hidetomo was always boasting that he had socked away money here and there to hide it from the tax collectors. He probably had one of his stashes right in the house, and the kid had found it and even had the key. She let Kazuki's penis slide from her mouth. If the million shows up tomorrow, I'll ask him straight out, she decided.

"And I think you know where your daddy is, too. And maybe you've already killed him . . ."

Kazuki jumped up and danced naked on the bed. "And maybe I've already killed him!" he called, his voice rasping along with the springs.

"How long ago was it? More than twenty years now, it must have been.

Just down there they had this woman, buck naked, up on a barrel. The guy she was married to was always trying to rent her out, forty thousand yen for the week. It was interesting around here back then. Remember, Gramps?" The old man laughed feebly. One of the few people who had been born and raised in Kogane-chō, he owned a shop in Hatsune-chō that was an odd cross between a drugstore and a convenience store.

"Your place is open all night. Do you really think you should drink so much?" his companion asked.

"My son and his wife run it now, so I don't really have to show up."

"So you've retired in leisure, have you? Lucky you!" The other man poured some more beer into his glass.

"Not me! Retirement these days is a joke . . . Well, want to go sing karaoke?" he said, standing to leave. He pulled out his wallet and settled the bill.

As Kanamoto watched the two duck under the curtain, he pictured the shop where the old man's son and daughter-in-law waited wordlessly for customers. He in his horn-rimmed glasses, she with her dagger eyes and wounded look. He waved his empty glass.

"Looks like this is becoming a bar, too," he said.

"But we only serve sake to you," said Sada. "Chihiro!"

Chihiro came out with a large bottle cradled in both arms and poured a glass for Kanamoto.

"Could I get some ramen, too?" he asked.

"Sorry. We've shut down the stove for the night." Sada poured some shōchū from his private bottle into a glass, thinned it with tea from the kettle, and settled into a chair.

From the moment the staff at Vegas had told him that Yuminaga was missing, he'd been convinced that Kazuki had killed him. He had no reason to think so, but all day, like a horsefly buzzing around his head, a voice had been droning: killed him . . . he killed him.

"Have you heard that Yuminaga's disappeared?"

"No, hadn't heard anything about it," Sada lied. Kanamoto wrenched the sake bottle from Chihiro's arms and set it on the counter.

"He took my bottle," she complained, though her voice was tinged with laughter.

"Seems he just vanished," Kanamoto said.

"Was he in some kind of trouble?" Sada asked, lighting a cigarette.

"None that I knew of." For a moment the droning stopped and it was very quiet inside his head, but then the blood and sake began buzzing again. "Suppose a kid you knew very well had killed his father. What would you do?" Kanamoto asked.

"Nothing, What would you do?" said Sada. "Go to bed," he told Chihiro who was eating pork ramen at the counter. She snatched a slice of pork in her fingers, stuffed it in her mouth, and padded up the stairs.

Kanamoto was unable to quiet his foreboding. It hadn't bothered him for almost thirty years, this trapped feeling that was less one of terror than despair. But when he had suffered from it, he had usually been able to wash it away with sake. Like a hangover, it would linger for a while, but if he was willing to put up with the loneliness and emptiness for a few days, finally he would forget it. He'd always thought of it as a train ride: if he just sat quietly, rocked along by weariness and resignation, he would eventually reach the end of the line. "No hope," he muttered, but he had no idea why he, a relative stranger to all of them, should feel so hopeless. He tried to rouse his brain, rusted from disuse, to ponder his own despair. After graduating from middle school, Kanamoto had become a longshoreman on the Yokohama docks. Eventually, he got involved in the enforcement business, going to work for the financial branch of a gang that controlled the waterfront. He became a bill collector, and by his own estimate there had been at least three people who had been driven to suicide by his more forceful techniques. But he'd never been particularly bothered by the work or felt particularly guilty about it. Two of his business acquaintances had been sent to prison for murder, and one of his own staff members had stabbed and killed the woman he was living with. Still, the crime he suspected Kazuki had committed was fundamentally different from these, and he was sure that until the boy's conscience began to torture him, until he became terrified of his own act and broke down crying, he would never be able to escape from his nightmare.

"When one of your boys kills somebody, what do you do?" Sada asked, his eyes fixed on Kanamoto.

"We usually suggest they turn themselves in."

"What if we tried that with Kazuki," said the old man.

People who turned themselves in were either suffering from a guilty conscience that trumped their fear of punishment or they were hoping for a lighter sentence for being cooperative. If either applied in Kazuki's case, he would have come forward a long time ago, thought Kanamoto. What if he went to the boy and urged him to confess but he refused to admit that a murder had even been committed? He could never bring himself to turn the boy in. For that matter, even if he wanted to, without a body for proof, he doubted the police would pay much attention. Kanamoto realized that he couldn't make a very strong case to Kazuki for giving himself up.

"Tell me," he said, "what would you tell a kid these days who didn't understand why he shouldn't kill?"

"I'd just say that kids shouldn't kill," said Sada. "Do you need a reason?"

"Then is it okay for adults to commit murder?" Kanamoto asked.

"Adults know they shouldn't do it, but someone will always wind up murdering someone else. But it's wrong for kids to kill." Still, if Kazuki came to him and admitted that he'd killed his father, Kanamoto wanted to be able to explain to him clearly why it was wrong.

"But why?" he said. Shaking his throbbing head, he looked up at Sada like a dog that had just been beaten.

"If life isn't sacred, then nothing else is. If people are going to live together, you've got to begin with that one rule: Thou shalt not kill. If you don't start there, then everything else falls apart, like the ribs of a fan when the linchpin is broken. But then there are always exceptions, like war. Once you're in a war, you can't be talking about life being sacred. And once you've made one exception, there will always be others—the country, the emperor, other things worth killing for. I forget where I heard it, but they say that if the emperor kills someone, it isn't even considered a crime. Did you know that?"

"No, but how could that be true?" said Kanamoto.

"I suppose because he's even more important than a president."

"Almost like a god, I guess."

"Almost."

This was more confusing still. The emperor was supposed to be a human being, but he was permitted to kill, while murder was forbidden to everyone else. Then how could you explain the idea of sin? Kanamoto tried to picture the white-haired man—about his same age—who could kill whenever he wanted.

"But you know, kids need logical explanations. Without that, I doubt we'd convince him," said Kanamoto.

"If you could explain, do you think he'd agree?"

"He killed his father!" Kanamoto cried. The fan blew through the Golden Pavilion like a sudden squall, and the two men were quiet for a while, as if the wind had blown the spirit out of them.

"Do you have any proof he did it?" Sada asked, apparently hoping to discourage Kanamoto.

"No." The sake he was pouring into his glass ran over and spilled on the counter. "Still, I know he did. But what can we do? We could tell him to turn himself in, but if he still says he didn't do it, there's not much we can do. Hey! Are you listening?" A fly was buzzing around the old man's head as he appeared to nod off. "This whole thing scares me. The world seems to have changed and I don't know why I'm hanging on." The fly stopped on the rim of his glass. When he brushed it away, it flew off to land on the wall or the fluorescent light. It was back a moment later, however, flitting from bald head to sweaty neck and rubbing its legs together as if to mock them. "At any rate, I don't see how we can help him."

"Did you know he sent over an altar for Shige," Sada said.

"Kazuki?"

"It's upstairs. I have no idea what he was thinking. Maybe he was drunk . . . You want to stay here tonight?"

"No, I'm going," said Kanamoto. As was his custom, he estimated the bill and left the money on the counter before ducking under the curtain. So, what did it mean to feel guilty? He stumbled out into the main street, tugged at his zipper, and began to piss. A car screeched to a halt in the street and a man rolled down the window. "Hey, asshole," he yelled, poking his head out, but when Kanamoto began walking toward him, penis in hand, he quickly rolled up the window and sped away. But what should he do? When he saw a story on the news about children killing someone, he had the odd feeling that he'd done it himself. But this time it was worse . . . it was Kazuki.

He zipped up his pants and began walking. When he heard that an adult had starved to death, it didn't affect him one way or another. But when he heard about a child starving to death, he felt sickened and lost his appetite for the rest of the day. Why? He staggered to a halt and cocked his head, catching sight of the hazy crescent moon out of the corner of his eye. The new moon always made him feel calm; the full moon made him feel lucky. Hearing that a child had killed someone made him feel . . . Some guy once told him that if a butterfly flapped its wings in New York, it would cause a typhoon in Japan. So if a kid killed somebody, perhaps the moon would fall from the sky. He suddenly realized that he was lying facedown in the street, and he was overcome with the desire to simply fall asleep. And why shouldn't he? What was wrong with sleeping in the street? Shit! If he was going to sleep, he'd better do it by the river. You just couldn't go around killing people. If you didn't understand that, you were better off dead. But why? Why? Children . . . they're our past, and at the same time our future. No one knows what's going to happen in the future, but everybody wants to know, wants to predict the future. That's what makes kids so reassuring—you can see the future in them, see what it'll be like once you're gone.

The moon wove its way between the clouds, its light shining on Kanamoto's drunken form.

Why did you think the old man and I have looked out for you all this time? Sada's not got much longer to live; why shouldn't he look to you for some kind of comfort? He just wants to have someone to look back at when he's crossed the river into hell—and what's so wrong about that? You may think he's being selfish, but that's the way it is when you get old. That's the way he's lived his life. He just wants to hold on to this one little shred of hope . . . As he caught sight of the Ōoka River, he lost consciousness.

"Do you want to get a drink?" Sugimoto called, stopping Hayashi.

"After we close?" he said, looking around skeptically. "It's past eleven now." Hayashi had left the office and was heading for the hall.

"Why wait?" she said. "Seems like you're always leaving during business hours. Were you here at all yesterday? I looked for you."

"That's odd. I was here."

Hayashi was older than Sugimoto and had been at Vegas longer, but at some point she had developed a closer relationship with Hidetomo. Though he knew that they'd been lovers soon after Sugimoto joined the company, Hayashi was fairly sure that there was nothing between them now. She was supposedly his accountant, but most of the actual bookkeeping was contracted out to a big accounting firm. Sugimoto was Hidetomo's partner in the tax evasion scheme, and everyone knew that she had her hands on the purse strings, so Hayashi was somewhat in awe of her. She had even handled the payoff of his gambling debts, for which he had been forced to bow and scrape to her. And never once, in all this time, had they had a drink together. So why was she inviting him now? She must be up to something. But the only thing she ever thought about was money, he chuckled to himself, so whatever she was planning, he would probably be able to get in on the action.

"Was there something you wanted to talk about?" he asked.

"I did want to ask your advice about something," she said, her forty-something cheeks tightening into a smile. "Shall we go in back?" she said, pointing toward Hidetomo's office.

"I see," he said. "Fine. I'll just finish up in the hall and join you in a moment." He bowed and walked out the door. She probably wanted to talk about Hidetomo's disappearance. But he doubted she would call him aside like this if she just wanted to air a theory about where he could have gone. During the first week, he'd thought that Hidetomo was probably just holed up with a new woman in a hotel somewhere, but that was seeming unlikely now. At this point, Hayashi was inclined to suspect the boss's lover, Mai. After that big fuss she made in the office, she'd called once to say she wanted to know the minute they heard from him—and then nothing. There was something decidedly odd about her behavior. Hayashi's current theory was that Hidetomo had wandered in while Mai was in bed with another man and had been murdered; then they'd buried his body in the mountains or somewhere. The theory was so crude that he'd refrained from mentioning it to anybody, but it occurred to him now that most murders were pretty crude. Still, just as you couldn't play poker if you were missing a card, any theory was just so many words in the face of the boss's absence. Since there hadn't been any kind of ransom note or phone call, the one thing that was certain was that it wasn't a kidnapping—at least not one that was meant to turn a profit.

But whether he was just missing or actually dead, the fact of his absence remained, and that meant their immediate problem was the future of Vegas. Though he may have been incompetent as a manager and shameless as a man, oddly enough, when Hidetomo was gone the life went out of the hall, and the noise and clamor itself echoed like a hollow lament. But the truth was that the missing card was not Hidetomo himself but someone to play the role of president. If they just had a joker who could fill in, Vegas could go on running without a hitch. It annoyed him that no one had come up with this simple solution. It would have to be discussed at the branch managers' meeting that would take place in five days. But there was no one in Group Icarus who was in a position to take over as acting president. The successor to the presidency was already decided, but there was no way they could have a middle school boy run the company. Then by process of elimination, it fell to him as general manager. Still, he could hardly nominate himself, and he doubted anyone would do it for him at the managers' meeting.

Hayashi, who had worked for nearly forty years as a glorified nail straightener in this little fiefdom of Kogane-chō, was aware that he lacked the wits to cut a deal with the other managers. He tried to convince himself that he should simply seize control now, but he could only muster the enthusiasm for a moment or two and then it faded. He had been passive for so long that his ambition had been reduced to a few smoldering embers that refused to catch fire.

Sugimoto was also worried about who would become acting president. She felt strongly that the only course was to pick someone as soon as possible and get on with business. Hidetomo had been fond of talking about his plans to reform and modernize Group Icarus, but the fact was he had absolutely no intention of doing so, and the business remained a privately held one-man operation.

She had taken the whiskey from the cabinet and was waiting for Hayashi with ice and glasses. He had spent about twenty minutes in the hall; when he entered the office, she offered him the boss's chair.

"Not there," he said.

"Don't be silly," she said, nearly forcing him to sit down. The smile that she had reserved for Hidetomo was now directed at Hayashi as she poured his whiskey. "Cheers," she said, flicking the rim of his glass with her fingernail.

Why should she be wearing more makeup today? I'd better find out what she's plotting, he thought as he raised his drink. And what, exactly, are we toasting?

"Needless to say, I want to talk about the boss's disappearance. What do you think's going on?" She had taken a can of ginger ale from the refrigerator and was pouring it in her own glass. "Oh, shall we order some sushi?" She was following the usual pattern when Hidetomo used this room.

"Someone would get wind of it," Hayashi said.

"Okay, then we'll just have a chat with our drinks," she conceded. "But what do you think happened?"

"I think he's been murdered and they've buried him somewhere, though it's probably not my place to say so."

"No, not at all. I want us to be able to speak frankly. And besides, that's the only logical explanation . . . I'm not much of a drinker, but I might have just a drop," she giggled, pouring a thin stream of whiskey into a glass of ice and mineral water. "And what do you think will become of Vegas?" she asked, the smile suddenly fading from her lips.

"Now that's a good question," Hayashi said. "Usually, when something like this happens, the wife or another relative would take over, but we've got a designated heir and he's still in middle school."

"Is he in the hall now?" Sugimoto asked.

"No, I haven't seen him yet today," said Hayashi. An image of Kazuki's face came to them almost simultaneously, and with it a deflated feeling. He had put in an appearance at Vegas nearly every day since Hidetomo had disappeared, giving cockeyed orders or chewing out the employees. In fact, there was nothing new in that, except that now it was clear that he felt he was running the place. His manner of speaking had grown more arrogant, and he'd taken to making comments on employee performance and the selection of prizes. When you tried to brush him off, he flew into a rage and became abusive. Of course, he was upset at his father's disappearance, but there was something almost humorous about the way he paced the hall, as if possessed. For Hayashi and Sugimoto, he was nothing but an obstacle to the smooth running of the business. Still, whatever he did, it was little more than a child's game, and they both thought it silly that a boy of middle school age would choose to interfere in the operations of a pachinko parlor.

"We need to decide who should become acting president at the branch managers' meeting," she said.

Feeling the effects of the whiskey, he tried to look solemn, as if he were already the company director confronting the pressing issue of succession. If she'd agree to nominate me, no one could oppose us.

And didn't she seem to be hinting she would? His spirits soared.

"Yes, I suppose so," he said, trying to restrain himself until he was sure of her intentions.

"I think it would be best if you'd agree to do it," she said, getting right to the point.

"I wonder if I'm qualified to fill in for the boss," he said, laughing tensely as he sat back in his chair.

"Don't be silly," she said. "You've been around longer than anyone else and there's nothing you don't know about pachinko. Or would you rather it was left to someone like Ōishi from the Tachikawa shop?"

"Not him!" he said.

"You see? There's no one else who can do it. You've been head clerk ever since the Treasure Ball days—it's your turn now!"

Sugimoto didn't think Hayashi had any real management ability. After all, he was just the nail straightener. He may have the title of general manager for Group Icarus, but he ran his own hall in the most outdated style, just managing to get by because it was in Kogane-chō and the original shop. Still, he had to take good care of Vegas, given that Hidetomo was paying him seven hundred thousand yen a month in salary, plus a bonus of five months' pay. Beyond that, there was cash, paid under the table, that amounted to more than two million a year. But he'd made the mistake of buying a condominium during the peak of the bubble years, paying 120 million; and though the value had since fallen to 70 million, he would still be paying the mortgage for the next thirty years. But under the circumstances, it hardly mattered whether he was capable or not; there was no one else to do it.

"I guess you could say the boss and I were joined at the hip, and there's not much I don't know about the place. But I'm getting old and the whole thing sounds like too much trouble. Why don't you do it yourself, Miss Sugimoto? You've really been his right-hand man."

"That would never work. But how about this? You and I could form a management team; I'll run the office and you manage the hall. We'll keep things running smoothly and wait for the boss to come back. It's the best possible plan. What do you think?" She smiled at him, satisfied that the conversation had proceeded exactly along the lines she'd hoped.

"Sounds like the right idea to me. Isn't much else we can do if we want to keep Vegas going." He realized he was playing right into her hands, but there was nothing else he could do. It would have been impossible for him to seize control by himself; he would need her help to succeed.

"Fine! It's decided then. You can announce it at the meeting," she said.

"I wonder if that's such a good idea," he said. "I'd rather you did it."

"Really? Well, then I'll have to be at the meeting too." She'd managed to get him to agree to her plan, but she was still exasperated by his lack of backbone. She licked her lips, suppressing the desire to scold him, and made him another drink, stronger this time.

"We have to figure out what to pay ourselves as acting presidents," she said. "How about an extra million a month each? Or perhaps you should get a million two. That sounds about right. Plus a suitable bonus, say five million every six months. At that rate, you could pay back your loans in no time."

Hayashi rubbed the stubble on his jaw. She isn't planning to take over, he thought, she's going to eat the place whole. He wasn't quite ready to accept that just because Hidetomo had gone missing they could suddenly do as they pleased with Vegas. Still, it seemed clear that if he teamed up with Sugimoto he could get his hands on some real money. After all, she's always had the key to the company vault.

"Well, all I know is that we've got to do our best for Vegas. I'll leave the matter of compensation up to you," he said. As they sat discussing their strategy for the managers' meeting, the door suddenly opened without a knock and Kazuki came striding in. Hayashi hopped up frantically and stood mumbling unintelligibly in the face of the boy's enraged look.

"What are you doing?" he demanded, charging toward them. "Who said you could drink in here? And during business hours! Get out of the way!" Hayashi scurried away from the table as Kazuki approached and stood at attention, waiting for the right moment to make his escape. "You think this is some kind of bar?" Kazuki bellowed, turning on Sugimoto. "What's with the hostess routine? Tell me!" Irritated, Sugimoto stared across the room. He sounds exactly like his father, she marveled. "Just because the boss isn't here, you think you can do whatever you want? You think you can get sloshed in his office during business hours? Is that what you're telling me, Hayashi?" He slammed his fist on the table.

"I'm afraid I have work to do," said Sugimoto. "You'll have to excuse me."

"You're not excused!" Kazuki screamed. "We're not done. Tell me what you were doing in here!"

"Now wait a minute," said Sugimoto. "I think it's disgusting how you're treating Hayashi-san. Didn't anybody ever teach you to respect your elders? I've held my tongue for a long while now, but I'm through. From now on, you keep out of the hall and the office. This is a business, and we have jobs to do. You wanted to know what we were doing here? Our jobs, that's what! We were discussing how to keep Vegas going!" Her indignation poured over Kazuki, and for a moment he just stared at her, astonished. She was probably flushed from drinking, he thought, but even so, he felt as though he was seeing how ugly and sinister she looked for the first time.

"What did you say?" he managed at last.

"I said that this is a business, and not a place for a kid to hang out."

"And when did you become king and get to order me around?" he said. "You really think you can do that? Who do you think you are?" His anger made his head hurt, and he found it difficult to raise his voice.

Thinking that it would be better to get things settled immediately, Sugimoto told Kazuki about their decision to run Group Icarus as a managing council. While she was speaking, Kazuki sat quietly, looking utterly passive, but this had the effect of unsettling Sugimoto and Hayashi, who glanced at one another anxiously, waiting for his outburst. Finally, his eyes moved from one to the other with a look of utter contempt. "Idiots," he hissed. "You two as president? And who do you think will buy that? You can't just decide something like that for yourselves? Hayashi, you think you're really up to the job?"

"Given the current emergency, we plan to get approval at the managers' meeting." Why do I let him make a fool of me? Hayashi wondered. This is the last time, he promised himself.

"Like I said, you're an idiot. Group Icarus is a joint stock company. Do you even know how a joint stock company picks a president?"

Hayashi's face froze in the same thin smile that it had when Hidetomo was badgering him. He had no idea what a joint stock company was; in his head, there was only the Treasure Ball Hall that he had built with this boy's grandfather. Vegas wasn't a company—it was a pachinko parlor.

"How about you, Sugimoto?" Kazuki said.

"You're talking about big corporations," she said. "That's just a formality for Icarus."

"A joint stock company's a joint stock company. Big or small. And the Yuminaga family owns 100 percent of the stock in this company. The stockholders pick the president—that's just common sense, which neither of you seem to have. On top of that, my father has already publicly announced that I'm to succeed him. Or hadn't you heard?"

"We have," said Sugimoto, her voice trembling. "But do you really plan to take over now?"

"You are just in middle school," Hayashi squawked, clinging desperately to his hope of big money.

"What if I am? Are you trying to say that dumb shits like you are qualified to be president and I'm not?" Kazuki leaped up and swept their drinks off the table. Grabbing the whiskey bottle, he smashed it against the wall. "The two of you as president? Don't make me laugh!

As of today, this is my office, and you're not to come in here without permission. Now Sugimoto, get this cleaned up, on the double. And when you're done, get rid of all the alcohol in here. Hayashi, at the next managers' meeting I want you to explain that I've taken over as acting president. Understood?"

No matter how much abuse Hidetomo had heaped on him, Hayashi had always laughed inwardly and let it roll off, but he couldn't put up with this. No, it would be wrong to buckle under to this boy. He was suddenly furious.

"Who the fuck cares how you run a joint stock company. This is a pachinko parlor. It's not some fancy business, so cut the crap! . . ." He was so exasperated he could hardly speak, and his voice trailed off into guttural moan.

"You're nothing but a green-assed brat . . . ," he managed to add, almost breaking down. "Why should we work for a little shit like you? If you're going to be president, I quit." Damn, he thought, as soon as he'd said it, but he repeated himself. "You hear me? I quit." His voice sounded lifeless but he had made his point.

"If you want to quit, go ahead," said Kazuki. "But first pay back the money you owe us. How much is it now?"

"I've worked her for the last thirty-eight years, since your grandfather and I started Treasure Ball. I have about thirty million in severance pay coming when I leave. Even after paying off what I owe, it would still be a fair amount."

"I'll think about your severance pay. But I've never heard of anyone in this business getting anything like that much. Have you, Sugimoto?" Kazuki could hardly conceal his delight at being relieved of the difficulty of having to fire Hayashi on his own.

"If Hayashi-san leaves, I'm leaving, too," Sugimoto said flatly.

Caught off-guard by this new threat, Kazuki could feel his stomach sink. What would he do if both of them left at once? Even if he could find someone to replace Hayashi, he knew that he would never be able to figure out the books.

"If Hayashi-san and I and all the other managers quit, do you think you can just run this all by yourself? What would happen if everyone went on strike at once?"

"How could they?" said Kazuki, getting to his feet nervously.

"Everybody's worried, with the boss gone. If Hayashi-san and I told them to, they'd strike. We've been here every day for twenty years or more, since long before you were born. You're living on another planet if you think a middle school kid can walk in and take over as president. If you think you can get around adults that easily, you've got a lot to learn." As she watched Kazuki hover above his chair, his eyes wandering around the room, she was sure she'd won. He's probably not eating right, she thought. No matter how tall he's gotten, he's really just a child, one who hasn't had much love from his parents. It's a shame to have to take him on like this. Now that she'd gained the upper hand, she almost felt sorry for him.

Kazuki could not come up with a way to counter Sugimoto's attack. Could they really organize a strike? If so, it would spell disaster. He had no idea what the losses might be, but the fear of ruin eddied around in his head.

"We understand that Group Icarus belongs to the Yuminaga family, but we want you to recognize us as acting presidents. In exchange, we'll go on depositing the president's salary to his account, seven million a month. Agreed?"

Die, bitch! The words bubbled up in his head, but he left them unsaid, allowing his anger and hatred to sink into his heart. And then, suddenly, a life preserver was tossed in the water right in front of him. I'll call him, he thought. Why didn't I think of it sooner?

"You go on home now," she said, as if shooing him out. "We don't want you cutting your hand, so we'll forget about cleaning up this time. But don't come around here busting things up again. You'll make me angry next time."

"You think I don't have anybody to back me up, but I do," Kazuki said, his voice sounding hoarse.

"And who would that be?" Sugimoto asked, her tone almost cheerful as she gathered up the broken glass.

"I'll bring him tomorrow," said Kazuki. "But if you apologize now, I'll forget the whole thing."

"Bring who?" said Hayashi, his lips curling in disdain, though he was racking his brain trying to imagine who the boy could mean. It's probably just a bluff; he knew almost everything about the Yuminagas' affairs, but he couldn't think of anyone who would come to their aid at a time like this.

"It's someone you know. Think it over; I promise you we'll take care of you tomorrow." His sudden idea had eased his fear, and he left the room feeling only slightly uneasy.

Hayashi and Sugimoto looked at one another.

"Who?" she said.

"My guess is, he's bluffing. There's no one—unless he means Miki-san."

"Miki?"

"His mother. She and the boss are separated. I don't think they ever divorced—you must have met her." Sugimoto recalled Hidetomo's wife, a scrawny, nervous woman with a tormented look on her face who pronounced each brittle word like twigs snapping off a branch.

"That could be trouble," she said, "if the wife shows up."

"Never happen. She left him because she hates anything having to do with money. She was brainwashed by some cult, and the last time she was here she made a huge scene, screaming how the whole place had to be torn down or her older son would never be cured. I think she even showed up at the ward hall at one point, trying to get them to change the name Kogane-chō—didn't like it because it uses the character for 'gold.'" Hayashi seemed almost uninterested now, lazily scratching the stubble on his face.

"Then we should be fine," said Sugimoto. "How about it, Hayashi-san? Partners?"

"I'd rather jump off the Bay Bridge than get pushed around by a brat like that," he laughed.

Kazuki tried calling Kanamoto on his cell phone, but no one answered. He's the only adult I can depend on, he thought, his hands gripping the phone so tightly that his knuckles turned white. He wasn't about to let dirty scum like Hayashi and Sugimoto take over, and while he didn't know whether Kanamoto would help him or not, there wasn't anyone else he could turn to. On his way home in a taxi, he continued to dial, but Kanamoto was out.

A note from Kyōko on the dining room table told him to heat up something in the kitchen. He wondered whether Kōki was asleep as he sat down and rested his head on his hands. He could not let them seize power, but the threat of a strike still bothered him. A low moan escaped his lips and he rubbed his eyes. Thinking it might feel good to get high, he considered calling Miho to ask if she could get some speed. She'd probably hop in a cab and come running over, but he knew that afterward he'd feel like shit. And he'd have shown weakness in front of his sister. Giving up on the idea, he got a cola from the refrigerator and whiskey from the sideboard and made himself a drink. Those two were stupid, but he'd learned that adults were calculating and had to be taken seriously. What was it adults had that he didn't? The reason he'd been forced to retreat when she threatened him was that she had more knowledge and experience when it came to managing the business. So all he had to do was fire her and hire somebody with even more experience. That was simple; but what about the problem of the strike? What could he do about that? Again, knowledge was the key. If he could find someone who knew all about joint stock companies and strikes, he was sure he could tell him what to do. He ground his teeth as he thought through his problems.

At some point he would have to take the university entrance exams and go off to college; but could someone who had quit school even take those exams? Who cares? He would be a self-taught man. Once he'd settled this current problem, he'd study at least three hours a day. But what should he study in order to run the business or handle something like a strike? He knew that law and economics would be useful, but the fact that he had absolutely no idea where to begin or how to go about studying these things made him feel furious and helpless at the same time. He staggered upstairs.

Every computer game he had ever played had a strategy book to go with it, and since the world itself was a big game, it followed that the key must be out their somewhere. He pulled the dictionary from his bookshelf and looked up "joint stock," "shareholder," and "strike," but he didn't see anything that looked like a clue to solving his current dilemma. Telling himself that he shouldn't sleep until he'd come up with some sort of plan, he punched at the cell phone again. This time, Kanamoto answered.

"I'd like to see you tomorrow morning."

"Tomorrow morning?"

"There's something I need to ask you about. In a hurry."

"Fine. Shall I come around to the house?"

"Yes. Is ten o'clock too early?"

"Ten is fine. I'll be there."

Kazuki put the phone down by his pillow and set the alarm for nine-thirty. After changing into his pajamas, he collapsed on the bed.

As he walked up the stairs, the gold characters for Group Icarus glowed on the frosted glass door, but the room beyond was dark. The door was slightly ajar and he could hear a voice inside. Pressing his back against the wall, he approached cautiously until he was able to catch the obscene tone of the voice but not what was being said. Slowly, however, he began to hear words and then phrases. The boss has been murdered—that was Hayashi. We need to tell the police—this time it was Sugimoto. Then it faded into a muddle again. He peeked in through the crack to see Sugimoto, Hayashi, and Kawabata sitting cross-legged on the linoleum around a large, flickering candle. They seemed to be practicing black magic, putting a curse on someone. How could he have killed his own father? said Sugimoto's oily voice. Kawabata started to say something, but then Sugimoto's laugh echoed through the room. Just as Kazuki brought his face closer to the door, Hayashi lit a cigarette in the flame of the candle and turned to look at him. He blew a cloud of smoke into the air where it hung above them. The phone rang. Without taking his eyes off Kazuki, Hayashi jerked his chin toward the phone where it lay on the linoleum. He's telling me to answer it. But why should I? Answering phones in the office is your job! he wanted to scream, but the words died in his throat. He'd have to use sign language. His left hand was numb and wouldn't move, so he used his right to manipulate his tongue. Hayashi gestured once more toward the phone, which was still ringing. Kazuki braced himself and glared at the receiver, certain he mustn't pick it up, that it was the detective calling. As Hayashi lit another cigarette in the candle, the phone stopped ringing. Sugimoto had used too much mascara on her eyelashes, and though she blinked them desperately, trying to keep an eye on Kazuki, she could see nothing through her fluttering eyelids. Kawabata, who had been watching him quietly all along, squinted and then stood to come nearer. At this point, Kazuki ran down the stairs and into Vegas.

The hall was pitch black. There were no customers, no employees, just rows of pachinko machines, flashing red, blue, and green. He had to hide before Kawabata caught up with him, but as he hurried up the aisle, the floor seemed to suck at the soles of his shoes like wet sand, and when he turned to look back, he saw that he was leaving tracks. At this rate, they were bound to find him. He would have to turn around after each step and wipe away the footprint. But who could have spread sand in the hall? He finally reached the rest rooms and pushed open the door of the women's room, but the employee he had attacked—the one Hayashi had said he would transfer to the Mita branch—was sitting on lid of the toilet.

What the hell is he doing here? As he turned to run away, he caught him by the neck. A yellow spot flickered before his eyes and he went limp, nearly losing consciousness. The grip on his neck loosened, and at that instant he spun around and planted his elbow in the ribs of his attacker. The man groaned as he clutched his chest, but Kazuki instantly grabbed the collar of his uniform and slammed his head into the wall, kneeing him in the stomach for good measure. The man staggered back, protecting his face with both hands as a woman might do; but the hinges on the door gave way, and as he fell, his hands flew up and Kazuki could see that it was—Kyōko. Her face had been grafted onto the man's body. She reached her out toward him, gripping his elbow and pulling him into her arms. Burying her face in his neck, she whispered something, but when he looked up to ask what she'd said, her head was raised as well and a faint sound escaped from her lips. She might have been panting, or laughing, but then the lips parted invitingly and Kazuki pressed his mouth against hers.

Now only their lips were touching, but she plunged her tongue into his mouth and his went into hers, each filling the empty space of the other. Their mouths seemed to become one as they sucked each other's tongues, until at last, needing to breathe, Kazuki pulled his lips away and opened his eyes. The smiling face looking back at him somewhat quizzically was Kyōko's for just an instant before it changed back into the face of the employee who should have been in Mita, though he now looked a bit like a squashed Noh mask. He raised his arm, and Kazuki closed his eyes, anticipating the blow. He shuddered, waiting . . . but no blow came. Cautiously, he opened his eyes, but the man was gone.

Kazuki spread his arms and flapped them, and his body rose gently into the air. He discovered he could fly down the rows of gaudy, flashing pachinko machines at incredible speed, just like in a science fiction movie, but as he turned a corner, he suddenly found Kōki and Chihiro, standing naked in front of him. There was a baby in Kōki's arms, but when he looked more closely, he realized it was actually a miniature dachshund. As he stood staring at the dog, it seemed to decompose before his eyes, the flesh dripping down between Kōki's arms. As it melted away, bones appeared, and then teeth. It's dead, he thought, carefully edging a bit closer, it must be dead if it's rotting like that. But as he bent down to look at the dog, its eyes looked up at him. Clear, black eyes—that reminded him of someone, though he couldn't think who. The eyes were full of pain, but the dog was alive. Perhaps it could be saved if they got it to a veterinarian. But when he reached out to take it from Kōki, his fingers sank deep into the dog's back. Rain. It seemed as if he had been walking in the rain for a long while, but also that the rain itself had just started. The road was filling with water, as if he were walking in a shallow river. He could see headlights approaching through the rain, but he couldn't raise his hand since he was holding the dog. The taxi went speeding by, spraying his pants—and then suddenly he froze, caught in the beam of a searchlight. The raindrops pelted him, shining now like sharp needles in the light, boring countless tiny holes in what remained of the dog's flesh. The last shreds of skin sloughed away, revealing the ribs; and within, the pink, pulsing heart. A sob escaped Kazuki's lips. It's over, he thought. Even if he could get him to a doctor, the most he could do would be to help him die peacefully. He wanted to fling the dog away and curl up in a ball, but he forced himself to keep walking. Die, die, die, he murmured, as he trudged down the road, unsure now where he was going. The noise from the cars faded and even the sound of the rain died away as the street fell silent. A strong wind was blowing but it made no sound. Headlights were approaching, and seeing a cab's "For Hire" light, he walked out into the middle of the street.

There was a squeal of brakes and Kazuki opened his eyes to find himself standing outside Kōki's room. When he looked down, he saw that the dog was still in his arms. The door opened silently, and he could see that the room was strung in a dense web of thread. He stepped in, but the thread immediately coiled around the dog's neck. He tried to brush it off, but it dug deeper into the flesh. The dog looked up at him with clear, peaceful eyes—eyes beyond pain, filled with resignation and forgiveness. At the moment those eyes met Kazuki's, the head nodded over, tearing away from the body, and the two halves of the dog fell at his feet.

When he peered in through the knots of thread, he could see Kōki and Chihiro, still naked, working to put together a crib. He tried to call out to them, to tell them that it was a dog, not a baby, and that its head had already come off, but his voice made no sound. And then the scene was swept away in a jumble of colors and shapes, as if he'd boarded an amusement park ride.

When the dizziness and shaking finally subsided, he found himself back in Vegas. The walls and ceiling seemed to be contracting, like the lining of an ulcerated stomach, and blood was leaking in places, dyeing the whole hall red. Though there were still no customers, the flippers on every machine were working at full speed and balls were pouring onto the floor. Kazuki pounded on one machine after another and then went running around frantically changing overflowing ball boxes, holding his hands over the chutes to stanch the flood. But the deluge continued, as the balls flowed down the aisle in the direction of the prize counter; and in each ball was a tiny reflection of Kazuki's face. He began to laugh. A muttering chuckle at first, but as he laughed, violence and darkness filled the hall along with great echoing peals of laughter. "I won! I won!" he screamed. His mouth was thrown open so wide he felt it might rip apart, but he couldn't close it. "I won! I won!" A fissure opened in the ceiling and an avalanche of balls poured down. Kazuki crouched down, arms above his head. He wanted to run away, but the path was blocked by the torrent of balls falling on his head, his hands, his back and arms. The pain was unbearable, as if he were being stoned, and then suddenly a cheer went up all around him and a new streams of balls poured from the ceiling, aiming right at him.

But then the hand he had cupped over his head for protection was covered by someone's palm. The hand felt warm and smooth, and he tried to hold on to it, but when he looked up, it was the same man. He seemed to be dissolving now, blood dripping from the tips of his fingers like drops from a melting icicle, his eyes flowing out of their sockets. His mouth opened wide and rice poured out—but not rice . . . maggots. Kazuki struggled to get away, but, buried waist-deep in pachinko balls, he only sank farther into the morass like a beetle writhing in sand. The hand that the man extended toward him closed into a fist. He'll kill me, Kazuki thought, closing his eyes.

When he opened his them, he was in the basement. It was a dream, he thought. Wiping his sweaty palms on his pajamas, he pulled open the drawer under the display case that held the swords. As he did, a shower of light broke over him, ghastly and golden, and he froze like a deer caught in headlights. The rays of light swirled around him, forcing their way between his lips. Once in his body, the light became a chilly liquid that slithered down his throat, piercing him like prickly thorns. Soon it had transformed into shreds of gold, but as he waited for it to float to the surface, it suddenly metamorphosed once again, this time into a huge moth that went flying around the room, landing gently on top of the underground vault. Kazuki crept up on the moth from behind, raised his foot, and stomped down on it. The sound of a soft body being crushed, and then the moth flew up in a wild arc. He stepped on it again, and a yellow liquid oozed from the abdomen. Picking it up gingerly by the wing, he held it in his hand and examined it before closing his fingers and crushing it. As he opened his palm a fine film of gold leaf fluttered to the floor. Countless solid-gold moths. No matter how long it took, he would kill them all, he thought, laughing hollowly. He straightened himself and a determined look appeared on his face as he crushed the moth nearest him; but as he opened his hand again, the moth flew away unharmed. When he opened his mouth in shock, the moth flew in and a scorching pain ran down his throat. The gold faded and an uncanny blackness engulfed him.

There was a terrible crunching sound, a gnashing of teeth. Kazuki opened his eyes. This wasn't the basement, it was his own room. He'd been dreaming. Reaching for the remote by his bed, he turned on the TV and turned up the volume. A woman in an apron was sprinkling a flowerpot of herbs with a small watering can. The time was superimposed in the upper left-hand corner of the screen: 5:26. Morning already. The garden show gave way to a commercial for instant ramen, followed by another for a stew mix. The same shitty commercials as always. He was sure he was no longer dreaming—he was awake now and watching TV. He wasn't crazy. No one was here. He was sane—but no matter how many times he told himself so, his heart continued to pound. He pressed the Rolex on his wrist to his ear, trying to match the regular ticking of the watch to his heartbeat, but his heart kept getting ahead. He had to calm down, he thought, reaching for a cigarette and his lighter. He watched intently as the first puff of smoke crept up the wall above him like a hungry ghost. The thought occurred to him that the man might appear in the smoke . . . but no, it was just smoke. It was just a dream. But if he had dreams like that too often, he really would go crazy, he thought, stripping off the sweat-soaked top of his pajamas and closing his hand around the golden dog tag that lay stuck to his chest. His mouth was still tingling, as if he'd been laughing in the dream, or sobbing, or both, and his head nodded over, as though he might fall back into the abyss of sleep. He was weary and he wanted to curl up and rest, but he knew he couldn't. There were too many things he had to do, way too many. He climbed out of bed, spread open his notebook for Japanese class, which hadn't been touched in months, and began making a list of things he needed to take care of. Impossible, he concluded almost immediately; he could never do all this alone. He would have to get someone to help, he thought, feeling as though his brain were shriveling up into nothing. The phone! That was the answer! With a phone, you could call anyone, anywhere in the world. He grabbed the cell phone on his desk and punched at the buttons.

"Hello! Hello! Hello! Hello!" The quiet sound of gold could be heard coming from the phone's tiny speaker. It was a dissonant sound, born of greed and beauty, the unbearable noise of silence. Fear attacked him once again and his heart began to race. He had to gather all the gold in the world and sink it to the bottom of the ocean. A sound wormed its way into his ears, the sound, it seemed, of his mind snapping. A gurgling sound, as when the pipes backed up, the sound of gold as it sinks down through water, passing among the sea creatures on its way to the bottom, settling at last in a cloud of murky sand. And there it would sleep forever, in the deepest sea where no light on earth could reach it.

In the first, brilliant light of day, the morning news was blaring from the TV. Kazuki was sure now he was finally awake, but his limp head refused to rise off the pillow. Only his right hand responded to his brain, so he had it fumble around for the remote that turned on the air conditioner. He felt a sudden chill and heard a sound like an airplane making a low pass. The air conditioner shouldn't sound like that, but he had no idea whether it was broken, or his ears were, or perhaps even his brain. He was frightened. He sensed that if he fell from the edge of sanity into the pit of unconsciousness, he would never come out again.

Sitting gingerly up in bed, he swung his legs over the side. He went to the window, opened it, and stuck his head out. As he did, someone reached around him and grabbed the windowsill; but when he turned to look, there was no one. He had pushed himself from behind. Do you want to jump? It's only the second floor, so you'd probably just sprain a leg. It's grassy down there. It would barely hurt—might as well forget it. But if you dived head first, you might break your neck. He stood bending out the window like a person trying to escape a fire, his teeth clenched to keep back the cry for help.

By the time he got downstairs, Kyōko had already made breakfast. He remembered that Kanamoto was coming, but when he checked his watch he found that it was still before nine o'clock.

"Good morning," Kyōko said.

"Ah," sighed Kazuki, his voice like steam rising from a pot. He went to the sink and washed his face. Drying off with a towel, he looked in the mirror . . . but the face was that of someone still wandering in a nightmare. Bloodshot eyes peered out from a pale, swollen, haunted face.

"Coffee," he said as he sat down at the table, making an effort to sound cheerful.

"I think there's instant," said Kyōko, taking a pan off the burner and replacing it with the teakettle.

"Someday I want to buy a little house where we can live together, just the two of us. A house that looks like a boat."

"Weren't you talking about a house with six sides where we could all live together?" Kyōko asked.

"Which would be better?" he said, sniffing the coffee. It had a mournful smell, like walking through fallen leaves. He reached for the cup Kyōko had set on the table. "And don't say that they'd both be fine. I hate that. I want to get away from everything, to be better somehow." After he'd eaten, Kazuki went down to the basement. Kōki arranged his collection of CDs in his room while Kyōko started to run the vacuum cleaner.

As he got closer to the house, Kanamoto found himself wondering where Yuminaga's body could be hidden. Dust had collected on the windshield of the imported car that stood unused in the driveway, and the lawn was overgrown and choked with weeds.

The door opened almost as soon as he'd rung. Kyōko laid out some slippers for him and led him into the living room without a word.

"Thanks for coming," Kazuki said, the impatience evident in his voice. "What would you like to drink?"

"Barley tea, or black tea, whichever," said Kanamoto, sitting on the couch.

"Her name's Kyōko," Kazuki explained. "You may not remember, but we once had a man named Yasuda working at the hall. He took care of me for a while. She's his daughter. She's a friend, but she helps out with the house." He rushed through this explanation as Kyōko retreated to the kitchen.

Kanamoto passed the well-wrapped golf club and a brown envelope to Kazuki before speaking.

"The change from Miss Miho's hospital bill and a receipt are in the envelope. But what was it you wanted to talk about?"

Kazuki told Kanamoto that Hayashi and Sugimoto had threatened to organize a strike if he didn't accept them as acting president and ordered him to stay out of the hall and the office.

"What should I do?" he asked when he'd finished, feeling almost happy that he sounded so pitiful.

"What do you want to do?" Kanamoto answered.

"I want to protect the business until my father comes home. I've got a responsibility. So I want to make it clear to them that I'm standing in as president."

"And you think you could handle being president?" Kanamoto could see that Hayashi and Sugimoto were up to something, but he wasn't sure he wanted to intervene on Kazuki's behalf.

"Since last spring, I've been learning all about the management of Vegas—my father wanted me to. I think I can do it, and I know I've got to try," said Kazuki.

Kanamoto watched the boy, as he stood there on his crumbling tower, with an uncomfortable mixture of loathing and pity. He had probably killed his father for no better reason than his desire for money and power. Kanamoto remembered a puppet play he'd seen as a child about the murder of a king. On the whole, the play had been rather boring, but one scene had made a strong impression: the snow-covered set at the moment the king had died had suddenly transformed into a blizzard of cherry blossoms. Kyōko set a glass of oolong tea in front of him, interrupting his memory.

"I suppose a copy of the certificate of incorporation for the company is somewhere in the office," he said to Kazuki. "But we could have a look at it if we went down to the courthouse. I think it might be better if I made a few calls instead, but it's a bit involved. Could I use a phone somewhere quiet." Kazuki led him to Miho's room.

"Who is he?" Kyōko asked when Kazuki came back to the living room.

"He's yakuza," he said. "But he's a great guy. He's one of the few real adults I know. Whenever I've got a problem, I call him."

"Is something wrong at Vegas?" she asked.

"Nothing we can't handle. I've got to go look for the incorporation papers," he said, standing up and stretching, as if chasing away his fears.

Kazuki remembered that when he'd hidden the bills and the gold bullion in the drawer under the sword case, he'd had to move some papers to the closet to make room. He went back to them now and sorted through them one by one. They were stock certificates, bonds, and other kinds of securities he didn't understand—probably more valuable than the gold, he thought. He'd have to look at them more carefully when he had time.

Kanamoto found Kyōko seated at the piano when he entered the living room.

"I used to play with you when you were a little girl," he said, smiling and sitting on the sofa. "You and Kazuki."

"Really?" she said. She had no memory of him or those days.

"You were only five or six. It's more than ten years ago now . . . Where is Kōki?" he asked.

"Whenever there's something important to talk over, he goes to his room to listen to music."

"You know," he said. "I think about Kōki-san when something's bothering me. It always helps calm me down. He's had so much pain in his life. I suppose it's wrong of me, but it helps."

"Could you tell me your phone number?" Kyōko suddenly asked. He looked at her skeptically but he took a notebook from his pocket, tore off a sheet, and wrote down the number.

"Is there something you'd like to talk about?" he asked, handing her the paper. She shook her head, folding the paper. Hearing Kazuki coming back, she stood.

"I found it," he said. "Is this what you meant?" He passed the document to Kanamoto.

"This is it," he said, glancing at the paper as he got to his feet. "Shall we go?"

When they arrived at the office, Kazuki led Kanamoto to the back room and pressed the intercom to call Hayashi and Sugimoto. At the sight of Kanamoto standing behind the boy, Hayashi seemed ready to turn and run. Sugimoto had never actually met him, but she knew of him from the Treasure Ball years when he had solved a number of problems as an unofficial "friend of the company." In particular, she remembered Hidetomo telling her how useful he'd been in getting a rival company to change its mind about plans to move in on Treasure Ball territory.

"You've heard of me, I think," Kanamoto said, breaking the silence. They nodded. "And are the two of you really planning to take over as acting president?"

"No, no, not at all," Hayashi said. "We were simply trying to think what to do in the boss's absence. Isn't that right, Sugimoto-san?"

"There are a number of pressing matters that somebody has to deal with," said Sugimoto.

"I'm sure that's true. But don't you think it would be better to consult with Kazuki as you make these decisions? This business belongs to the Yuminagas, not to you two. No matter how long Yuminaga is missing, that doesn't give you the right to take over and do as you please . . . And which one of you told Kazuki that he was no longer welcome here?"

"That's another matter altogether," said Sugimoto, sounding like a witness summoned to court. "It has to do with a little incident we had. Kazuki beat a dog to death with a golf club and then threw a whiskey bottle. This is an office, you know."

"If it is, then what were you doing with dogs and whiskey here? Perhaps the boy simply thought they didn't belong." Kanamoto turned to look at Kazuki.

"They were drinking during business hours," Kazuki put in, amazed at how easily Kanamoto could twist their words.

"We were simply concerned for the welfare of the company," said Sugimoto, her face beginning to look more and more like a Kogane-chō whore. "Can I ask then, are you proposing that Kazuki-san serve as acting president?"

"And would you have some objection?" Kanamoto asked, looking at her with a hint of sympathy in his eyes.

"You're in middle school!" she wailed, turning on Kazuki, her face growing bright red. "Where on earth do they let schoolboys be company presidents? Tell me! Where does that happen? Don't talk nonsense. You plan to use the boy to grab control," she said, looking now at Kanamoto. "But we won't let you!"

"He may be in middle school, but he's also director of Group Icarus. I don't know where you fit in the pecking order, but it's safe to say you're somewhere under him. According to commercial statute, the director represents the company and manages business operations. Kazuki has been director of Group Icarus since he was in elementary school." He studied the dumbstruck expressions on their faces for a moment and then went over to the bookshelf, took down a volume on commercial law, and threw it on the table. "Check for yourself. Article 254 of the Commercial Code specifies which classes of people are disqualified from becoming directors, and there's not a word there about a minimum age. So it's only natural that Kazuki-san should become acting president, and it's legal as well. Any questions?" Hayashi and Sugimoto sat motionless, staring at the cover of the book. "The only questionable thing is your telling the company's director that he can't come to his own office. And another thing—threatening a strike unless you're made president is not only a form of blackmail, in some courts it would be taken as a criminal breach of your official trust as officers of the company."

"That was the farthest thing from our minds," said Hayashi. "We were prepared to do whatever it took to help the company, up to and including resigning. We're willing to sacrifice everything for Vegas— how can that be a breach of trust? That's going too far." He was watching

Kanamoto, wondering when he should play what he considered to be his trump card: the threat of quitting Vegas.

"If you really want to help the company, then you shouldn't be talking about quitting. This is the darkest hour for Vegas, and you need to decide whether or not you're willing to cooperate with Kazuki-san to save it."

In the end, Kanamoto got them to agree to support Kazuki in exchange for three hundred thousand yen a month each in additional compensation. Then he chased them out before they could launch into what promised to be long justifications for everything they'd done. But when Kazuki said there was one more important matter he wanted to discuss, Kanamoto rose to go, saying he had an appointment and it would have to wait for another time.

"After this, you'll have to manage on your own," he said. "I don't want you to think you can rely on me to solve all your problems." With that, he turned and left the office.

Out on the sidewalk, he found himself staring back in at Vegas. With only those two to help him, he thought, he wouldn't last long. He listened to the electronic din, like the echo in a badly eroded cave, surprised once again at how naturally these seemingly incongruous lines of men and women in front of the pachinko machines blended into the cityscape. He turned and walked toward Hinode-chō Station.

The late-summer sun was fading quickly, as if anxious to be done with the day. But the last rays of light lingered on the surface of the Ōoka River, buoyed up by the dark water beneath. Kazuki stared at the flickering sunlight, like leaves bobbing on the surface of the river. From time to time he looked up at Kōki, who was waiting on a bench in a small park, listening to his Walkman. When Kazuki had called his mother the night before, saying he wanted her to meet them in the restaurant of the New Grand Hotel in Yokohama, Miki had refused. But when he proposed meeting on the Shirogane Bridge instead, she had agreed instantly: five o'clock at the end of the bridge. It would probably have been better to meet at Chōja Bridge, which was closer to Hinode Station, but Kazuki harbored a faint hope that the view of the park from Shirogane might bring out her maternal instincts and help him convince her to come home.

Now she was fifteen minutes late, and he was sure she had stood them up. But just as he was turning to go back to the park, feeling anxious and angry, Miki appeared, crossing Sakae Bridge. She marched up to him on her wiry legs, hostility and wariness showing on her face.

"Where's Kōki?" she demanded. The white lace girl's parasol she carried had the odd effect of emphasizing the blotches and wrinkles on her face. Kazuki pointed toward the bench in the park across the way. His brother, glowing orange in the late-afternoon sun, seemed about to float up and blow away.

"Shall we go get something to eat?" Kazuki suggested, falling in step next to her as she set off toward the park.

"I'm not hungry," she said, hurrying ahead of him and into the park. Kōki made no move to embrace her as she came up to him, barely glancing her way before turning his rapt gaze toward the sky. Having missed the chance to speak to him, she lowered herself quietly onto the bench.

"If you're not hungry, then maybe we could at least go get something cold to drink," Kazuki said.

"What an awful smell," Miki said, grimacing. One bench away, a homeless man lay on his back, using an old leather bag as a pillow. A black cat was stretched out on his stomach, fluttering its eyes in time to the man's snoring. From time to time its tail would brush against the man's thigh, but he went on sleeping, oblivious to the cat.

"So let's go somewhere," said Kazuki. "It's too hot here."

"No, we're fine here," she said, taking a handkerchief from her bag and wiping her forehead and neck.

"But it stinks, like you said, and it's hot!"

"What's the matter?" Kōki said, surprised at Kazuki's sudden show of anger. He stood, removing his earphones.

"Nothing," said Miki, returning the handkerchief to her bag and smiling.

"It's been a long time," Kōki said, leaning against his mother's shoulder and rubbing his cheek against hers.

"You seem well," she said, turning away from him to fold the parasol.

"You look worn out," Kōki said, pushing his face back close to hers.

"I'm just getting older," she said, opening the parasol again.

"I'm getting married, Mama!" he cried. Miki put her hands over her ears. "I'll tell you the name of the person I'm going to marry. It's Chihiro." Shielding her face from Kōki with the parasol, she looked up at Kazuki.

"Who is he talking about?" she said. "Chihiro?"

"She's a friend," he said.

"You can't be serious," she said. "They're getting married?"

"What's her other name, Kazuki?" Kōki asked, hopping up on the bench and peering over the top of the parasol.

"I don't know," he said.

"Liar!" Kōki shouted.

"Well, maybe Grandpa Sada adopted her, so I guess it's 'Nakada.' But I'm not really sure."

"Nakada! That's it, Mama! It's Chihiro Nakada." Kōki sat down on the bench, giggling. He held his breath for a moment and then burst out laughing again.

"Kōki can't get married," Miki said. "Do you understand? And there's nothing good about marriage anyway. So you mustn't think about it or even mention it. Understand?"

"But didn't you get married?" Kōki asked, his mouth contracting into a pout.

"But I didn't like it at all. That's why I quit being married. You remember, dear. Mama got divorced."

"But you had me and Kazuki and Miho," he said, smiling at her benevolently. Miki glanced over at the cat perched on the vagrant's stomach. It would have been better if I hadn't, she thought. The one thing she really regretted in her life was that she had given birth to this unfortunate lump. And Kōki aside, the other two were likely to continue the line, to give birth to yet more miserable children sometime in the future. No matter how much she herself sought the faith, there was no wiping out the sins of the Yuminagas. For all eternity, their blood would never know the kind of peace that had been granted even this beggar sleeping here beside them.

"You must never have children," she said, "That is hell." The words slipped out before she knew what she was saying.

"Would it have been better if you hadn't had me?" Kōki asked, his voice trembling, thin, and high.

"No, of course not," Miki sputtered. She wanted desperately to talk about something else, but, unable to hit upon a topic, she simply began to slowly close the parasol.

"Well, I'm going to marry Chihiro and she'll have my babies," Kōki announced.

"No! I'm telling you, you mustn't!" She was sorry the moment she'd said it. Perhaps she was the crazy one?—screaming at the absurd wishes of a child.

"But why shouldn't he get married?" Kazuki shouted. "You have no right to tell him anything! You should apologize!" Kōki pressed his palms over his ears as Kazuki grew more agitated. The black cat jumped down from the man's stomach, stretched its front legs, and walked away. The man sat up almost immediately and looked around. Catching sight of the cat heading for a drinking fountain, the man pulled a packet of dried sardines from his leather bag and hurried after the animal trilling "Here Blackie! Here Blackie!"

Why did people keep cats? Kazuki wondered idly. Even this man who had given up his job, his house, and his family still had this pet. But maybe a pet wasn't such a bad idea after all—they could get a dog and a cat. It would liven up the house, and it would make Kōki happy.

"I'm sorry. Mama was wrong. Kōki, I'm awfully tired; I think I'd better be going home."

"Don't work yourself to death," Kōki said.

"Why don't you come to the house to rest before you go?" said Kazuki, trying to make his voice sound gentle. "He's not home."

"Why? Where is he?"

"In Korea, I think," Kazuki replied, stealing a look at Kōki's face.

"Still?" she said. "But it doesn't matter, I can't set foot in that house."

"Papa . . . is . . . miss . . . ing . . . and . . . won't . . . be . . . com . . . ing . . . back," Kōki intoned, watching Kazuki's face.

"What does he mean?" Miki demanded.

"We haven't heard from him since he left for Korea," Kazuki replied without hesitation.

"Mama's been missing too," said Kōki, resting his hand on her shoulder. "I think it's time for her to come home."

"Missing? How can Yuminaga be missing? What's going on?" She set the parasol, still open, on the bench and looked doubtfully at Kazuki.

"Don't ask me," said Kazuki.

The vagrant came back with the cat, lay down on his bench, and began to feed the animal the dried sardines.

"That house is possessed by evil spirits," Miki muttered, looking down at her lap.

"That may be," said Kazuki, trying to dismiss the subject, "but I wanted to see you today because I have a favor to ask. While he's gone, I need to take over as president of the company, but I wanted to get your approval."

"Please, Kazuki, don't do it!" she cried. "I promise not to criticize anymore, but please don't do that. You mustn't go to that evil place, you mustn't allow yourself to be polluted by those evil balls."

"But I have to," he said, in a tone knotted with bitterness.

"No!" she screamed, her voice like a slap in the face.

"Fine! Then how are we supposed to live? I have to do it, for Kōki and Miho. You don't have to do anything—just tell anyone who asks that I'm the president for the time being. That's all. You may not know it, but the rest of us have to obey something known as laws."

"Those are the laws of this world," she said. "The true law comes from somewhere far beyond this world. You must try not to worry. We all dwell in the palm of the Buddha's hand."

"But what'll happen to Kōki?" Kazuki said.

"Ah, but that's just the point. You'll go on looking after him for as long as you both live. If you ever abandoned him, it would be the end of you. He is your one virtuous deed, and you'll never leave him. Do you understand?" She stood, turned to face Kōki, and pressed her palms together in prayer. Then, as he waved and smiled at her, she picked up the parasol and turned again, as if breaking the bonds that tied them. She walked away, though her steps now were slow and faltering.

They heard a scream. As they left the park, they could see someone leaning out over the railing on Ōta Bridge. As they got closer, Kazuki realized that it was the same woman he'd seen several weeks earlier yelling for someone to return her bag. She was saying something now, too, but he couldn't make out the words.

"She's saying that 'if you think something without acting on it, it's the same as never thinking it,'" Kōki said. "And that 'only the wind can dance in the sky, but those who fail to understand are truly hateful.'"

"Let's go home," Kazuki said, grabbing his brother's arm and steering him away from the bridge.

"She says it's all in the stroller."

Give me back my diary! My diary! Give it back!

The woman suddenly screamed. The setting sun dyed the surface of the river a dull orange.

"She wants a diary, Kazuki. Buy her one or she'll jump."

"Even if we bought her one, it wouldn't help," he said. "She wants her own back."

"Hey!" Kōki called, turning toward the woman, "it's gone! You'll have to write it again!" The woman grasped the railing and crouched down. Her mouth opened but only a dribble of foam emerge. "I think she's crying, Kazuki. I want to help her."

"She needs an ambulance," Kazuki said. "I'm sure someone will show up soon. Let's go home." But Kōki continued to stare at the woman, who was curled now in a tight ball.

Kazuki and Kanamoto were walking along the canal that met the river at the Band Hotel. From the way he had handled things with Sugimoto and Hayashi, Kanamoto had made it clear that he could take care of problems neatly and quickly. Kazuki knew that he would be unable to run Vegas without his help, so he had phoned to ask if they could meet once more. When Kanamoto had suggested getting together at his house, Kazuki had no reason to refuse.

Pleasure boats were tied up in the Shin-Yamashita Canal like cars in a parking lot, and the street was lined with a mixture of apartment buildings and old warehouses, a few of which had been converted into clubs or bars. Fifteen years ago, Kanamoto had used all his savings to buy a small warehouse, and now he lived on the remodeled second floor. The first floor still functioned as a warehouse, filled with goods of some sort that a friend had asked him to store. The living quarters above were simple, consisting of a cavernous space with little more than a floor, an exterior staircase, and a washroom added. There was no bath and no kitchen. The furnishings consisted of a bed, a small table, and a chair. Beyond that, the only other objects in the room were a telephone and a refrigerator.

Kazuki had imagined that Kanamoto would live in a traditional Japanese house or an old-style apartment, so he was surprised to find a place that reminded him of the lofts he had seen in American movies. "Nice!" he said. "I wouldn't mind a place like this."

"Can I get you something to drink?" Kanamoto asked, going over to the refrigerator. Kazuki shook his head, and Kanamoto took a glass and a bottle of gin from the top of the refrigerator. "Have a seat—but I'm afraid it will have to be on the floor," he said.

"Do you have a bath?" Kazuki asked, folding his legs under him and leaning against the wall.

"No. I go to a sauna two or three times a week," he said, pouring some gin in the glass.

"Have you ever been married? Or had kids?"

"No, neither," said Kanamoto.

"But aren't you lonely here by yourself?"

"Well, I suppose not. I haven't led what you could call a regular life, and it's a little late to start worrying about whether I'm lonely or not. I am pretty sure that I'm better off without a family. Even if I had married, I don't think I'd have had any idea how to treat a wife or kids. I'd probably have beat the kids and run around on my wife. I suppose if you want to get married, you have to be prepared to live a regular life." He suddenly stopped talking and drained his glass, laughing at himself for pontificating about something he knew nothing about.

Kazuki was excited at the prospect of the first true man-to-man talk he'd ever had; and he was sure that no matter what he wanted to ask about, Kanamoto would give him an honest answer.

"And what is a 'regular life'?" he asked.

"Don't take anything I say seriously," Kanamoto laughed. "I'm basically full of crap. I suppose I mean a family that eats breakfast together, and then gets back together for dinner, and does that year in and year out."

"Are there really families like that?"

"Some people can't do it because of their jobs, but it's really more an attitude problem. Still, I imagine there are families that do—lots, probably, though I don't know any." Kanamoto was anxious to bring the conversation around to more important matters, but the boy was simply happy to be visiting him at home. Maybe Kanamoto would suggest he stay over? And he might let them have Kōki's birthday party here next month; he could invite Chihiro, Yōko, Kyōko, her sister Haruko, Miho, and maybe even his mother.

"Kōki's birthday is next month on the ninth. Would you mind if we had the party here?" he asked.

"No, I suppose that wouldn't be a problem," Kanamoto said, rather ambiguously, caught off-guard by the innocence of the boy's question.

"It would be great if we could get Sada to come, too . . . ," Kazuki said.

"Was there something you wanted to talk about?" said Kanamoto, cutting him off. Feeling as though he'd been doused with cold water, Kazuki fell silent, studying his fingernails. What if Kanamoto refused to help him? He could feel his heart pounding as his sense of helplessness grew. What should he say? He probably hates me, that's why he refused to hear me out about the birthday party. He swallowed and looked at Kanamoto, tempted to tell him there was nothing he wanted to talk about and go home.

"I want to hire you as a consultant at Vegas," he managed to say at last. "I can't protect the place all by myself. I want you to help me; I need someone strong. I'm asking you from the bottom of my heart." Kazuki felt as though he ought to be down on his knees begging, but instead he just looked down, his face a deep scarlet.

This is probably the first time in his life that this boy has asked anyone for help, thought Kanamoto. He had seen any number of grown men in this position, presidents of small companies and the like, swallowing their pride and pleading for his help. But what would make a boy of this age so fearful, so anxious for his protection? Adults were much more willing to eat crow and ask for help, but children almost never did. When the news reported the latest case of a child committing suicide because he'd been teased in school, Kanamoto was always sure that the victim had suffered from his own pride—a realization that filled him with a mixture of admiration and pity. He was old enough to see the similarities between the disillusioned and damaged children of today and the youth gangs of the past. Both were willing to lose everything rather than sacrifice their fragile pride. But at his age, he knew that it was almost always better to give in when your opponent had the upper hand; still, young people invariably chose their own destruction rather than submitting, as if there were some invisible line in the sand they could not cross. How different this was from adults, and even the yakuza gang members he knew best. Not one of them would fall on his sword over something as trivial as pride. So perhaps now, in the very act of humbling himself, this boy was declaring himself debased, and thereby declaring his manhood.

Since the day he had gone to Vegas to lay down the law for Kazuki, he'd been sure that the boy would be back to ask for his help. At that point, he'd thought, if he handled things right, he might get him to open up, perhaps even confess to his crime. And in time, they might even have discussed what Kazuki could do to make things right. But now that he was standing in front of him, Kanamoto stood silent, at a loss for words.

"So you won't help me?" Kazuki said, waiting for the anger and hatred that he knew he should feel for Kanamoto. Either emotion would help get him through this.

"I'm sorry. I can't," he said at last.

"Why?" Anger and hatred had deserted him, leaving only a plaintive wail.

"I don't suppose you could tell me what's bothering you so much that you come to someone like me for help," said Kanamoto.

He's not a parent, or a teacher, or a cop—so why is he looking at me like that? He's scared and sad at the same time, as if I were some dying animal he was about to put out of its misery. Kazuki turned away.

"It's because your father isn't here. If he were, Hayashi and Sugimoto would never have run amok. But they're not the point; if he were here, you wouldn't have to worry about Vegas at all. Kazuki, tell me where your father is?"

"How should I know?" he said. He really is yakuza, Kazuki thought, strong-arm tactics and all. He glanced at the door, wondering whether he could still escape.

"I think you do know," Kanamoto said.

"Why would you think that?" Kazuki managed to say at last. Trying to act unconcerned, he rubbed his hand across his forehead, feeling the slippery mix of sweat and oil. Kanamoto's face suddenly seemed to loom over him, like the fish-eye view through the peephole in their front door.

"Do you think of yourself as a child or as an adult?" Kanamoto asked.

"I'd like a Coke," Kazuki replied.

"I don't have any."

Ignoring him, Kazuki crawled over to the refrigerator, found some cold oolong tea, and began drinking right from the bottle. Kanamoto could not tell whether this was the behavior of a real child or a cunning adult who wanted to avoid having to talk by acting childish.

"Which do you consider yourself?" he asked again.

"It's obvious, isn't it? I'm not a child or an adult," Kazuki said.

"But if you had to pick one or the other?" Kanamoto sighed, disappointment showing on his wrinkled face.

It was true that Kazuki had not thought of himself as a child since about the time he turned nine; on the other hand, he had never really thought of himself as an adult. Did he really have to choose? No matter how many times he asked, his answer would be the same: he was neither. But why this question now? Whenever adults asked obvious questions like that, it meant they were setting a trap. Kazuki decided the best strategy was to keep his mouth shut. If he refused to say anything, there wasn't much Kanamoto or anyone else could do; he would clam up and Kanamoto would give up.

"You don't want to say?" said Kanamoto. "In a way, that decides it then: if they want to, children can keep quiet no matter what they're asked or by whom. But there are times when an adult just has to speak, even if he'd rather not. Particularly when he has an obligation to the person asking the questions. I think it's fair to say that you incurred a debt to me the other day at Vegas, am I right? But if you think of yourself as a child, you don't need to answer. Your silence is your answer."

"But I told you—I'm not a child or an adult. I'm fourteen!" said Kazuki.

"To me, anyone who isn't an adult is still a child. That's why society sets boundaries, eighteen or twenty years old, and says that's when a person reaches adulthood; and that's why certain things are forbidden to children who haven't reached that age—alcohol, tobacco, driving a car, sex, and all the rest. That's society's way of saying that these things aren't good for growing children, or that the child just isn't ready for them. But it's also true that not every child develops at the same pace, so it's natural that some children may think they've become full-fledged adults even when they're still quite immature. Children like that tend to think their parents and teachers, and adults in general, are all idiots, that they're no more mature than they are. And the fact is, there are plenty of very immature adults rumbling around in the world. So when children see these adults for the fools they are, they think they can no longer be children—and as a result, you have lots of children out there convinced that they're adults, children who then want to tear down the adult world, stage a coup d'état of sorts. Those seem like pretty natural feelings, but what I'm trying to say is that they need to ask themselves whether they're really all grown up or if they've just convinced themselves they are. I guess if the answer is yes, that they've really grown up, then you could conceivably have a ten-year-old or a fourteen-year-old adult." Kanamoto paused to take a gulp of gin before continuing. "You think of yourself as an adult, don't you Kazuki? You've realized that you have the same desires and strengths as an adult."

Right! Kazuki thought. So what is it you're trying to say? I've known since the time I was nine that adults are idiots—my father, my mother, teachers, the stooges at Vegas—they're all stupid, filthy liars who do nothing but get in my way. You're right, I became an adult at nine.

"But it wasn't so easy trying to run Vegas, was it?" Kanamoto said. "Part of the problem was your lack of authority, but in general adults don't like kids ordering them around. That's why you found it so hard to get things done; you have to get people to do them for you, but adults can be difficult that way. It's impossible, really, at your age. That's why it would be better to stay in school and wait until you're all grown up."

"Can you really grow up at school?" Kazuki demanded. "You say that because you don't really know how horrible school can be."

"You're right, I don't really know whether school is the place to grow up. But if not school, then where? For my money, school is still the place—I know that much about it. And there just isn't anywhere else."

"But I don't want to go," said Kazuki.

"Then you need to find your own place, somewhere to wait until you've finished growing. Somewhere other than Vegas."

Then again, thought Kanamoto, maybe Vegas is as good as any place. If Hidetomo had allowed Kazuki to quit middle school and come to work at Vegas, not as the president's son but as a regular employee, things might have worked out. It was against child labor laws, but if he'd started him exchanging balls and cleaning toilets, none of this would have ever happened. If he'd worked him hard and paid him the same as any other grunt, if he'd treated him like a man, taught him how to be a proper heir, he would probably have been suited to be a branch manager in a few years.

"But even you must see that you can't be president right now," he said aloud. "You need to wait until you're grown up before you take over; and you needed your father, at least until that point."

What do adults have that I don't have? Kazuki wondered. Nearly all my problems come from adults who think I'm a child and refuse to let me into their little adult club. That's why I can't get things done, why people don't do what I want them to. What I need is the ability to manipulate people with smooth talk, like Kanamoto can; and for that, it seems you need to know all about the law. He promised himself again that from now on he would concentrate on studying—not just commercial law but all different kinds as well. He would ask Kanamoto to tutor him, to teach him to be eloquent and persuasive. If he agreed, he would stay over here from time to time and Kanamoto could be his teacher. He wanted to learn it all: the gin-soaked expression, the dusky voice, the cruel superiority. But most of all, he wanted Kanamoto to love him. He looked at the older man with eyes that asked what he could do to make himself loved, how he could capture Kanamoto's heart.

"I've got gold ingots," he blurted out suddenly. "Do you want them?"

"You have?" said Kanamoto. "How did you get them?" He remembered the day Kazuki had asked him the price of gold when they'd met under the train tracks, the day he'd taken the golf club from him, the day Sugimoto had said he'd beaten the Doberman to death. That was the day.

"Before he died, my grandfather said he'd give them to me, not my father. They're much cooler than plain old money, but you can have them if you want them."

"I don't really need them," said Kanamoto.

"Why?" Kazuki regretted asking this before the words were out of his mouth, but he hadn't been able to stop himself.

"What would I do with them? You're saying you'll give them to me because you don't need them? If they're really so important, you should keep them. If not, they're not such a great present anyway."

"You hate me, don't you?" Kazuki said.

Kanamoto said nothing.

"Please be my father!" The words slipped out of his mouth without Kazuki quite knowing what he'd said.

Kanamoto was stunned again by the boy's innocence—he might have been four instead of fourteen. For nearly his whole life, he must have been looking for someone strong and reliable to take the place of his father and mother, someone in whom he could place all his trust, without the fear of being betrayed. Kanamoto remembered when he had played hide-and-seek with Kazuki years ago in Kogane-chō. If he hid longer than usual, when he finally did emerge, he would find the boy standing in the middle of the alley, fists clenched, trying to control his anxiety. Kanamoto would let out a soft meow, like a lost cat, and the boy would look around nervously, finally wandering in his direction until he found him and grabbed him in a fierce grip. He could still remember the strength in the small hands and the soft cheek against his. Somehow, the boy had aged ten years while he was covering his face for the next game of hide-and-seek, but in reality he was still his younger self, standing there, in the middle of the alley. Please be my father! He forced himself to drive away the pleasant echo of those words.

"I can't take the place of your father," he said. "I'm not that kind of person." Kazuki's mouth moved but no sound emerged, like a goldfish gulping for oxygen on the surface of a muddy pond. He's crying, thought Kanamoto—or, he wants to cry but can't. "You killed your father, didn't you?"

A gasp escaped from Kazuki's lips and his eyes, which had been staring off into space, dropped slowly to focus on Kanamoto. "I did not," he said.

They were silent, frozen for a time. How long? Kazuki wondered. There's no clock in this room. The Rolex usually fastened to his wrist wasn't there today. "Is that so," Kanamoto said at last. Surprised at the sadness in his own voice. He wondered for a moment if, in fact, he did think of the boy as his son—but he tried to banish the thought as quickly as it had come into his head. Still, it was true: for the first time in his life he found himself genuinely concerned about someone else. He had decided he was prepared to commit himself to Kazuki the moment he had heard that Hidetomo was missing, despite the fact that they had no blood relationship. But why? Something had taken hold of him, something instinctual that was far stronger than anything that could be called love, but he had no way of knowing exactly what it was. And he was attempting to deny it, to cut the bonds that held him to the boy. They stood looking at a small boat that had been tied up in the canal but was now drifting out toward the dark sea.

Anyone else would have been fine, Kanamoto thought, but why this boy? Many years ago he had slept with a Kogane-chō prostitute who came to him afterward to say she was pregnant with his child. "I'm going to get rid of it tomorrow," she'd told him, almost cheerfully. He had felt at the time that she wanted to be connected to someone who wasn't a customer or a friend by a story that was about something other than sex. Was he doing the same thing now? Trying desperately to tie himself to someone through a shared story? The story of the boy and his crime?

"So you won't help me?" Kazuki said. Not only won't you help me, you know I killed him. He could feel the hatred building inside, and it helped him regain his composure. "If you think I killed him, why don't you go and tell the police?"

"To tell the truth, I'm not too fond of the police, so you have nothing to worry about on that score. I'm not threatening you. But if you've been siphoning off money, then you're going to have to worry about more than just Hayashi and Sugimoto; they'll be lots of guys coming around for a cut, and they won't stop until they've stripped you clean."

"So you are yakuza, after all," Kazuki blurted out.

"What? Oh . . . yes, I am. Though you could also say that I'm the sort of man who could never be yakuza. In any case, I haven't been like this all my life—I know a little bit about how nice people should behave."

"I had no idea you were such a filthy scumbag," Kazuki spat out. "But I'll never forget that you let me down like this, and someday I'll pay you back. Remember that." He stood to go, but Kanamoto grabbed his shoulder and held him back.

"How can you kill your own father and still not feel anything?" Kazuki's eyes opened wide for a moment, as if he wanted to plead for something. But almost immediately they seemed to become dark pits and then he closed them.

"I didn't kill him so I don't know, but I do know that it would be better to kill him than to want to kill him and never have the balls to do it. Feeling sorry for something you've already done is bullshit. How many times have you ever regretted what you did?" He hurried out of the room.

Kanamoto leaned against the wall and poured gin from the bottle straight down his throat. He would try to ignore everything from now on—that was the only solution. The whole idea of trying to connect with someone had been wrong from the beginning. There was no one else out there—he was all alone. If he ever met another human being again, it would be the day someone wandered in to kill him, to sink a knife in his heart. He wondered whether he would forgive the person—or want to kill him. Or, more likely, it would be just like it had always been: a human connection based on some profit-loss calculation, and the killer would pass by, remaining just another stranger. He wondered what Yuminaga had seen at the moment he'd been murdered by his own son. Or perhaps the boy had killed him while he was sleeping, giving him no time to see anything, to think anything. He could hear the sound of a boat engine from the canal. He'd wanted to dig a canal to connect himself to the boy, but in the end, he'd failed.

Kazuki was walking along the same canal. When he was small, Kanamoto, Sada and Shige, and the others in Kogane-chō had been kind to him, but now that he thought about it, they had all been strangers, even then. Not one of them had ever understood how he really felt. But it didn't matter. He didn't need anyone. From now on he would fight, and no matter what, he would win. In the end, money could solve everything. If worse came to worse, he could always give Sugimoto a pile of money and buy her as an ally. He would give her one of the gold bars tomorrow to see what kind of effect it had on her. It was bound to work. He'd tell her that it was just a little present. He suddenly felt that he was in over his head, but he didn't care . . . just as long as he didn't drown.

Since she'd started coming to the house, Kyōko had tried to make sure she behaved like a housekeeper, but every once in a while she would be embarrassed to realize that she was acting more like a wife. Then she would get quiet for a while. As a model for how a housekeeper should behave, she had only the housemothers at the orphanage where she and her sister had grown up, women for whom she felt nothing but hatred and who she had no intention of imitating. These women had made no effort to hide their feelings of superiority as they cared for the children, and their silly pride only made the children feel more worthless. But there were times when she could sense a similar atmosphere in this house. Like the children at the orphanage, these two boys had been abandoned. In the orphanage, the laws of society had governed their every moment and there had been no private space at all; while here, they were cut off from society, as if the whole house had been locked and sealed like some underground bunker. If you added her age to those of the two boys, it still didn't equal that of one old person, so when you got the three of them around the dinner table, it was more like camp than a real family. It was, after all, summer vacation, she thought.

"Aren't you going to eat?" she said, setting a crystal ashtray that she had just washed in front of Kazuki. Without answering her, he turned on the TV with the remote and began churning through the channels. He stopped for a moment at a cooking show where a man in a chef's hat lopped off the head of a live fish and filleted it with a few strokes of his knife. A commercial for instant ramen came on and the volume was suddenly too loud. He lowered it and went back to surfing: a commercial for makeup with a smiling woman's face filling the screen; news, with the announcer's solemn face reporting that stock prices were lower. As she set a cup of tea in front of him, Kyōko realized that the only reality that reached this house was the one that filtered in through television.

"Do you have a driver's license?" he asked suddenly.

"No," she said.

"Could you get one? I'll pay for driver's school."

"I don't have plans to drive anywhere, so I don't believe I'll be needing a license," she said, blushing at the formality of her own words. "Kōki has been saying that he'd like to see fireworks, so I've bought some. Would you like to set them off?"

Kazuki tapped the ash of his cigarette awkwardly against the rim of the ashtray, scattering it on his untouched omelette. Shooting off fireworks in the yard was the kind of happy family activity that made him feel nostalgic and somehow embarrassed. Nothing like that had happened in this house for years, and he wondered now whether it was possible to suddenly start up again. "I thought it was raining," he blurted out, feeling annoyed and self-conscious.

Kyōko opened the small window in the kitchen and stuck her hand out. She stood for a moment and then came back to the table.

"It's not raining," she said.

"They were saying on TV that it would start this evening," he said. He left the table and went into the living room, resting his hand gently on Kōki's shoulder as he sat playing the piano. "Fireworks," he whispered in his ear. Kōki finished playing the last few bars of the piece.

"Can we?" he said, hugging Kazuki.

The three of them went out in the garden, and Kazuki handed out the fireworks, lighting each in turn with his lighter. Three streaks of lightning flashed through the darkness, and they watched as the sputtering balls of flame spread into fragile flowers of red threads, before vanishing into pale afterimages. It was a fleeting banquet of color, passing from the memory almost before it had faded from sight. Then they lit Roman candles and sparklers and smoke balls one after another, scattering sparks into the air with a whirring noise. Their eyes glowed red then yellow then green as the flames and smoke spewed from the fireworks. Kōki's face crumpled into ecstatic laughter, as Kazuki brought his hollow cheeks closer to the flames, not bothering to avoid the sparks.

"Kōki, which would you rather see, a big fireworks show or a volcano erupting?" Kazuki himself knew he would prefer the volcano, a real eruption, not a video, with real lava and ash engulfing a town.

Kōki thought for a moment. "Fireworks," he said. "They're so pretty."

"Oh!" Kyōko said, looking up at the sky. A single raindrop struck her, and then, in the space of a breath, the downpour started. "Rain!" she cried, glancing over at Kazuki.

He began setting off the remaining fireworks one after the other, red, orange, blue, and green fireballs erupting into the night. But the fuses were increasingly difficult to light. The rain was running off his head, matting his hair to his forehead. The wheel on the lighter burned his hand as he looked up from his work. Kyōko and Kōki had disappeared. He lit the fuse of a rocket, but when he raised his head to follow its path, the raindrops struck his face.

Back in the house, he shook the rain from his hair and then went around turning out lights.

"What are you doing?" Kyōko shrieked. The beam of his flashlight crawled across the floor, stopped at her feet, then crept up to her face.

"Fireworks," he replied, setting a rocket in the ashtray on the table. When he lit the fuse, Kōki screamed "Water!" and started flailing his arms, knocking over the floor lamp. Their shadows flitted across the ceiling like lassos of light, there was a whooshing sound, and suddenly the room was filled with beads of colored fire. Sparks filled the house, ricocheting from the walls and ceiling, the floor and the furniture. Finally, the casing of the rocket came to rest on the piano pedals, as a fountain of fading sparks glowed dimly, reflected in the ebony surface of the instrument. When the room had grown dark again, Kazuki could be heard laughing hysterically, like a shrill, whistling Roman candle. The red and green standby lights of the air conditioner, the TV, the video, and other machines glowed faintly around the room. As Kazuki went around turning on the lights, they found Kōki with his hands pressed tightly over his ears. He slowly dropped one hand to his heart, gazed at Kazuki for a moment through glazed eyes, and then disappeared up the stairs.

The darkness under the floor in the basement spread out behind Kazuki's eyelids. Total darkness, darkness that illuminated darkness itself like a kind of negative light. He rubbed his chest, feeling affection for the darkness in the vault, darkness so much like that in his own heart.

Kyōko moved around the room, picking up the debris from the rocket and setting the lamp upright. "Did you want to talk about something?" she said, straightening the shade. "If not, I'm going."

He looked into her eyes for a long time and then went down the stairs and opened the door to the basement. He waited, looking back over his shoulder, until he saw her following him. Her calves first, then her knees, her thighs and hips, chest, and finally her face. Her expression was tense.

Kazuki closed and locked the door, pushed her down on the rug, and rested his hand on her blouse. She grabbed his wrist, trying to push him away, but he covered her mouth. Her eyes opened wide and she tried to scream, thrashing her arms and legs and mumbling as if she were sinking underwater. The buttons on her blouse popped off and her white bra was visible underneath. Then suddenly, she went limp, looking up at Kazuki for a moment before closing her eyes. Her body was slack, lifeless. He watched the veins pulsing on her long, white neck as he slid the straps of her bra from her shoulders and unhooked the clasp. Unsnapping her skirt, he pulled it off; then he slid the white lace panties down around her ankles. He stood, looking down on her naked body, as he unfastened his own belt and stepped out of his pants. He penis was still soft. I can't do it, he thought, his desire crumbling into lumps in his stomach. He wrapped his arms around her to arouse himself, taking her face in his hands and sucking her lips. As he plunged his tongue in her mouth, he pried her thighs apart and felt between her legs. She was still dry. Even when he he took her nipple in his mouth, she made no sound. He raked his teeth across her breast and forced his finger in up to the first knuckle, but her muscles closed around it, stopping him from pushing in. When he increased the pressure from both teeth and finger, she moaned and arched her back on the floor. As he began to move his finger in and out, he felt his penis stiffening, but she had drawn her knees up to her chest and he couldn't enter her. Growing frustrated, he knelt over her and held her head with one hand, his penis with the other. He rubbed it against her lips, but she refused to open her mouth. Reaching over to the nightstand, he opened the drawer, fished out a condom, and ripped open the package.

Holding his penis, he slowly entered her. He moved carefully at first, making sure not to slip out, and then gradually his hips began to thrust harder and faster. The gold pendant slapped on his chest, and Kyōko's back rubbed along the rug. He grabbed her legs and pulled her toward him, bringing his hips down on her with his full weight. She bit the back of her hand, smothering her cries. Stretching out, he pressed his face into hers and began to thrust again, feeling her heart beating under his. He suddenly thought of the other heart, no longer beating, that lay beneath them, and he wasn't sure whether he was having sex to forget that corpse or having sex here because he was thinking about it. He realized that the sightless eyes were looking up at him. Turning his head, he could see him sitting on the edge of the bed, sour broth gurgling from the hole that had once been a mouth in that face that was now like the flesh of a ripe tomato. Liquid, like seawater thick with plankton, burbled from the mouth, as if he were trying to laugh, and his purple cock stood erect in his lap. Kazuki closed his eyes, concentrating as he started to come. The cacophony of rain, laughter, the creaking of the bed all mixed together, drilling into every corner of his head, washing away the darkness. In one instant, he felt chills running up his spine and then hot pleasure gushing from him; he felt liberated and captured all at once. In the final moment, they clung desperately to each other.

For a while he lay on top of her, matching his breathing to hers. He held her around the hips, laying his cheek low on her stomach. A sour yet slightly sweet odor rose from her body. She ran her fingers through his damp hair as if she were stroking a cat.

At last Kazuki rolled off, stretching out on his back with his arms under his head. In the silence, he could hear a sound, one that he knew he'd been hearing now for days. At first it resembled the crackle of fish grilling or the bubbling of simmering stew. From time to time there was a sound like steam rising from boiling water. He wondered for a moment if there really was a fire under the floor, if the body hadn't given off its oils and burst into flame—but that was absurd. Still, perhaps gas had built up from the decomposing flesh. If he could force sulfuric acid into the vault, perhaps he could erase the memory. It wasn't just the noise coming from below—the whole house seemed to shudder with fear of the body buried under it. A clamor went up all at once from every particle of the house, from the boards and plaster and wallpaper, from the mice nesting in the ceiling and the cockroaches scuttling around the kitchen, even from the dust mites that bred in every corner. This is the sound a ship makes as it runs aground on the rocks, thought Kazuki. The house is sinking. That dead man has opened a hole underneath and water is flooding in. He turned to wrap his arms around Kyōko, and she stroked his back. It was only when he was touching her that the buzzing was still and the beating of their hearts set up a pleasant rhythm. He pulled away, leaving a small space between their bodies and felt her nipples rubbing against his chest; and then he pulled her back, crushing her against him and pressing his mouth to her ear.

"Do you smell something bad?" he whispered.

"Yes," she said, almost inaudibly. She sniffed at the odor without moving a muscle, as if the smell were seeping in through her skin.

"Blood," he said, and then fell silent. She looked at the face lying next to hers and it suddenly seemed as though blood were flowing from his mouth. A shudder ran through her. "There's a body under here," Kazuki said, sitting up and running his hand over the rug. As Kyōko waited for him to go on, her eyes bore into the ivy pattern on the Persian rug and a pallor crept over her face, as if mold were suddenly growing there.

"I killed him," Kazuki said, looking at her. His eyes narrowed and the corners of his mouth turned up. It looked to her as though he was trying to smile.

"Who?" she asked, sitting up.

Kazuki pulled off the condom, wrapped it in Kleenex, and tossed it in the trash. Taking several more tissues, he wiped the semen from his penis and then set the box of Kleenex in front of Kyōko.

"Who did you kill?" she asked again in a tiny voice, as if there were someone listening under the floor. Kazuki put a cigarette in his mouth and flicked his lighter.

"Him," he said, staring at the cigarette. Kyōko tried to get up, but he grabbed her wrist and pulled her back to the floor. "I killed him, and the body's right here under the floor."

She realized she had probably known what had happened long before when he had first asked her to come to work as their housekeeper, and now that he was telling her, she was hardly surprised. She was more frightened to be sitting on top of a corpse than she was to be alone with this boy who had killed someone.

"When?" she asked, unable to stop trembling. It was as if a weak electrical current were flowing through her body.

"A few days before you started coming," he said.

"That was two weeks ago."

"So, a little over two weeks. That's why he's starting to stink." He took a deep drag on the cigarette and started to cough. From somewhere came the sound of dripping water. There must be a leak, Kazuki thought. But we're in the basement, he reminded himself, looking up at the ceiling.

"What are you going to do?" she asked, looking over at the empty bed as if she had suddenly gone blind. Where did he kill him? she wondered. And how does he have the body hidden down there?

"I'll handle it," he said.

Realizing that he was staring at her, she was suddenly frightened. She started talking to cover her fear.

"You should probably go to the police. You can't keep a body down there forever. No, that's the only thing to do, go and confess . . ." Feeling suddenly uncomfortable, she broke off. Her words were meaningless, but silence was worse. She took a deep breath and continued. "You know you have to go to the police; you can't live like this." She had no idea what she was saying. "If you don't say anything, it'll only make things worse. It'll all fall apart. And then you won't ever be able to make things right. Turn yourself in. I'll go with you. Please! Please go!" She stumbled over the words, as if running in terror, and yet she needed to go on. But she wasn't running away; she was sinking with him, never to rise again. Finally, she fell silent, feeling the words drown within her.

Kazuki suddenly felt hungry. But he didn't think he could eat. If he ate now, he would almost certainly throw up. He stubbed out his cigarette in the ashtray, coughed, and then studied the cigarette box. Taking another for himself, he offered the box to Kyōko, but she shook her head.

"Don't you care at all?" she asked, her voice sounding distant and hollow. She stared at the knives in the case with eyes as hollow as her voice.

"No," he said. His eyes were almost smiling as he looked at her. Having confessed, he felt relaxed, as if all his problems had been solved, and a bit sleepy. He yawned. He wanted to take a bath with her and then fall asleep upstairs listening to the rain. He took her hand. Her damp palm rested under his like a thick piece of meat. Why was it so warm? Did she have a fever? He set his other hand on her forehead.

"I'd like you to help me get rid of the body," he said. She shook her head. "We've got to bury it in the yard. It'll rot there and turn to dirt. No one will ever find out. I'll plant a tree over it. What kind would be good?" he asked, just as her fingernails dug into the back of his hand.

"Don't say you don't feel anything. It frightens me."

"Are you going to tell the police?" he said.

"Even if they sent you to a reformatory, you'd be out in a few years. If you tell them your father beat you, it would probably be shorter than that . . ." Her voice trailed off into silence, in part because Kazuki was no longer listening, but also because she wasn't sure the words needed to be said. What should she say? What should she try to make him feel? She thought she knew, but she couldn't put it into words. The word "crime" danced around in her brain, but silence came rushing from her throat. She could feel her chest constricting, cutting off her air, as if the walls and floor were pressing in on her.

"If I went away, what would happen here? What would happen to Kōki? To Vegas?" he said, as if remembering something that had slipped his mind.

Looking as though the questions had taken her by surprise, Kyōko paused and folded her hands in her lap. He grabbed her by the arm, pulled her down, and tried to scramble onto her again, but her hand shot out and slapped his cheek.

"Stay here tonight," he said, a note of supplication creeping into his voice for the first time.

"I'll sleep in the maid's room," she said. What should I do? She was nearly at the point of praying.

As the sound of Kyōko's footsteps receded in the distance, the scene of the murder that he had kept out of his head until now began to replay itself. The face twisted with terror, the blood spattering the walls, it all came back in vivid detail. He fluttered his hands in front of his face, as if trying to drive away a bee. Something was coming for him, not fear itself but an ill-natured vengeful spirit. And it wasn't just in this room; he would have to live with this fear of ambush from every dark alley he passed, every corner he turned. Even when he sat stock-still like this, it was there, the rotting corpse clinging like a bat inside his head. But why had he confessed? What had he been hoping for? Comfort? Help? Did he really think Kyōko could give him either? All he'd done was wake up this evil spirit. He stood up and went over to the display case. He stared for a moment at the Japanese sword, hesitating like a boy debating whether or not climb a tree, wondering whether he'll be able to climb it or not. The blade was the work of the swordsmith Bizen Osafune Nagamitsu. As his accomplice, it would never breathe a word of what had happened; but on the other hand, it would never be there to listen to him. The sword felt heavier than he remembered. As he drew it from the sheath, a flash of light ran down the blade. Brandishing it over his head, he turned to face the vengeful spirit. The room was suddenly filled with an oppressive silence that he felt he had to cut through. The floor beneath him creaked and the point of the sword trembled. The spirit seemed to appear momentarily in one spot only to vanish again, as if teasing him. A boiling sound seemed to crawl up from under the floor, and he swung the sword.

The intercom tone sounded and when Kyōko went to check the security monitor, she found a man with a graying crew cut staring back at her. The man identified himself as Uchida from the Isezaki Police

Station, and she pressed the button to open the gate. A moment later, the bell rang and Kyōko opened the door to find a middle-aged man in a short-sleeve shirt, his gray suit jacket folded over his arm.

"The boy—I think he said his name was Kazuki. Is he home?"

"Wait a moment, please," she said, going upstairs. She looked down at him a moment as he slept, his legs drawn up to his chest and his arms crossed over them as if for protection. "A policeman's here," she said. He sat up, swallowing hard as his eyes flew open. "He says his name is Uchida, from Isezaki Station."

"Tell him I just woke up and ask him to wait, but don't let him in." Kazuki forced his legs into his pants and sat back on the bed. There's nothing going on with the case, he thought, so why would he suddenly show up here? The game's started. This is the opening gambit. He stood up. As he looked down the stairs, his eyes met those of the detective standing in the entrance and he flew into a rage. "I said you shouldn't let him in!" he screamed at Kyōko.

"She didn't," said the man, the smile on his face vanishing as he spoke. "I let myself in while she was upstairs."

"Mind if I call your station?" said Kazuki. "I'm sure they don't approve of their officers barging into people's houses."

"You're right, and you're welcome to call if you like. But I'm not really here on official business. I just happened to be in the area and I was worried, so I thought I'd stop in. Could we sit down for a minute?" He patted Kazuki on the shoulder as he opened the door to the living room. In a moment, he was seated on the couch.

"You can't search the house," Kazuki said, realizing how pitiful he sounded.

"I'm well aware of that. You live here with your father and your brother and sister? And who was the young woman? Your sister?"

"The housekeeper."

"Mind if I smoke?" the detective asked, taking a pack of Hi-Lites from his pocket and lighting one before Kazuki could answer. He reached over to pull an ashtray toward him. "Pretty young for a maid.

So, it looks like your father hasn't been in touch. How long has it been? Two weeks? I'm beginning to think he's got himself mixed up in something. Looks that way to me, anyway."

"Mixed up in what?" Kazuki asked, using his anger to calm himself.

"I don't know. There're a lot of possibilities. Might have been a car crash; some people when they realize they've killed somone in an accident will take the body somewhere and leave it. I'm not saying that's what happened with your father—just that those kinds of things do happen."

Kyōko came in with glasses of barley tea and set them down on the table.

"How old are you?" the policeman asked suddenly. "And why aren't you in school?"

"What's that got to do with it?" Kazuki screamed.

Why is he so upset? the detective wondered, looking more closely at the boy. Maybe young people these days are more emotional; or maybe it's just this one. At any rate, I don't understand kids anymore— and I'm not sure I even want to. I guess you could say I can't stand them. They're smart but cruel, and basically worthless. They have no manners, no discipline. Remembering that a month earlier he had ended up kicking a high school kid who was blocking the door of a convenience store as he was trying to leave, he tried to calm himself. He leaned toward Kazuki, deciding to give him a scare.

"You must have thought about where your father is. I'd like to hear your theory."

"Hmm," murmured Kazuki. "I'm afraid I don't know."

"You don't? I see. Well, let me ask about something else instead. I get the feeling that drinking and smoking are pretty much standard for middle school and high school kids these days, but I'm wondering if Hōsei students do stuff like that. And you hear a lot about bullying— that go on at a fancy place like that, too?"

"I wouldn't know," said Kazuki.

"How about you? You smoke?"

"I refuse to answer on the grounds that it might incriminate me," Kazuki muttered. I'm not taking that bait, he thought, determined to outmaneuver the policeman.

A smile crept over the detective's face but he seemed at a loss for words as he sat staring at the boy. Taking the Fifth? He doesn't even seem to be joking. He's hiding something—assault, drugs, theft, rape? No, nothing that serious. Alcohol or tobacco, more likely, or at worst threatening some kid at school. He took a sip of his tea, discouraged by the boy's hostility. When he heard at the station that Hidetomo Yuminaga had disappeared, he'd felt right away that it was foul play. But even if it was a murder, they couldn't begin the investigation without some proof that something had happened. If they ever got proof, though, it was unlikely he would be put in charge of the case. So he'd wanted to have a look around Yuminaga's house. He'd thought it wouldn't take more than a few minutes, but now here he was, locked in a battle of wits with this odd boy. In the old days, if you yelled at a kid or gave him a good thrashing, he'd fight back, but nowadays he was more likely to call his lawyer. This one's a particularly rude little shit, he thought, rubbing his palms over his suddenly grim face.

"Have it your way," he said. "There's just one thing I'd like to ask you: what time did your father leave the house on the day he disappeared?"

"I don't know," Kazuki answered. He's probably got a miniature tape recorder hidden in his pocket, so I've got to be careful what I say. He sat very still, hands gripping his knees.

"What do you mean, you don't know? He left, didn't he? If he didn't, we've got a problem here. When your father disappeared, you must have given some thought to where he went, and when you saw him last—or didn't you? It's always important to determine the spot where somebody disappeared and the last person to see him. Or are you telling me he never came home that day?" The officer's tone was more urgent now.

"I left early that morning," Kazuki said. He's toying with me, trying to get me flustered. But he's just fishing, and this isn't an interrogation, he reminded himself, trying to stay calm.

"Miss! Could you come here a minute?" the detective called, turning toward the kitchen.

"I told you! We don't know anything!" Kazuki said, his face coloring with anger.

The policeman suddenly noticed Kōki standing in the doorway, one eye looking at him and the other at the boy. He shuddered and looked away. "This your little brother?" he asked.

"My big brother," Kazuki said, almost panting. The smoke billowing from the detective's nose and mouth was filling the room and he wanted to open the window, but his feet felt glued to the floor and he couldn't move. He was beginning to sweat. Reaching for the remote, he lowered the setting on the air conditioner.

The detective turned to look at Kyōko, who was standing next to Kōki, staring at the floor.

"Do you know what time Mr. Yuminaga left the house that day?" he asked.

"I don't know," she said.

"You don't? Was it your day off?"

"I didn't come to work here until after he disappeared, so I wouldn't know. Is this an interrogation?"

"An interrogation or just a simple question—why does everybody care so much? But now I'm curious, why did you hire a maid so soon after your father left?" His cool eyes fell on the boy's trembling knees.

"That's it!" Kazuki screamed. "You can't come snooping around people's homes, asking anything you want. Get out! Get out!"

"It's simple enough to come back with a warrant and ask the same questions," said the detective. "You sound like any dumb thug demanding his rights."

"Fine, then try arresting me!"

"Now you don't want to start talking like that. You've already made yourself a suspect. I'm going to start looking into this, and you better hope I don't turn up anything." He sneered at Kazuki as he got up to leave. Walking slowly through the hall, he glanced at the staircase. It was tempting to go up, if only because he knew how much the boy would hate it, but he fought the urge and stepped outside. "Okay, we're out of here," he called to the young officer waiting in the garden.

"Nothing suspicious out here," said the other man.

"If there were, we'd be digging by now," said the detective with a faint smile. "I wonder if we can start asking around at Hōsei?" He glanced back at the house.

"They say Yuminaga is on the board of directors."

"Why would they put a guy who owns pachinko parlors on the board of a school like that?"

"Because he gives them money, I guess. I heard he was paying for a new building."

"Well, if one of their directors is missing, seems like they'd be willing to answer some questions. We can slip in the questions about the boy along the way."

"But we wouldn't be going ourselves, would we?"

"The Welfare Bureau's always slow, so we might consider it."

"At any rate, Yuminaga's on every watch list there is, so the guys in charge won't be able to ignore it much longer."

"Do you want to try planting a story in the weeklies? We could hint that it might be a murder."

"You don't really think the boy did it, do you?"

"I don't know what to think anymore, but it doesn't seem likely. Or maybe it does? . . ." At the sound of the gate opening, the detective looked around to find a young woman on crutches approaching them. The two men bowed and began walking toward her.

"Can I help you with something?" she said.

"We had some business with Kazuki but we're through," said the detective, and they hurried out the gate.

"That must be the daughter," said the younger man. The detective nodded, recalling the faces of the three Yuminaga children and the young maid.

As she entered the living room, Miho glanced doubtfully at Kyōko and then turned to look at Kazuki. "There were a couple of strange men in the garden. Any idea who they were?"

"Detectives," he said.

Miho had almost no reaction at all when Kazuki explained that their father had disappeared.

"Who's she?" she asked, nodding toward the kitchen when Kyōko had gone.

"The maid quit, so I asked one of Yōko's friends to help out." Kazuki had been staring at the ashtray where the detective's cigarette lay smoldering, but suddenly he looked up. "How's your leg?" he asked.

"Not bad," said Miho. "Looks to me like you're the one who's messed up." She studied the dark circles under his eyes and the swollen lids. "I've found an apartment," she added, her voice cloyingly sweet.

"You said half a million."

"Have you got it?"

"I've got it."

Miho hobbled up to the closet in her room, calling for Kyōko to bring some boxes. A moment later there was a knock at the door. "Come in," Miho said, looking back over her shoulder to stare at Kyōko. Kyōko stared back for a moment before losing her nerve and hurrying quietly from the room. Odd girl, thought Miho. If she has something to say, she should just say it. Probably hooked up with Kazuki . . . but she's about my age.

She set the box in front of the closet and began stuffing it. That man missing? Not likely, she thought. Why would that bastard go missing? He's with one of his girls. So what should I take with me? And what to toss? To start with, all the school stuff is trash. But just as she was making this decision, she suddenly felt as though her head had been lopped off and launched into space, and she stood without her crutches and collapsed on the bed. He must have been murdered . . . but who did it? She stared at the wall for a while, watching the colors drain from the posters, and then started stuffing the boxes again. It was obvious who had killed him. Shit, he didn't need to go that far. Her eyes were blurry with tears. Still, who cares? It didn't matter to her one way or the other. There really wasn't much here she needed; three boxes would hold everything. She could have them delivered.

The envelope Kazuki handed her in the front hall contained a million yen, twice the amount she'd asked for.

"Thanks," she said, tucking it in her bag. She slipped into her sandals and pulled herself up on the crutches. As she reached for the doorknob, she suddenly turned to face him. She told him she was on his side, that he had to be strong. Hidetomo's disappearance meant nothing, but if Kazuki were to leave them, she and Kōki couldn't survive. The instant the door slammed behind her, she knew she would never come back. She stared blankly at the line of orange light shining through the clouds on the horizon.

As he sat in the taxi heading toward Mai's apartment, Kazuki imagined what was about to happen. And then, right through until the sex ended, it all unfolded like a videotape, just as he had imagined it. But just because reality had followed his imagination like a script, it didn't mean that it had been monotonous or boring. Part of the pleasure in sex was the tension and surprise of traveling through an unknown land, but there was also a more familiar sort of pleasure that came from the fact that it happened just as you knew it would. If you wanted a different thrill every time, you would have to sleep with lots of different women, but then you would never know how nice it could be to get to know every aspect of a single woman's body. The desire for a lot of women was a failure of the imagination, and a man who lost interest in one woman had, in fact, lost his ability to imagine. It occurred to him that Mai's body was something golden, like a swollen foie gras, force-fed on desire, an hors d'oeuvre permitted only to those who themselves possessed enough gold. He reached for the pack of cigarettes on the bedside table.

"I'd like to be paid for my grief over your father," she said. "If we throw in the money to formalize our new relationship, it would come to something like fifty million. I think that's reasonable. When you come this time, could you bring along a deposit book?" She felt like an idiot talking to a middle school student like this, but she had no other cards to play.

"How would I have that kind of money?" he asked.

"But you killed him, didn't you? If you didn't, why did you put the million in my account? How could you be spending your father's money like that if you didn't know he was dead? How could you be sleeping with me? If you thought he was still alive, you'd be too scared. Tell me! You killed him, didn't you?" She pulled her body away from his, brushing her long hair back behind her shoulders.

Kazuki was disappointed by this show of childish calculation. It ruined his image of her as mindless desire, marred the beauty of her pliant body. This woman should never think; she should wage all her battles in the realm of the flesh. Mai sat sipping a cocktail. As he stared at her nude, white body, he was suddenly tempted to beat her just enough to bring out bruises, but he knew his self-control would give way and he gave up on the idea. Still, he wondered, opening and closing his fist, what would she look like writhing on the bed after he'd hit her?

"I've been in charge of the household budget for years," he said. "A million is small change—I've always got that lying around. And I'm the official heir, so I have to look after things while my father's gone—you included."

"You killed him, I know it! Tell me. I won't tell anyone."

"Why would I kill him? Do I look like a killer?" Kazuki sneered at her as he pulled on his underwear. The only people who suspected him were Kanamoto and this woman.

"Why don't you stay here tonight?" she said, her tone somewhere between an invitation and a threat. As she stood to follow him, she suddenly realized she was naked. Going to the dresser, she pulled a man's shirt from the drawer, slipped into it, and fastened a few buttons.

"My father didn't stay over, did he?" Kazuki said. If you think wearing his shirt is going to rattle me, you're fooling yourself, he thought.

"You don't really think he's coming back, do you?" Tears were shining in her eyes as she sat down back on the bed. She probably doesn't know herself whether she's acting or really feeling something, he thought.

"Why do you think I killed him?" he asked. Mai giggled and frowned, like a child caught being naughty.

"I'm sorry I suspected you," she said. "But there's been a lot of talk about kids killing. So I thought maybe you . . ."

Kazuki laughed. Bingo! That's correct! But I'm sorry! We have to disqualify you for faulty logic, for failing to use your brain.

"I did kill him," he said.

"Really? Now you're lying. Really? You really did it?" Nervous now, she edged back to the middle of the bed.

"Of course I'm lying . . . aren't I?" He collapsed in a fit of apparently uncontrollable laughter, as Mai sat, pale and tense, trying to decide what to believe. If it were true, then she'd been having sex with a murderer . . . But whether he did it or not, she decided it was time to get her money and get out. Since Hidetomo had disappeared, she had been thinking of almost nothing but money during every waking hour. Money, money, money . . . she had to get her hands on enough money so she could stop thinking about . . . money. If she had to keep thinking about it like this, she'd go crazy . . . thinking . . . about money.

"If you can't come up with a lot of money, I'm in a fix. I can't just sit around here getting my monthly allowance, waiting for your father. If you can get me the fifty million, I could open a shop or a bar or something. And then you could come by whenever you felt like it. What do you say? Please! It's just fifty million." She grabbed his arm and tried to pull him back onto the bed, but he shook her off. He stood, slipping on his pants. "Are you going? Before you leave, tell me what you're going to do. Wait! . . . If you don't give me the money, I'll go to the police or to Vegas and tell them you killed him. Is that what you want?"

Ignoring her threats, he left the apartment and started walking. No matter how much she screams, nobody's going to listen, he told himself.

The reason adults couldn't imagine anything that fell outside of their own narrow self-interest was that they were convinced that everyone else was acting selfishly as well. Still, even if they would never believe he was a murderer, she might convince them that they'd had sex and that he'd paid her the million yen. He pictured the suspicious faces of the Vegas staff, and then ran through the legions of threatening adults until he arrived at the detective who had come to the house. He, at least, would be curious where the million had come from and why he'd given it to Mai. The woman was dangerous, he thought.

He suddenly realized that the headlights of a car seemed to be coming up behind him. He jumped aside and pressed his back against the wall, narrowly avoiding being hit by a station wagon. He aimed a spitball of fear and loathing at the retreating taillights, ricocheting off the car and heading back toward Mai. He started to walk, finding himself suddenly wrapped in darkness, as if there had been an unexpected disturbance in his brain waves. He realized he'd entered a tunnel. He could see a faint light in the distance; if he walked toward it, eventually he'd find his way out. He would have to kill her. If he got rid of every scrap of evidence, no one would ever suspect him. A man disappears, his mistress is murdered—who would ever think the son had done it? The social fabric was tightly knit by fixed ideas and self-interest, and anything that wasn't caused by one or the other was likely to slip through a hole or a tear. In fact, adults didn't seem to realize how extraordinarily susceptible children were to the same things that motivated them—fixed ideas and greed. With kids committing so many crimes, you would think that adults would realize that the motives weren't so different. But the media and the police, at least, seemed indifferent. The only people who had noticed were weak-willed women like Mai who were prone to taking mental shortcuts. Who knew what the rest of them were thinking? They seemed incapable of imagining any sort of human conflict that didn't fit their own narrow ways of thinking, that didn't come down to greed or selfishness. So when they're confronted with a crime that couldn't be attributed to either, they immediately chalked it up to thrill-seeking or something equally as gratuitous, the result of some mental or emotional defect—anything to avoid finding out that their ideas are tired, their interests compromised. Children don't kill cats for fun. But for adults, who have it fixed in their heads that cats are pets, the children and the cats should be connected by some inviolable link.

Kazuki was beginning to hallucinate as he walked through in the tunnel, and each time a car roared by, he would press his back against the wall as if to avoid being hit. If Mai turned up dead, there would probably be an investigation, some sort of inquiry. And that detective might end up running it—best to be prepared for that. He would at least be asked about meeting Mai at the Vegas office, being invited out to coffee with her, about coming back an hour later. But if he said he hadn't seen her since then, that would probably be the end of it. If she'd talked to anyone about having sex with him, that could present a problem, but he doubted she had. He had a feeling she didn't have anyone she could open up to, anyone to confide in. And even if she had, it didn't really matter. He was a fourteen-year-old boy. Who would believe that he was fucking his father's twenty-eight-year-old mistress? He could simply deny it, and if there were no proof linking him to the murder, he was home free. He felt relieved, as though tightly knotted shoes had suddenly come unraveled. He turned to look back the way he'd come and was shocked to see that there was no tunnel at all, just a wide empty street. But what had he been cowering from all that time? At any rate, as soon as he'd finished the preparations, he would kill her—tomorrow, or the next day at the latest. Before he did, though, he wanted to do her one more time. He chuckled, imagining himself buzzing her intercom and telling her he wanted to come up to talk about the money. No one knew what he was thinking, what he was planning to do, and no one could stop him. He was free. He broke into a sprint, as if he were running, terrified, through a dark tunnel.

As he stared at the sword, he could feel himself settling into the idea of killing Mai. The sword, by its beauty and strength, was able to illuminate the fathomless nullity of the flesh, to purify it and return it to nothingness. If it were possible, he would like to kill her with a sword. He tried to picture the blade as it pierced her soft, white belly, to imagine her flesh as it trembled under the thrust. If he were to give her the fifty million she was demanding, he would be all but admitting the murder and exposing himself to blackmail for the rest of his life. He might even lose Vegas. No, if he didn't kill her she would steal his soul with her great nothingness. He had the sudden feeling that her body had melted in his head and was floating free above him. If things went on like this, his brain cells would be fried. But if he did it with a sword, he would have to cut her up to get rid of the evidence. Boiled human flesh rendered enormous amounts of glistening, white fat, but he'd read somewhere that if you then grilled it or fried it, it was as delicious as the best beef. He slipped the sword back in the sheath and returned it to the cabinet. Taking a shorter knife off the shelf, he tucked it in his backpack. He ran his hand along the computer cable he'd packed in case he decided to strangle her, and then zipped the bag shut. Sensing someone was watching him, he turned to find Kyōko standing in the doorway.

"How'd you get in? The door was locked!"

She started to walk around the room, ghostlike in the light of the lamp. Her face was blank, unaffected by Kazuki's scream.

"I asked how you got in!" he repeated. For a moment she continued walking, ignoring the question.

"I need to talk to you," she said at last, sitting down in the middle of the rug and turning to face him. There was both fear and pity on her face.

"But how did you get in?" he said again, almost inaudibly. She raised her hand and a key dropped out as she pointed toward the wall. Why hadn't she noticed it before? A row of potted pulmeria lined one side of the room, filling the air with a suffocating fragrance.

"The smell is getting worse," she said.

Kazuki leaned over and sniffed at the rug. The odor was still there, but he didn't think it was getting stronger. It was bearable now. If you didn't know what was under the floor, you might simply think it was just a basement smell.

"You think we should burn it with gasoline?" he said, looking at Kyōko for any sign that she might help him.

"I want you to turn yourself in," she said. The moment she had heard him confess to murdering his father, Kyōko had understood why she was involved with Kazuki: it was her mission to get him to surrender.

When she was thirteen, some boys had dragged her into a storage closet at the orphanage and forced her to suck them. After that, they had raped her. As she watched them on her, she had seen the look in their eyes, the look of boys victimizing someone else to escape their own sad reality. And she saw it now, in Kazuki's eyes. They were convinced, then and now, that they could save themselves by hurting someone else. If she'd met up now with those boys from the orphanage, if one of them had come up to her on the street, she imagined she would probably go out with him. In part, she still wanted revenge—she couldn't deny it. But she also wanted to erase the fact of the rape itself, to revise the memory by establishing a new relationship. She realized now that she had been waiting all along for the day when Kazuki had pushed her head down and demanded that she suck him. In the instant that he forced his penis into her mouth, the memories of that day in the storeroom had exploded like a land mine, scattering themselves like the shower of semen. It was just another form of bodily excretion—if she could think about it like that, she could be done with it. She could go on living, damaged perhaps but living. The pride she had salvaged as a thirteen-year-old had survived as a kind of tumor buried deep in her chest, and in sleeping with Kazuki, she had been asking him to make compensation in place of the boys in the closet. Still, she'd been disappointed by his sexual inexperience and had started to think about how to leave him when this other land mine had exploded in an unexpected spot, and the sparks from the blast were beginning to burn her. A person who did something he shouldn't do had to be punished . . . If she ignored that fact, she would be forced to spend the rest of her life with penises in her mouth. Soul-Hackers? These boys were hackers who forced their way in and destroyed whatever they found. She would have to put an end to the game.

"Why should I turn myself in?" he said, plucking petals from a pulmeria.

"Because you did something you shouldn't have," she said.

"You shouldn't kill people?"

"You think it's okay?" A wide grin spread over his face. She smiled back weakly.

"It may be against the law, and for most people it may be a bad thing, but not for me."

"Would you say that if someone killed you?"

"If someone tried to kill me, I'd kill him first. But if he got to me anyway, then I'd be dead and it wouldn't matter. I wouldn't really care if they charged him with murder or not, and I wouldn't care if they punished him." As he spoke, Kazuki felt a fresh surge of energy. Why was it wrong to kill? Even now, all over the world, countless murders were being committed and no one could stop them, no one was even trying. The desire to kill came on people like a giant unseen hand, and once it had you, there was no getting away from it. If it were really wrong to kill, why were the movies and comic books full of such incredible slaughter scenes? Reality was becoming fictionalized, and fiction was becoming more real. "If I've done something wrong, then I'm willing to accept punishment," he said. "But they've got to catch me first. If they come to arrest me, I'll go quietly because I'll know they've beaten me. But why should I stick my hands out for the cuffs when they haven't gotten me yet? Guys surrender when they know they don't have anywhere left to run. I still think I'll win the game." He stood up and began lining the rug with the flowerpots. The shadows of the plants swayed on the walls and ceiling as he worked.

To Kyōko, it appeared that the shadows were moving Kazuki. She unzipped the backpack and took out the computer cable and the knife, setting them down in front of him as he stood like a tombstone in the middle of his makeshift garden. The basement room had become a graveyard, the cable and knife, offerings at the grave.

"Who are you going to kill this time?" she asked.

"Just one more and it's over," he said, his voice almost kindly.

She was suddenly surprised that it had never occurred to her that she could be the next victim. Me? She put her hand over her heart. Kazuki smiled, shaking his head. The tension suddenly broke, like a taught string that snaps, and Kyōko felt helpless. She wanted to cry or scream, but helplessness had sucked up every sound, and a deep silence took control of her body. While she'd lived at the orphanage, she had often pressed her ear against her arm to listen to the rushing blood. If you listened quietly and carefully, you could hear the flow in the veins like the murmuring of a stream in the distance. At other times, if instead you placed your palm over your ear and pressed hard, you could hear the sound of the wind blowing or a rumbling deep in the earth.

"It would be better if you just turned yourself in," she said in a tiny voice, as if determined not to upset him.

She remembered that she'd felt she was turning herself in when she went to talk to the director of the orphanage about the rape. She had promised herself that she wouldn't tell anyone, but when her period stopped, she had no choice but to confess. The director was devoutly Catholic and behind her back the children referred to her as The Nun. She sat and listened to the story without interrupting, but Kyōko could sense the irritation and coldness in her eyes. When she'd finished speaking, she realized that the woman had heard nothing but the fact that her period was two weeks late. "Please return to your room," was all she had said. Three days later, Kyōko had been taken to the hospital by an instructor and the housemother. The boys who had committed the crime received no punishment; but she who had done nothing was made to lie spread-eagle on the operating table while the fetus was scraped out. And thus the matter was settled. Her confession had been punished as the shameless act of an orphan who failed to understand her place.

"What would you do if I were raped?" she asked suddenly.

"I'd beat the shit out of the guy, and if you wanted me to, I'd kill him."

"Because it's unforgivable?"

"You think you should forgive someone for that?"

Why had she insisted then that she wanted to have the baby? She had screamed and cried for two days, refusing the abortion. The teacher had spirited her into the orphanage infirmary, as if she were being kidnapped, and they had forced her to change into a hospital gown and lie on a stretcher. She had tried to escape while they weren't looking, and in the end she caused such a scene that she had to be restrained. She had been terrified of the operation, but the real reason was that her pride wouldn't let her do it. When the anesthesia had worn off, she found herself staring dizzily at the ceiling. The teacher placed a Bible by her bed and urged to read the book of Job. During the three days she spent in the infirmary, she read it over and over, but it never brought her any peace. Job's darkness and agony were frighteningly real to her, and she understood immediately that her only option was to wander like Job in the desert. Her belly still ached. As she pressed her hands over it, she repeated a verse from what she had read, reciting it over like a curse: Why died I not from the womb? Why did I not give up the ghost when I came out of the belly?

"You think it's unforgivable because you think rape is wrong," she said at last. "That's why you'd punish him. So what if someone killed me?"

"It's not punishment, it's revenge. I can't forgive anyone who takes what's mine."

"And if I didn't forgive you?"

"Why?" Her words stung him and he looked at her blankly.

I don't forgive you, you or those boys, and now I've got to stop you. The crimes of children reproduced themselves, closing their victims in cages built of nightmares. After she'd had the abortion, Kyōko had lived in silent terror her last two years at the orphanage, lived in constant fear of the boys who waited for her, wriggling in the chaotic darkness like spiders or bats. Once she left for the outside world, it took a full year for the darkness to begin to dissipate, to brighten into something resembling shadows. Now she lived in a perpetual dusk, the half light of evening, but Kazuki was dragging her back into the darkness of death where no ray of light could penetrate.

"Just hear me out then, and don't interrupt. First, I want you to turn yourself in. If you do . . ." She took a deep breath and looked at him. "I'll marry Kōki." Kazuki was so startled he could only stare at her with his mouth hanging open stupidly. "Kōki is eighteen and I'm seventeen, so it's perfectly legal. If you turn yourself in, you'll be in the reform school four years at most. In the meantime, Kōki will be president of the company, but I could work at Vegas and look after things. Kanamoto-san could help me if something difficult came up. If he told them to, I'm sure that Hayashi and Sugimoto would cooperate. And when you got out, you could take over."

It isn't Mai I'm going to have to kill, thought Kazuki, glancing down at the knife on the floor, it's this one. She's been worming her way in here to get revenge for her father's suicide.

"It wasn't this man under the floor here who made your father kill himself," he said, his face convulsing with anger. "That's all a lie! I didn't think you would try to pull something like this. And where did you get the idea that Kanamoto would help you?"

"I talked with him today," she said. "He promised to protect us no matter what happens."

"So the two of you have been plotting behind my back!" he screamed. In his head, the computer cable had begun to coil like a snake.

"Then you don't trust me? You can't trust anyone, that's what Kanamoto-san said. He said you just can't do it."

"Why is Kanamoto suddenly such an expert? The man's a gangster, a murderer!"

"I trust him. There aren't many adults like him."

"He's a double-crossing bastard. You both are. But you just watch out! I'll show you!" Though he was glaring at her with a threatening look, Kyōko couldn't help feeling that she was watching the struggles of a drowning man. Even when he reached out for the cable, she felt oddly calm. I suppose I want him to kill me, she thought. There was that other time, when she had fashioned a noose out of some rope and hung it over a beam in that storage closet—why hadn't she been able to die that time? She'd sat looking up at the noose for more than an hour, until the rays of the sunset had come creeping in through cracks in the door. Why did I think I wanted to live then? And why should I still have the will to live now? What purpose does my life serve? But if he would turn himself in, I think I could manage to survive at least as long as he was in jail . . . Suddenly discovering the selfish motivation that lurked behind her proposal, she felt herself on the verge of giving up. Kazuki wants to add his poison to my personal hell, she thought.

"I trusted you," he said. "That's why I told you everything." There was no sign of fear in her eyes as she watched him reach for the cable, but she held out her hands to stop him. Run, why don't you? I'll strangle you from behind. Go ahead and scream! Help! His eyes wandered around the room. She was right: he never had been able to trust people. Perhaps he had trusted Yasuda and Kanamoto and the old folks at the Golden Pavilion, but he was a little boy then. How was he supposed to trust anyone now? He wouldn't even know what it felt like. To trust, to kill—it was all the same to him. People were always trying to form close ties . . . too close, ties that needed cutting . . . cutting. Why would you ever need anyone else like that?

"Then trust me now," she said. "You've got to believe in something to go on living. If it isn't religion, then at least in somebody. At least one other person."

"What do you believe in?" he asked.

"I believe in myself. I've always tried to believe in my other self." For a moment, Kyōko could feel anger swell inside her and threaten to spill out, but as quickly as it came, it faded away, leaving only a vast expanse of emptiness. Words were useless now. Trying to explain to him why it's wrong to kill was like trying to explain to a child why the sky is blue. The word "trust" was like a mirage. You could see it with your eyes, but if you tried to touch it, it vanished in your hands. No matter how thirsty you were, you could never drink the water from this oasis. There had been two of them that day, staring up at the noose in the closet—the self that so much wanted to die, and that other pitiful self that could never decide. And in the end, she had been forced to accept the self that embraced this meager life and chose to wander alone through the wilderness, the self that unraveled the noose and walked out of the storage room. "That's why I haven't killed myself," she said. "And why I don't believe in killing others."

"What's that got to do with me?"

"Why did you tell me you killed you father?" she asked.

"Because I trusted you," he said.

"Then go on trusting me! I trust you. Let me help you, please. Turn yourself in." Kazuki yawned, no longer even angry, just amazed at the woman's egotism. It was as though she were asking him to jump off the roof. She must be an idiot, though in a different way than Mai. He would have to take care of Mai soon, he decided, but he was still unsure what to do with this one. "Then you don't trust me," she said, standing to leave. His hands reached again for the cable but stopped in midair, his fingers still flexing. "No matter what happens, I won't tell the police," she said. "I won't tell anyone. I promise. I'm going now." She didn't know herself whether the words had come out clearly or not.

"Will you be coming back?" he asked, but before she could answer, he had forgotten his question, as if the blood to his head had been suddenly cut off and brain cells were dying. Why was he here? What was he doing?

I won't be back. There's no point in seeing you again.

He could hear what she was saying, but he had no idea why she wouldn't be coming. And he was growing frustrated that he couldn't spit out the words he wanted to say. His head shook back and forth like a petulant baby. He couldn't remember the words. You know . . . You understand what I'm trying to say . . . I mean . . . The more he hurried after them, the more the words seemed to retreat into the distance. Why do you have to actually say something for people to understand you? When he'd asked whether she'd be coming back, what had she said? He couldn't remember. This had never happened to him before—his head was blank.

So, I won't.

He strained every nerve to catch the sound of her voice as it struck his eardrums. But what was she saying? He took her hand, pulling her toward him as he fell to his knees.

Stay. Just a little.

He'd said something. Given time, he thought he'd be able to sort out what he'd said and what she'd said, but for now it was a jumble. She was pulling her hand. He was barely holding on, but she seemed unable to get away. Her lips were moving, but nothing was coming out. She stared at him, a desperate look on her face. His consciousness was returning bit by bit, as if a blocked artery had been bypassed. He knew now that she'd said they would never see each other again. But that was too sad, unbearably sad. If he lost Kyōko, he'd lose everything. His arms and legs began to shake, his teeth chattered. The trembling spread out through his body, growing stronger as his knees knocked against the floor. It hurt! He tried to stop shaking but he couldn't. When his grip grew so tight that Kyōko screamed, he finally let go of her hand and kicked out at the pots of flowers. Working quickly, he rolled back the rug, pulled up the tape, and lifted the cover to the underground vault.

A powerful wave of nausea swept over her and Kyōko vomited. Her eyes seemed to cloud over, and she rubbed them with the backs of her hands. When she had managed to cover her nose, she looked up to find Kazuki peering down into the hole, as if trying to sniff out the decay. He seemed to pant for a moment, and then convulsions rippled across his back and he vomited as well, spewing his guts down into the vault. When he was done, he bent over and reached in, trying to drag out the body. She opened her mouth to scream for him to stop, but the nausea rose in her throat, blocking the words, and she coughed violently instead. She slipped off her T-shirt and used it to wipe sweat and tears from her eyes and nose. Then, balling up the shirt and pressing it against her face, she edged toward the hole. When he turned to look at her, she could see that Kazuki's face was covered with sweat and his eyes seemed to bulge from his head. He had swung one leg down in the vault and was about to lower himself in when Kyōko pounced on him and dragged him back out. Averting her eyes, she slid the cover back in place.

Even after she had unrolled the rug and replaced the pots, the smell still filled the room. Kazuki's groans, full of resentment and despair, grew louder and louder.

Do you trust me? Trust me?

Kyōko found a clean pillowcase in the cupboard and used it to wipe Kazuki's mouth. Then she wiped the slime of the decomposing body from his arms and legs. As she worked, he continued to mouth some silent complaint over and over. "Do you trust me?" she said, cradling his face in her hands. The eyes that looked up at her were filled with tears.

She took him up to the bath and got in with him to wash his body and his hair. After that, she dressed him in clean underwear and pajamas and lay him down on the bed. Then she scrubbed herself again, and brushed her teeth until her gums bled.

Kazuki lay in the bed, his eyes open but unseeing. A single ray of moonlight pierced his eye. Suddenly, Kyōko was standing over him. She bent and brushed her lips against his, then stroked his cheek and his hair with her long, pale hand. Gently closing his eyes, she slipped out of her nightgown and lay down next to him. Before I turn myself in, I'd like to take a trip. But where? To the zoo. The bed rocked peacefully, like a boat anchored in a calm sea.

They left the house on a clear, late-summer morning; but the sun was growing brighter by the minute, mercilessly revealing Kazuki's pale, sunken face. He had grown thin, and his coloring was unhealthy, like a cancer patient who was losing organs one by one. Kyōko had wanted to know why he needed to go to the zoo, what he wanted to do or see there, but she'd been unable to ask him. She was even unable to walk next to him, choosing to follow behind, holding Kōki's hand. She sensed that his heart was like a tidal pool cut off from the sea, but she was unsure whether it would simply dry out in the August heat or whether the waves might reach it again and restore it to life.

As they passed under the gate to the zoo, they were suddenly suffocated by the odor of animal dung warming in the sun.

"I want to see the elephant," Kazuki murmured, as if talking in his sleep.

Kyōko stopped in front of a map, shielded her eyes from the sun for a moment, and then looked around. When she pointed out the direction, Kazuki and Kōki lumbered off like two donkeys carrying heavy loads.

The cicadas were crying in the trees, but the sound was oddly thin, as if there were cotton in his ears. And the scene passing in front of his eyes seemed somehow removed from reality, dissolving into a dream moment by moment. All the animals—the ones that had been snatched from the rain forest as well as those brought from the ice-crusted Arctic—were wilting under the summer sun and the clouds of smog. Kazuki noticed a leopard pacing back and forth in a small cage.

Its low groan followed him as he passed the latticed shadows of the cage. As he came up to the giraffe, it lifted its head and squinted, as if listening for some distant sound. After a moment, however, the heavy lashes lowered, covering its eyes. When Kazuki moved a step closer, the eyes opened again and the blue tongue shot out toward him like another animal. When had he had the dream? He was trying to go visit his mother, but the apartment was surrounded by wire. A giraffe pushed its neck up over the wire, and at its feet a flock of birds fluttered about like butterflies. When he managed to find a hole in the wire and slip inside, the giraffe swung its neck in a wide arc and buried its head at the base of its neck, forming a ring. Feeling frightened, he had run up the stairs, brushed aside the bamboo blind in front of the door, and charged into his mother's apartment. The tatami mats were covered with the same small birds he had seen outside, but when he looked again, he realized they were origami. Somewhat relieved, he took a step into the apartment to look for his mother, but as he did, there was a high-pitched wail and something warm latched on to the back of his leg. Craning around, he had found the giraffe staring him in the face.

A monkey was looking up at him, swinging its long tail back and forth. It hesitated a moment and then came up to the bars. But when Kazuki in turn came closer, the monkey jumped back, leaping up on its swing and dangling from the top of the cage by its tail and one hand.

When Kazuki stopped again to wipe the sweat from his face, he found himself looking at a gorilla. The gorilla cocked its head thoughtfully to one side for a moment, then slowly, robotically, lowered itself into a squat to cover the floor with shit. A sign posted next to the cage warned visitors against getting too close to the bars since the animals were known to throw their own feces. But this gorilla seemed to have no such intentions; it merely watched Kazuki attentively with its jaundiced eyes.

By now, Kazuki was growing tired of these animals whose lives seemed so peaceful and lazy, and he was beginning to regret having come. Why had he thought he wanted to spend his last free day at the zoo? But where should he have gone? He suddenly pictured himself, face pressed up against a train window, staring out at the sea. Then the train passed through a tunnel, and a grassy, windblown plain opened up around him.

In the elephant pen, there was not a single shade tree, nor, at the moment, any elephants. The concrete expanse was broken only by the occasional pile of dung, but then Kazuki noticed a yellow puddle of urine that had not yet dried, suggesting an elephant had been there recently. It must be resting in the windowless concrete building that formed the back of the enclosure. It was probably time for its lunch. The outer wall of the pen had apparently once been painted the color of custard, but years of sun, wind, and rain had faded it to dirty sand. Kazuki was disappointed that the elephant was not there, but he also felt somehow relieved. A fundamentally sacred animal like the elephant, when shut up in a zoo, lost its sanctity. Of all the animals here, the elephant was the least suited to life in the zoo. It should never live anywhere but in the forest or on the savanna. The merciless sunlight that shone down on the concrete rocks and drinking trough revealed to Kazuki the absence of myth in this place.

In front of the elephant pen stood some trees, and lined up in their shade were three benches. On the right-hand bench sat a vagrant who had fallen asleep bent over the newspaper spread on his lap. Sweat was dripping from his face onto the paper, spreading out in a dark stain. Another man came up to him as Kazuki watched and began shaking his shoulder and yelling for him to wake up. His voice was too loud for the zoo, and Kazuki wondered if he was drunk, or perhaps deaf.

The left-hand bench, which was half in the sun, was occupied by an ordinary-looking teenage couple who were busy making out. The girl wore a white tank top printed with large sunflowers over a green miniskirt. She talked to the boy with an affected lisp as she rubbed up against him, flapping her arms and legs like a small child and blowing bubbles from the bottle they had bought at the shop.

Kazuki sat down on the middle bench, next to two middle school girls who were listening to the same minidisk player through two sets of headphones. Kōki, who had been following behind, finally caught up to Kazuki and stood in front of the bench. The girls stood up and left. Kōki's face was flushed from the sun, and drops of sweat clung to the fuzz on his upper lip. A fly stopped for a moment on the spot of miso soup from breakfast on Kōki's white shirt, busily rubbing its hairy front legs together before flying off. It grazed Kazuki's face and then buzzed noisily around his ear. While he was brushing away the fly, Kōki had stooped down by the bench to scatter a swarm of ants that were covering a dead cicada. As the ants rushed off in every direction, Kōki crushed them with the sole of his shoe. Picking up the cicada, he held it out to Kazuki. The head had been smashed and one wing had come off. When Kazuki hesitated to take it, Kōki held it carefully for a moment in his cupped hands and then shoved it in his pocket.

"Where's Kyōko?" Kazuki said, realizing that he had not turned back to look for them since they'd entered the zoo. He had not even been conscious that he'd come with someone.

"She's gone to buy juice," Kōki said.

A boy who appeared to be about five years old was sitting on a bench opposite them. Could he have come to the zoo by himself? The brim of his baseball cap was shading his face, but they could see his plump legs that he held perfectly still, as if he were sitting on a bridge, dangling them in the water. In fact, only his right hand moved, as he slowly lowered a metallic blue yo-yo and wound it up again. Kazuki stood, as if in a trance, and walked toward the boy. "Could I borrow it a minute?" he said. Snatching the yo-yo, he quickly showed the boy walk-the-dog and around-the-world and then handed it back. There was no sign at all that the boy was either upset or impressed by Kazuki's demonstration. He simply let the yo-yo unroll again as he watched the older boy go.

When Kazuki turned around, Kyōko was approaching with a paper cup in each hand. "Which would you like, Coke or orange juice?" she said, holding up the cups. Kazuki took the cola without a word. He seemed ill at ease, as if he were about to run off somewhere at any moment, and Kyōko found herself looking for any sign that he might be changing his mind about turning himself in.

"Where are the peacocks?" he asked.

"Peacocks?" she echoed. "Hold on a second. I'm going to give this to Kōki." While Kyōko went over to the bench where Kōki was waiting, Kazuki wandered off to look for the peacock cage. Passing the emus, he came to the ostrich pen. The long white neck above the black-feathered body reminded him of a priest. The sign said that they lived on grassy plains and grew to a height of two meters, making them the largest birds in the world. The ostrich stood almost motionless, like a philosopher pondering some deep mystery, apparently having forgotten that while it couldn't fly, it was able to run at speeds of up to fifty kilometers per hour. Farther along was another pen. In the middle stood an oil palm surrounded by yuzuriha, dracaenas, and rhododendrons, and next to it was a flock of flamingos.

Kazuki wandered along imagining what it would be like if all the animals escaped at once. But . . . then he suddenly realized that animals were out of their cages. Two gorillas, one sitting on the ground and another just getting up—and the people passing by didn't seem to notice that they were free. At first he thought they must be statues, but they were real gorillas; and as he was staring at them, an enormous hippopotamus came lumbering into view, its slick, black hide shining in the sun. The hippo stopped in front of Kazuki and opened its mouth so wide that even the enormous body disappeared behind the gaping throat. Kazuki stood and walked along with the hippo for a while, but still none of the visitors even looked their way. Strange, he thought, watching the hippo plod off toward the entrance, very strange. But when he rubbed his eyes and looked again, the zoo had returned to normal. How would you go about setting all the animals free? he wondered, heading for the elephant house. Even if you crept in at night, the cages would be locked tight.

The smell of dried grass and dung filled the elephant house, which was divided into four pens. In the half light, Kazuki could make out the silhouettes of four elephants, four tattered brown trunks methodically curling around bunches of fodder and raising them slowly to four waiting mouths. The back left leg of each animal was secured in a shackle. I had no idea that the smell of dung and grass could be so soothing, Kazuki thought, taking a deep breath. He gazed at the bed of dried grass as if he were looking at the spot where he'd been born.

"What are you doing here?" said a zookeeper who was passing through the house.

"What happens to the animals if we have an earthquake?" Kazuki asked.

"The zoo's built to withstand earthquakes," said the keeper. "No need to worry about that."

"But if there were an emergency, you'd let them go, wouldn't you?"

"Well, that's not likely. The monkey's might escape, but the pens for most of the animals are earthquake-proof, stronger than most of the buildings around here." The zookeeper had an utterly average face, the kind you would never remember having met him just once, like an anonymous executioner.

"So the animals can't escape?" Kazuki persisted.

"I don't think you'd want them to. Do you know how much damage an elephant in heat can do? And who do you think they'd come after? Us, that's who. I'd hate to think what would happen if they got out. The elephants alone could trample people to death and turn over cars, no problem." A thin smile played over the man's mouth as he head toward the outdoor yard.

In a major earthquake, highways and skyscrapers would collapse; it didn't seem likely that these cages would survive. And if they did crumble, then all the animals would escape at once. Suddenly feeling as though the earth were shaking under his feet, Kazuki fell on his stomach and pressed his ear to the floor. He could hear it—the unmistakable sound of a tremor. Getting up, he left the elephant house. His heart was racing, probably due to the heat or anemia. He was beginning to break out in a cold sweat, his ears were ringing, and he felt dizzy. The ringing gradually faded, replaced by the sound of a voice. He shook his head to drive it away, but then he recognized who was talking—it was his own voice. A stream of taunts and curses and rebukes was pouring from his mouth. What was he saying? All of this anger and hatred must have been stuck inside his mouth. He could feel his body stiffen in resistance. Are you still fighting this?

It's time to surrender. It was the barely perceptible consciousness of his crime that he was both resisting and trying to accept. He had agreed to turn himself in out of fear of losing Kyōko, but from the moment he had entered the zoo he'd been rocked by the sense that he had done something very wrong. This thing called a crime was a form of human debt that had a unique spiritual shape, like some rare animal. No, that was bullshit—anyone could commit a crime. Kazuki wanted the heat of the sun to fry his brain and drive him crazy. But no matter how much he wanted to escape himself, he never could. A man who couldn't bring himself to commit suicide, who wasn't lucky enough to go insane, was forced to go on living in agony, locked in that cage called the Self. Until the moment of his death, he was doomed to be a prisoner for the crime of Self. Still, if an earthquake comes, then everything that walks on the earth will be pardoned. Compared to the destruction of a great earthquake, the crimes humans could commit were trivial, hardly worthy of the name. Dead or alive, wouldn't the crimes of those pinned under the rubble be paid for? That's why he was no longer interested in escaping punishment. All he asked was that when the earthquake came, he would be forgiven for the fifteen or twenty seconds that the ground would tremble. The innocent and the guilty alike would be shaken, and for those few seconds they would all come face to face with that punishment known as death. For Kazuki, earthquakes were miracles.

The whole zoo had fallen still, as if waiting for something. Then suddenly, as Kazuki watched in a trance, the flock of beautiful pink flamingos rose into the deep blue sky. After circling for a moment, the birds flapped several times, as if in prayer, and then turned east and disappeared.

Suddenly a roaring sound could be heard deep in the earth. It grew louder and stronger until it split the ground and burst into the sky. The pavement underfoot began to shake and cracks spread in the asphalt. The cages began to rock and collapse, fences buckled and fell. Then, a numbing cry filled the air, a thunderous sound ran through the rolling ground, and an elephant rose from the rubble and charged out of the zoo. Kazuki tried to follow it, but his feet caught in the crumbling sidewalk and he fell. Trying to catch himself, his hands were cut on the wire of a broken fence, and he watched as pinheads of blood appear on his palms and began to drip to the ground.

In the woods where the gorilla pen had been, two apes stood howling on the roof of their collapsed cave. Nearby, the concrete wall that had surrounded the tiger pit had fallen and the cages had broken apart. Three tigers were creeping cautiously from the ruins, heads bowed. Owls and eagles and hawks and birds of all kinds were taking off into the smoke-filled sky. Other animals passed Kazuki on their way out of the zoo—a bloody polar bear, a limping orangutan, kangaroos, crocodiles, a rhinoceros. The cries of animals mingled with the sounds of explosions and sirens. Kazuki managed to stand up. He hurried along the path, which was still trembling with aftershocks, and finally made his way out the gate.

Where the city had stood that morning when they'd come to the zoo, now there was nothing but a mountain of rubble. Flames rose from the remains of toppled buildings, sending dark smoke billowing into the air. Above the crumpled houses, hot winds swirled in an eerie dance, occasionally finding a lick of flame to blow into a pillar of fire.

Kazuki looked up and caught sight of a condor perched on a tilting telephone pole. As it looked out over the ruins of the city, the bird sat so still that it might have been a dusty trophy in someone's study. But then a strong aftershock threatened to topple the pole, and the condor flew off, only to land again on the roadbed of a collapsed highway. The enormous concrete pillars that had supported the road were twisted like pretzels. Kazuki tried to follow the bird, but it was soon hidden in the thick smoke that swirled and billowed, darkening the summer sky.

Seven penguins waddled past him in a line, their lustrous black heads swaying as they headed off toward a flaming taxi. Kazuki bent forward to catch the last one, but the penguin let out a cry, brushed aside his hands, and flapped off toward a ruined house. As it approached, a brick fell from the wall, striking the bird on the back and knocking it to its belly, where it lay scraping its tiny wings on the ground. Kazuki scooped up the injured bird and hugged it to his chest, but it struggled wildly, swinging its head back and forth. Finally, he let go and it hopped from his arms. He stopped for a moment to rub the soot and smoke from his eyes, and when he looked again, the penguin was gone.

Several cars were buried under the ruins of a pedestrian bridge, but one of them suddenly began to move. The hood was crushed and the windshield was shattered, but behind the wheel sat an orangutan. It bared its teeth and jumped up and down on the accelerator, sending the car lurching forward, right toward Kazuki. As he caught sight of the bloody face of a man sitting in the backseat, he felt his stomach drop. He looked familiar, he thought, edging backward.

But it couldn't be . . . At that instant, the car exploded and was engulfed in flames. The sharp smell from the fire filled his head as a blast of hot air struck him in the face. The wind tugged at this clothes and his heart began to race.

The animals had not so much returned to the wild as been seized by madness and panic. A zebra ran under a collapsed arcade for shelter, while the rhinoceros was stabbing at a traffic light with its horn. A lion charged headlong at the burning screen in a ruined movie theater, and an elephant stood frozen in the middle of an intersection, staring up at the sky and whipping its trunk back and forth. Kazuki tripped on his shoelace, and when he bent over to tie it, a peacock feather floated down in front of him. Looking up, he saw the bird struggling in a knot of telephone wires like a butterfly caught in a spider's web.

Sensing something behind him, he turned around to find a Korean tiger bearing down on him. Crouching suddenly, it pounced, burying its fangs in his shoulder. He tensed for a moment, but as the teeth drove in deeper, he went limp. He was vaguely aware of a line of sharpshooters, glimpsed in silhouette on the roof of a damaged building. A noiseless burst of flame shot from the barrels of their guns, and the weight of the animal on his back became heavier, pinning him to the ground. The pavement in front of him was dyed red, and he could feel the warm blood pouring over his head. A moment after Kazuki had pulled himself out from under the animal, it began writhing and vomiting blood. Finally, it collapsed and lay still in the rubble.

He crawled up on a mound of broken cement and then crawled down again. The half-demolished buildings stood stoically, as if they were neither ashamed of nor frightened by their own listing forms. Kazuki dropped to his knees to pray, but he had no idea what words to use or what to pray for. He heard a baby cry somewhere nearby. In here, he thought. He pushed his way into a building and stopped to listen. He heard the cry again, but it was very weak. If he didn't find it quickly, the baby would die. He began moving bricks and boards, and with every one, the cry became louder. His bloody hands worked feverishly, but when he'd cleared the last of the debris, all that emerged was . . . a cricket.

Kazuki closed his eyes and wrapped his hand around the gold pendant that hung next to his chest. He took a deep breath and a shudder ran through his body. He was afraid to open his eyes, but he thought he could hear a voice. His ears were ringing like they did after he'd been slapped around or shouted at. "Kazuki! Kazuki!" It was his brother's voice. When he opened his eyes, everything around him was dim, like shadows in the dark, but Kyōko and Kōki were standing nearby in a pool of brilliant light. They were holding hands and waving at him. Were they beckoning for him to join them? Or waving good-bye? Around them, the sky was cloudless and the brilliant sunlight made the scene sparkle, dazzling his eyes. He blinked, focusing on their silhouettes as they rose into the sky. They seemed very far away, a limitless distance, a distance that would never again be narrowed. Still, they also seemed to be walking toward him, though with each step their faces became more blurred, until he could barely see them . . . But then they were by him, each grabbing an arm and lifting him from the earth.

"Are you all right?" Kyōko's chest was pressed up against him, reminding him how her body had felt when he'd held her in the basement.

"Yes," he muttered, trying to give her a reassuring smile. But to Kyōko, the grin appeared feeble and twisted.

Kazuki turned and took a tentative step. And then he saw it. His eyes clung to it like those of an animal with its face pressed up against the cold bars, desperately looking out. It was the one and only sign that the world still existed, that this spot where he was standing was real and not a dream, that he was still alive—it was the cage. He realized he was standing in front of a cage, not a place for healing but for punishment. He gasped for breath, sorrow welling up inside him as if his lungs were being wrenched from his chest. His face was damp—with tears or sweat, he didn't know—and a salty taste filled his mouth.

Two fingers reached out and pinched his cheek until it hurt, and suddenly Kōki was staring him in the face, poking him in the ribs with his thumb and reaching up to tickle him under the jaw. His eyes shimmered like a pool in the dead of night.

Kazuki pulled a faded photograph from his pocket. It was the picture of his family standing in front of the elephant pen. He was in the middle, holding hands with Kōki and Miho, and behind them were their parents, his father's hand resting on Miho's shoulder, his mother's arm around Kōki. It was this same zoo. His father stared sadly into the camera. Kazuki had looked at this picture many times before, but he had never noticed this sadness in his father's eyes. He looked down at his own hand, the one that had killed his father, and then moved it slowly to cover Hidetomo's face in the picture. Suddenly, he pulled out the disposable camera he'd bought at the station.

"Let's take a picture," he said. Ripping off the wrapper and turning the knob on the camera, he looked around for the right spot. A family was approaching, the mother pushing a stroller while her husband held hands with their small boy. "Excuse me, but could you take our picture?" Kazuki asked, running over and handing the camera to the father.

The three of them lined up in front of the empty elephant yard. Kazuki stared straight at the dark hole in the camera and tried to smile. He had no idea whether Kyōko and Kōki were smiling as they held his hands on either side, but at that moment, everything inside his head was exposed.